Until All The Gods Return

Tim Frankovich

WARPSTEEL
PRESS

Praise for *Until All Curses Are Lifted*

"An inherently riveting read by an author with a genuine flair for originality and a distinctively engaging and entertaining narrative storytelling style, *Until All Curses Are Lifted* by Tim Frankovich will prove to be an immediate and enduringly popular addition to community library Science Fiction & Fantasy collections."
– Midwest Book Review

"Frankovich leads readers down twisting paths, traveling with unforgettable characters, in a story with evocative depth.
Highly recommended!"
- Eric Wilson, NY Times bestselling author

"I was part of this world. I cared for its people. Even the leper assassin Kishin tugged at a corner of my heart. I genuinely cried over a pivotal scene at the temple of Theon, the one that proved just how powerful a mother's love can be. I felt shivers when the two seemingly separate tales of Marshal and Seri finally intertwined. The good people are set on their sworn duties and even the most villainous of creatures had something significant to fight for... I can't wait to read more."
- Elle Espiritu, Reedsy Discovery

"I enjoyed this book almost more than I can say."
- Lelia Rose Foreman, author of the Shatterworld Trilogy

Praise for *Until All Bonds Are Broken*

"Brings one to the absolute brink of astoundment, leaves one staggering from all the action and thrill of the story! I'm still agog and reeling from my amazement to the events unfolding. I've read books that I found difficult to put down, but I found this one totally impossible not to carry on. Almost like a obsession, it draws one in, then pulls even harder until one is completely immersed."
-Beba Andric, Goodreads review

Books by Tim Frankovich

Heart of Fire

Until All Curses Are Lifted
Until All Bonds Are Broken
Until All The Gods Return
Until All The Stars Fall

Dragontek Lore

Viridia
Incarnadine

For John & Shannon
Keep reading & gaming together

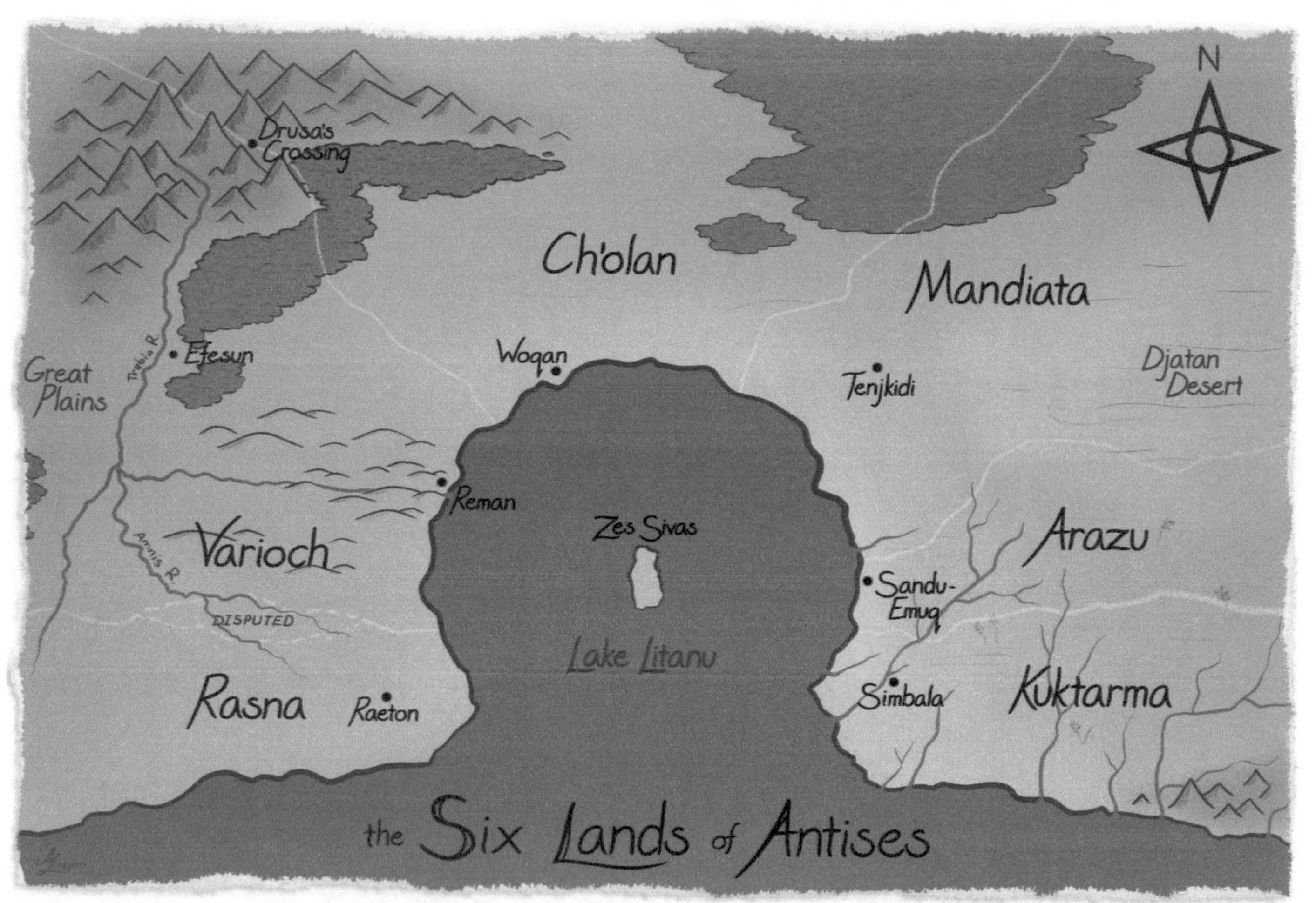

N
Ch'olan
Mandiata
Drusa's Crossing
Great Plains
Trebia R.
Efesun
Woqan
Tenjkidi
Djatan Desert
Reman
Zes Sivas
Arazu
Sandu-Emuq
Varioch
Annis R.
DISPUTED
Lake Litanu
Simbala
Kuktarma
Rasna
Raeton
the Six Lands of Antises

(((1)))

"You need to go, and go quickly."

Jamana looked up to see Master Korda's imposing shape looming in his doorway. Since their arrival in Tenjkidi five days ago, his mentor had barely spoken to him, let alone come to his room. Jamana scrambled to his feet from behind the desk.

Master Korda glanced out into the hallway, but did not move any further. He shifted his feet, appearing almost nervous, a concept Jamana had never associated with this man.

"Go where, Master?"

"Back to Zes Sivas," Korda answered. He took one more look down the hallway, then entered the room. In two long strides, he stood beside the desk and in front of Jamana. He glanced down. *A History of the Lords' Betrayal* lay open on the desk where Jamana had been studying it. "And take this book with you. Neither of you are safe here any more."

"I don't understand."

"Must I spell everything out for you?" Master Korda bent over the book and paged through it. Finding the page he sought, he pointed to a paragraph. Jamana looked down and read it. He started out loud, but Master Korda hushed him, so he continued silently.

"Prior to the Great Cataclysm, all of the nations boasted their own gods. These were dark times. The gods were capricious, throwing nations into conflict at a whim, or demanding undue sacrifices. Akhenadom's proclamation of a single god, one that loved his people, came as a great relief to many."

Jamana looked up. In his time reading this book, the same theme had recurred multiple times: the dangers of the ancient gods of the early nations. And now, after a thousand years, those gods were returning. Two of them roamed this very palace. Of course the book was not safe. But why him?

Master Korda bent in close and spoke in a very low voice. "The remaining Masters on Zes Sivas need to know about what is taking place here, and they are not responding to my messages. I don't know if they're even being received. You must go in my place and tell them all."

Jamana nodded. "But why is it not safe?"

Master Korda closed his eyes for a moment. When he opened them, he looked to the door once more and then back at Jamana's face. "Because you, my acolyte, know the truth. You have a strong faith in Theon. I have noticed this about you. I do not believe you can remain silent for long in these conditions."

Jamana hesitated. His faith in Theon had been strong a year ago. But so much had happened since then: the earth shaking, the murder of some of the Masters, Dravid's injury, Volraag's murder of Lord Sundinka. It seemed much harder to believe in a god who ruled over such chaos. Yet if the book were true, these "returning" gods were far worse.

"If anyone asks, I gave you permission to visit your family," Master Korda said. He stepped back and spoke louder. "Pack your things and hurry on, acolyte. Things are happening that you will not want to miss!"

Jamana bowed his head and closed the book. As Master Korda left his room, a sense of urgency overtook him. He scrambled to find a satchel large enough to hold the book along with his few belongings. Within a few minutes, he finished packing, left his room, and made his way toward the palace doors.

• • • • •

"Why do you doubt, acolyte?"

Jamana almost jumped out of his skin. Komadi, the court mage, approached him from the palace doors. He gave his blue robes an extra flourish as he came to a stop.

"What do you mean?" Jamana asked. He shifted the satchel on his shoulder. Komadi eyed it before responding.

"I saw you approaching the doors with a bag, as if you were going somewhere. So I asked myself: why would anyone choose to leave when facing such historic and world-changing possibilities? The only answer I could come up with was… doubt."

"Master Korda has given me permission to visit my family," Jamana said. "I haven't seen them in over a year now." He felt a twinge inside, since that much was true. Actually visiting his family had vanished from his thoughts the moment they had entered the palace and met the gods.

Komadi studied him for a moment. The smile that spread across his face unnerved Jamana more than his challenge. Komadi had been instrumental in the arrival of the gods to Tenjkidi. He never stopped bragging about it. If Jamana were truly in danger, Komadi would be his most dangerous foe aside from the gods themselves.

"Family is important, even for we mages," Komadi acknowledged. He started to turn, then paused as if struck by another thought. "Before you go, acolyte, I must show you something." He took a few steps down an adjoining hallway and motioned for Jamana to follow.

Jamana glanced toward the palace doors, so near. He took a deep breath and turned to follow Komadi.

The other mage led him toward the east side of the palace. A sprawling construct, the palace contained more rooms than any building in existence, as far as Jamana knew. Perhaps the citadels on Zes Sivas would rival it, if they were counted as a single structure. But at least the layout of this palace made sense.

"As you know, other worlds adjoin ours," Komadi said as they walked, speaking in an almost-condescending tone. "Harbinger and Nummotem speak of one close to ours, where the gods have chosen to dwell. It is from there they came to us." He led the way up a flight of stairs to the second floor.

"The Otherworld," Jamana said. "A friend of mine visited it."

Komadi shot him a skeptical look. "When Nummotem came to us, he brought something else from that world," he went on. He stopped walking and gestured down the hallway, where it ended in a balcony. "Come see."

Jamana stepped past him, noting how Komadi's eyes darted briefly toward his satchel. "What are we—" He broke off as he looked down from the balcony.

Below them lay a high-walled courtyard. At one time, it had no doubt housed a pleasant garden with walkways between flowering plants and shady trees. Several other such gardens lay at various points along the palace exterior. But this one had been torn apart. Trees lay split apart on the ground, their roots ripped from the earth. Flowers, grass and walking trails alike had been crushed beneath heavy footsteps. Claw marks decorated various points along the brick walls, some of them frighteningly close to the top.

And in the center of this devastation lay the creature responsible. Jamana's hand trembled as he rested it on the balcony's railing. He had seen large creatures during his travels, and his friend Dravid had regaled him with stories of even more down south in Kuktarma. But this… nothing he had seen or heard of compared.

The creature's hairless skin appeared covered in large hexagonal scales with occasional rough protuberances. Its four legs lay under it as it rested, but not asleep. Its cat-like eyes moved back and forth above its curved snout. It looked more muscular than any creature Jamana knew. How did the walls even hold it in?

Seri. She had seen one of these when she visited the Otherworld. It terrified her then and it terrified Jamana now.

"Spectacular, isn't it?" Komadi asked. "Such a monster of pure power. Yet it bows to Nummotem at a single word. Truly, only a god could control such a thing."

"Amazing," Jamana said, and meant it.

The creature rose to its feet and shook itself, cascading dirt all around. It took a few steps toward the palace, revealing three massive claws on each of its front feet.

"Tunaldi, they called it," Komadi said. "The gods use them to ride… and to hunt."

"To hunt?"

Komadi looked at Jamana and his smile returned. "When unleashed, the tunaldi can find sources of magic, or… those who use magic. They are relentless. Unstoppable. Yet totally within the control of the gods."

Jamana could not repress a shudder.

"Yes, frightening. But also inspiring, don't you think? That the gods could command such power. And they offer it to us to do with as we will."

"What about the Laws?" Jamana said before thinking.

"The Laws of Cursings and Bindings?" Komadi snorted. "The gods are beyond them. And soon they will set us free from them as well."

"Why would you want that?" Jamana exclaimed. "Do you want people able to harm others without consequences?"

Komadi rolled his eyes and sighed. "Acolyte, you have much to learn. For serious crimes, the gods themselves will execute punishment. There will be difficulties, of course, but the freedom offered by the gods is worth it. Freedom from the Laws. And freedom from Theon."

"How can— but—" Jamana sputtered out. He didn't know what to say in response. Of course some people hated the Laws, but he had always assumed those people to be the ones who would commit crimes if they were able. But freedom from Theon? The very idea was blasphemous.

"Think carefully, acolyte," Komadi said, turning away with one last pointed look at the bag. "Enjoy your time with your family. But don't be gone long. We have a pilgrimage to take."

Jamana glanced down at the tunaldi, then started down the hall. His curiosity overtook him. "A pilgrimage to where?" he called.

Without looking back, Komadi answered, "To the high place in Kuktarma."

(((2)))

Jamana made his way to the outskirts of Tjenkidi. Haste would be his greatest ally now. If anyone were watching him, it would not take long for word to return to the palace telling of his movements. West, toward the coast, instead of east, toward his family's estate.

What would be his best method of travel? He could find a ride on a barge moving down the river to Lake Litanu. Safe, but not very fast. Or he could go overland. Merchants and other travelers were always going back and forth to the capital city. Yet they would not be very fast, either.

He tried not to let Komadi's words trouble him, but he could not erase them from his memory.

He looked up the road that circled around the southern side of the city. At its corner just within his view, it passed by the great temple to Theon. He watched as a trio of pilgrims entered the gates, and a pair of horses emerged, though it looked as though only one held a rider.

All his life, he had valued his identity as a devout follower of Theon. It had been a tough choice between entering the priesthood or becoming a mage, as he believed both to be chosen servants of the god. How different his life would have been had he chosen the priesthood. Instead of running in fear right now, he would be up there in the temple... also in fear. What could the priests of Theon be thinking about the old gods? Were they as frightened as Jamana, or was their faith unshakeable?

The horses appeared to be coming his direction, but soon disappeared in the crowded street.

Were these returned gods even real? Jamana had never given much thought at all to the gods his people had worshipped before coming to

Antises. Why should he? Theon was the only god he needed. Wasn't he?

Jamana looked back the way he had come, half expecting to see the tunaldi's massive bulk racing down the street after him. He saw nothing but the usual crowds of city dwellers, all busy about their chosen tasks. Were they even aware of how Antises changed around them?

The Book of the Law said there were no gods above Theon. Yet didn't that very statement imply there were gods below him? These beings held great power, power unlike the magic of Antises. Perhaps they truly were gods, of a sort. Regardless, if Komadi spoke true, then these gods stood in opposition to Theon, hoping to end his laws. That could not be.

Jamana straightened and shifted the bag on his shoulder. His task was clear. Yet still he hesitated.

"You look almost lost, young acolyte!"

The voice jolted him and he whirled, expecting Komadi or even one of the gods. Instead, two horses stood behind him. An elderly man with a scraggly beard sat atop one of them.

"Theon's blessings on you this fine morning!" the rider said when Jamana did not answer right away. "Is there a way I can help you, acolyte?"

"Theon's blessings to you, revered father." Jamana found his voice. "I was… that is, I am looking for the best way to the coast."

"Ah, the best way is always by horse," the old man said. "Or camel, perhaps. But I don't have a camel." He glanced around. "I do seem to have two horses, however. And I am also traveling to the coast."

"I can pay—" Jamana began.

"We'll deal with that later. I'm itching to get moving right now. Climb on up here." He leaned over and patted the other horse's neck.

Jamana grinned. It felt like he hadn't grinned in quite some time. It also felt right. He mounted the horse with a little difficulty, thanks to the awkward bag, then settled in.

"What is your name, young acolyte?"

"Jamana, sir. And yours?"

"Let's ride!" The old man patted his horse on the flank and set off on the road west, toward the coast. Jamana hastened to catch up.

•••••

As they journeyed, Jamana found his traveling companion talkative, but only on certain subjects. He chattered at length about the condition of the temple and the priests therein.

"Are you a priest, sir?" Jamana asked.

The old man hesitated a long moment before answering. "Yes. Yes, I am." That was the most personal information Jamana managed to get out of him for the entire first day of riding. Somehow, he never got around to even sharing his name.

He did press Jamana for his own personal information, however. He asked about Zes Sivas, and the Masters. He seemed to know quite a bit about how the island and its occupants lived and worked, far more than anyone Jamana had ever spoken with, aside from mages themselves.

From what he could tell, the old man was not Mandiatan. His skin appeared somewhat lighter, perhaps from Arazu or Kuktarma. But his accent did not sound like either of those. Jamana couldn't place it at all, which he found very perplexing.

The sun traveled across the sky until it lay before them. With no clouds to shield it, Jamana had to squint against the brightness. It certainly made it easy to keep going the right direction.

"I presume you're returning to Zes Sivas now," the old man said. "Been visiting home?"

"Master Korda and I came to visit the new Lord," Jamana answered. "It has been a difficult time."

"How so?"

Jamana jerked in his saddle. "Are you a stranger to Antises itself? Surely you know of what has happened over the past few months!"

"I know many things. But I wish to hear your side of the story. Tell me, acolyte, of the fall of the Masters."

Jamana shot a look at his companion. The fall of the Masters? That seemed an overly dramatic way of describing it. Not to mention most of the Masters still lived, as far as he knew.

But as he related the story of the shaking ground, the treachery of Volraag, and the deception of Curasir, he realized the Masters truly had fallen. Or perhaps a better word would be: failed. They failed to see through Curasir, failed to stop Volraag from murdering his own father and Lord Sundinka, and failed to find any solution at all to the earthquakes. Even worse, they failed in remembering their own history, something that still baffled Jamana to the core.

"History should be a guide to us," the old man said. "It can warn us of failures that others have made, so that we may avoid them."

Jamana blinked and looked around. He didn't remember what he had been saying to prompt that response from his companion. And the sun would soon be out of sight. How had it gotten so late?

"This should be a good spot to camp for the night," the old man observed. "Unless you'd like to push on through the darkness?"

"No, no. This should be fine." Jamana's stomach rumbled, complaining of its emptiness. He had eaten a few bites along the way, pieces of bread and cheese from his bag, but they did not stop for a midday meal. At the same time, he remembered the possibility of pursuit. He looked back the way they had come, seeing nothing.

The old man slid from his saddle. "I believe some rest will do us good. We can set out early in the morning."

Jamana nodded and joined him in preparing a meager campsite. Between the two of them, they had little enough to eat, yet it seemed just the right amount. His stomach satisfied, Jamana idly reached out for magic, a practice he tried nightly before bed. Being still far from Zes Sivas, he expected to find little if anything.

"You might try over by that broken palm," the old man said. "Wild magic often crops up where nature is damaged."

Jamana got up and took three steps toward the palm before he realized the significance of his companion's statements. He turned slowly on his heel to look down at the old man.

"Who are you? You said you were a priest, yet you know… how did you know I was looking for magic?" Jaman shivered, feeling cold sweep over him. He needed to know what this meant. Everything seemed to hinge on this man's identity.

"Ah." The old man sighed deeply. "I've said too much." He started to get to his feet, then slumped back down. "I really miss that staff," he muttered.

"What do you mean?" Jamana demanded. "Who are you?"

The old man leaned back and chuckled. "You are not ready for that answer. For now, just accept that I am a servant of Theon, and a friend to any other servant of Theon or lover of Antises."

Jamana rarely let his temper grow, but this was one of those times. His hands shook and he clenched them into fists. "You… you expect me to… just accept that? I can't trust you!" He grabbed for his bedroll, intending to gather everything up and leave.

"Stop it!" The old man's voice vibrated with something Jamana didn't recognize. Yet somehow, he felt obligated to obey. "Close your eyes. Reach out with your senses. What do you sense from me?"

Jamana opened himself up, and directed his senses toward the old man, just as Master Korda had taught him in those early days. At first, he felt nothing.

One moment, there was nothing. The next, it seemed like someone had opened a door to reveal hidden glory within. Magic erupted from the old man. Jamana staggered back at the overwhelming force of it, though none of it was directed at him. An instant later, it vanished. He felt a trickle coming from the direction of the broken palm, but nothing else.

Jamana sank to his knees. His temper had vanished, but he shook now from the impact of the moment.

"I've been around a while, Jamana," the priest said in a soft voice. "And in that time, I've learned how to conceal many things." He sighed and looked to the east. "Unfortunately, I just announced myself to any who might be watching."

"Then... why?"

Ancient eyes peered into Jamana's own in the darkening twilight. "Because it's that important for you to trust me, acolyte. If Antises is to survive, if we are to stop these so-called gods, then so many of you must do your part. And I do not have the time to persuade you all, one by one. Will you trust me?"

Jamana's mind whirled with the implications. Priest and mage. How could it be? And the power. Surely it was on a level equal with the Lords. Or even greater. Power alone did not require trust. The gods commanded great power. But this man spoke the name of Theon and proclaimed himself against the gods. Was that enough?

"I will trust you. For now."

The old man snorted. "That's all I ask."

(((3)))

The kiss lingered on his lips and in his memory, an echo of what might have been, and, when he dared to hope, what yet could be.

Dravid leaned on his staff in the glow of the Otherworld's stars and thought of Seri. Always Seri. He needed to constantly remind himself of her, that her life continued because of what he had done. Without that reassurance, he would have long since given up.

The former member of Marshal's squad known as Wolf, now revealed as an ancient god named Calu, had demanded a price to save Seri's life. The price was Dravid's enslavement, probably until he died. Such was the cost of making a deal with a god.

"Hey, crip! Get a move on!" The ugly voice intruded on Dravid's reverie and he took a step forward. The army moved on again, and so must he. He glanced at the other slave who had reproved him. Dravid never learned his name, but he sounded antagonistic every time he opened his mouth. He blustered, but he was a coward, terrified of offending the gods or the Durunim who also served them.

Most of the other human slaves seemed to have been taken from the primary world from Varioch and Rasna, though a few came from Ch'olan. Even if Dravid hadn't been missing a leg, he would be an oddity among them.

He looked out over the slow-moving army of Durunim, the strange warriors of the Otherworld. They seemed like Eldanim, yet so frightening. Their bizarre skin absorbed all light, appearing completely black one moment, but iridescent the next. Dravid tried to avoid them as much as possible.

His duties thus far had been vague. Calu required Dravid to wait on him at the morning and evening meals, and any other time the army stopped. He complained about Dravid being slow, but had not given him any punishment for it. Other slaves were not so lucky. Their masters, the other gods, were fickle and some were quick to anger. Dravid had seen open wounds on faces and scars on the backs of many of his fellow humans.

Far ahead among the crowd, a chariot of some kind detached itself and circled back. Dravid watched it kick up dust as it moved. Considering the size of this moving army, he would think the whole region should be covered in a dust cloud. Though Marshal's grandfather had destroyed a huge portion of the army, others had come to join, swelling its ranks back up to at least its original size.

The one thing Dravid couldn't determine was their destination. He had no sun to provide compass directions, and the landscape was wholly unfamiliar. The stars probably provided direction for those who knew them, but of course he didn't.

The chariot came to a stop almost directly in front of him, throwing dirt and debris into the air. Dravid and the other slaves around him choked on the dust, coughing and trying to escape the cloud.

"Cripple!" a voice cried out. Dravid stopped, coughed again, and waited for the dust to settle.

As it did, he found himself looking into the face of the creature pulling the chariot. Up until now, Dravid had done his best to avoid the various animals he saw among the gods and Durunim. This one stared back at him, not with intelligence, but a gleam of something antagonistic and challenging. It snorted and jerked its head up. Vaguely horse-shaped, the head was topped by two spiraling horns that jutted backwards above its neck. The rest of the creature also resembled a horse, though somewhat lower to the ground with thicker legs. Dravid thought it must be brown, with a lighter underbody, but that might be the dust.

His eyes moved beyond the animal to the chariot it pulled and the god who stood there, looking down at him. Golden-skinned like all of them, he wore red and yellow clothes draped over his muscular body in multiple layers. A tall crown sat on his head, matched in gaudiness by enormous earrings. He tapped a long scepter of some kind against the chariot wall and chuckled.

"Do you recognize me, mortal?" Like all the gods, the charioteer's voice vibrated with the magic inherent to his nature. Every time one of them asked a question or gave an order, Dravid felt compelled to obey.

"No," he answered.

The charioteer looked sad. "Not even from old drawings in books, perhaps?"

Dravid shook his head.

"Then it is as the others said. You truly have forgotten us." The god heaved an enormous sigh and looked away for a moment. "Your people once knew me well. I am Vayan. I am one of the gods of your people, from long ago, before you named your new land Kuktarma."

Dravid didn't know what to say in response. His education had not gone into any detail on ancient gods, beyond deriding them as false and forgotten.

The god studied him, waiting for recognition perhaps. When none came, he gave a short nod. "I have persuaded Calu to turn you over to me. He grows weary of a slave who cannot keep up."

"And you won't?" Dravid bit his lip. That might have been too impertinent.

Vayan laughed. "Unlike Calu, I recognize your impediment and will allow for it." He leaned over the chariot wall and stared intently. "I also know of your other abilities and I am fascinated. I will know more."

Dravid nodded.

Vayan straightened and gestured. "You may sit at the rear."

Dravid made his way to the back of the chariot and sat. He had barely pulled his leg up from the ground when Vayan snapped at the beast and the chariot lurched into movement again.

Only then did Dravid notice the chariot itself appeared to be entirely fashioned from the golden magic wielded by the gods. Dravid himself could channel the same magic, except he could only create small items, and then only for a short period of time. The power to create something like this—with moving parts!—staggered him.

He almost fell the first time the chariot struck an uneven spot. He had nothing to hold on to. This would not end well, unless…

Dravid held his staff at chest level against the two side walls of the chariot. He concentrated and reached out. A familiar heat rose within his chest. He pulled at the chariot wall and was delighted when he managed to reshape a small piece of it. He wrapped it around the staff, then repeated the process on the other side. Now he had something to keep him in place.

Not a moment too soon. The road grew rough. Dravid held on to his staff. And Vayan laughed.

• • • • •

Dravid didn't know what to make of this strange god. He drove his chariot like a maniac, swerving here and there. Sometimes Dravid thought he deliberately selected the roughest terrain. Since the chariot moved faster than the rest of the army, Vayan would take it out far ahead of the main column, then spin around and shoot all the way back to the rear.

Throughout all this, Dravid could only hang on, wondering. What would happen when they finally stopped for the night? What did Vayan want from him? Most important, Dravid considered his debt to Calu paid. He had said Dravid would serve him until death… "or until I grow tired of you." Isn't that exactly what had happened?

"Tell me of Kuktarma!" Vayan called over his shoulder.

Dravid turned to look at him, though it made for an awkward position. "What do you want to know?"

Vayan shrugged. "The royal family. What are they like?"

Now there was a subject Dravid could talk about. No one knew the stories of Lord Meluhha's sons more than Dravid. But where to start?

"Lord Meluhha rules over Kuktarma. He has seven sons and one daughter. The eldest son became engaged to the daughter of Lord Sundinka of Mandiata. However, things did not go quite as planned. What happened was…"

Over the next two hours, Dravid told story after story. Vayan listened to them all, voicing a question only now and then. During a break, while Dravid tried to decide which story to tell next, he noticed Vayan had let the chariot slow. He took a deep breath, but before he could say anything else, Vayan spoke up.

"When we return to power, I believe I will have this seventh son exiled."

Dravid blinked. Exiled? "I, I don't understand."

"He irks me. He saves people from the consequences of their actions far too often."

"Isn't that a good thing? Sometimes?"

"Pain is necessary. Until I take it away."

"Take it away?"

Vayan waved dismissively and gave the reins a snap. The chariot sped up again. "I don't like him."

"Uh, these stories are not… they're not all completely accurate, you know." Dravid hated to admit it, but circumstances demanded the truth. "Many of them actually happened to previous royal families. They're… adapted to the current Lord and his family. It's how we do things in Kuktarma."

"I am aware," Vayan said. "It was done that way before your people came to this place also."

"Then…"

"The seventh son's character is still revealed by his position in the stories. Were he not the kind of person so described, the stories would not continue."

Dravid didn't know how to answer.

The chariot moved ahead of the main column again. Vayan let it go a little further before turning around. Once they started back toward the rear, he spoke again.

"Your people have not forgotten how to tell stories. That is well. But they do not know the right stories any more. That will have to change."

"What are the right stories?"

"Stories that honor your gods and direct you to them for what you need." Vayan lifted his hand in a wave to another god who responded with a brief wave of his own. Dravid watched as they passed. The other god, imposing in size even among the others like him, sat atop the largest of the creatures known as tunaldi. Dravid couldn't see as clear as he'd like under the starlight, but the god's clothing seemed similar to his own people's.

"Who was that?" he asked Vayan.

Vayan shook his head. "You have even forgotten him? How far you have fallen." He glanced over his shoulder down at Dravid. "That was Murdak, greatest of your gods. He leads this journey."

"Where are we going?"

"I understand you have seen power in your world, and you have seen a taste of our power from Calu, no doubt," Vayan said, ignoring his question. "But all of that pales next to the power of Murdak. Though you remember him not, that much you should know first and foremost."

Dravid watched Murdak and his steed grow smaller as the chariot raced away. On one hand, knowing the leader of this group would be important if they were to be defeated. On the other, he couldn't help but wonder about the power Vayan described. Did Murdak's power rival that of the Lords of Antises? Or Marshal?

(((4)))

Jamana and his traveling companion looked down at the coastline of Mandiata. The river flowed into Lake Litanu here, beside the city of Kombori. From their hilltop advantage, Jamana could see far out into the lake. Only two or three ships were visible out on the water, none of them moving very fast.

"Wind," the old man murmured. "That is a sign. And not a good one."

"What do you mean?"

The priest shook his head. "It means the end draws closer than we would hope. Unfortunately, it also means we must part ways here, young acolyte."

"Already? Shouldn't we enter the city first?"

"I am not going to the city. And neither should you, for that matter."

"I shouldn't?" Jamana felt foolish, repeating questions like this.

The old man smiled. He pointed back the way they had come. "Pursuit is coming. The city is the first place they will look for you."

Jamana shifted in his saddle and stared back over his shoulder. He could see nothing along the road to Tjenkidi. How close was this pursuit?

"I told you that I did not have time to persuade everyone one at a time," the priest said, looking down at the water. "And so, I will leave it to you to do some of the persuading."

"Persuading who?"

The strange old man turned his eyes on Jamana. "When you see the leper face-to-face, you must deliver my message to him. Not before, mind you. When you see him face-to-face."

"The leper?"

"You will understand."

"But… what is the message?"

He held out a small scroll tied with a red ribbon. Jamana took it and looked it over, before slipping it into the bag with the book. Nothing this old man said ever made much sense.

"I will need my horse, I'm afraid."

With some reluctance, Jamana dismounted and handed the reins of the horse to the priest. He had grown to enjoy riding the past couple of days. "Thank you for your assistance," he said. "Where should I go, if not the city? I still need passage to Zes Sivas."

The old man stared down at the coastline. His eyes moved along it toward the north, as if he could see much more than could reasonably be seen from this point. At last, he pointed that direction. "Go north along the coastline. In time, you will find the help that you need."

Jamana scratched the side of his head. "That's all? Just go north?"

"That will take care of everything, I believe." The old man sat back, a satisfied look on his face. "Yes, that should do quite nicely."

"Then… then I will bid you farewell." Jamana pulled the bag with the book onto his shoulder. "Thank you again."

He took several steps down the hill before the old man called out. "Wait!"

Jamana turned back. The priest dug into his large sack, moving through items Jamana could not see. "Just a moment."

At last, he brought out something. "Ah, this should work." He spurred the horse forward to catch up to Jamana, and offered the object down to him.

Jamana took it. He smelled it before his eyes confirmed it. "Bread?" It even felt warm beneath the cloth wrap. How was that possible?

"Yes. You may find it helpful."

"Thank you…" Jamana opened one corner of the wrap. Bread. No question about it.

The old man spurred his horse and turned toward the south. Over his shoulder, he called, "We will meet again, young acolyte. We will meet again!"

• • • • •

Jamana circled the city to the north and reached the coastline, as the old man had advised. Every few moments, he couldn't help but pause and look around. Somewhere nearby, Komadi was searching for him.

Who else would it be? He had to avoid the other mage until… until he found the help the old man talked about.

He climbed over a sand dune bristling with tall weeds and slid down the other side. He stood and checked the book at his side. Then he looked up.

His heart sank. The coastline leading toward the north had to be the most inhospitable landscape he had ever seen. Uneven sand dunes covered in dense patches of weeds and tall grasses intermixed with rocks of all shapes and sizes. In some places, the vegetation seemed to shift from the sand to the rocks and back again without a break. How could he find his way through all this?

"You a priest or somethin'?"

Jamana tensed and swiveled toward the voice. To his relief, he saw a stranger. He looked like a beggar, perhaps, dressed in rags, hunched over as if he expected someone to attack him at any moment. Jamana breathed easier.

"You're wearin' robes." The beggar gestured, and only then did Jamana notice he had no hands. Both arms ended in stumps.

"Mage," Jamana said. "I'm a mage, not a priest."

The beggar nodded, as if he understood. "You lookin' to go that way?" He pointed with one of his stumps up the beach.

"Yes." Jamana swallowed and looked back again. "I need to go that way." It wasn't the most articulate conversation he had ever been a part of, but he couldn't think of anything else to say.

"If you got any food, I can show you."

Jamana pulled the bag tight against him as his breath caught. Food? He opened the bag, reached in, and brought out the loaf of bread the old man had given him. He looked at it, and for a moment considered putting it back and taking out some of the dry rations instead. But he knew that wouldn't be right. He held the loaf out as an offering.

A slow smile spread across the beggar's scruffy face. He moved carefully forward, as if afraid to startle his benefactor. He placed his two stumps on either side of the bread and took it. He cradled it between his arms, lifted it to his face and sniffed.

"Oh, that's the good stuff, that is." He somehow tucked the bread into a large pocket in his raggedy outfit. Then he pointed north. "This way, mage."

Once the beggar started, he moved with surprising speed, guiding Jamana along a winding path he never would have found on his own. At times, it seemed to come to a complete end against a solid rock wall.

The beggar would look around for a moment, mutter something, push aside a few weeds, and uncover the path's continuation in another direction. Other times, it would lead into a patch of tall grass and disappear completely. The beggar pressed on, and when they emerged from the grass, the path waited for them on the other side. Amazing.

Equally amazing was the way the beggar maneuvered without any hands. He had no trouble scrambling over rocks and dunes alike, climbing up small inclines, pushing his way through the plant life. At one point, he led the way up a sheer cliff by bracing his stumps on either side of a narrow cleft in the rock and scooting his way up. Jamana had more trouble doing the same with his hands.

He wanted to ask the beggar's story, but didn't want to offend. After all, the beggar might leave him out here to fend for himself. He could never find his way through this maze alone. But why both hands? It could be some kind of horrific accident, of course. But it seemed rather unlikely. No, a curse would be the most likely explanation. Hands? Cursed for stealing something, no doubt. Something important.

They had been traveling for about an hour when a distant sound caused both of them to stop in their tracks. A roar echoed across the rocks, a roar unlike any of the wild beasts of this region. Though he had never heard it before, Jamana knew at once where it came from. The tunaldi.

"What is that?" the beggar demanded. He hunched down even smaller than his usual posture.

"It's after me," Jamana said. "Some kind of creature called a tunaldi. They're trying to find me with it."

"Why? What did you do?" The beggar took several steps back away.

"I am innocent of wrongdoing." Jamana spread his hands. "If I had done evil, would I not be cursed? The man who guides this creature is serving evil, though I am thinking he does not fully understand it."

The beggar took another step back, his eyes darting around. "How do I know? Maybe he's in the right and you're lyin'."

Jamana lowered his chin and fixed his gaze on the beggar's face. "I am a servant of Theon, and a friend to any other servant of Theon or lover of Antises," he repeated the words the old man had used on him. "If that is not enough to convince you, I do not know what will."

The beggar watched him for a few moments longer, then gave a short nod. "Good enough." He turned and resumed his progress, though with a little more speed. Jamana followed with a sigh and a nervous glance back.

• • • • •

In time, Jamana and the beggar emerged from between two enormous rocks and looked down on an open beach. Smooth sand stretched along the water as far as the eye could reach.

"I think you can find your way from here," the beggar said.

"Thank you," Jamana answered. The beggar nodded and disappeared among the rocks and brush. Was he the help the old man had promised? If so, he hadn't been around for very long. Jamana sighed, adjusted the bag on his shoulder and set out down the beach.

He soon discovered there was a trick to walking along a sandy beach. Too close to the water and his feet would stick and sink in the water-logged sand. Too far from the water, and the loose sand became even harder to walk through. He had to maintain just the right distance from the water's edge to find the right consistency of sand upon which to walk.

Another roar echoed through the rocks behind. Jamana stumbled, looked back, and tried to pick up his pace. Had that roar been closer than the last one? It sounded louder. Or was that his imagination?

A few moments later, another roar reached his ears. Definitely closer.

Jamana spent so much time glancing over his shoulder, he failed to keep a watch on his path. An odd-shaped hole in the sand caught his left foot. He barely managed to get his hands in front of him to break his fall. The impact with the sand didn't hurt much, but a sharp pain in his ankle did.

He lifted his face and stared down the beach. A haze hung over the sand, and the water shimmered. Gentle wavelets stirred the surface as they flowed in. A pair of dark figures pulled a rowboat to shore in the distance. Or did they? He blinked and didn't see them any more. The haze seemed to grow.

"Jamana!" The voice rang out behind him. He climbed to one knee and looked back.

The tunaldi perched like an enormous lizard atop one of the last rocks. Two figures sat on its back. Jamana could not make them out, but the voice had sounded familiar.

Jamana moaned and scrambled to his feet. He tried to run, but the pain in his ankle almost made him fall again. He limped with excruciating slowness. The moisture fled from his mouth.

He glanced back. The tunaldi bounded down from the rock and

raced across the beach. It would overtake him in a matter of moments.

He looked ahead and blinked. The rowboat and the two figures. They did exist, and they were closer than he had thought. He faltered toward them, reaching out a hand in supplication.

Something struck him from behind and he plowed into the sand again. Caught by surprise, he didn't break his fall this time. He spit sand and tried to push up again. The weight struck him again, but this time it pressed down, forcing his entire body down into the wet sand. Water soaked into his robe and chilled his skin.

"Careful! We want the book he carries." That voice had to be Komadi, but it came from so high above.

Jamana struggled against the unbearable weight. Water and sand pushed past his lips and into his mouth. Every time he tried to push himself up, he succeeded only in digging his hands down deeper.

A roar slammed against his ears with immense pressure, and the weight on his back vanished. Jamana flailed until he got his face up, spitting sand and gasping for air.

"If you can move, do it!" an unfamiliar voice yelled.

Jamana struggled to pull himself out of the sand, and glanced back. The tunaldi stood only a couple of feet away, though it held one front leg off the ground as if injured. He could now see Komadi on its back, along with… was that Harbinger? Wonderful. He had been chased down by a monster, a mage, and a god.

But a young man stood between Jamana and the creature. A gold-trimmed red cloak hung down his back beneath long blond hair. In his right hand, he held a sword dripping with blood; in his left, he spun an odd-looking flail. "Been wanting to fight one of these since Talinir did it," he muttered.

"Are you insane?" demanded Harbinger. "You think to stand against one of the tunaldi?"

In response, the monster roared and lunged forward at the young man. He dodged to the side with surprising speed. A quick swipe with his sword didn't seem to do much damage, but he grinned all the same. From this angle, Jamana could see pale skin and a short beard. Rasnian or Varioch? A long way from home, either way.

Jamana pulled his bag out of the sand and managed to get to his feet, though his ankle continued to throb with pain.

The tunaldi swiped at the annoying warrior with its massive claws. One of them snagged the edge of the cloak and pulled loose the gold trim.

"Now look what you've done! I really like this cloak."

Jamana tried to blink sand out of his eyes. Who was this man? And did he really think he could take on this monster? Jamana took a halting step backward. As he did, his magical senses kicked in. He almost lost his balance again. An overwhelming source of power reverberated right behind him.

Before he could turn around, a hand rested on his shoulder. "Will you be all right, acolyte?" The voice sounded odd, as if the speaker didn't fully understand how to pronounce each word. Jamana turned his head and looked at another young man, short and also fair-skinned, but horribly scarred across his face.

"A little help here?" the blond warrior called.

The scar-faced man turned toward the conflict. "I thought you wanted to fight it."

The warrior dodged another lunge from the tunaldi, but lost his balance and fell. He scrambled backward on the sand. "Some of us don't have a warpsteel blade!" he yelled.

"Wait!" Harbinger touched the creature from above and it came to a stop. He stared at the scarred man.

"What are you doing?" Komadi demanded.

In response, Harbinger swung his leg over the side and slid down from the creature's back. He approached the scarred man with arms spread out. "Great one!" he exclaimed. "Allow me to introduce myself. I am—"

"You look like Forerunner. Are you like him?" the scarred man interrupted.

"Forerunner is one of my order. He—"

"Not any more. He's dead." The scarred man looked up at Komadi. "You'd better get down too. This creature does not belong in our world, and I'm not going to let it stay."

"You?" Komadi seemed about to argue, but then gave a sudden intake of breath. Maybe he finally sensed what Jamana had from the start: the scarred man held an unbelievable amount of power within, power beyond that of a Lord, even. Maybe more than the gods. Komadi scrambled down, though not as gracefully as Harbinger. The tunaldi stood still, eyeing all of them, but poised to attack if given the order.

"Ah, this creature belongs to Nummotem, god of Mandiata," Harbinger said. "I do not think he would be pleased if anything were to happen to it."

"I don't care." The scarred man pointed at the ground beneath the tunaldi. Jamana felt vibrations through the air as unleashed power flowed from the man's outstretched arm. The sand exploded outward in all directions. Jamana shielded his face with his arm, but tried to keep watching.

The tunaldi roared in surprise and anger. It attempted to leap forward, but its back legs had already sunk down into the moving sand. Its front legs scrambled for solid ground, but found none. In only a few moments, all four legs had disappeared into the sand. Water flowed in from the lake, and the tunaldi continued to sink. Its roars changed tone from anger to fear. Jamana turned away and tried to plug his ears. The sound was horrible, but it didn't last long. When the sound stopped, Jamana looked back. The scarred man lowered his arm. No sign remained of the tunaldi, buried beneath the wet sand of the beach that rippled beneath a new shallow inlet.

For a moment, no one spoke. The blond warrior moved up next to the scarred man. "All right, I'll admit it. That was impressive. I expected you to just blow it away."

"Seri said I need to learn new ways to use my power. I'm trying."

Did he say Seri?

"Your greatness," Harbinger said, finding his voice. "We seem to have an unnecessary conflict here. This acolyte stole an item from the royal palace, and we were merely trying to recover it. He—"

"I know who you are." The scarred man glared into Harbinger's face. "You are not wanted in this world any more than that creature. Leave now, before I send you to join it."

Komadi pulled on Harbinger's sleeve. He hesitated only a moment before nodding and joining the mage in a quick retreat down the beach.

The scar-faced man turned and looked up at Jamana. "Are you all right?" he repeated.

"I am well, thanks to you," Jamana said. "You are… I have so many questions. I do not know which one to ask first."

The warrior laughed. "Pick one. And then let's head for the boat. We should get off this beach, just in case."

"Did you mention the name Seri?"

<h1 style="text-align:center">(((5)))</h1>

Jamana rested in the bow of the rowboat while his two rescuers pulled at the oars. Marshal and Victor. He repeated their names in his head. What a remarkable coincidence, to be rescued by someone who had met Seri. And possessed such power!

"You must be the lost King," he said, breaking the silence.

Marshal glanced at him. "People say that," he acknowledged.

"He is," Victor said. "He just doesn't want to admit it."

"And Seri found you, just like she wanted." Jamana chuckled. "Of course she did. Of course."

"You should know that Seri is not with us," Marshal said. "We are going to follow her, though."

"We'd be a lot further along, if we hadn't stopped for you," Victor added. "Marshal says he felt strange power coming from your direction, which is why we showed up. Lucky for you."

"You saved my life," Jamana said. "I am in your debt. I do not understand, though. You are following Seri? To Zes Sivas?"

Marshal and Victor exchanged a glance. "No," Marshal said. "She is…"

"She's in danger," Victor finished. "I'm Bonded to her, and I can tell."

Jamana furrowed his brow. "Then you should not have stopped for me! You should rush to her aid!"

Marshal rocked his head and licked his lips. "It's not exactly like that."

"I do not understand."

"It's a long story," Victor said. "We'll tell you on the ship."

"Ship?"

Victor nodded ahead. Jamana turned and looked.

A vessel with its sails furled sat waiting for them not far ahead. It looked to be about forty feet long with overlapping hull planks, and a single mast in the middle. Several figures moved about on the deck.

"Think Tich can repair my cloak?" Victor asked.

"You can ask," Marshal said. "I'd be scared to."

"All women scare you."

Jamana listened to the banter between the two men and smiled. They sounded like he and Dravid once did: two friends who knew each other well. Yet there was something else here. The connection between these two felt stronger. They had a bond that had endured much.

Sooner than Jamana expected, they pulled up next to the ship. A short, blonde woman leaned over the side and smirked down at them. Her skin tone resembled Jamana's rescuers, though hers appeared much more tanned by the sun.

"Sorry, men," she said. "While you were gone, we tossed the captain overboard and took over the ship. We've decided to leave Antises and go into piracy."

"What's piracy?" Victor asked.

"Your innocent ignorance is only cute up to a point," the woman said. "Who's your new friend?"

"This is Jamana, a mage acolyte," Marshal said. "Toss down the rope, Tich."

"I told you. Things have changed. To come on board, you have to swear loyalty to the new captain."

"Who's the new captain?" Victor wanted to know.

"I am, of course."

"Tich…" Marshal rolled his eyes.

At that moment, another figure came up behind Tich. Jamana blinked. One of the Eldanim! At least he didn't look much like Curasir. He still had the same angular features, but darker hair and…

"Marshal!" the Eldani cried. "How am I supposed to protect you if you run off without me?"

Marshal chuckled and held out his hands. "I have the powers of a King and a Lord now, Talinir. What do you need to protect me from?"

"He just buried one of your tunaldi," Victor added.

"All the power in the world won't protect you from a knife in the dark," Talinir argued. "Don't do that again."

A tall, Ch'olanese man walked behind the other two and glanced down at the rowboat. "Are you two going to just keep talking, or help them on board?" he asked. As if it meant nothing either way, he moved on across the deck.

"Sorry, captain," Tich answered, tossing a rope down to Marshal.

Jamana squinted. "If that was the captain, what was she saying…"

"You have to get used to Tich," Victor said. "She's a curious thing." He took the rope from Marshal and pulled himself up hand-over-hand.

In a few moments, all three of them stood on the deck. Jamana looked around. Besides the captain, Tich, and the eldani, he only saw a couple of other sailors at work on tasks he didn't understand. They also appeared Ch'olanese. "Whose ship is this?" he wondered.

"It belongs to an… acquaintance of ours," Marshal said. "He's down below. You probably won't see much of him."

Despite the warm air and lack of wind, Jamana shivered. His wet robes clung to his body. Tich appeared to notice his discomfort.

"All right, acolyte. Follow me. Let's find you some more suitable clothes. Up here, we like to stay above the water, not bring it with us everywhere."

Her tone sounded harsh, but without malice. Jamana glanced at Marshal, who nodded. "Go with her. Once you're dried off, we'll talk."

Jamana turned back to Tich. She motioned with a jerk of her head and led the way to a hatch. Up close, Jamana re-evaluated his first impressions of the female sailor. She couldn't be much older than himself, if that. She carried herself with a strange confidence bordering on swagger. Her hair, shorter than Victor's, looked like she had cut it herself. She wore a white shirt with a neckline a bit too low for Jamana's comfort, trousers, and sturdy boots. A large knife hung from one side of her belt, and from the other hung a coin purse that jingled with each step.

After they descended the ladder into the hold, Jamana looked around at a bewildering arrangement of hammocks, barrels, crates, and various tools, ropes and other items he couldn't identify. Tich led the way to a large chest and pulled it open.

"We have a lot of spare clothing in here. All sizes. Most of them are from dead people I've pulled out of the lake myself." She shook her head. "So many people drown out here. It breaks the heart. Anyway, you should be able to find something to fit you." She looked him over again with a raised eyebrow and stepped out of the way. "Maybe."

Jamana set down the book. Its wrappings should have protected it from the water, but he should check it soon. He shivered again and began to sort through the clothing.

"What's that thing?" Tich asked.

"A book."

"That's a big book. Not so easy to carry around. Must be important."

"Very important." Jamana held up a pair of trousers that appeared to be near his size.

"I used to read a lot myself. The Lord's Library in Raeton. My mother took me often and I read everything I could. That's how I learned eleven different ways to kill a man. No, wait." She looked up and mouthed something silently. 'Twelve. It was twelve. I used number four against the librarian when he tried to hurt me. That's why I ended up here."

"You're from Rasna, then." Jamana finally found a shirt, but it looked exceedingly large.

"That's where I started, sure. Been to all six lands since. Find what you needed?"

"I think these will do."

"Better change then. I can hang up those robes to dry somewhere."

Jamana waited, looking at her. She glanced around. "What is it?"

"Forgive me. But I have no desire to change clothes in front of you."

"Oh. You're one of those." She turned her back on him. "Go ahead, bashful."

What kind of a woman was this? As Jamana struggled to extricate himself from the wet robes, he wondered what Dravid would think of her. His friend always had more of a way with the girls. Jamana had known many girls back in Mandiata, but ultimately, they all seemed so similar. Then he had met Seri and she had destroyed his expectations of the female sex. But Tich… As he finally got the robe over his head, he caught her glancing back at him.

"Excuse me!"

She jerked her head back. "Sorry. I thought you would be done by now."

Jamana pulled on the new clothes as fast as he could. As anticipated, the shirt hung very loose. He tied it and the trousers around his waist with a weather-beaten belt. "I'm done."

"About time." Tich turned around and looked him over. "You're a big man. That shirt must have belonged to old Captain Snert. He was enormous. Died in his sleep. We had to rip the door frame open to get his body out of the cabin."

Jamana cocked his head and peered at her in the low light. "You talk about death a lot."

She shrugged. "Everyone dies. So we all have that in common."

"Everyone also lives."

Tich gathered up the discarded robes. "Do they?"

(((6)))

Marshal looked over the back of the ship—the stern, Tich and the captain called it—at the coast of Mandiata. It was sheer chance that brought them to this spot in time to help Jamana. Or was it? Aelia, his mother, would have called it the hand of Theon. No doubt the priest Nian would say the same.

When Seri and Volraag left Ch'olan by ship, Marshal had despaired. To his shock, the solution to their problem had come from Kishin, the assassin. Though badly wounded, he led Marshal, Victor and Talinir to his home and from there to this ship, which he owned. Assassination paid well, apparently.

Unfortunately, they had made little progress on the water. On the first day, the winds had died and not returned, except in brief periods. Rather than sail out into the open lake, the captain of the ship, a rather grumpy individual known as Atzam, had insisted on staying close to the coastline.

Marshal agreed with the decision, though Victor did not. If they sailed deeper out into the lake and lost the wind, the only port nearby would be Zes Sivas. Marshal did not want to go near that place just yet. He knew he would have to, eventually, but for now, following Seri was the priority.

"Any change with her?" he asked out loud.

Victor sat sprawled on a coil of thick rope. He looked up in surprise. "What?"

"Seri. Any change?"

Victor thought for a moment. "I haven't felt any sudden pulls or anything. She's still in danger, but not severe."

Marshal nodded. Victor's bond to Seri created an efficient guide. For now, they could follow at a slow pace. Surely, Volraag's ship could not move any faster than theirs.

"What would you do if I told you her danger was severe?" Victor asked.

Marshal looked over his shoulder at his friend. "I don't know. Probably try to use my power to get to her faster."

"How?" Victor snorted. "What would you do? Fly?"

"Maybe."

"Ha."

Silence fell. Marshal watched one of the other sailors toss a line of some kind over the railing down into the water. He knew of three other sailors on board, besides the captain and Tich. Unlike Tich, the others showed no interest in their passengers. Marshal wasn't sure they even spoke the common language.

"Here they come," Victor noted. Marshal turned back to see Tich and Jamana emerging from the hold.

"How many stories do you think she's told him?" Victor got to his feet.

Now Marshal snorted. "Four or five at least. The question is whether she's brought up her parents yet."

Victor shook his head. "She's crazy."

"Nian told a lot of stories too," Marshal recalled. "But his…"

"His were funny. And they felt real. Something is always off with Tich's."

Marshal didn't answer as the other two drew near. Jamana wore shirt and trousers similar to the other sailors now, but the shirt was far too large for him.

"Here's your acolyte," Tich said. "He insisted on changing in front of me. Bold of him."

Jamana's mouth dropped. "I did no such thing!"

"I'm not complaining. He's not bad looking, now that we got those robes off him."

"Thank you, Tich," Marshal said. "We'd like to talk alone now."

Tich shrugged. "Like I want to hear anything you boys have to say." She turned on her heel and headed toward the bow.

"What a strange woman," Jamana said.

"Wait a few days." Victor stretched and yawned. "You haven't heard anything yet."

No one said anything for a moment. Jamana tugged on the overlarge shirt. He looked awkward and unsure of himself.

"I suppose we should share our stories, then," Marshal said at last. "Where should we begin?"

"Tell me of Seri and Dravid," Jamana pleaded. "I have not seen them in months."

"We met them… oh, it's been weeks now…" Marshal looked to Victor for confirmation.

"A couple of months by now, surely."

"Maybe so. Summer hadn't begun, I don't think. They were traveling with Forerunner, who was a herald, I guess, for those in the Otherworld that are coming back."

"The gods," Victor added.

"They are already here!" Jamana said. "This is why I am trying to get back to Zes Sivas. And protect the book. The gods have returned!"

Marshal straightened. "I saw the one on the beach; he was like Forerunner. Are you saying there are more?"

Jamana nodded. "At least one. Nummotem. He claims to be one of the ancient gods of my people."

"He's saying this in public?"

"He is in the palace itself! And he promises to change everything. Even the Laws of Cursings and Bindings!"

Marshal and Victor exchanged a quick look. "How?" Victor demanded.

"He doesn't say. But he says more gods are coming back, and they're going to meet them."

"Where?"

"A high place in Kuktarma, I was told."

Marshal pushed away from the railing and paced. "This isn't good. They're moving faster than we thought."

"You know they've probably brought an army through the other gate already," Victor said. "The one in Varioch."

Jamana looked from one to the other. "But what does all this have to do with Seri and Dravid?"

Marshal sighed. "Victor, try starting from the beginning and telling him the whole story. I don't think my voice can handle it." He leaned against the railing again and listened as Victor began in Drusa's Crossing and started telling everything.

How long ago had that been? Winter had been losing its grasp when they set out, and they must be at least mid-way through summer. Months. Months that had changed his life in so many ways.

Hearing Victor speak of his mother brought too much pain. Marshal turned and looked out over the water again, pulling his thoughts inward, descending into himself as he always had while still under the curse. Aelia hated it when he did that. But she wasn't here any more, was she?

Here in his own thought-world, no one else existed. Victor's voice became a buzzing sound that no longer mattered. He knew this wasn't good for him; these thought processes led him to almost killing himself before, if Victor hadn't intervened. But he had no desire to hear his mother's story again.

A hand touched his shoulder. He shoved it away and turned, words of reproach for Victor on his lips. But Talinir stood there, looking at him with that angular face which somehow managed to show concern and care. Marshal blinked.

"…and then Marshal buried the high place!" Victor's voice faded back into clarity. "He's got the powers of a Lord and the King now. He's probably more powerful than anyone in Antises has ever been!"

"But… Dravid is still in the Otherworld?" Jamana wrung his hands together.

"He's all right," Marshal said. "I'm bound to him. His danger is… not significant right now." The Binding to Dravid pulled at him all day, every day. It wasn't strong, but it served as a constant reminder of his own failures. Another thing he needed to deal with… and soon.

"How can you say that?" Jamana demanded. "He is a slave to one of those… gods! Or whatever they are!"

"You'll have to trust me," Marshal answered. "I will go find him. Soon."

"But we're following Seri, you said."

"Yes."

Jamana looked back to Victor. "And you are bonded to her. How much danger is she in?"

Victor hesitated. "Not a lot at the moment. She's with some bad people, yes. But she has Ixchel with her."

Jamana nodded. "That is the best news you've told me this whole time." He looked out over the water. "I trust Ixchel to protect her. She is… impressive."

"That's one way of putting it." Victor chuckled.

Jamana opened his mouth to ask another question, but Marshal held up his hand. "Wait. I need to think for a moment."

He stepped away from the other three. Let Talinir and Victor answer Jamana's question for now. They could do a better job than he could, anyway. Right now…

Jamana's news troubled him. The gods were moving faster than he expected. They could, after all, travel between the worlds without the portals. He had seen it done by the Durunim they met before. Marshal drew his warpsteel sword and looked at it. With his new power, he believed he could cut his own way into the Otherworld any time he wanted.

But the gods did not want to come one at a time. They wanted to bring their armies to this world, to dominate the people of Antises as they had in the distant past. They wanted worship and power.

Victor was right. They had left behind the portal in Varioch. Volraag must have opened it. Armies of Durunim would be pouring through. Would they move to conquer Varioch or Rasna at once? He had no way of knowing.

The portal in Ch'olan was useless now. Marshal had made sure of that. The army on the other side would have to march across the Otherworld to one of the other portals.

Jamana's news about the pilgrimage to the high place made everything worse. Volraag and Seri were heading in the same direction. Unless Seri could convince him otherwise, Volraag would open the portal. Who knew what would emerge?

Marshal noticed Tich watching him from the opposite side of the ship. He ignored her and returned to the other three in time to hear Talinir explaining the origin of the Durunim.

"Tell me about this book you carry," Marshal said. "Why is it important?"

Jamana hesitated only a moment. "It is the story of the Lords' Betrayal. It tells much of the early history of Antises."

Marshal leaned forward. "You mean it tells how the Laws of Cursings and Bindings were created?"

"It… tells much of those days. And how it was corrupted."

"Can they…" Marshal didn't know exactly how to ask. "Could the mages learn from this book about how to… undo it all?"

"What do you mean?" Jamana's eyes widened.

"We want to end the curses," Victor said. "That's been our goal all along."

"But… but that is what the gods want as well. Why would you want that?"

"The curses are a harsh judgment on people. There is no mercy. It's not right." Marshal felt his face getting hot.

"But there would be no judgment at all!" Jamana protested. "No consequences for wrongdoing!"

"I don't have all the answers," Marshal said. "But I know that judgment should come from other people. Just rulers, perhaps. Not from blind magic that cannot know circumstances or feel sympathy. Do people deserve punishment for what they do? Sometimes, sure. But sometimes… people shouldn't get what they deserve."

Jamana looked like he wanted to say something else, but didn't.

"Can the book guide us?" Marshal repeated. "Can the mages learn from it?"

"Perhaps."

Marshal nodded and looked toward the open water. "Our course is decided then."

Victor stood. "I thought our course was to follow Seri."

"It is. But we're making a stop along the way."

"Where?" Talinir asked.

"We're going to Zes Sivas."

(((7)))

When the army came to a halt for the night, or whatever one called it in the Otherworld, Dravid learned more about his servitude to Vayan. A nameless servant introduced him to two other human slaves: Tiur and Lasa, both from Rasna, stolen from their homes like the people in the village of Tungrorum. Together, the three of them erected Vayan's elaborate tent and worked on preparing his supper.

"I'm afraid I'm not much use to you," Dravid said. "A one-legged slave is not very helpful."

Tiur shrugged, a gesture barely noticeable on his large frame. "We've been managing with just the two of us," he answered. "Every little bit you add is something we did not have before." He stirred a mixture of meat and herbs frying over a small fire.

Lasa, a dark-haired young woman, looked tiny next to Tiur. She smiled, though Dravid did not sense much warmth from it. "Vayan keeps us busy, but he is not cruel, like some of the gods."

"Did you two know each other before coming here?" Dravid asked.

They glanced at each other. "I do not remember," Tiur said. "Nor I," Lasa added.

"You don't remember?" Dravid frowned. "Have you forgotten your lives in our world? How long have you been here?"

Lasa shrugged this time. "I'm not sure. A long time."

Tiur removed the frying pan from the fire. "Lasa, I seem to have misplaced the platter. Have you seen it?"

Lasa looked around. "I didn't see it when we unpacked, but it must be here somewhere."

"Oh, I can help with that!" Dravid focused and felt the familiar warmth spread within as he accessed his power. He gestured in the air and golden light flowed from his hand. He shaped it into a large oval, then offered it to Tiur. "This should work."

Tiur and Lasa stared at him. "You possess the power of the gods!" Lasa whispered. "How is this possible?"

"A question I wish to explore myself!" Vayan's voice startled all three of them, as he emerged from the tent. "Tiur, use the platter Dravid has provided. I'm sure it will be splendid."

In a few moments, the slaves finished with Vayan's meal and carried it into the tent, followed by the god. As Tiur set the platter on Vayan's personal table, Dravid realized his error. He could not maintain a magical structure indefinitely. During the chariot ride, he had only reshaped the magical structure Vayan himself created. The platter, though, was all Dravid. And the longer he kept it substantial, the more he would feel the effects.

Vayan sat and took a bite of the meat. "Excellent as usual, Tiur," he proclaimed. The slave bowed and exited the tent. Lasa remained near, holding a pitcher to refill Vayan's drink should he desire. Dravid, unsure as to his place, looked around. He took a halting step toward the exit.

"Stay, Dravid." Vayan motioned with his fork. "We still have things to discuss."

Dravid stood still, growing more uncomfortable with each passing moment. His chest grew tight, the familiar burning sensation within moved up his throat, drying out his mouth. The heat built up behind his eyes. He put his hand over them and gritted his teeth.

When he could bear it no longer, Dravid pushed back against it. Each time this happened, it grew harder to shut it off. What if he couldn't shut it down someday? Would he burn alive from the inside out? The thought almost panicked him, but he kept his focus. The heat diminished. At the same moment, the platter vanished. Vayan's food plopped onto the tabletop. Lasa's eyes widened, and she took a step back.

Vayan chuckled. "And there we have the answer to one question!" He looked up as Dravid leaned hard on his staff and almost fell over. "You have a strict limit on the time you can hold a shape. Interesting."

Dravid nodded and rubbed at his eyes. He licked his lips, trying to generate saliva. Noticing this, Vayan lifted his water glass. "Lasa, give him a drink."

The slave girl complied. Dravid guzzled the entire glass down and handed it back with a grateful smile. She nodded, and stepped back again, eyes still wide.

Vayan removed the crown from his head and set it on the table beside his scepter and the spilled food. He ran his fingers through perfectly smooth black hair that fell to his shoulders. "Calu was somewhat vague on how you acquired such power," he said. "Perhaps you can elaborate for me."

Dravid considered for a moment, but could think of no reason to lie. "I tried to absorb power from Forerunner. It almost killed me, but somehow, it worked. I guess. Since then, I've been able to do what you saw." Before Vayan could speak, Dravid asked his own question. "Is Calu very high among your hierarchy?"

Vayan snorted. "Him? He's a god of Rasna. He has no place among this gathering, but is tagging along rather than cross all of the land by himself." He picked up a piece of meat from the table, eyed it for a moment, then popped it into his mouth. He chewed, swallowed, and leaned back in his chair.

"I suppose it is remotely possible that no mage of your world ever tried to absorb the power of a god before, but it seems unlikely." His gaze swept over Dravid, and he narrowed his eyes. "Is there something different about you, I wonder?"

"You mean besides missing a leg?"

Vayan's eyes glanced briefly at the stump of Dravid's left leg, then flickered back to his face. He shook his head; his earrings made impressive arcs as they swung with it.

"No, no. It would be something within." He jumped to his feet and crossed the tent to Dravid's side. Vayan walked in a circle around him, staring down as if to penetrate his soul. "I can sense the power within you, and a tiny spark of your world's magic. But nothing else. Curious."

Vayan took a step away from Dravid as if to return to his chair, but stopped instead. He clenched one of his fists and bowed his head, grimacing. Before Dravid could ask, he shook his head and moved on. Before sitting, however, he spun back and stared once more. Dravid shifted his weight on the staff, not sure what else he should do or say.

"Tell me of your pain," Vayan suggested. The abrupt change in topic caught Dravid by surprise. He blinked twice.

"My pain? You mean from my leg?"

"No, let us start with something smaller. A recent pain, perhaps?" Vayan took his seat.

The kiss popped into Dravid's head, but he would not tell Vayan of that. He thought of helping Marshal, and the fight against the curse-stalkers. He had emerged from that battle with surprisingly little pain for himself, but...

"That scar on your left hand," Vayan said. "Tell me about it."

Dravid looked at the back of his hand. The burn mark, from the curse-stalker. Of course. "A monster attacked me," he said. He gave a brief description of the battle with the curse-stalker and how Ixchel rescued him. He still wondered why her rescue had not bonded them. Forerunner's power, perhaps?

"So you bear more than just the one scar?"

"No." Dravid shook his head. "Forerunner healed me. Only this scar remains."

Varan clapped his hands. "A perfect opportunity. You have shown me your power. Now I will show you mine." He jumped back to his feet and approached Dravid again. "Normally, I would have you kneel, but I suppose I can make an exception for your situation."

"What are you talking about?"

"I take my people's pain away. It soothes me, and relieves them. Is it not a wonderful relationship?"

"I don't understand."

Vayan entwined the fingers of both hands and then pulled them apart. A web of golden light connected them. He reached down and placed the web over Dravid's face. The magical construct felt cool against his skin, still warm from his own magic use.

"Tell me the story again," Vayan instructed. "This time, leave no detail out."

Dravid frowned, but Vayan's voice still resonated with magic. It was difficult to defy. He started again, telling of how Seri had left him alone and the curse-stalker attacked. He told of Ixchel's rescue, the slaying of the beast, and Forerunner's healing. As he spoke, he thought he felt an occasional pulse of energy from the web of light on his face, but nothing of consequence.

When he finished, Vayan pulled the web of light away. It dissolved back into his hands. The god's head leaned back, eyes closed, mouth open in what looked like... ecstasy? Dravid's eyes darted toward Lasa, who still stood near the door of the tent, pitcher in hand. Her eyes no longer appeared wide. Instead, he thought he saw a tear glisten before she wiped it away. Noticing him watching, she hung her head.

"Exhilarating!" Vayan proclaimed. He spun on his heel and danced back to his chair. He collapsed on it as if exhausted.

Dravid blinked. What had just occurred? They had discussed how he gained his magic, and then... Vayan asked about pain. Didn't he?

"Tell me, Dravid." Vayan's voice slurred a bit, like an intoxicated man. "Where did you get that scar on your left hand?"

Scar? Dravid lifted his hand and looked at both sides. The back of his hand boasted a two-inch long reddish scar, like a burn of some kind. Where had that come from?

"I... I don't remember."

For some reason, a chill swept over Dravid. The hairs on his arm lifted. Why? What was happening?

Vayan looked at him through half-lidded eyes. "We will have many more of these conversations, my friend," he said. "You have much to share with me."

(((8)))

Jamana wandered about the deck of the ship, though he didn't have much room to move about. The ship seemed much smaller once he spent a full day on board. How had he ever thought it was big? He made his way to the prow and looked ahead. Zes Sivas shouldn't be too far. Would he be able to see it today? The wind continued to be temperamental, giving the ship very little movement.

Marshal tried using his power to propel the ship forward, but had little success. He made some big splashes, but couldn't find a way to push against the water at the proper angle.

Jamana sighed. A normal voyage to Zes Sivas would take two days with a good wind. He had no concept of how long it might take now.

A thump came from below his feet. He glanced down, despite knowing he wouldn't see anything through the deck. A private cabin lay below him here, didn't it? The owner of the ship stayed within. Kishin, the others called him. A cursed assassin who had switched sides to join Marshal's cause. He hadn't emerged from his cabin since Jamana's arrival.

"Summer's always like this." Tich. How had she approached without his notice? As if to emphasize her lack of stealth, she jingled the coin purse at her belt. "Late summer even more so."

"You mean the winds?"

Tich nodded. "A little unusual this early, I guess. But I heard once about a Mandiatan ship that sailed out south of Kuktarma into the sea during late summer. The winds died while they were too far from land. When the winds returned in the fall, another ship found it. Everyone on board had starved to death. Except one man. He ate the others."

"Have you ever seen it? The sea?" Jamana tried to ignore the morbid side of her story.

"Seen it. Never sailed on it. I grew up in Rasna, remember? We're next to the sea. It's not much different from this." She swept an arm out, indicating the water.

"Do you have family still in Rasna, then?"

"No."

Her curt tone made Jamana shut his mouth. Not a topic to explore, evidently. He looked back out over the water. Lake Litanu seemed endless enough to him. He couldn't imagine the sea that lay beyond Antises, water stretching on and on for weeks, they said.

"Lord Tyrr killed my parents." Apparently, Tich did want to explore the topic. She jingled the coin purse again.

"I'm sorry." Jamana turned back to look at her.

She stared back with an intensity he hadn't seen in her before. "They were wild mages."

Jamana almost gasped. "Were they on board the ship Lord Tyrr brought to Zes Sivas?"

Tich didn't answer.

"If so, then I believe it was actually Lord Volraag that killed them. Lord Tyrr was using them to—"

"It doesn't matter," she cut him off. "Lord Tyrr wanted all the wild mages found. He found them and took them. Now they're dead."

"I'm very sorry."

"Don't be. They probably deserved it. Don't you regular mages believe that wild mages are an abomination or something?"

Jamana jerked back as if he had been slapped. "No, I do not. There are some among the Masters who believe that, but it is not taught to us. We—"

"Never mind. Sorry for mentioning it. I need to get back to work." Tich spun on her heel and sauntered away.

Jamana watched her go, even as Victor approached. Victor greeted her, but she didn't answer. He looked at Jamana and raised an eyebrow. Jamana shrugged, not knowing what to say.

"Let me guess: she told you about her parents," Victor said when he reached Jamana's side.

Jamana nodded. "She did that. I am thinking it is not a topic she enjoys."

"Are you kidding? She tells it to everyone. And I think I've heard at least three different versions of the story now."

"Then I am perplexed."

Victor chuckled and leaned against the railing. "She's a strange one. Tells stories all the time, but almost always brings up her parents' death. And other people's death too." He paused. "Come to think of it, almost all her stories are about death."

"Perhaps..." Jamana hesitated. "Perhaps it is her way of dealing with the grief?"

Victor turned his head to look at him. "You think so?"

"It is possible. Volraag killed the wild mages on Lord Tyrr's ship only a few weeks ago. The pain must still be real to her."

Victor squinted against the sun's reflection from the waves. "If that's really when they died. I don't know." He looked across the water, then back at Jamana again. "You think we should pity her, then? You're an interesting man."

"I think all of Theon's children deserve our care," Jamana said. "Tich no less than anyone."

"Huh. Maybe you should have been a priest instead of a mage."

"You are not the first to say that."

• • • • •

Marshal watched Victor talk with Jamana. The acolyte's words and the book changed many things. He thought he knew what to do now, but everything would require precise timing.

"Talinir," he called. The Eldani warden stood only a few feet away, as he often did when Marshal stood on deck. The fact that he and Victor had been able to slip away from him the other day was a fluke. Marshal regretted it, but they did have fun rescuing Jamana.

"What is it?" Talinir asked, approaching.

"The Binding between Victor and I worked even when one of us was in the Otherworld. Is there any reason they wouldn't work over there?"

"I do not know. Your Bindings are a form of magic that we have never been able to study. But if yours worked, I would assume they all would. After all, your curse did not vanish in the Otherworld either."

"I can feel Dravid. His danger is increasing." Marshal instinctively turned in the direction he knew Dravid to be: somewhere toward the northeast. But in another world.

Talinir frowned. On his already severe face, it always looked frightening to Marshal, though he knew the Eldani did not intend it that way. "Yet how can you go after him, follow Seri, and go to Zes

Sivas with the acolyte all at once? That is what troubles you?"

Marshal nodded. He looked toward Victor again. "We're not Bonded any more, so I can leave Victor. But I don't suppose you'll let me travel the Otherworld alone, will you?"

"Not a chance. There is much you do not know. Even with your power, you can be taken by surprise. You need a guide."

"I could travel much faster on my own. I can almost fly, you know."

"What a superb way to let them know you're coming."

"I'm not afraid of the so-called gods."

Talinir's frown deepened. "You should be. Their power is different from yours." Talinir lifted his arm and pulled back his sleeve. "Just a touch did this to me." Most of his forearm pulsed with a darkness beyond black. Faint lightning seemed to crackle across it every few moments.

"It looks like…"

"The Durunim." Talinir pulled his sleeve back down. "The gods transformed my people into those things. Your mother was right, though she didn't know all the details. We fight a war against ourselves."

"But the Durunim are coming here now. Your people are probably not having to fight as much." Marshal didn't mind having long conversations with Talinir. Unlike everyone else, Talinir never winced or looked askance at Marshal while he talked. He knew his voice still didn't sound right sometimes, and even Victor couldn't hide reactions to it.

"I suppose not," Talinir agreed. "They will be relieved, I'm sure."

"We will need their help before this is all over."

Talinir shook his head. "You tried going to them for help once already."

"That was different. Momma wanted them to lift my curse. Now we're fighting the same enemy."

"If the Durunim all leave our world, the Eldanim will be happy to see them go. I do not think it would be easy to persuade them to chase the enemy into another world."

Marshal couldn't argue with that. Yet at some point, someone would have to go to the Eldanim again. They might be the only hope for defeating the gods and their armies, especially if the second portal were opened.

Thinking about it reminded him of the people they had met in Intal Eldanir. He had at least one friend on the high council that could be persuaded. But he knew almost nothing about the rest of the Eldanim leaders. They had not been the least bit interested in helping remove his curse, especially after hearing the prophecy.

"What do you think she meant? About the stars falling?"

Talinir had looked away. He jerked his head back. "What?"

"Lady Sir… whatever her name was. The one who read my future. What do you think she meant?"

"I'm sure I don't know."

"But you could guess?"

Talinir hesitated. "The nature of the stars themselves is… a subject of some debate among my people," he said.

"Are they alive?"

"What?"

"Are the stars living beings? Seri thought she saw one when her Bond was broken. It took away her star-sight."

Talinir did not answer for a few moments. "I do not know what she saw," he said at last. "I have never seen a star descend, nor do I know of anyone who has."

Marshal could not help noticing Talinir had not answered the question. He had a clever way with words. But it wasn't worth pursuing right now.

"All right. So if you come with me into the Otherworld, how fast can we move?" He looked back toward Dravid's direction.

"If we have need of speed, we should be able to travel fairly quick."

"Faster than you led us through Varioch?" Marshal smiled and glanced at the Eldani.

Talinir scowled. "You know we were trying to avoid being found. We can move much faster in the Otherworld."

"Good. We'll need to." Marshal pointed. "Dravid is that direction, but moving. I think he's with the Durunim army that's on its way to the third portal."

"Which Volraag is trying to open."

Marshal nodded. "We need to rescue Dravid, stop Volraag, rescue Seri, and deliver Jamana and his book to Zes Sivas." He paused. "And probably have some thought about what to do if we fail at any of these tasks."

"Everything is not up to you, Marshal."

"It's not?" He pointed out at the water and released a burst of magic. A spray of water exploded into the air. "I have the power of a King of Antises. By all accounts, I am the King. If it's not up to me, then who is up to?"

"You have help. You have friends. Trust them."

"You think Seri will stop Volraag."

"I don't know. But she went with him for a reason."

Marshal considered it. "I need to think for a while."

Talinir nodded and moved away, but only a few feet. Marshal had the feeling he would never be out of the warden's sight again.

He needed to plan, but his thoughts returned to Talinir's non-answer about the stars. Thinking about them made him long to see them again. His hand strayed to the hilt of his warpsteel sword. With it, he could sunder the barriers between the worlds, cross over, and look at the stars again. He had no doubts that with his new power, he could do it. It would be easy.

And it would be selfish. He could not behave that way. Not with so much riding on his actions now. So many people depending on him. He might not want to be King, but until this crisis was solved, his actions were just as monumental as a King's.

Talinir had not answered the question. He believed something about the Otherworld's stars, but he didn't want to talk about it. Curious.

Lady Sira... Siratel. That was it. The old Eldani woman saw stars falling in his future. What could it mean? Would he cause the stars to fall? Through his success or his failure? The vision had terrified Lady Siratel. In his mind, he saw her waving in the darkness of her room, pushing Eniri away, repeating "they fell!" over and over.

Eniri. He hadn't thought of her in a very long time. Her kindness to him had made a difference in his life. Outside of his mother, she had been the only female in his life who didn't seem to mind his company... at least until Seri.

Seri. Such an amazing woman. If he were to be a King, she would be an amazing queen, he had no doubt. And the prospect of seeing her each day brought a smile to his scarred lips. But the smile faded as quickly as it came. Seri betrayed him. She left him to go with Volraag, his half-brother and greatest enemy.

Victor said she had a plan. She must have a plan, because she had reminded him to follow her. But it felt wrong, completely wrong. Even if she knew what she was doing, Volraag could not be trusted. And his personal assassin even less. Despite Victor's assurances, Marshal worried. What was Seri thinking? And how did it factor into what he now had to do?

(((9)))

Dravid found another advantage to being Vayan's slave the next day. Vayan arranged for him to ride in the wagon which carried the god's tent and supplies. Tiur and Lasa sat together at the front, controlling the beast that pulled the wagon, while Dravid relaxed in the back. He could get used to this.

Or so he thought for the first few minutes. Then the wagon hit the first large bump and he almost fell over. The army followed no roads, and the uneven ground made riding in the wagon even bumpier than it had been with Vayan's chariot. Tiur and Lasa endured without comment, or at least none that he could hear. It would have been nicer to sit closer where they could talk.

Instead, only his own thoughts kept him company as the army plodded along. He had no obligation to stay now. His debt to Calu was fulfilled. The payment for Seri's life. But neither did he have a way to escape. If he slid off this wagon and let the army proceed without him, he would be alone in the Otherworld. As he looked around, trying to see beyond the dust-choked column of Durunim, he could not imagine surviving for long on his own here.

No one would be coming to his rescue, either. He had practically told her not to. Seri expected him to live out his days as Calu's slave. If he were to escape, he would have to do it himself, at a time and place where he had a chance. A chance to… return to his own world?

That would require another portal. He sat up straighter. Of course. This army would be heading to the third portal. "Idiot." Why hadn't he thought of that before? And when they reached the portal, he could escape. Maybe. Somehow. All he needed to do was please Vayan and not get into any kind of trouble until then.

When the army paused at what must have been midday, Lasa climbed off the front of the wagon and joined him in the back, much to his surprise. Company, especially female company, would be very welcome.

Lasa was nothing like Seri. Small, pale-skinned, and nervous, she seemed always on the verge of collapsing in fear. Dravid wasn't sure where that came from, since he had seen no mistreatment from Vayan as yet.

"You are in grave danger," she told him when the wagon began moving again.

"I think my situation has improved," Dravid countered. "I'm riding instead of walking. And Vayan seems much nicer than Calu."

She shook her head and looked around, as if worried someone might hear them. "No, no. You don't understand." She took a deep breath. "What do you remember of last night after dinner?"

Dravid frowned. "Vayan wanted to know more about how I got my power. Then he went to bed. We cleaned up and fell asleep ourselves."

Lasa shook her head again, and her whole body trembled. "He did something to you, and you don't even remember it. Worse. You don't remember something else."

She took his hand in both of hers. Her touch was cool. Despite himself, Dravid felt pleased by it. Lasa turned his hand over and rubbed a spot on the back of it.

"This scar. Do you remember where it came from?"

Dravid looked at his hand. Hadn't someone else asked about that recently? The scar looked like a burn of some kind. But try as he might, he could not remember anything about it.

"I don't know," he admitted.

"Doesn't that… seem strange to you?"

Dravid shrugged. "Memories fade. I have a small scar on my thigh, and I have no idea where it came from either."

"But a scar of this size?"

"What are you trying to say?"

Lasa released his hand. "Last night, you told Vayan the story of the scar. How it came from a curse-stalker."

"You must be mistaken."

"You did. You told him the whole story. And how a warrior—a woman!—rescued you from the beast."

"Ixchel?"

Lasa nodded. "And then Vayan took it."

"What do you mean?"

"This is what he does. He finds stories of pain, and he takes them."

Dravid felt dread rising up within. "He takes them? I don't understand."

"He pulls the story from your memory. You no longer remember it. But he gains… pleasure from it."

A god who gained pleasure from others' pain? The very sadism of it repelled Dravid. "How? How can that be?"

"I don't know. It is his power."

"Can the other gods do the same?"

Lasa looked around, agitated to be answering so many questions. "I don't know."

"Has he… has he done this to you?" Dravid glanced over his shoulder. "And Tiur?"

Lasa nodded. "Many times. I… I remember very little of my days before coming here. And then, I know that I was at first in service to a different god, who… who abused me. Or so Tiur tells me. I have no memory of it."

Vayan seemed so friendly. So curious about humanity. But if Lasa was right, he did it all for his own sick purposes.

"He always takes his slaves from other gods," Lasa explained. "Ones that he knows have been abused. Then over time, he takes their pain."

Dravid struggled with the implications. "But… our pain, our memories… they shape us. It is what makes us who we are!"

"He lets us keep our joy, our good memories. But without the bad memories to give them context, they lose their meaning as well." Lasa also glanced over her shoulder. "Tiur is almost a shell now. He has even forgotten what Vayan does to him, though I've tried to remind him. Vayan grows tired of him and will get rid of him soon."

"And you?" Dravid almost didn't want to ask.

Lasa looked down. "I hold on to a few memories. He wants them, but I try not to tell him. With you here now, he will forget about me for a while."

"Because he wants my pain."

Lasa touched his scarred hand again, and looked down at his stump. "It is not just physical pain he craves." Her voice grew stronger in earnestness. "He wants emotional pain even more. Abandonment. Lost friends. Lost loves." She lifted her head and looked up at the stars. "I think… I think I was in love once."

Dravid recoiled. His greatest pain right now was the loss of Seri. He could not lose that memory! That kiss. That embrace. Would Vayan take it from him? Would he forget Seri altogether? He looked down at Lasa. How much had she lost? The sick dread roiled his stomach.

"Thank you," he said at last, "for telling me."

Lasa nodded. She slid off the back of the wagon and walked beside it. She looked at Dravid. "I hope you remember this conversation."

"Why wouldn't I?"

She looked so sad, Dravid almost reached out to touch her. She closed her eyes and wiped away some of the dust from her face. She looked up at him one more time.

"Because it caused you pain."

(((10)))

Seri pointed at the map on the table with far more confidence than she felt. She glanced at Rathri, the assassin, and then focused on Volraag. "The portal is in northern Kuktarma. I can guide you there."

"So you have said," Rathri answered, his rasping voice like gravel to her ears. "But why should we trust you?"

Seri felt Ixchel move a little bit closer to her side. In her mind, she thanked Lady Lilitu again for deciding she needed a bodyguard. Without Ixchel, she never would have had the courage to continue this course of action.

She ignored Rathri and pointed at the coastline. "With the slow passage we've had so far, I think our best bet is to make port in Arazu and cut across toward the portal. It would be the shortest route."

"You do not answer the question. As usual." Rathri gave an exasperated sigh. "Lord Volraag, this woman is useless. We can find the portal on our own."

Volraag turned his head to look at Rathri, but not without wincing. Seri couldn't help feeling sympathy for him. Victor's flail had torn apart his jaw. Even with the magic that flowed through his body now, the healing process seemed to be taking a long time.

To think she had once thought him handsome! He still possessed some of the good looks that drew people to him: his hair, those eyes… But his lust for power had twisted not just his heart, but his physical body. Absorbing power from the god Calu had increased his muscles, to be sure, but in a grotesque way. None of his finely-tailored clothes fit properly now. And if his damaged face never fully healed… he might never pass for a normal human again. Fitting then, that he spent his time with this leprosy-ravaged assassin, hiding in this cabin most of the time.

"You need me," Seri insisted. "Time is of the essence, and I can guide you quickly."

To be honest, Seri didn't know the exact location of the portal. She had a good idea of its general whereabouts from her reading, but it could be anywhere in the vicinity she kept referencing. Volraag and Rathri didn't need to know that, though.

"Ridiculous." Rathri glared at her.

She slammed her palm down on the table, letting a tiny burst of magic escape with it. The table vibrated. She glared back at Rathri. "Who made you his Lordship's mouth?" she demanded. "He can think for himself!"

"But not speak for himself, thanks to your friend."

"I'm trying to help him!"

"And yet you fought against him at the Ch'olan portal."

"I fought to save lives. You tried to kill me!"

"You fought alongside Lord Volraag's bastard half-brother."

"I left him to come with you!"

This argument had been building since they first boarded Volraag's ship. Seri and Rathri exchanged barbs on a regular basis. The assassin did not trust her, but only Volraag's opinion mattered.

"Ixchel and I can leave right now," Seri declared. "You can put us on shore anywhere."

Volraag raised a hand. Seri and Rathri fell silent. The young Lord looked from one to the other. Then he pointed at Seri, and then at the map. With his finger, he traced the route she had suggested.

"So you agree with me?" she asked.

Volraag nodded.

Seri leaned over and put both hands on the table. "Very good. You communicated. Now imagine what it was like for your half-brother, who couldn't even do that much for eighteen years."

Volraag's eyes stared back into hers, then wandered down her face and settled somewhere just below that. She glanced down and jerked upright. Had her robe been hanging open? She glared at Volraag. He smiled with the side of his mouth that still could move.

Seri stormed out of the cabin, followed closely by Ixchel.

• • • • •

Out on the main deck, Seri found a place far from Volraag's cabin and sat down with her back to the ship's railing. Though this was the fourth ship she had been on this year, she had no desire to stare out over the water. Sometimes, it gave her a queasy feeling in the pit of her stomach.

Ixchel approached. She glanced all around, making sure no threats were near, then settled onto the deck cross-legged, facing Seri.

"I suppose you don't approve of how I handled that," Seri said. A stray wisp of hair fell in front of her eyes, and she tucked it back.

"Do you wish to know what I think?"

Seri sighed. "I'm pretty sure I know, but you may as well tell me anyway."

Ixchel cocked her head to the right. "In all our encounters with others, with each new person we have met, I have supported you. Over and over, I have told them, 'My lady does not lie.'" She paused. "I cannot say that here."

Seri nodded. "Because I am lying."

"Yes. It troubles me greatly. And I do not understand it."

Seri put her head in her hands and groaned. "I don't understand myself. The old King told me we needed him. And Dravid." Mentioning Dravid's name added to her consternation. Marshal promised to rescue him. But they had no way to communicate, no way to know what might be happening in the Otherworld.

"Why do we need him?"

"I don't know! But somehow, I have to convince him to help Marshal. It's the only way to make everything right again."

"I do not understand. Make everything… right?"

"Ugh. I can't even explain it to you. How can I convince him?" She lifted her face and waved in the direction of Volraag's cabin. "Especially when I can't ever talk with him without that freak at his side!"

"Do you wish the assassin removed? I could fight him." Ixchel drew one of her daggers and scratched at the deck with it.

"No, no. Don't do that. He fought both you and Victor together. I wouldn't want you to take him on alone."

"You doubt me?"

"What? No! I just… He's frightening, Ixchel." Seri looked away. "He terrifies me. And I don't… I don't want to risk losing you."

"He is a formidable opponent," Ixchel admitted after a moment of silence.

"Yeah."

They sat without saying anything. The heat, while not as oppressive as it had been in Ch'olan, made Seri uncomfortable in her mage's robes. A breeze would be a relief, but there had been no wind lately. Seri heard the slow movement of the ship's long oars down below. A group of Varioch sailors pulling at the oars kept them moving, but their progress seemed almost nothing.

"I don't know exactly how it will work," Seri said. "But the King said that it would take all four of us: me, Marshal, Dravid, and Volraag. We would be needed to fix things. I'm assuming he meant the troubles with Antises."

"The earthquakes?"

Seri nodded. "I understand that the King's power, which Marshal now has, will be needed. And Volraag's, since he's now a Lord. So we need the two of them and the other Lords together at Zes Sivas. Like at the Passing. But... I don't know what Dravid and I have to do with it. We're not Lords."

"It will be difficult to persuade Volraag to return to Zes Sivas. And the other Lords will not be pleased to see him."

"I know! And we can't let him open the third portal, either!"

"Yet that is where we are going. And you said you would guide him there."

"I did. But I don't even know where it is, exactly. Just the area."

"But why guide him?"

Seri's smiled, but felt no pleasure. "That's where I'm lying. It's the only way I can think of that he'll let us stay with him. And I need time. Time to persuade him."

"But you cannot even talk with him. Because of Rathri."

Seri nodded.

"I think I understand a little better," Ixchel said. "I wish you had told me all of this when we first joined them."

"Things were crazy. And, and I had just lost Dravid."

"He is not dead."

"No, he's a slave. And it's all my fault."

"He did it to save your life. It is a noble thing."

"It doesn't feel noble."

"To you, maybe. But it does to him. Were he a member of my order, he would be greatly honored."

"How so?" Seri straightened up a little.

Ixchel put her dagger away. "When a Holcan dies in the act of saving the one to whom she is pledged, those who remain hold a special ceremony in the plaza between the pyramids in Woqan. Her body is carried by her sisters down the full length of the plaza, and entombed within the oldest of the pyramids. If her body is unavailable, an empty shroud is carried in her place."

Seri smiled. "That sounds like a great honor. Does it happen often?"

Ixchel shook her head. "No. True danger is rare in Antises, with the Laws in place."

"Not for us."

"I would say that your story is an exception. Such danger is very rare."

"Lucky you. You get assigned to the one woman in Antises' recent history who has a real chance of getting killed." Seri almost laughed.

"I am fortunate indeed."

Seri ducked her head to hide her smile. "Right. You consider that an honor."

"It is the purpose of my training."

Seri considered everything for a while. "So what can we do about Rathri?"

"I have an idea."

(((11)))

One of the great advantages to travel by ship was the view at night. Marshal took the steps to the forecastle, where he stretched himself out on the bowsprit and gazed at the sky. They weren't the stars of the Otherworld, of course, but the beauty still appealed to him. Here, also, he could see the moon, or half of it anyway. In its light, he could see across the small ship. The only other person on deck was the helmsman on the aftcastle, on duty and hoping some wind might yet turn up.

Marshal watched the stars for a while, trying to identify some of the constellations Aelia had tried to teach him as a child. Growing up on the side of a mountain meant he never saw the full arc of the sky like he did now. In the Otherworld, he knew the stars had something to do with magic. But here? What did they mean? Nian the priest, in one of their many conversations, claimed that some of the stars were actually other worlds, completely unknown. The thought fascinated him. Were there ways to reach those worlds, like crossing into the Otherworld he knew?

He shifted and a motion on deck caught his eye. Someone else had emerged on deck. Talinir might have noticed his absence and come to check on him.

But no. The shape was human, not Eldani. Marshal watched as the figure strode to the main mast and put his back to it, facing the forecastle. Moonlight glinted off metal. A sword? The figure shifted into a battle stance, and Marshal could see two swords in his hands now. Not Victor then. Kishin.

He hadn't seen the leper assassin since they had boarded his ship. He seemed to be recovering from his injuries. His movements, as he shifted into various stances, looked smooth and crisp. He swung both swords in multiple arcs, moving through a complex pattern. Talinir had taught Marshal and Victor the value of working through such patterns, but this one went beyond anything he knew.

Kishin moved faster and faster, leaping into the air at times, spinning, aiming kicks at imaginary opponents, ducking, dodging, even rolling. He moved to the base of the forecastle and back, shifting around the mast and the stairs leading down to the cargo deck, all the way to the base of the aftcastle. Then he spun and began the whole process again.

Marshal watched, fascinated. He knew Kishin to be a formidable warrior. His motives, though, remained a mystery. Could he be trusted now? He had tried to kill Marshal on multiple occasions.

Kishin completed his exercise with a forward lunge ending in a kneel as he thrust both swords down into the deck. He stayed motionless for a few moments before standing and visibly relaxing.

Marshal rose and descended the stairs to the main deck. Kishin made no move as he approached.

"Impressive,"Marshal observed. "How long have you trained to do this?"

"All of my life," Kishin said. He pulled one sword free from the deck and returned it to its sheath.

"You know, I'm sure Victor would appreciate any training you could offer. He's had some, and we fought in the army briefly, but I know he'd love to learn some of those moves you were just doing."

"Training from him?" Kishin nodded toward the forecastle. Marshal looked up and saw the silhouette of Talinir watching them. How long had he been there?

"Guess I can't escape from him again, even on deck." Marshal chuckled.

Kishin pulled the second sword from the deck. "I have no desire or inclination to be a teacher."

"It was just a suggestion. If you wanted some other way to help. That's all."

Kishin stood silent. At last, he put the second sword in its sheath. "The ship is my help to you," he said. "It is all I have to offer now."

"But your skills, you—"

"I had my chance at redemption," Kishin interrupted. "I was healed, purged of my curse. But I could not change who I am. I killed again, and lost it all. Again."

"But you did that to save everyone." Marshal hadn't seen Kishin kill Tezan, but Victor and Talinir told him what happened.

Kishin shook his head. "It doesn't matter. I could have wounded him, stopped him some other way. But I chose to kill. I am a killer. I will not pass those skills on to anyone else."

"And if we run into more trouble on our journey?"

"The ship is yours. I can do no more." Kishin moved past Marshal to his cabin beneath the forecastle.

Talinir descended and came to stand beside him. "What was that about?"

"I don't know," Marshal said. "He's a confusing man."

"And confused as well, I believe."

Marshal nodded.

At that moment, he felt the air move across his scars. He looked up. The mainsail rippled ever so slightly, then billowed. The helmsman's cry confirmed what he already knew: "Wind!"

●●●●●

When the army stopped for another evening, Dravid tried to push aside his fear. What would Vayan ask of him tonight? Would he be able to resist? And what would Vayan do if he did resist?

As before, they erected the tent and Tiur cooked the god's meal. When Vayan arrived, he did not come alone. A tall and slender goddess accompanied him. Dravid tried to think of Seri, but the goddess' beauty overwhelmed him. Her elaborate but loose clothing barely covered the essentials. Sensuality surrounded her like an aura, pulling at his desires in spite of his best efforts not to look at her.

When Dravid helped Lasa bring the meal into the tent, they found Vayan and his companion lying together on his enormous bed. Vayan rolled away from her and jumped to his feet. "Ah, excellent! Place the trays on the table, Lasa. Leave the pitcher, and you may go."

"And this is the cripple, then?" When the goddess spoke, Dravid's attention turned to her. She rolled onto her stomach on the bed, facing him with curiosity in her eyes. Her golden skin radiated health and so much more. Dravid wanted to touch it, more than anything else in the world at the moment.

"Ah, yes. This is Dravid, from Kuktarma. One of our people, you know." Vayan took a drink. "Dravid, this is Dursa. I suppose you don't remember her, either?"

"I... I think I would remember her." Dravid stared, knowing his behavior was inappropriate. Yet he couldn't stop.

"Ha! Yes, I would think so. How your people managed to forget her, I can't even imagine. Come, Dursa, Tiur is quite a good cook. Perhaps the best I've had." Vayan took a bite before settling on one of the stools beside the table.

Dursa got to her feet and strolled to the table. Her every movement revealed more beauty. Dravid took a step toward the table himself.

Vayan frowned. "Ah, yes. That could be a problem. Dravid!"

His name in Vayan's voice pounded against his ears. Dravid staggered and looked at the god.

"You will not look at Dursa again unless I tell you to. Do you understand?" Vayan's voice vibrated with strong magic. Dravid could not resist. "I understand."

"Good. Then we may eat in peace." He offered the other stool to Dursa.

With the goddess' pull on him broken for the time being, Dravid's mind returned to the danger of Vayan. "Shall I leave, sir?" he asked, hoping his voice would not reveal his fear.

Vayan, eyes on the goddess, waved dismissively. "Wait by the wall," he ordered. "I will have use for you soon."

Dravid obeyed. With the command not to look at the goddess still influencing him, he stood and watched the floor. He listened to the pair as they ate and exchanged flirtatious comments, sometimes crossing into explicit details of what they desired to do to each other later in the evening. Dravid had never heard such flagrant language, even among the young men of his age back at school in Kuktarma. He felt heat rising within him, and not the magical kind.

Vayan finished eating first and leaped up from his stool. He clapped his hands and Dravid turned to him. "Now, before you clean up here, Dravid, the goddess and I require a story from you."

"Of course, sir. Shall I tell you another tale of Kuktarma?"

"No, no." Vayan rolled his eyes. He knelt beside Dursa and massaged her hand, moving up her arm. "I want a story of you."

"There's little to tell, I'm afraid."

"Nonsense." Vayan released the goddess and wove golden magic between his hands into an elaborate pattern. It reminded Dravid of how young children played with threads.

Vayan approached and Dravid trembled. This could not be good. But what could he do? He couldn't run. He couldn't disobey. In that moment, he realized he had truly become a slave in every sense of the word. Vayan held complete control over him.

The god placed the web of golden magic across Dravid's face. Coolness radiated where it touched his skin. He gritted his teeth and gripped his staff tighter.

Vayan glanced back at Dursa. "Now. It must be a fine story, since I have a guest. Tell me…"

"How did he lose his leg?" Dursa asked.

"Yes! An ideal selection!" Vayan focused on Dravid. "Tell me how you lost your leg."

"It—it's a boring story, sir. A rock fell on me." Dravid felt a heavy strain on his mind by telling so little. He wanted to blurt out everything, but struggled to keep it to himself.

"Nonsense." Vayan looked into his eyes. "I want to hear everything, Dravid." He paused and stared deeper. "Every. Single. Detail."

Dravid tried to grit his teeth, but the words forced their way out of his mouth. "I was in hiding, on Zes Sivas, because my Master had died and I didn't want to go home."

"Your Master died? Tell me about that!"

Dravid recited the facts about the death of Master Simmar, being sure to include Curasir's name. The false Eldani was here with the army somewhere, he knew. Master Simmar's death had caused Dravid some pain, but he had only known the man a few weeks. His method of death was more traumatizing than the death itself.

"Fascinating. Now tell me about your leg."

"There was an earthquake. My hiding place collapsed. My leg… was trapped beneath a large stone."

"And then?"

Until now, Dravid had managed to avoid speaking of Seri in any way. But she came into the story at this point. If he mentioned her, would Vayan recognize the emotions he held toward her? Dravid tried to concentrate. If he could form a magical construct and hold it, it might help seal off his throat…

But Vayan held him firm. "Focus," he commanded, and Dravid obeyed. "What happened next?"

"Two of my friends, fellow acolytes, found me. They—"

"Tell me of these friends."

"I… I…"

Dravid felt pressure building up on his head, everywhere the web of light touched his skin. Vayan's commands pushed past his willpower, demanding his obedience. Without any of Antises' magic to defend himself, he was completely helpless. He could not disobey.

He gripped the staff even tighter and tried to think of something else. The staff itself. Victor gave it to him. It came from the pilgrim that had joined them on their journey to the portal. For a brief moment, Dravid wondered what had happened to him.

"Tell me."

The pilgrim. Topleb said pilgrims considered the portal a sacred place, not to the old gods, but...

"Theon help me," Dravid whispered. If he could not resist Vayan's power on his own, perhaps calling on another power would make a difference.

Vayan backhanded Dravid across the face, sending him sprawling to the ground. Dursa stood in surprise. "Vayan?"

"Never mention that name!" Vayan commanded, his voice vibrating both with magic and rage.

Dravid's head felt like a hammer had struck him. His consciousness wavered.

Bursts of golden magic spewed from Vayan's fingers and dissolved in the air. He knelt next to Dravid and whispered, "Your people's obsession with that imaginary creature is what took you from us, what led us to this very moment. You will not speak of it again in my presence!"

Dravid could not respond. His ears rang, his vision blurred, and he felt like vomiting.

Vayan stood, and the goddess moved next to him. "Come, Vayan. Be done with him for now. You should pay attention to me. One might think you prefer torturing this slave to the pleasures I can provide."

Vayan glared down at Dravid. For a moment, Dravid thought he would shove the goddess away. Instead, he turned toward the tent's door. "Tiur! Lasa!"

The other two slaves appeared almost instantly.

"Take this one out of my sight! Do not let me see him again until I order it."

Tiur hastened to Dravid's side and hauled him up. Lasa picked up the staff. As they left the tent, Dravid looked back with his blurred vision and saw Vayan and Dursa tumbling onto his bed. Yet even there, Vayan turned and shot one last look toward him. He had angered a god, and the consequences might have only begun.

(((12)))

Ixchel ran her finger along the edge of the wood and examined her carving work. The practice swords were crude, but they would suffice. The greatest difficulty had come in finding two pieces of unused wood aboard this ship.

She stretched and took a deep breath. She could be honest with herself, though she would never admit it to Seri: she feared Rathri. The leprous assassin possessed an uncanny skill. Seri knew Ixchel fought with Victor against him without success. She did not know that Ixchel had fought against him again, this time with the aid of the Eldani. And again, the assassin fought both of them without giving ground. Ixchel knew she did not have a chance against him alone.

But she did not need to beat him today. Though it galled her, losing would accomplish just as much as winning in this case. She approached Volraag's cabin and knocked on the door.

"Go away," Rathri called from inside.

"I wish to see you," Ixchel answered.

After a moment, Rathri opened the door. He looked over the young woman, eyes noting the practice swords she held. "You can't be serious."

"I have no one with which to train or test my skills here," Ixchel said. "Would you do me the honor?" She offered him one of the swords.

Rathri considered her for a long moment. He took the proffered sword and looked it over. "Did you make this?"

Ixchel nodded.

Rathri snorted. He tossed the wooden sword onto the deck. "A waste of your time."

"You refuse me?"

"No." Rathri drew one of his swords. "But I train with real blades."

Ixchel's face showed no reaction, but her mind raced. Even a training match with Rathri, using real swords, could result in serious injury. And then Lady Seri would be defenseless. Yet if she did not accept, Seri would not be able to speak with Volraag as she desired. The risk might be worth it. Maybe.

"Very well." Ixchel tossed the other practice blade aside and drew her short sword. She stepped back and let Rathri emerge from the cabin. "Rules?"

Rathri's eyes swept the deck. "No rules."

Ixchel shook her head. "No harm to any others," she said. She wouldn't put it past the assassin to hurt one of the sailors if it benefited him.

"Fine."

"Do we fight until first blood, then?"

"No. We fight until one of us yields."

Ixchel nodded. She stepped out into the most open area of the deck, picked up her shield where she had left it, and slid into a defensive stance. "When you are ready."

Rathri smiled. He spun his sword in a complete arc through his fingers, an altogether unnecessary display. Ixchel already knew his skill. Moments of extra swordplay, especially when it served no combat purpose, would do nothing to impress her further. He had no reason whatsoever for such an action, unless…

Rathri attacked. Ixchel managed to get her own sword up in a parry, but it was a near thing. Then she understood. The purpose of the spinning sword action had been to merely make her wonder, distract her. And it worked. She filed the knowledge away and entered her combat zone.

When Ixchel fought, nothing else mattered. Only her weapons and her opponent. And her charge, if she were present. But she wasn't. This… was pure combat. All her training—days, weeks, months of practice—took over her movements. She barely even recognized what she did most of the time, so instinctive had it become. Her eyes focused on her opponent, watching his moves, his patterns, searching for any flaws, any missteps.

Rathri had none. Every opponent she had faced in her life, even the Blademasters who trained her, possessed some slight flaw in their fighting style. Perhaps they leaned to the left ever-so-slightly when defending. Perhaps their peripheral vision was weaker on the right, leading to a slower reaction time on that side.

Rathri did none of that. Every movement he made flowed from the previous move. Some of his movements seemed impossible for a human being. Ixchel knew she would not be able to duplicate them. Yet they seemed second nature to the assassin. It took Ixchel only a few seconds to realize he outmatched her beyond reason. She had hoped fighting him one-on-one, instead of with Victor or Talinir, would help her be able to understand him better, to perhaps make an impact against him.

She had no hope of that now. All she could do was keep him distracted long enough for Seri. And even that might be difficult.

Rathri drove her across the deck with ease, attack following attack with relentless ease. "Do you feel tested?" he asked. "Or would you like to yield already?"

"The exercise is not over."

"No one in this world can best me, girl. You… are nothing."

In that instant, as Rathri brushed aside her parry and cut a light scratch on her neck, Ixchel believed him.

• • • • •

Seri watched Ixchel and Rathri face each other, swords drawn. Her curiosity made her want to stay and watch, but that would defeat the purpose. From the quarter deck, she slipped into the hallway unseen. Three cabins opened from the hall: the captain, the helmsman, and… Volraag. She considered knocking on the door, but every minute counted while Ixchel fought. She opened the door and stepped inside.

At her unexpected entry, Volraag rolled off his bunk, dagger in hand. He stood up and cocked his head at her, obviously surprised.

"I know, I know," Seri said. "I'm sorry to surprise you, but I wanted to see you without Rathri around, and this is my only opportunity, and I need to hurry…" She trailed off, staring at him.

Volraag tossed the dagger back onto his bunk. He stood shirtless, staring back at her, waiting. Seri swallowed and re-evaluated her earlier thoughts about the grotesque nature of his new muscles. They were actually… quite impressive in this dim light.

Volraag lifted both hands, palms up, as if to say, "I'm waiting."

"Right. All right. I need to talk with you about all this. And I can't do it in front of Rathri. He might try to kill me."

Volraag shook his head.

"You don't want him to, I know, but I don't know that he'll follow your wishes. He's pretty scary."

Volraag gave a short nod.

Seri didn't know what to do with her hands. She started to lean forward on to the table, then remembered the last time she had done that and jerked back up. She put her hands behind her back.

"I don't understand why you want to open the portals in the first place," she said. "What do you gain from this?"

Volraag considered for a moment. He opened a drawer below his bunk and took out a few sheets of paper, some ink, and a stylus. He set them all on the table and wrote a single word on the first page: "Power."

"They promised you power? You aren't getting enough from murdering the Lords and taking theirs?"

Volraag's eyebrows narrowed.

"What good will it do you if they conquer Antises? That's their goal, you know."

Volraag's eyebrows went back up. Did he not understand this?

"The gods. The Durunim. They had an army waiting on the other side of the portal that you were opening. That's why Marshal buried it. Do you understand me?"

Volraag nodded.

"And, and that means they've probably brought an army through the first portal, in your homeland! Have you heard anything from home?"

Volraag shook his head.

"That's probably because they've been invaded! And now you're going to open the third one? Why? What good is power if, if Antises is overrun?"

Volraag sat down on the edge of his bunk, leaning forward. He did not answer.

"Listen, back on Zes Sivas, before… before you started murdering everyone, I thought you were a reasonable man. You saved me from your father, and listened to me when I told you about Tezan, though I guess you only did that because you were able to twist it to your advantage." Seri stopped and took a deep breath. "I guess I'm just saying that I think you have it in you to be a reasonable man. If you're anything at all like your brother—"

Seri broke off as Volraag's face darkened.

"Forget I said that. Listen, I wouldn't have come with you if I didn't believe that you were important to all of this." She waved her arms around.

Volraag wrote on the paper again. "Guide?"

"Yes, I said I would guide you. I still will. But I don't want you to open the portal. I want to talk you out of it. And..." She paused, wondering if she should tell him everything. "And I want you to help us. To heal Antises."

Volraag eyed her for a moment, then wrote, "How?"

Was he actually considering it? "We need to gather back at Zes Sivas for another Passing," she said in a hurry. Volraag shook his head immediately. "No, listen to me. Now that Marshal has the King's power, that can be added to all of yours and truly heal the land. We have to, before the earthquakes get worse and, and everything is torn apart."

Volraag wrote, "No," paused for a moment, then added, "Tyrr."

"Lord Tyrr? I know you've been at war, but surely—"

Pouding footsteps interrupted her, followed by swift banging at Volraag's door. A sailor threw the door open, eyes wide.

"Your Lordship, someone's gone overboard!"

• • • • •

On her first day on board, Ixchel memorized the entire layout of Volraag's ship. When Rathri pressed her back in his opening barrage of attacks, she knew exactly how far across the main deck she could retreat before reaching the forecastle. She angled her steps back toward the starboard side, knowing the stairs waited for her.

Rathri aimed a flurry of blows directly at her, which she caught one after the other, on her shield. Nothing more than brute force, but it drove her further back. She took the first step up.

The assassin aimed a swipe at her legs, throwing her just off-balance enough to give him another opening. Instead, he spun away from her, leaped onto the railing itself, and ran past her to the forecastle where he dropped back onto the upper deck, facing her.

Ixchel stared. The movement, the balance... he could not be human.

"Do you see now?" he mocked.

"I see that you are a worthy opponent," Ixchel said, her voice calm. "It is something I have been missing for some time."

Rathri gave a short bow. "If it's any consolation, you are quite skilled for one so young. But the difference between us is something you will never overcome, even with one of your lifetimes of training."

"What are you saying?" Ixchel took advantage of the moment to launch her own attack, a feint with her shield followed by a quick slash below. Rathri batted it aside without moving.

"I am saying it takes longer than your lifetime, however long that may be, to reach my skill level. Are you always this stupid?"

How old was he, then? Ixchel had no reason to doubt his word, yet she did.

"You lie."

Rathri stepped back, abandoning any pretense of a defensive pose. "I do not. Your Lady is the one who lies."

Ixchel winced inside. Seri's untruths did bother her. She wanted to defend her, yet to do so would be lying herself. Honesty was a hallmark of the Holcan. Honesty, and protecting one's charge, no matter the cost.

She feinted a stab toward Rathri. He dropped back into a stance. Ixchel took the moment to leap onto the railing herself. She caught hold of a rope there with her left hand, stabilizing her position. It sacrificed the use of her shield, but the higher position gave her other advantages.

Rathri nodded, either in respect or resignation: she couldn't tell. He pushed forward, aiming downward strokes at her feet. Ixchel deflected them with her own sword. Not her preferred way of using her weapon, but it worked for now. She hit the last deflection extra hard to push Rathri's sword arm back.

With a swift stroke, Ixchel cut the rope loose from the railing. She swung out over the water and circled back down, where she dropped onto the main deck into a crouch, sword and shield at the ready.

Rathri dove over the forecastle's railing, flipped in the air, and came to a landing three feet away from her. Behind him, she could see several of Volraag's sailors watching, their mouths agape.

Ixchel had little sense of time passing while fighting. How long did Seri need with Volraag? When could she yield to this opponent with honor?

Even as she blocked another underhanded swing from Rathri, she knew. She could not yield. Not because she felt any stubbornness or misguided sense of pride. But because the assassin was pure evil. And evil must be stopped.

Ixchel changed her tactics. She grew more reckless, pushing her own attacks in spite of Rathri's own. Every thrust, every slash, she turned back on him, knowing that eventually her movements would leave her open.

It happened when Rathri backed to the stairway leading to the quarter deck. He put one foot back on the first step, then used it to leap to her right, just as she lunged forward in a thrust. For a brief moment, Rathri slipped into position on her open right side. A brief moment was all it took.

Rathri's sword pierced her side, cutting through the scar tissue left by the curse-stalker months ago when she saved Dravid. A gasp escaped her mouth.

"Not first blood, but first serious blood," Rathri noted. "Do you wish to yield now?"

"I do not."

"It would not matter. I would not hear you if you did." Rathri swung his sword with such force that it lodged in Ixchel's shield. He leaned into it. "With you out of the way, your precious Lady will be undefended."

"Monster." The wound in her side bled freely. It would weaken her, very soon.

"Yes." He shoved harder. Ixchel stumbled back against the stairs and the railing.

Rathri jerked his sword loose, then aimed a slash at Ixchel's feet. Instinctively, she leaped. In that instant, Rathri reached out with his hand. Some force, not unlike the Lady's magic, struck her shield and threw her back. She let the shield fall as she flipped. She caught hold of the railing with her left hand. Her feet caught the edge of the deck, but she stood outside the railing.

Rathri kicked her shield across the deck, where it tumbled down the cargo hatch. He smiled again. Until that moment, Ixchel had never been unnerved by his disease-ravaged face. But now… something like true fear pierced her with that smile. Never before had she recognized such helplessness on her own part. She could not stand against this foe, no matter what she did.

Rathri aimed a blow at her left hand. She parried it with her sword, but it was a near thing. Rathri's sword slammed into the railing a few inches from her fingers, cutting a wedge from the wood.

He lunged forward with a speed he hadn't shown before now, taking her breath away. His left hand caught her right wrist and held her sword away.

"Any last words?"

Ixchel thought of Seri. "My Lady..."

"Yes?"

"I cannot swim."

Rathri shoved her.

Ixchel fell.

(((13)))

Seri followed Volraag and the sailor out onto the main deck, a sick feeling gathering in her gut. Volraag turned and bounded up the stairs to the quarter deck and the aftcastle. Seri did her best to keep up.

Sailors crowded the aftcastle, leaning over the railing and staring down at the water. Rathri stood on the quarter deck, wiping off his sword. Ixchel was nowhere to be seen.

The captain of the ship, a tall nobleman of Varioch, turned as they approached. "No sign of her, your Lordship."

"Her?" Seri blurted.

The captain spared her a quick look. "The warrior woman." He pointed at Rathri. "They were fighting up and back all over the ship. And then she went over."

Seri pushed her way to the railing and looked down. The rowers had stopped, leaving the ship rocking gently in the waves. Seri saw nothing more than the lake's surface.

"Ixchel..." she breathed.

"She went straight under," another sailor confirmed. "I never saw her come back up."

"Ch'olan, weren't she? They don't spend a lot of time on the water."

"The leper shoved her right off."

"Do we lower the boat, captain?"

Seri turned to hear the answer. The captain pursed his lips, glanced at Volraag and then out over the water. "Has anyone seen any sign of her?" he asked. He received a chorus of negatives. He looked back to Volraag. "Then I see no reason to lower the boat, your Lordship."

Volraag nodded shortly. He and the captain both looked toward Seri. She wanted to contradict them, to scream that Ixchel was all right, that she waited just below for them to toss her a rope or lower the boat or...

She was gone.

Seri looked back at the water. How could it be? Her bodyguard, her constant companion, her dearest friend... lost to the waves? Ixchel was too strong, too skillful for such an end. She—

A dry chuckle broke the silence behind her.

Seri spun to find Rathri staring at her with his bright eyes surrounded by death. Some of the sailors, already moving away from the railing, paused to see them facing each other.

"You did this," Seri managed to say.

"Of course I did." Rathri slid his sword back into its sheath. "We fought. She lost. As does everyone who faces me."

"You monster."

Rathri tilted his head. "She called me that. Right before she told me she couldn't swim."

Seri felt a trembling beginning in her hands.

Rathri took a step closer. "And now you have no one to protect you." His hand dropped to the hilt of a dagger tucked into his belt. "No one to ward off a blade in the dark of night, while you sleep..."

"Lord Volraag!" Seri said as loud as she could manage, almost choking from the warring emotions building up inside. "Do you allow such threats to your companions?"

Volraag looked placidly from one to the other. He stepped to Seri's side, facing Rathri. He put his hand on her shoulder, then wrapped his arm around her, keeping his eyes on the assassin. The implication could not be clearer. Protection.

"Little girls always need someone to protect them," Rathri said. "So pathetic."

Seri pushed Volraag away. One emotion won out. Anger. She took a step toward Rathri.

"You don't really know who I am, do you?"

Seri blinked, activating her star-sight. She waved her hands in slow, meandering circles. To the others watching, she appeared to be making random movements, or perhaps preparing some form of conjuration. In actuality, she absorbed every ray of magic she could find, regardless of color. The power grew and grew within her.

"I am Seri-Belit, mage of Arazu. The power of Antises is mine to command. And the closer we draw to Zes Sivas or one of the portals, the more my power grows!"

Seri took another step forward, and let power flow out of her foot. The aftcastle rumbled. The sailors murmured and backed away. Two of them hastened down the steps to the quarter deck. Rathri and Volraag stood still.

"This display is pointless," Rathri snarled, but he drew his sword.

"I don't need a weapon," Seri responded. She let more of the power flow out from her feet and downward pointing palms. She rose into the air a few inches above the deck. One of the planks splintered beneath her. The remaining sailors fled down the stairs. The captain himself paused at the top step, torn between his fear and duty to his Lord.

Seri allowed a tiny flow of power to rush up through her scalp, cascading her hair into the air around her. She knew it didn't mean anything, but it had to look fabulous.

"So you can shake things. It's not—"

Seri spun in a circle, gathering every bit of magic she could. From her point of view, she grabbed three purple rays, one large blue one, two red ones, and more that came so fast she couldn't identify them. When she felt she couldn't absorb any more, she threw her right palm forward, launching an enormous burst of power—not at Rathri himself, but at his sword.

Like the clod of mud on that early day in her training, the sword exploded in Rathri's hand. Multiple shards struck the assassin. He staggered back and almost fell over the railing toward the quarter deck. One shard sliced across Volraag's arm, but he didn't flinch. One piece spiraled back toward Seri, but the power vibrating out from her deflected it over the side of the ship. The captain fled.

Seri settled onto the deck, being careful to avoid the cracked plank. She let the power fade. In truth, she had very little power remaining after that display, but she wasn't going to let Rathri know it.

The assassin pulled a three-inch shard of his sword out of his thigh. He looked up at Seri. Another shard protruded from his right cheek. He pulled it out as well. Blood gushed out, looking shockingly bright against his deathly pale skin.

"Well played," he murmured, causing a new flow of blood to spurt out of his cheek. Seri winced.

Rathri stepped carefully over a six-inch shard protruding from the deck, and made his way to the stairs. He took one last look at Seri, then descended.

Seri stood alone with Volraag. The young Lord shook his head. Seri watched his face. The damage made it difficult to understand his expression. Was that admiration in his eyes? Or something else? She would settle for indifference at this point.

Volraag bowed. Seri's heart skipped a beat. He bowed to her. That was good, wasn't it?

The Lord turned and followed Rathri. Seri, alone, looked back out over the waves.

She felt drained. Almost as much as when she helped Marshal in the Otherworld. She might pass out at any moment. Wouldn't that be a fantastic ending to her display of power?

Carefully, keeping her head high, she descended the stairs and made her way toward her cabin.

• • • • •

She descended to the quarter deck and then down to the main deck. She turned, head still held high, and entered the mess. Passing by a trio of sailors who stared at her with frightened eyes, she opened the door to her cabin and walked inside. When the door shut behind her, she collapsed. She slid to the floor and took several deep breaths.

Her emotions, her senses, even her magical abilities, all seemed thrown off. Everything that had taken place in the past few weeks all came crashing together in her mind.

Looking up, she saw the two bunks she and Ixchel had been sharing the last few days. Ixchel insisted that Seri sleep in the top bunk, so that potential attackers had to get past her to get to Seri.

And now… no one would protect her. This door didn't even have a lock, as the room was usually taken by the ship's officers.

But protection didn't matter. Seri could handle herself. Maybe. At least she had given that impression to everyone on deck.

What mattered was Ixchel. She was gone. Seri couldn't bring herself to even think the word "dead." Surely Ixchel still lived, somehow. Swept away in the waters so that they couldn't see her or retrieve her. She would wash ashore somewhere, wouldn't she? And then try to catch up on her own.

The thought, as far-fetched as it sounded, gave Seri some comfort. The alternative—that Ixchel had drowned—could not be true. It couldn't.

She lost Dravid. She left Marshal behind. And now she lost Ixchel.

Tears began to slip from her eyes, and she felt a sob building up. The sailors outside the door could not hear her crying. She could not show weakness.

Seri crawled to the bed, the lower bunk that Ixchel used, and buried her face in the blanket. Only then did she let the sobs escape. After a few moments, she crawled into the bed itself and cried herself to sleep.

(((14)))

Marshal watched Victor for his reaction. His friend's face wrinkled in consternation. "I don't like splitting up," he said at last.

"Neither do I," Marshal answered. "Except for short trips to the Otherworld, you and I have been together since we left home." He glanced at Talinir, who didn't add anything. The three of them stood beside the main mast on deck.

"Then I should come with you."

"I need someone on this side, and no one else is left." Marshal sighed. "And let's be honest. Our Bonds control us. Mine pulls me toward Dravid. His danger is growing by the hour now. And yours takes you toward Seri."

"I almost jumped in the water and started swimming yesterday afternoon," Victor admitted. "Something happened. Something bad. But it's gotten better now. Her danger has gone down... some."

Marshal nodded. "All those years you had to deal with me... I finally understand a little of what you went through."

Victor chuckled. "Good. You deserve to know. You annoyed me so —"

"Zes Sivas ho!" came a shout from the front of the ship.

They all looked up. The wind continued to blow in fits and starts, giving the ship enough momentum over the past day and a half to make it this far. And now their destination had been sighted.

"Have you ever seen Zes Sivas?" Victor asked Talinir.

The warden shook his head. "Not on this side of the worlds, at any rate. It's... not very nice on the other side."

"I want to see."

The three of them made their way to the forecastle, where they joined Jamana, Tich, and two other sailors. Marshal looked ahead in the direction indicated. From this distance, he could make out a dark spot of land and some towers rising from it.

"Not much to see," Marshal said, but he felt something stir within. Unless he wanted to, he usually couldn't feel the magic filling his body. But at the sight of Zes Sivas, that magic began to move about, creating a very odd sensation.

"Not yet," Jamana said. "But when we get closer, you will see. The Citadel of Kings and the Citadel of Mages! The heart of Antises itself."

"It's not all that," Tich said. "I've seen it three... no, four times. Some rocks. Some walls. Not much to it."

"It is where our history began!" Jamana insisted. "Where the lands were divided among the peoples. Where the Laws of Cursings and Bindings were enacted. Where the Lords betrayed the mages and—"

"And where wild mages come to die."

Jamana fell silent. Marshal winced. Tich's parents. Lord Tyrr brought them here and Volraag killed them, along with many others.

"How do you think they'll react to the return of a King?" Victor wondered.

"The return of what?" Tich asked.

Jamana frowned. "They will probably demand proof. After Tezan deceived so many, they will not be quick to believe."

"Well, we'll just have to see what happens." Marshal wasn't all that interested in proving himself to the mages. Zes Sivas was a stepping stone, a brief stop on the way to where he needed to be. A thought occurred to him. "Your Master Mage stayed back home, you said. How many Masters are even left here?"

"I am not sure. Varioch and Arazu may have sent new Masters by now. If not that leaves only..." He thought for a moment. "Master Tzoyet of Ch'olan. Master Ganak of Kuktarma. And Master Plecu of Rasna."

"Kuktarma. That's good." Marshal exchanged a look with Victor. "He'll be the one you'll need to appeal to."

"Right. Are you sure I'm the right person for this job? I'm not a diplomat, you know."

Marshal gestured at Jamana. "You have Jamana to help you. I'm sure he can do some convincing."

"Convincing of what?" Jamana asked.

"Kuktarma needs to know about Volraag and the portal," Marshal explained. "They need to send someone there, in case..."

"In case of what?"

"In case I can't get there in time."

Tich snorted. "You people are just gallivanting all over Antises, aren't ya? Reminds me of an old man I met in Rasna. Said he'd visited all six lands many times. Gotta admit. I haven't made it to Arazu yet."

Marshal watched the towers of Zes Sivas draw nearer. "I go where I have to. Where I am drawn." And the island did draw him. It pulled at the magic within. Magic calling to magic?

"A good tavern draws me right now. Anything like that on your island, mage boy?"

Jamana stuttered an answer, but Marshal stopped listening. The Bond with Dravid pulled at him, drawing his eyes away from the island and toward the northeast.

"Soon," he whispered. "I'm coming."

• • • • •

Dravid's head wobbled as the wagon struck another bump. His vision still blurred every few minutes, and his head throbbed with constant pain. His neck also ached from the force of his head snapping to the side when Vayan slapped him.

He had never been struck so hard by anything. Not since losing his leg had he suffered such continuous and severe pain.

Lasa checked on him every hour or so, but said little. Her sad eyes haunted him each time she left, and he remembered her words of the day before.

He also remembered almost everything about the night before. Vayan had tried to take his memory of losing his leg. He didn't think it had worked, though he wasn't sure why. Some of his recollections of the earthquake seemed a little vague, but he didn't think he had lost any specific details. Most importantly, he remembered Seri and Jamana coming to his rescue. But trying to recall even that much made his head ache even more.

He lay back against the packed tent and somehow managed to fall asleep again.

In the evening, Tiur and Lasa did not ask much from him, and Vayan did not summon him. Throughout the day and night, he drifted in and out of consciousness, pain his only constant.

The next day brought more of the same. The pain lessened a little, but never left him. At least his thoughts became more clear. He could remember everything; at least he thought he could. He still had no memory of the burn scar on his hand.

That night, Lasa examined the bruise on his head again. "It looks better, but I know little of medicine," she declared. She looked into his eyes with her usual anxiety. "Can you see all right?"

Dravid nodded. "I haven't had any blurred vision today, I don't think."

"Perhaps it will heal all right, then." She hesitated. "Normally, one of the gods could heal it with a touch. But they do not do so when it is a punishment."

Dravid looked up as Tiur walked by, carrying a sack of flour. He would be preparing the evening meal soon.

"Lasa… you called Tiur a shell. Does he remember anything of his life in Antises?"

Lasa stood for a moment, thinking. At last, she sighed. "I'm sorry. I have to concentrate to remember that name. Antises. Our world."

Dravid grimaced. Even the name?

"Tiur remembers…" She glanced over at him. "He remembers that he had a life before this. And faces. Faces come back to him. He tells me of them sometimes. But he doesn't remember their names."

"I'm so sorry. When I met the two of you, I had no idea…"

"How could you? We are—"

"Lasa! Attend me!" Vayan's call interrupted their conversation. He kept Lasa busy for the rest of the evening. Relieved not to be called himself, Dravid sought sleep once more.

And so a third day passed. The pain in his head faded to a dull ache. That evening, he managed to help with the tent set-up and meal prep once again. After all was completed, he found his sleeping mat and relaxed. Perhaps tomorrow, the pain would be totally gone. He lay back and looked up at the stars.

Then Tiur stood over him, looking down with his usual passive expression. He gestured toward the tent.

"The master wants to see you now."

•••••

Seri kept mostly to herself during the next day. She heard the news of the wind that brought relief to the rowers. At least it meant they would soon leave this ship for good. And perhaps just as important, she would be home.

Throughout the voyage, Seri had pondered the wisdom of seeking aid in Arazu. Lord Enuru and Lady Lilitu had fought against Volraag on Zes Sivas. They both possessed great power. But the Lady had been in league with Curasir. Did she understand who and what he was? Curasir deceived Master Hain and the other Masters, of course. Had he done the same with her?

If not the Lord and Lady, who? Her parents? They were wealthy, but what could they do against the power Volraag now wielded… or even Rathri's martial prowess?

Perhaps it would be best not to involve anyone at all. Yet her heart ached at the thought of passing through her home and not seeing anyone she knew. After all, she was all alone now. No Ixchel. No Dravid. No Marshal or Victor. Seri stood alone, surrounded by foes of great power.

And despite her demonstration on the deck, she knew the further they traveled, the weaker her power would be. The greater the distance from Zes Sivas, the fewer rays of magic she would find. It would be stronger near the portal, but it was still very far away.

Evening arrived before she heard the call. Arazu had been sighted. Seri gathered herself and strode out onto the deck with much more confidence than she felt. She resisted the urge to look for Rathri. Instead, she looked ahead, over the water.

In the deepening twilight, she spotted the lights of the city. Sandu-Emuq, capital and greatest city of Arazu. Her eyes sought for familiar silhouettes in the darkness: the dome of the temple, the towering pinnacles that surrounded the palace. She thought she could make them out, but she would have to wait until morning to fully see what she knew to be there.

Home. Here she grew up. Here she studied at the university. Here she conceived of her dream to become a mage. That dream, now a reality, had turned out much different than she had ever anticipated.

"Welcome home," said a quiet voice behind her.

Seri spun to see Volraag. "You can speak now?"

"Just a little," he whispered. His words sounded painful, though his injured jaw barely moved. He handed her a piece of paper. "Your instructions."

"Instructions? Why would you think you could give me instructions? I—"

Volraag tapped the paper. Seri looked down and began to read:

"If you were sincere in our discussion in my cabin, you will follow these

instructions to the letter. It is vital to both our goals." Seri glanced up at him with narrowed eyes, but then looked back at the paper. *"In the morning, go ashore and announce yourself to the Lord and Lady. Tell them what you wish, but do not mention my presence. Otherwise, enjoy the day.*

"Tomorrow, I will arrive separately and request the famous Arazuan hospitality."

Seri groaned. By Arazu law, no one, not even the Lord, could reject a request for hospitality. Volraag would be safe in the Lord's palace for three days. After that, the blessings of hospitality would be withdrawn. But of course, Volraag would know that and plan for it. She kept reading.

"I will attempt to negotiate with the Lord. This will give time for Rathri to procure our traveling materials. We will leave on the second day, if all goes well."

Seri looked up. "Once you leave the hospitality of the palace, you will no longer be safe," she pointed out.

Volraag nodded to indicate he understood. "Negotiation," he whispered.

He hoped to work out some form of agreement with Lord Enuru? How could they possibly agree to let a Lordslayer—Seri felt quite proud of the term that popped into her head—go free? "I don't see how that will work," she said.

Volraag smiled. "Trust me."

Seri looked around the deck. She saw no sign of Rathri, though in the darkness, he could be waiting in the shadows a few feet away, and she wouldn't know it. Perhaps Volraag was sincere. Seeking peace with Arazu would be a first step, but a small one. They weren't the ones he had wronged the most, after all.

"All right," she said. "I'll try it your way."

<h1 style="text-align:center">(((15)))</h1>

"Where do we land?" Marshal turned from the view of Zes Sivas and looked at Jamana.

"There is a quay on this side of the island, beside the Citadel of Kings, but it collapsed during the first earthquake. We always use the dock on the far side—the south side, that is."

"Hmmm." Marshal looked back at the island, then to Victor and Talinir. "What do you think?"

Victor shrugged. "I mean, if you're going to declare yourself to them, why not show up where the King should show up?"

"But the quay has not been repaired," Jamana said. "The ship cannot enter there."

"We can take the rowboat."

"Yes, but… no one will be there to greet us. They won't be expecting it."

Marshal smiled. "All the more reason."

In short order, they lowered the rowboat and set out toward the island. Tich and one other sailor came along to pull at the oars. Marshal, Victor, Talinir and Jamana did their part as well.

Marshal looked back at the ship, wondering if Kishin were watching. The assassin had not come out on deck to say farewell, and there was no sign of him now. Apparently, he had been quite serious about staying out of everything now.

Marshal turned back, pulling at his oar. Zes Sivas. The Citadel of Kings. He stared up at the towers that stretched high into the sky. The one on the left had fallen apart, no doubt from one of the earthquakes. But even so, the structure looked impressive, far larger and stronger than anything he had seen even in the capital city of Reman. And his ancestors had lived here. Ruled here, for that matter. He didn't know how to feel about that. He had no desire to make the citadel his home, let alone take on the responsibility of ruling all of Antises. And yet...

"Do I have to do all the work here?" Victor complained.

Marshal jerked out of his thoughts and pulled on the oar again. Victor grinned at him.

"I should have come alone first," Jamana said. "And prepared the way for you. Then they would be here to greet us."

"Perhaps someone saw the ship," Talinir suggested.

They approached the ruined quay. At one time, it had apparently been a U-shaped stone-and-concrete structure. Most of it looked intact, but some buildings or other structures had collapsed into the water. No ship could fit past all of the debris.

The rowboat, though, could pull right up to one end of the quay. Tich jumped up onto the surface and tied off the boat. One by one, the others joined her.

When Marshal stepped onto the quay, his foot slammed down with more force than he intended. His second step did the same. The magic within him seemed to rush down his legs, pulling at the magic beneath the ground. For a moment, he stood still, wondering if he could even walk on this island. Talinir noticed something amiss, and placed a hand on Marshal's shoulder. The touch broke the odd spell. Marshal breathed a sigh of relief and took a few more steps. The magic still pulled him down, but he could control it. In fact, he felt more powerful than ever. Here, he could do anything.

Jamana, wearing his robes once again, hefted the bag with the book and looked around. "I actually haven't been to this area except once," he admitted. "I think we can just follow this path up to the citadel. Then we can either enter and move through it, or go around to the Citadel of Mages." He set off, and the others followed.

"Someone approaches," Talinir noted.

The others all looked, and soon they also saw a figure hurrying down the stone path toward them. He looked small, wearing orange-colored robes like Jamana. Another acolyte?

"Adhi!" Jamana cried, and rushed ahead to meet him. Marshal and the others followed, amused to see Jamana throw his arms around the smaller acolyte and lift him off the ground in a massive hug.

Once Jamana set him down, the young man tried to smooth out his robes and looked around at the group with a nervous smile. He reminded Marshal of Dravid, though quite a bit smaller and not as...

gregarious.

"It is good to see you, Jamana, but why have you come on this side of the island?" the acolyte, Adhi, asked. "If I had not been working on clean-up nearby, no one would have seen you."

"But you did! This is fortuitous, I am thinking!" Jamana seemed much more boisterous all of a sudden, an enormous grin on his face. Perhaps he was relieved to get back to familiar surroundings. He gestured at Marshal. "This, my friend, is Marshal, the lost King of Antises. The real one, this time!"

Adhi looked at Marshal. He didn't express shock or disgust at his scars: that was a good sign. He nodded. "We must tell the Masters."

Victor pointed to a small, grassy area near the quay. "How about if we wait right over here?"

"That should be... acceptable." Adhi took Jamana's arm and drew him up the path. Marshal heard them talking rapidly to each other until they were out of view.

•••••

"You are absolutely certain of his claims?" Adhi demanded.

Jamana nodded. "More importantly, Seri was certain of his identity."

"Where is Seri? And Master Korda?"

"It is a long story. I have so much to tell you."

Back at the Citadel of Mages, Jamana noticed a great deal of work had been completed in his absence. Much had been repaired, though some glaring bits of destruction remained as testimony to the earthquakes. They entered the dining hall and Jamana placed the book on one of the tables. At last, it was safe again. After a moment's consideration, he took the small scroll from the bag and secreted it in one of his pockets. He had yet to meet a leper, but who knew when— or if—the old man's prophecy would come true.

Master Ganak appeared, his bulk and unique clothing unmistakable. "What is this, acolytes? Has Master Korda returned already?"

"No, Master," Adhi replied. "Only Jamana here... but he is not alone. He has brought... ah... another young man claiming to be King."

Master Ganak only nodded. "Whoever he is, he possesses great power. We were just about to go see what this meant. On the north side, is he?"

"Yes, Master. At the quay."

"Over here!" Master Ganak called. Masters Tzoyet and Plecu emerged from the hallway and joined them.

"Lead the way, acolytes."

Jamana nodded. None of these three were his Master, of course, but being in their presence immediately cowed him. Whatever they might think of Marshal, he would not color their expectations. A few other lesser mages joined the party and followed behind. As they walked, some servants and workers joined as well. The word spread quickly, it seemed. It would not approach anywhere near the size of the group that had welcomed Tezan when he arrived, but to be fair, the population of the island had greatly decreased since then.

Marshal stood waiting for them. Victor and Talinir stood a few feet behind him, while Tich and the other sailor—Jamana felt embarrassed for not remembering his name—waited on the quay. Marshal stood resolute, shoulders back, arms behind his back, legs spread in a solid pose. Murmurs swept through the crowd. What must they think of this scarred young man?

Master Tzoyet, the most senior of the Masters, took the lead. "Are you the claimant to the throne?" he asked in a loud voice that silenced the crowd.

"I claim no throne," Marshal answered. "I do, however, claim that I am Marshal, son of Aelia, daughter of Evander, and that this line is descended from the Kings of Antises." His words confused the crowd, not least because of his odd speaking pattern. Jamana had grown somewhat used to it on the ship, but he knew how it sounded to people hearing it for the first time.

"You clearly possess great power," Master Tzoyet observed. "From whence does it come?"

"The power is mine by inheritance. I possess the Lord of Varioch's power, passed down from Varion. And I possess the King's power, from my mother and grandfather."

That created quite a stir in the crowd.

"Varion was your father?"

"Varion raped my mother. He is my father only in that sense."

"I… see."

"What is wrong with your voice?" Master Plecu demanded. "And those scars! You do not look or sound like a King!"

"My scars came from a curse-stalker. And I apologize for my voice. I have only been using it for a few months. Prior to that, I lived under a curse that kept me from speaking."

At the mention of a curse, the crowd exploded. Master Tzoyet lifted his staff high and waited for everyone to fall silent again.

"You say 'prior.' Do you then claim to…" He hesitated. "Have you been freed from a curse?"

"My mother lifted my curse. She died in the temple of Reman."

The explosion of voices was even louder this time. Jamana had to step forward to keep from getting shoved about as the crowd grew exceedingly agitated. No one here had any doubts about the significance of that claim.

Master Plecu's voice rose above all. "You claim not only the power of a Lord, but to be the King, AND to have a curse lifted! You expect us to believe all of this?"

"Whether you believe me or not is ultimately not important to me," Marshal said.

At this, the murmurs fell silent again. Not important? How could it not be important? Jamana exchanged glances with Adhi and grinned. This couldn't be what the Masters had ever imagined the return of the King would be like.

"Then why have you come?" Master Tzoyet asked.

"I have come to warn you. I have traveled far in these past months, and seen much. For much of that time, I traveled with your mage, Seri of Arazu. And what we have learned should concern you greatly." He pointed to Jamana. "Your acolyte there can tell you what he has witnessed. The ancient gods, or at least some beings claiming to be the ancient gods, are returning to Antises."

"Blasphemy!" Master Plecu muttered. No one else spoke. Jamana noticed Tich and the other sailor had moved much closer, listening intently with everyone else.

"These gods, or whatever they are, crave power. They do not intend good things toward us."

"What do you think needs to be done, then?" Master Ganak asked.

"It should concern you most of all. Lord Volraag is helping them. He is even now on his way to Kuktarma." The crowd noise grew again, and Marshal raised his voice to be heard. "He intends to open a portal there, allowing the gods and their armies to enter your land."

"Preposterous," Master Plecu said. "Why should we believe you?"

"I have told you who I am. What I have witnessed. Jamana can tell you more."

"Come," Master Tzoyet said. "Share with us in detail. We can gather in one of the great halls." He gestured toward the citadel.

"I cannot." Marshal shook his head. "I have an urgent mission to undertake."

"This is ridiculous," Master Plecu cried. "We still have nothing but your word as to your identity. Prove it to us. Show us the Heart of Fire!"

Marshal looked uncertain for the first time. "I... I'm not sure what you mean."

"If you truly are the King, show us the Heart of Fire!" Plecu repeated. "Even the false king Tezan could do that much!"

"I do not have time to waste showing off my powers—"

"Because you have none!" someone else in the crowd shouted.

"I've seen his power!" Jamana shouted back.

"Prove it!" another mage yelled. Loud cries of agreement joined him.

Marshal glanced over his shoulder at Victor and Talinir. Then he drew his warpsteel sword. Jamana had seen it briefly on the ship, but it gleamed even brighter here for some reason. The crowd quieted. A drawn weapon on Zes Sivas. The only other time that had happened in recent history was during Volraag's rampage.

"I will not perform for you," Marshal declared. "But as I said, I have an urgent mission to undertake. That mission... is in the Otherworld."

He lifted the sword. As Jamana and the others watched, the air itself seemed to warp around the blade. Marshal closed his eyes and placed his other palm against the sword. He seemed to be concentrating. He mouthed something none of them could hear.

Then he turned to his left and in a swift motion, slashed the sword from left to right. A rip appeared in the air, a tear in reality itself. Darkness bled through. Gasps erupted from almost everyone assembled. With three more slashes, Marshal cut open a doorway: a doorway to the Otherworld.

Along with everyone else, Jamana stared into the dark landscape that lay beyond. The perspective made his brain hurt. It looked like a doorway, but it had no depth to it, and behind it, he could still see Zes Sivas and the lake. Within the portal, he couldn't make out much of the ground, but the lighting captured his attention. A strange light, a dark light, poured out of the doorway. Jamana crouched to get a better view angle. From there, he could see enormous stars in the sky of the Otherworld. Seri had spoken of those stars, and now he knew why. They were immense, multi-colored, and spectacular.

Marshal turned. "Talinir?" The Eldani nodded. He made some sort of gesture, running his open palm in a line down the center of his body, then entered the doorway. Marshal stepped to the very edge himself, then turned back.

He looked first to Victor. "I'll see you at the portal." Victor nodded.

He looked back at the residents of Zes Sivas. "Believe what you choose to believe," he called. "I go where I must. When I return here one day, it will be time to heal this land. For good."

He stepped into the Otherworld. Behind him, the edges of the the doorway lost their cohesiveness. All four sides shrank, moving in on themselves.

A figure broke from the crowd and ran toward it. Jamana took a step as well, recognizing her. Tich! The portal was closing. She would never make it. At the last moment, she dove, arms forward. Her streamlined body shot through the last vestiges of the doorway.

It vanished, leaving no trace of the Otherworld, Marshal, Talinir, or Tich.

<h1 style="text-align:center">(((16)))</h1>

"What are you doing?" Marshal cried. He stared as Tich got to her feet, brushing off her clothes. She gave an extra pat to her money pouch, jingling it as she often did, and adjusted a coil of rope hanging across her shoulder.

Talinir stood with sword drawn. "That was very foolish, girl. Why have you come here?"

"I'm not a girl. I haven't been a girl since someone betrayed my parents to Lord Tyrr." She looked up at Talinir's sudden increased height. "Whoa. What happened to you?"

"Don't avoid the question. What are you doing here?" Marshal demanded.

Tich shrugged. "I was bored with sailing back and forth across Lake Litanu. The opportunity presented itself to do something different and exciting." She looked around at the Otherworld ruins of Zes Sivas. "Not that I'm all that impressed so far."

"Try looking at the stars," Marshal grumbled. She did so. "Oh."

While Tich gazed upward, temporarily at a loss for words, Talinir moved next to Marshal. "What should we do with her?"

Marshal lifted his sword. "I open the portal again and we throw her back through, I guess."

Talinir put a hand on his wrist. "Don't. In fact, it would be better if you avoided the use of your magic as much as possible."

Marshal shot a look at the warden. "What do you mean?"

"I'm serious. Why is Talinir now tall man?" Tich interrupted.

"When you fought Curasir here, you were lucky," Talinir said, gesturing widely at the desolate landscape and ignoring Tich. "And at the portal, you were already surrounded by an army, so it didn't matter. But if we are to travel rapidly here… you should avoid using magic. Any large display will attract attention, both from the wildlife and possibly the Durunim and their masters."

Marshal sheathed his sword. "You might have mentioned that before."

Tich took a couple steps away. "I guess it's just an Eldanim thing, huh?" Her head drew back suddenly. "The lake is gone."

"Noticed that, did you?" Marshal stomped over beside her. "Apparently, we're stuck with you. Talinir says if I use magic to send you back, it might attract enemies." He looked her over. "You didn't even bring any supplies, did you?"

Tich spread her hands. "What can I say? It was an impulsive decision. I have my rope and canteen. Good news: I don't eat much."

"None of us will." Marshal didn't know what to think. Out of all the possibilities of a journey through the Otherworld, this had never occurred to him. He had considered what to do if Victor insisted on coming, but Tich? She was a sailor on Kishin's ship. She had no knowledge of anything they had been through, no investment in their struggles. Why? He ran both hands through his hair.

"Come on, it's not that bad," Tich said. "I might be helpful. What is your 'urgent mission' here, anyway?"

Marshal pointed to the northeast. "We have to rescue a friend from an army of Durunim and evil gods."

Tich stood still for a moment. "Well. That should be interesting."

Talinir approached. "I don't see any signs that our arrival has been detected. We should be able to move out."

"What's happening back on Zes Sivas right now?" Marshal asked.

"Victor and the acolyte have gone with the Masters. Everyone else is dispersing." He paused. "Your fellow sailor, Tich, is quite irritated with you."

"Heh. He deserves it." She blinked and looked at Talinir's face. "You can see both worlds?"

The Eldani nodded.

"Wondered what those weird eyes meant."

Marshal climbed onto some debris and looked around. "All right. We know the army is probably on its way to the third portal. My sense of Dravid is still northeast, but moving. We should probably head east to intercept them." He looked down. "Talinir, lead the way."

Talinir looked down at Tich. "Follow. Do not stray. There are hidden pits, and predators beyond what you've ever seen."

"I saw a tiger in Kuktarma once. Great big cat."

"One of the tunaldi would eat it."

"That's pleasant."

As Talinir continued trying to communicate the seriousness of the situation, Marshal finally took time himself to look up at the stars. As always, their majesty overwhelmed him. He could stare at them for hours and never grow tired of the sight.

"Marshal? Let's go."

Marshal pulled his eyes away and nodded. As he fell in behind Talinir, he wiped away a tear.

• • • • •

Jamana couldn't take his eyes away from the empty spot where the magical doorway had stood. What was Tich thinking? Why would she want to go with Marshal to the Otherworld? It made no sense.

The crowd erupted, everyone talking at once.

A large hand landed on his shoulder. "Acolyte! It appears we must speak with you," Master Ganak said.

Victor pushed his way forward. "You must speak with me too!"

Master Ganak looked him over. "What a curious magical conundrum you are," he murmured. Jamana didn't think anyone else heard it. "Very well," he said louder. "You may join the Conclave as well. We must hear everything."

The Masters led the way, passing by the empty Citadel of Kings and approaching the damaged Citadel of Mages. Master Ganak kept his hand on Jamana's back, escorting him with them the entire way. Victor followed close behind, looking all around and trying to take everything in. As they entered the citadel, Jamana picked up the bag with the book.

Master Tzoyet took the lead inside and led them to the Conclave's audience chamber. Jamana had been here several times, most notably when he first arrived on the island and faced questioning from all six Masters.

Today, only three took their places on the raised seats elevated in a semi-circle above the rest of the circular room. Jamana stood before them. Victor moved to his side. Eight blue-robed mages also joined them, the highest-rank outside of the Masters. They sat behind Jamana and Victor. No one else was allowed inside.

"Did you know Tich was going to do that?" Victor whispered.

Jamana shook his head. "I am as shocked as you."

Victor chuckled. "Now Marshal has to deal with her. I don't envy him."

Master Tzoyet rapped his staff on the floor for silence, an unnecessary action since everyone else already waited quietly in anticipation. He looked down at Jamana, ignoring Victor for the moment.

"We have heard many claims in the past few minutes," he said. "Our job as Masters is to evaluate them and come to the truth of the matter." He looked at the other two. "It is hard to even decide which of these claims to consider first."

"The kingship," Master Plecu said.

Master Tzoyet nodded. "Indeed. For if that claim is true, it will shape our opinion of the others. Acolyte Jamana, tell us what you can of this Marshal of Varioch."

Jamana bowed. "Masters, I will gladly tell all that I know, but Victor here has known Marshal his entire life. Perhaps you should hear from him first."

"We will hear from him in due time. For now, we will hear from one of our number. You."

Victor scratched at his beard. "This is as bad as the Eldanim high council," he muttered.

Jamana hesitated, then began with the fight on the beach. Unfortunately, that meant he had to explain why he was fleeing from another mage, the identity of Harbinger, a description of the tunaldi, and so on. It took some time to even get to Marshal's part in the story. When he described how Marshal confronted the pursuers and then buried the creature, it sparked quite a bit of interest from the Masters.

"A Lord could command such power," Master Ganak observed. "And by his own admission, he is the son of Varion and holds his power."

"Did you see any further evidence of his power, or anything that would lend credence to his claim to be the lost King?" Master Tzoyet asked.

"I saw what we all saw," Jamana said. "He opened a door to the Otherworld. Until that moment, I did not know such a thing was possible!"

"We did see that," Tzoyet said. "What it means, I do not yet have the wisdom to know."

"Of course you do!" Victor burst out. "You just don't want to admit it!"

"You have not been given leave to speak yet." Master Tzoyet glared at Victor. "We will hear all you have to say momentarily. But know this: we have heard from false claimants to the throne before now. We will take any such claim with careful consideration and a great deal of skepticism."

Victor rolled his eyes, but said nothing.

"There is one other thing," Jamana spoke up. "This body dispatched Seri-Belit to seek for the lost King. She found Marshal, and she believed in him. Is that not significant?"

"Unfortunately, Master Korda is the one who sent the Arazu mage on her mission," Master Ganak said. "And he is not here. Nor is she, I notice. Why is that, if she was the one who found him?"

"She is… attempting to stop Volraag from opening the final portal, I believe."

"Indeed? Interesting."

"This is preposterous," Master Plecu growled. "A bastard from Varioch can not possibly be the true King of Antises."

"And why is that?"

"Lord Varion was not in the line of the Kings!"

"I do not believe anyone has made that claim," Master Tzoyet observed. "Indeed, the young man said the Kingly line came through his mother."

"Ridiculous."

"We must hear more." Tzoyet turned to Victor. "Tell us who you are, and what you know of this."

Victor glanced around. "Ah, well, my name is Victor. I come from the village of Drusa's Crossing in Varioch. I've known Marshal my entire life."

"And his mother?"

Victor nodded. "She was a healer in our village. Marshal… he did various jobs, whatever anyone would give him. No one cared much for him, because of the curse."

The Masters sat up. "Tell us of the curse."

Victor described the struggles Marshal endured, explaining how the curse came from Lord Varion's actions. At the Masters' prodding, he recalled all he could from their early life, and especially the journey that led to the temple at Reman, where Aelia died.

The Masters got stuck at that point. They demanded Victor repeat the temple events over and over. They wanted every detail, even though Victor could only repeat what Marshal had told him about much of it. The lifting of a curse meant more to them than anything else being discussed.

"The timing is right," Master Ganak pointed out. "We all felt it that day."

"The conjunction of events is so… irrational," Master Plecu said, no longer antagonistic. "It seems inconceivable that the lifted curse would happen to a… a King."

"Who better?" Master Tzoyet suggested. "If it truly is him, then he has grown up knowing the ways of the Laws, their purposes and their failures."

"I'm sure this is all very fascinating to you," Victor interrupted. "But I think you've forgotten the most pressing issue. Gods. Armies. Remember?"

"We have not forgotten that part of the story," Master Tzoyet said. "But for now, we must discuss this business of the curse. We will summon you when we are ready to hear more."

"Discuss? We don't have time to discuss! We have to alert Kuktarma. We have to have an army waiting at the portal, in case Seri fails to stop Volraag! Don't you understand?"

"These are momentous events, of course," Master Ganak agreed. "But you fail to see the true significance of the lifted curse. That must occupy our thoughts, at least for the time being."

"This is insane!"

Jamana caught Victor by the arm. "Let it go, Victor. Let's talk outside." He leaned in and whispered, "Trust me."

Victor glared at the Masters, shook off Jamana's arm, and stalked out of the chamber. Jamana bowed to everyone else and hurried after him.

•••••

"So what was that back there about being the King?" Tich wanted to know.

"I'm not the King," Marshal grumbled. He climbed over a rock, following Talinir's lead. Only ten minutes into their journey and Tich's questions had gone beyond irritating.

"But the others think you are, and you obviously have serious magic power or something." She vaulted over the rock with ease.

Marshal didn't answer.

"I'm going to keep asking, you know. I heard enough on the ship to know the others take it seriously."

"Fine. Yes. I am descended from the Kings of Antises and I have the power. But I don't want to be King. I want to end it all."

Tich stopped. "End all of what?"

"The Laws. Cursings and Bindings. All of it."

Tich whistled, then hurried to catch up. "That's ambitious. Like something only a King would do."

Marshal rolled his eyes and kept walking.

"Why don't you want to be King? Wouldn't that help you?" Tich kept talking. "Everyone would have to do what you say. So you could order the mages to help you get rid of the Laws."

"I don't think it works that way," Marshal said.

"Why not?"

"A King must do more than give orders," Talinir broke in. "A King and his land are one. He holds its destiny in his hand. He must love it, guard it, and care for it beyond his own needs and desires."

"That's some high-sounding talk," Tich said. "Reminds me of a guy I met in Kuktarma. He talked like that. I really liked that guy." She paused. "But I think my boss killed him."

Marshal winced at the reminder of Kishin. He had no desire to dwell on how many people the assassin had killed in the past. On the other hand, Talinir's words stirred something inside him. Even if he wanted to, could he be the kind of person Talinir described?

"When you say a King and his land, do you mean the actual land? Or the people of the land?"

Talinir looked over his shoulder at him. "Both. But I suppose the people more so. A King must be selfless, putting their needs above his own."

"The Eldanim don't have a King."

"No, we do not. We have a Council now, with which you are acquainted," Talinir admitted. "But that doesn't mean I don't know what a King should be. We had a King once, and he failed to be those things."

"And that's why you have a council?"

Talinir nodded. "My people thought too much power in one man's hands led to corruption."

"Like our Lords."

"Yes. That is why a true King must be these things I've described. Selfless. A servant of others."

"No wonder you don't want the job," Tich muttered.

Talinir stopped, and dropped to one knee, facing Marshal. "You have the potential to be that kind of King, Marshal."

"I don't want—"

"I know you don't want it. And that's part of what makes you right for the job."

Tich snorted. "A lot of people don't want a job. That makes them right for it?"

Talinir kept his gaze fixed on Marshal. "There will come a time, a moment, where you will have to decide. Where you must take on that responsibility and protect your land and people... or absolve yourself of it all. Forever."

Marshal stared back at him. What could he say to something like that?

Talinir got to his feet and turned away. "In the meantime, we have far to go, in your quest to protect another one of your potential subjects."

Marshal resumed following the warden, but his thoughts remained on the Kingship. Thankfully, Tich stopped asking questions for a while.

(((17)))

Marshal lay back and watched the stars. Come what may in all the many journeys and hardships he had to face, at least he had moments like this. And the stars. They never changed. Glorious. Magnificent. He couldn't think of enough words to describe them. If he could be King of this place, it might be worth it. Whenever he got tired of responsibilities, he could watch the stars.

"Ouch," Tich said. "Guess there are bugs here too."

Marshal didn't get up. "Something bit you?"

"Yeah, I think it was a thrummer."

"Oh?" Marshal lifted his head. "They usually come after me..." Even as he said it, three of the tiny insects buzzed around his head.

"Some people are like that, I hear," Tich said. "Things used to come after both my parents all the time. I was an afterthought to them. Made me almost feel insulted."

"They're drawn to magic." Marshal held out his arm and let two of the insects land on it. The third one disappeared from view.

"You're letting them bite you?"

"Watch."

Marshal felt barely a pinprick from the tiny bites, but the insects began to glow. The longer he let them stay, the brighter they grew.

"Whoa." Tich moved closer. "I've seen them glow a little before, but not like that."

Satiated, the insects rose into the air, shining like miniature stars themselves. Marshal waved in the air and made them circle higher. He felt another pinprick on the back of his neck. That's where the third one went.

Marshal and Tich watched the insects move about above their

heads. After a few moments, the third thrummer joined the first two. They danced in circles with the stars of the Otherworld as a backdrop. Marshal wondered why they stayed, but guessed they might be reluctant to leave such a potent source of magic.

"Marshal?" Tich said.

"Yes?"

"Whatever else happens here… this makes the whole thing worth it. I could never see a sight like this in our world."

Marshal couldn't argue.

• • • • •

"I'm having a hard time getting used to no sunrises."

Marshal didn't respond to Tich as he gathered up his meager supplies. Morning in the Otherworld didn't look any different from any other time of the day or night.

"No sunsets, either. Is there even a moon here?"

"No moon," said Talinir. "Just the stars."

"Endless night. That's what you should call this place: the realm of endless night." She picked up her short coil of rope and looped it over her shoulder. "That's not necessarily bad. Some people might enjoy an endless night. There was this one port in southern Rasna. People said that because it was so far out on a peninsula, it was outside Antises, and therefore, outside the Laws of Cursings and Bindings. I never tested it myself, mind you, but a lot happened there that probably doesn't happen elsewhere very often. Especially at night."

"Talinir, did we make good progress yesterday?" Marshal asked.

"Not bad, for humans. We should do better today." The warden lit a small fire and blew on it.

Tich stretched and surveyed the sky again. "On ships, we use the stars for navigation. I'm guessing you do that here all the time, Tallman?"

"Many of the stars move about, but there are some that are consistent." Talinir pointed to a purple star that dominated one area of the sky. "That one is always in the north, for example."

"Your North Star is purple. I don't know what to think of that."

Marshal frowned. "You say they move about? What do you mean by that?"

"The stars are bound by nothing," Talinir said. "They shift positions from time to time. It is their choice. There is no pattern to it." He placed a pot of water over the fire.

"That's disturbing," Tich said. She jingled her coin purse. "Stars in our world move, but they have a specific path they follow."

"Our stars are different."

"No kidding. But you know the ones that don't move?"

"As a warden of the Eldanim, I know all the stars."

"What does that mean? Warden?"

"It means I know how to survive out here."

"I really want to know," Tich said. "What is a warden?"

"I am a protector for my people. The wardens travel the Otherworld, watching for threats to our city, Intal Eldanir."

"You have a city here?" Tich looked around. "Why would you ever leave it?"

"I didn't want to," Marshal said.

"You've been there?"

"It is the duty of a warden," Talinir explained. "Someone must keep an eye on the rest of the world."

"In your case, an eye on each of the worlds," Tich pointed out. She laughed at her own joke.

Marshal thought of something. "Talinir… we're still walking through Lake Litanu in our world. What do you see over there right now?"

"Not much."

"You see under the water right now?"

"Yes, but it's early morning. Not a lot of light is getting down to this depth. It's mostly dark." He paused. "Except for that one fish that has its own light."

Tich looked at him with narrowed eyes. "You're making that up," she accused.

"I'm not the one who makes things up."

"So why aren't you protecting your city now?"

"I made a promise to Marshal. Until his quest is complete, I stay with him."

Tich glanced at Marshal. "Lucky you. Kind of like a Bond, huh?"

"A little."

"I knew a couple of sailors that were Bonded. One saved the other from falling overboard near some sharks. After that, it was hard to keep them apart. We used to come up with excuses to separate them, just to see how long the Bonded one could handle it. Took him into town once and got him drunk enough to get into a fight. The other guy ran from the dock all the way to the inn without stopping. By then the fight was over. Without the Bond pulling at him, he passed out from running so hard."

"I've had a lot of experience with Bindings," Marshal said.

"I'll bet you have."

Tich raised her canteen and took a quick drink. She looked around again. "There is water here, isn't there?"

"Yes, but it can be very hard to find." Talinir smiled. "Good thing you've got a warden of the Eldanim with you. Ah, this water is boiling. Would anyone else like some tea?"

Marshal smiled. "With sugar?"

"Of course. What good is it otherwise?" Talinir pulled out a small pouch, then frowned. "Oh."

"What is it?"

Talinir's entire demeanor drooped. "This is the last of the sugar."

•••••

Jamana led Victor to the dining hall and procured meals for both of them. Victor shook from his anger, but he still had an appetite. While he ate, Jamana tried to explain the Conclave.

"The Masters like to debate everything in great detail. Since there are only three of them right now, perhaps they will be able to move faster than usual."

"Faster? We should be heading out right now, on our way to Kuktarma!" Victor gestured with his fork. "We don't even know how long that wind is going to last, for one thing!"

"They are also very wary, because of Tezan's deception, Volraag's attack—"

"Marshal isn't Volraag!" Victor interrupted. "If they can't see that, then they aren't anywhere near as wise as they're supposed to be." He paused. "But that one Master is from Rasna, isn't he?"

"Master Plecu? Yes."

"This isn't going to work." Victor put his fork down. "He'll never accept Marshal, because we're from Varioch. Lord Tyrr would never allow it."

"The Conclave of Mages is not beholden to the Lords—"

Victor reached into a pouch, pulled out a deck of cards, and slapped it down on the table. "This would disagree with you."

"What?"

"Mages and Lords, the game." Victor flipped some cards out onto the table. "It's been around for centuries. And it's all about the Master Mages fighting against the Lords… but the Lords win just as much as the mages. This has been known for hundreds of years. We can't trust that the Lords aren't pulling any strings here."

Jamana looked over the cards. He knew of the game, of course, though it wasn't played very much in Mandiata. Victor made a good point, though it rankled. The Masters, if they truly were Masters, had been chosen by Theon. The Lords had not. He knew which side he would follow if a conflict ever arose.

"What do you suggest we do, then?"

Victor gathered the cards and shuffled them without looking. "I don't know. I didn't want this, anyway. Marshal's the one who thinks. I usually just hit stuff."

Jamana didn't know what to say. He had only known Victor and Marshal for a few days. He was basing everything he believed about them on his experience on the beach… and Seri's recommendation.

Adhi slipped onto the bench beside him. Jamana grinned at seeing his young friend.

"The Masters are still cloistered," he reported. "You must have given them much to think about."

"We didn't even get to talk about the most important stuff," Victor griped.

Adhi nodded. "Your friend, the, ah, King, said an army was coming to Kuktarma."

Victor looked him over. "Your home?"

Adhi nodded again.

Victor let out a deep breath. "Yeah, it's an army. A big one. And every soldier in it is… well, they're nasty."

Adhi folded his hands together, but his thumbs twitched as he placed them on the table. "Tell me."

Victor described what he had seen in the Otherworld: the Durunim and the gods. Jamana thought of Harbinger riding the tunaldi. If the other gods rode similar beasts, and possessed the power of Nummotem, AND commanded an army of some kind of evil Eldanim… he did not see how the armies of Antises could stand against it. And they wouldn't even all be trying.

"Others are on their way to Kuktarma," he broke in.

"Marshal will be heading there, once he finds Dravid," Victor said.

Jamana shook his head. "But there is another army… well, maybe not an army. But a large group of people. A pilgrimage. Nummotem is leading it from Mandiata."

"Across Arazu?" Adhi said. "That will be a long journey."

"No longer than our own from here," Jamana pointed out. "And Victor hopes to find an army on the way."

"Then you'll come with me?" Victor asked.

Jamana shrugged. "Master Korda tasked me with returning the book to Zes Sivas, and telling the Masters about the return of the gods. I have done that. He clearly wanted the gods opposed. Going with you will honor his wishes, I am thinking."

"The army of Kuktarma is formidable if it can be roused," Adhi said, looking off in the distance. "But, ah, that may be difficult."

"The key is Master Ganak," Jamana said. "Will he be persuaded, do you think?"

Adhi hesitated. "I do not know. He is… Master Ganak is a proud man. He believes strongly in his own power, and in the might of Kuktarma."

"This is bad," Victor muttered. "Without him, I can't persuade anyone in Kuktarma. I don't KNOW anyone in Kuktarma!"

"You know me." Adhi's smile left as quick as it came, as nervous as he usually appeared.

"I've barely met you, but—"

"I can help you," Adhi declared, sounding more confident than Jamana had ever heard him. "I will tell Master Ganak that I am escorting you to Simbala to meet with Lord Meluhha."

"You can do that?"

Jamana stared. He would not dare to even think about "telling" Master Korda what he was going to do. Yet Adhi seemed sure of this, somehow.

"I will. Your ship still waits, doesn't it?"

Victor nodded.

Adhi got to his feet. "Let us give the Masters one day. If they do not decide to help, we will go to Kuktarma ourselves." He looked from Jamana to Victor. "Is this acceptable?"

"Yes."

"I believe so."

"Good." Adhi turned and walked away. Even his walk appeared firmer and stronger than what Jamana knew. This was Adhi?

Victor picked up his fork again. "That kid surprised me. Is he always like that?"

Jamana had no idea what to say.

(((18)))

Seri walked down the gangplank onto the dock of Sandu-Emuq. The last time she had been here, she was on her way to Zes Sivas to become a mage. Now she returned as one, much sooner than anyone would have anticipated.

Her blue robes attracted stares from the dockworkers. She held her head high and moved with a confidence she did not feel.

Volraag's ship sat beside three others currently waiting at the docks. Two of them were flat barges, unloading lumber. Arazu imported almost all of its building materials: ore, lumber, stone. In return, they exported vast amounts of wheat, barley, and other crops that grew prolifically in the southern fields.

Seri needed transportation to the palace. Of course she could walk, but it felt inappropriate to arrive at the home of the Lord and Lady on foot. She made her way to the main road from the dock and sought out a carriage. It did not take long to find one of the horse-drawn vehicles and pay the driver. In short order, Seri relaxed on the single passenger seat in the small four-wheeled carriage. The driver raised eyebrows at her robes, but said nothing.

As the carriage moved through the city at a leisurely pace, Seri delighted in how much she recognized. Less than a year had gone by since she left, but it felt so much longer. She noticed some new construction, but most of the buildings looked exactly the same. The vast majority were simple structures with flat roofs, though a handful of domes and vaulted roofs appeared here and there. Off to her right, Seri caught a glimpse of the temple, the largest vaulted structure in the city.

The carriage passed by a long series of circular brick columns dating back to the earliest days of Arazu. This oldest part of the city prided itself in its artistic and educational edifices. And in the center of it all lay the palace.

She could see it now ahead of them: an enormous circular structure with a dome atop a larger roof that angled toward it from all sides. Towers stood at six equidistant points around the dome. Each tower, built of white stone, rose to a pinnacle above an open viewing floor. In times of emergency, before Seri's memory, lookouts would be stationed in the towers, watching in all directions.

Occasional red stones scattered throughout the building's walls and towers created a fascinating pattern. Throughout her life, Seri had spent hours trying to map the patterns in her mind.

Captivated by the mental exercise yet again, Seri sat still when the carriage stopped. She could not help but wonder what Ixchel would have thought of all this. No doubt she would evaluate its defensive capabilities. Seri almost laughed.

"My lady?" the driver asked.

Seri cleared her thoughts, thanked him and stepped down. The early morning sun cast long shadows from nearby columns. She approached the open doors where a pair of guards waited, armed with long spears. She paused before them.

"I am Seri-Belit, mage of Arazu," she announced. "I seek an audience with the Lord and Lady."

One of the guards knocked on the doorframe. A moment later, another man appeared in the doorway. Tall and wizened, he looked Seri over with keen eyes. She recognized him: a functionary of some sort, though she couldn't remember his name.

"The Lady said you might come," he said at last. "Follow me."

That statement threw her off. How could the Lady possibly know? She obeyed, following the functionary through a curving hallway which circled the main part of the palace. As they walked, Seri admired the detailed murals that lined the walls. They depicted all of the major events of Antises' early history, from Akhenadom leading the people out from the Great Cataclysm, to the claiming of the lands, to the enacting of the Laws of Cursings and Bindings.

One mural in particular brought Seri to a stop. She had only seen these once before, so obviously, she would have missed some things, but this? She stared at a drawing clearly portraying the Passing. It held one clear difference between the Passing she had observed: in the center of the mural stood a noble figure, arms outstretched. And before him pulsed an enormous ball of light.

The Heart of Fire.

"Shall we?" The functionary's question broke her out of her reverie. She hurried after him until the hall led to another set of massive doors. These, Seri knew, were a gift from one of the early Lords of Kuktarma. They depicted intricately carved images of the two Lords of each land clasping hands, but in a much more abstract artistic style than Arazu's more realistic designs.

The functionary knocked once, then pushed the door open enough to squeeze in. He beckoned Seri to follow him.

Inside, she looked around at the receiving hall of the Lord of Antises. Its lengthy tripartite design was divided by more circular brick columns. At the head of the central section stood two large carved wooden chairs side-by-side. Seated on the elaborate chairs, Lord Enuru and Lady Lilitu waited for her. Seri couldn't help noticing the Lady's chair was just a bit smaller than the Lord's.

Lord Enuru's long black hair and beard had a bit more gray in it than the last time she had seen him. As before, he wore only multiple layered skirts and elaborate jewelry. He wore no crown this time.

Neither did the Lady. Her gown was teal with billowy sleeves and bare shoulders. Her jewelry looked identical to what she had worn on Zes Sivas, including the frontlet with its white crystal on her forehead.

"Seri-Belit, mage of Arazu," the functionary declared in a monotone. He nodded once to Seri and left the room.

Lady Lilitu immediately rose to her feet and came toward her. "My dear Seri, so good to see you!"

Seri attempted to bow, but the Lady took her arm and embraced her, as she had done on Zes Sivas. When they pulled apart, the Lady held her by the shoulders and looked her over. Seri couldn't help but look into her eyes, searching out the star they both possessed. Curasir called it an unusual wild magic, but the other Durunim they met called it her heritage. Something else she was determined to solve while here.

Lord Enuru stood near his chair, but did not approach them. "We did not expect you to come back so soon," he said. "We have not yet selected a new Master. Have the others sent you to check on our progress?"

"You did not expect her," Lady Lilitu said. "I did. And she has her own purposes now." She looked at Seri and smiled again. "Come. We were just about to break fast. Join us, and tell us all that you will."

Seri followed the couple into an antechamber where a sumptuous meal of breads and fruit had been laid out. She had eaten little since Ixchel's fall, but the smell of the fresh bread made her stomach growl. When the Lord and Lady began to eat, she joined in.

Lady Lilitu eyed her thoughtfully. "Has your bodyguard abandoned you?" she asked.

Seri almost choked on a mouthful of buttered bread. After all she and Ixchel had been through together, she had forgotten Ixchel's assignment to her had come because of the Lady.

"I… I lost her, my Lady." Seri struggled with the right words. "She died saving me."

Lord Enuru shook his head. "You seem to find danger wherever you go," he observed. "Most peculiar for a woman your age."

The Lady rolled her eyes. "I see that it is a recent hurt," she said to Seri. "You have my sympathies."

Seri nodded. She took a sip of water, not sure what to say next. She had rehearsed what exactly she should tell them, but the question about Ixchel had thrown her off.

"My Lord makes a point," Lady Lilitu said. "You have been traveling?"

"Yes, my Lady." Seri took a deep breath and began. "After the attack on Zes Sivas, I was dispatched by the Masters to seek out the lost King. I have traveled through Varioch and Ch'olan without success. And now I come here."

Lord Enuru absently tossed an apple and caught it. "Interesting choice of destinations. Wouldn't it make more sense to search all six lands?"

"Perhaps," Seri admitted. "But there are three locations of power—high places they are called—and I believe the lost King would be drawn to them apart from Zes Sivas. Magic calls to magic, you see. The first high place lay near the border of Varioch and Rasna, the second in Ch'olan, and—"

"And the third lies south of our border in Kuktarma, to the east," Lady Lilitu interrupted.

Seri nodded. Of course she would know.

"Tell me of Varioch," Lord Enuru said. "It seems they went to war with Rasna, perhaps in the same area where you traveled. What is that upstart Volraag up to there?"

Seri told what little she knew of the war, then admitted she also knew little about doings inside Ch'olan. She did not mention the opening of the portals or Volraag's involvement. Many times throughout the conversation, she noticed the Lady's eyes on her. Those eyes so full of wisdom undoubtedly saw right through her. How could Seri possibly hope to deceive her? And why should she, anyway?

The functionary entered the room and whispered something to Lord Enuru. He sighed and set aside his half-eaten apple. "It appears I am needed elsewhere, as is so often the case," he said, getting to his feet. "It was good to see you again, my young mage." He bowed to his wife. "My Lady." She nodded in return and he followed the functionary out of the antechamber.

Lady Lilitu took a deep breath and let it out. "Oh, good. Now we can stop talking about boring politics and war," she said. She ran her fingers along the edge of the table. "Tell me something more interesting. What have you learned of magic in this time?"

Seri's mind raced. Now she could ask more direct questions of her own. But she had to tread carefully. "I have learned much, My Lady. Most particularly, I met an unusual man in Varioch. He called himself Forerunner."

If the name meant anything to the Lady, she did not show it. "A mage?"

"No, he was… I'm not sure how to describe him. He was a being of pure magic, but not the magic of Antises. He claimed to be a representative of the old gods."

Lady Lilitu cocked her head. "Indeed?"

"His magic was unlike anything I've seen before, except… yours, my Lady. And he also had stars in his eyes. Like we do."

"Ah. I see." She reclined on her dining couch. "And so you come to me, looking for answers."

Seri could only nod.

"I told you that I would be your next teacher, when you had learned all you could from the Masters. And that we would have a talk about the sources of power in this world. Since then, many things have changed."

Seri frowned. Was the Lady going back on her word?

"Long ago, before you were born, I met a man. He was not unlike this Forerunner you mention. He possessed a power unlike any I had seen in this world. I questioned him incessantly, wanting to learn the secrets of this power. He would not tell me for weeks, but I persisted. Over time, I began to learn from him."

The Lady paused and took a drink from her goblet. "These meetings always took place at night, which is what led to those silly rumors about my meetings with 'night spirits,' by the way."

Seri's eyes widened. "I never gave any credence to those stories, my Lady."

"Over time, this man showed me how to reach beyond Antises and summon the power from another world." She tapped a fingernail next to her eye. "When I first did so, the star appeared in my eye."

"Did he have stars in his eyes also?"

The Lady nodded. "Three, at least. I'm not sure if that is some indication of his level of power or something else obscure I don't understand yet."

"I… I can see magic," Seri said. "And sometimes, I can see into the Otherworld. I've even transported myself there."

Lady Lilitu sat up. "Your powers are growing faster than I anticipated, then." She smiled. "I told you. You will be something far greater than a Master at the Conclave."

"I don't understand." The story was intriguing, but Seri could not reconcile it with what she knew of the gods so far. Nor did it match with the origin of her own star-sight.

The Lady got to her feet and approached her. She knelt beside Seri and ran a hand through her hair. "Dear Seri, I want to tell you much more, but I can't. Not yet."

Seri's face must have shown her confusion, because the Lady laughed. "But it will not be long. You have to talk with someone else first. It is not my place to tell you what she should."

"Who is that?"

The Lady's smile grew even larger. "Your mother, my dear."

(((19)))

Jamana opened the book one last time. He regretted not finishing every page, but the writing was difficult and sometimes out of order. It needed someone more skilled to study it. The Masters would handle it.

He looked at the last page he had been reading. Aharu wrote extensively praising her son, Nehesy, for his zeal and courage in defying the old gods. A mother's right, to be sure, but hardly beneficial for the current crisis. That was another problem: half of the book covered events and people that had nothing to do with the historical events that most concerned Marshal and his purposes.

Jamana closed the book and took it to Master Tzoyet's quarters. After being invited in, he set the ancient tome on the Master's desk. "Master Korda instructed me to return this to you," he explained. "He believed it was not safe in Mandiata."

Master Tzoyet looks down at the book. "*A History of the Lords' Betrayal,*" he read. "Yes, this created quite the stir when you found it. I look forward to studying it more. Thank you, acolyte."

"There is more than that," Jamana said. He hesitated, knowing this would be controversial. "Marshal hoped this would give you insight into how the Laws of Cursings and Bindings were created."

"It no doubt will," Master Tzoyet agreed. "Why did that concern the claimant King?"

"He, uh, he wants to rescind the Laws."

Master Tzoyet stared at Jamana without saying anything. He grew uncomfortable under the Master's intense scrutiny.

"Why did you not mention this in the Conclave?" the Master asked at last.

"I did not think it relevant."

"Not relevant? The fact that the most powerful man in all Antises wants to undo our most fundamental Laws? You did not consider this relevant?"

Jamana ducked his head. "When you say it in that manner…"

Master Tzoyet put a hand on the book and murmured something in the ancient tongue of Ch'olan. He looked up at Jamana. "I will have to tell the other Masters about this."

Jamana nodded.

"Is there anything else you have failed to mention, acolyte?"

"Nothing of consequence, Master. Has the Conclave made any kind of decision yet?"

Master Tzoyet eyed him again. "We are mostly convinced that this Marshal is the one for whom a curse was lifted. And that he possesses at least a Lord's power. Whether he is the lost King or not is still under debate."

"And the returning gods?"

"That is a subject for which we have no decision to make."

"We must warn Kuktarma! Surely, you can send a message—"

"We cannot," the Master interrupted. "Our usual means of communicating with our homes is not… working very well right now. Master Plecu, in particular, has not heard from Rasna in some weeks."

"Because that portal is open!" Jamana paced a few steps away before he remembered his place and returned to his spot in front of the desk. He did not pretend to understand the Masters' secretive communication system, but to stop it must require powerful magic. "The invasion has already taken place for Rasna and Varioch. All the more reason to inform Kuktarma."

"It may be as you say, but we cannot leave here. The island has never had so few Masters in residence, as it is."

Jamana bowed. "Then I will be leaving, Master. Under Master Korda's instructions, I must continue on with my mission."

Master Tzoyet nodded. "That seems wise. I wish you well, acolyte."

Jamana turned in frustration and hurried out. How could the Masters be so calm and uncaring about this? If the portal were opened, Kuktarma and Arazu would be overrun, as Varioch and Rasna were no doubt experiencing now. Then it would be only a matter of time before the gods and their servants spread their rule to Mandiata and Ch'olan. All of Antises would fall under their control.

And what would happen then? Jamana could only imagine. He went in search of Victor and Adhi. They needed to leave as soon as possible.

• • • • •

"And it was right about then that I realized she actually *was* the daughter of Lord Tyrr, and I had just called her a prostitute."

Marshal somehow kept himself from rolling his eyes. Tich's stories always took things just a step too far to be believable. Still, it provided some relief from the monotony of walking across the barren wasteland of the Otherworld. If they were back in their own world right now, they would still be beneath the waters of Lake Litanu.

"I don't understand why you are telling us this," Talinir said.

Tich shrugged. "It's how I pass the time. You don't have to listen."

Marshal felt a tug at his heart. The Bond to Dravid pulled him forward. Dravid's danger must be increasing, though not in a sudden, desperate manner. This danger seemed persistent... and growing.

"Can we move faster?" he asked Talinir.

"No." Talinir stopped, looking toward the east. "In fact, we must find a place to conceal ourselves." He pointed at a large dust cloud some distance away. Marshal couldn't make out anything within it, but it did seem to be coming toward them.

"Are these the predators you talked about?" Tich asked.

"No." Talinir gave no other explanation. He led them south, away from their intended path. Marshal felt the ache of the Bond's pull grow stronger as he moved in the wrong direction.

Talinir found a ridge beneath a short overhang. The three travelers crowded beneath it. From this vantage point, they could watch the dust cloud without being easily seen. Marshal waited with curiosity. In his brief visits to the Otherworld so far, he had never encountered any of its fauna. Of course, the curse-stalkers came from here. But it seemed inconceivable that anything could live in such a wasteland.

Especially something that could create such a large cloud of dust. As it drew near, Marshal saw enormous shapes moving through the cloud. Definitely not curse-stalkers.

"They will pass closer than I anticipated," Talinir murmured. "Still, we should be safe here."

"Safe from what? I still can't see," Tich complained.

"Hush. Watch."

Marshal stared. At the head of the dust cloud, a gigantic creature suddenly appeared. Its body, supported by four massive legs, had to be the size of Marshal's cabin back in Drusa's Crossing. Its head sat atop a neck as long as one of its legs. A spinal ridge began at the back of its head and ran all the way down its back and halfway down a long, tapering tail waving in the air behind it. Its head was the most bizarre of all. Though long like a horse's, it shared no resemblance to any other creature Marshal knew. Above its narrow mouth, its nostrils bulged and hung down in an elongated appendage that swung from side to side.

Other creatures of the same kind emerged from the cloud behind the leader, though none of them were its match in size and girth. The closer they came, the more Marshal could feel the ground tremble with their footsteps.

"I did not expect that," Tich said.

"Quiet," Talinir warned.

As the creatures passed by, moving toward the west, Marshal realized something else. He could sense magic from them. Though faint, it felt familiar to what he experienced around Talinir and the other Eldanim. Apparently, everything here had magic coursing through its veins.

Once the herd passed, Tich turned to the warden. "Would those things have attacked us? They didn't look like carnivores to me."

Talinir held up a hand, still watching through the dust. "They are not the threat," he said in a low voice. "The predators that stalk the herd are."

Marshal tensed. Talinir was right. Something else prowled through the dust cloud, not as massive as the herd creatures, but still very large. As it emerged into his sight, he recognized the hexagon-shaped scales and the curved snout: tunaldi.

Tich took a step back. Her foot kicked a pebble loose and it clattered down into a crevice.

The tunaldi's head whipped in their direction. It took a step toward them.

Marshal looked past the creature and selected an outcropping about the size of a man. He concentrated on focusing his power, not to throw a burst of energy, but to build up the energy, the magic, within the rock itself. To his delight, it worked. The rock exploded in a shower of shards. The tunaldi spun in that direction and bounded to investigate. Another one, slightly smaller, joined it.

"That was foolish," Talinir whispered. "The display will attract them for only a moment. Then they will understand magic has been used and follow it to its source."

Indeed, the creatures looked like they were sniffing the air. As one, they both turned toward the hidden watchers.

"Is it too late to open that portal back to our world?" Tich asked.

"Swords," Talinir said. "We'll have to fight. Don't use your magic unless you have no choice." He and Marshal both drew the swords. Tich watched them.

"Stay here if you can," Marshal said. Then he and Talinir climbed out to face the approaching beasts.

(((20)))

Seri paused at the stairs. She hadn't felt this nervous since her arrival at Zes Sivas so long ago. No, this was worse. Her nervousness at Zes Sivas had been filled with anticipation. This nervousness was filled with... dread.

For her entire life, Seri had enjoyed a good relationship with her parents. They treated her well, supported her dreams, sent her to the Lady's university, and encouraged her to apply to Zes Sivas. Yet with the Lady's words today, all of that had been thrown into question. Nor could she forget Forerunner's reference to her "heritage."

The stairs led from the street to the front door of her parents' mansion, the home in which she had grown up. Until a few months ago, the only place she had ever lived. But now she feared to open its door: a wooden import from Kuktarma like the throne room's. Her father, Ekur, spared no expense in making his family's dwelling as lavish as his wife desired. While most of the other homes in this area were made of the same white stone as the palace, this home's outer wall consisted of reddish granite imported from Mandiata.

"This is stupid, Seri," she said out loud. "They're your parents. They've always loved you."

Taking a deep breath, she climbed the stairs, gathered her resolve, and opened the door. Inside, she entered a large courtyard lined with circular brick columns, smaller but not unlike the ones in the palace. Ekur could afford the best here as well. He arranged the grain trade for several hundred farms, shipping their crops to all five other lands of Antises.

On the far side of the courtyard, a figure appeared on the second floor balcony above the columns. "Who's there?" a man's voice called.

"Seri!" she called back.

"My Seri?" He hurried across the balcony and down the curved stairs in the corner. As he rushed to meet her, Seri could not resist a gasp of joy. Her father looked no different from the day she left. His beard may not have been as spectacular as Lord Enuru's, but it was black and full and curly. As a child, she had delighted in burying her hands in all of that hair hanging down across his bare chest.

She ran forward to meet him; he caught her up in a massive hug and spun her around. "Let me see you, let me see you," he chortled, setting her back down and stepping back. "Blue robes! So you were not exaggerating in your letters. You truly are a full mage!"

Seri shoved at him. "Of course I am! I would not lie to you, Father!"

"It has been some time since your last letter," he chided. "Your mother has been quite concerned about you."

"Where is she?"

"She is here somewhere. One moment. Ninsha!" He stepped away and called toward the back of the house. "Ninsha! Come see who has come!"

"What is it?" Seri's mother emerged from beneath the balcony, wiping her hands on a small cloth. Her gray hair sparkled in the afternoon sunlight, cascading down over her shoulders, conservatively covered by the bright yellow gown she wore. A green belt with a large jade at the front completed her outfit. She put a hand to her mouth. "Seri?"

"Mother." For a moment, Seri didn't know what to do. Then her instincts kicked in and she rushed to her mother. The women embraced one another, and tears flowed. Ekur stood back with a proud smile on his face.

"Look at her, Ninsha," he suggested. "Doesn't she look wonderful?"

"You do indeed," she said. "Though these robes are in need of a good cleaning. As could you, I believe."

"I've been on a ship," Seri protested. "I couldn't wash very well there."

"Excuses."

"Mother!"

Ekur summoned a servant Seri did not recognize and ordered supper to be brought into the courtyard when it was ready. Then he led the way to benches that surrounded his tiny garden near some of the columns on the left side of the courtyard. "Tell us what has happened since your last letter," he said.

Seri took a deep breath. Unfortunately, she had to tell them the same story she had told the Lord and Lady, to maintain secrecy. She hated not telling them the full truth, but the opportunity to convert Volraag to their side was too important. She also found it difficult to talk about Dravid, so she left out what happened to him for now.

"Then you are not here for long?" Ninsha asked.

"No. A day or two at most," Seri said.

"Pity." Ekur stood and stretched. "It would be nice to have you about again. As it is, I'm afraid I have a meeting with the owner of our trading fleet shortly, and—"

"But I must ask you both something important!" Seri interrupted.

They both looked at her with raised eyebrows. "What is it, my child?" her mother asked.

Seri pointed to her left eye. "What do you see here?"

"Your eye?" Ekur wondered.

Ninsha shot him an exasperated look, then bent in to gaze into Seri's eyes. "It… it looks like a sparkle, a sparkle that does not diminish." She leaned back. "How curious."

"It means something. Lady Lilitu has one too. And the strange magic-user I found in Varioch had four of them in his eyes."

Her parents looked at each other, but said nothing. Seri trembled. They knew something! They were hiding something from her!

"The Eldani that I met on Zes Sivas claimed it was wild magic." Seri's words came out in a rush. "But another one said it was my heritage. And I was told to ask you about it."

Seri waited. After a moment of silence, Ekur asked, "Who told you to ask us?"

"Another mage that I met. And Lady Lilitu. She told me this morning."

Silence again. Seri couldn't bear it. "What is it? What is the problem?"

Ekur looked at his wife again. "You will have to tell her," he said. "I cannot. I will not."

Ninsha nodded. "I will take care of it."

Ekur bent and gave Seri a kiss on her head. "I love you, my daughter," he said. "Never forget that." With those words, he turned and left the courtyard. Seri's eyes followed him in confusion, then turned back to her mother.

"What is going on?" she whispered.

Her mother shifted and adjusted her gown. "I don't know how to tell you," she admitted. "It was my hope that this day would never come."

"Why?"

She put out her hand and Seri took it. Looking up, she was surprised to see tears in her mother's eyes. With her next words, Seri's heart shattered.

"We are not your true parents."

•••••

Marshal took a few steps away from Talinir at his instruction. He kept his eyes on the approaching monsters. This was his own fault.

"Don't worry too much about their teeth," Talinir advised. "Their claws are the main threat, and they can move much faster than you expect them to."

"Weak points?"

"Not very many. Their skin is remarkably tough. The warpsteel blades will pierce it, but only just. Try to aim for the head and neck area, if you can. If the opportunity presents itself, the underbelly is also weaker."

The only way he would see the underbelly of the creature is if it were above him. Marshal didn't think that likely… or at least he hoped it wasn't likely.

The two beasts separated, moving toward each of their targets. Marshal felt somewhat relieved that the smaller one had chosen him.

The first time Marshal had seen Talinir in combat was against one of these beasts. Talinir won the fight, but had been seriously injured. "I'm nowhere near your skill," Marshall called. "I don't think I can do this without magic."

"You're better than you think you are," Talinir said. "If you can't kill it, keep it busy until I can help you." With that, Talinir lifted his sword and charged his creature.

Marshal had no time to watch him in action as the beast in front of him chose that moment to pick up its pace. It roared at him, a snarling explosion of sound that vaguely reminded him of wolves on the mountains back home. Marshal dropped into a defensive pose, one foot back, and waited.

Victor didn't get far against one of these either. Maybe he should…

The tunaldi lifted one enormous paw and swiped at him. Unable to dodge in time, Marshal tried to block it with his sword. The warpsteel blade clanged against giant claws. The impact knocked Marshal off his feet, but at least he held on to the sword.

Jaws came toward him. He stabbed at the open mouth as he tried to scramble to his feet. He missed, but managed to stab into the creature's nostril. A screeching roar in response made him stagger another couple of feet back. The creature's breath smelled of decay and rot and… magic. Somehow, even its breath held magic. Seri would be fascinated by that.

Thinking about her almost got him killed. Another swipe of claws hit the rock where he had been standing, gouging into the stone. Marshal struck at the creature's leg, but his sword rebounded off its scales.

"You gotta do better than that, King Scar!" Tich's voice startled him. The tunaldi's paw swept back and backhanded him. He rolled away from it before leaping back to his feet, sword at ready again.

Tich stood on top of the tunaldi. How she had gotten there, he couldn't imagine. She dropped a loop of rope down around the creatures head and yanked back on it. She braced her feet against the back of its head and held on.

"What are you doing?" Marshal cried.

"I once rode a bull like this in Kuktarma! Only about half the size of this thing, but just as ornery. One of their priests taught me how to do it. I think he fell in love with me, but it never would have worked out."

Marshal wanted to shake his head in disbelief. Even in this situation, she kept babbling on with an outlandish story. If she weren't so obnoxious sometimes, it would be amusing.

"This is not the same thing!" Marshal tried to run in a circle to get behind the creature, but it turned with him. Tich's rope had no effect on it. When Marshal stopped, it tried to slash at the annoyance on its back, but its claws couldn't reach her.

"Ha. I guess I can stay here as long as I can hold on."

"What good does that do?"

"It'll get tired eventually."

"Before you do?"

Tich didn't answer.

The tunaldi lunged once more at Marshal, forcing him to run backward. As soon as he did, it turned its attention to Tich again. It rose on to its hind legs and shook.

"Devouring fire!" Tich screamed, unable to hang on to anything but her rope. And that didn't do her much good. She flew off the creature's back and hit the ground hard, rolling. Somewhere along the way, she finally let go of the rope. At the end of the roll, she slammed into an outcropping and lay still.

Marshal had only seconds to save her life. He launched himself into the air with a burst of magic. As the tunaldi opened its mouth to bite into Tich's unconscious body, Marshal landed on its back. He slammed his sword down, channeling as much magic as he had time for into the warpsteel blade. It tore through the thick scales on the creature's back and stabbed deep. "Now." The magic within the sword exploded inside the tunaldi, tearing its organs to shreds. It gave a low moan and slumped to the ground, its nose pushing Tich's body into an awkward position atop it.

Marshal closed his eyes and let himself relax, but only for a moment. *Talinir!* He spun to see what had become of the Eldani warden.

To his relief, the other tunaldi lay dead as well, flipped over on its back. Talinir pulled his sword from its neck and looked at Marshal. He shook his head and approached them.

"Had to use magic, did you?"

"It was the only way." Marshal slid down off the creature and moved to Tich's side. He pulled her out of the way. She didn't look badly injured.

"Let me see." Talinir bent over her. He checked her limbs, then brushed her hair back, revealing a large bruise. He touched it and muttered, *"i hatel dahanir."* He got back to his feet. "The stars should heal her now."

"Is that like what you did to me back at your city?" Marshal asked.

"You were all but dead," Talinir said. "What they did for you then is far beyond my skill."

Marshal looked back at the tunaldi corpses. "Since I used magic, do we need to run? Or hide?"

Talinir turned in a circle, gazing in every direction. "I do not sense anything immediate," he said. "But it would be best not to linger here. Gather our supplies. I'll cut some meat off one of these beasts to take along."

"You can eat them?"

"Oh yes." Talinir nodded. "The flavor can be somewhat coarse, and a bit greasy, but it is quite savory." He looked at the ruins of the tunaldi Marshal had killed, then hurried to the other one.

Marshal decided not to watch him. He removed Tich's rope from the tunaldi's neck. She might want it back. Once he had gathered the gear from under the overhang, he came back to her side. Talinir joined them with a large slab of meat. He pulled some thick cloth of some kind from his pack and wrapped the meat. Once he stored it, he bent and picked up Tich. He nodded to Marshal. "Let's go."

Marshal closed his eyes for a moment, sensing the Bond with Dravid. He pointed. "That way."

They set out again, but he couldn't help wondering what else the Otherworld might throw at them. At least the stars were still here. He glanced up at them to be sure.

So beautiful.

(((21)))

The shock of her mother's statement left Seri frozen. "I... I don't understand."

Ninsha spoke with slow, careful words. "We have raised you from birth, and loved you as our daughter. But I did not give birth to you."

"Then who did?" Seri shot a look in the direction her father had departed. "Did Father have another wife? A lover?"

"No, no, no. Your father is a faithful, good man. He would never do something like that to me, to us."

"Then..."

Her mother closed her eyes and took a deep breath. One of the tears escaped and ran down her cheek. She brushed it away and continued, "We had been married for three years. Three years with no children. I despaired. To think that I would never hold a child in my arms... I sank into darkness, my love."

Seri waited, her heart barely beating.

"One day, your father received a summons to the palace. He was gone less than an hour before he returned and told me to come with him. I did not want to leave the house, but he urged me. I followed him and we returned to the palace."

She hesitated.

"Only... we did not enter through the main doors. Your father took me around to another door hidden from view on the east side of the palace. He explained that he had been instructed to do this. A servant let us in and we were told to wait in an empty room. I asked him what was happening. He said only that he had been instructed to bring me there.

"After a few minutes, the door opened and Lady Lilitu entered. In her arms, she held an infant. It was you, Seri-Belit."

Seri didn't breathe. She had no idea how to respond to this.

"You could not have been more than a few days old. The Lady did not tell us where you came from, only that you were now without parents. She told us your name, and asked if we would take you."

Ninsha's words grew earnest. She leaned in closer. "You were such a beautiful baby. I fell in love with you in that very moment. You did not come from my womb, Seri. But I chose to be your mother. I chose you."

"When I was offered to you." Seri regretted the words as soon as she said them. Her mother recoiled. "I'm sorry. I'm sorry. I just… I don't know what to think of this."

"You are my daughter." Ninsha emphasized each word. "I love you and have always loved you. Nothing changes that. Nothing."

Seri released her mother's hand and lifted it to run her fingers through a lock of Ninsha's hair. "But we have the same hair."

Ninsha smiled and brushed away another tear. "As do many of the women in Arazu." She chuckled. "It's a very common hair color, my love."

Seri glanced back at the door. "Why did Father not want to tell me?"

"He does not like to be reminded of it. To him, as to me, you are our child. It is why we never told you." She hesitated. "And because the Lady asked us not to."

"Why would she do that?"

"Because she wanted you to have a normal life, with normal parents."

Seri's mind raced and warred with her emotions. Confusion. Anger. Betrayal. Fear. She cycled through all of them in moments. She jumped to her feet and walked in a circle around the garden. "I don't know what to think," she said. "I'm lost here. If I'm not your child, then whose am I?"

"You are our child!"

Seri kept going. "I don't even know where I came from. Where did the Lady find me? Did she give me this name, or did someone else? You didn't even name me!"

"We loved you. It didn't matter that—"

"It matters to me!" Seri snapped. She put her hands to her head. "I can't believe this. I can't believe all this is happening. I lost Dravid. I left Marshal. I lost Ixchel. And now I don't even know who I am!"

Ninsha rose to her feet. "You are my daughter, Seri-Belit of Arazu. That is who you are!"

"Am I? Who is that? Who is Seri-Belit? I've never even liked that name!"

"Seri…"

"I just… I need time. I need…"

"Seri…"

Seri stood still, trembling. Her mother came around the garden toward her, more tears in her eyes.

"I… I'm losing everything, mother. I can't lose you too."

"You will never lose me, dear one."

Ninsha wrapped her arms around Seri again. At first, she resisted, standing stiff but trembling. Could she trust this? Could she believe? And if she did, what if… what if she still lost everything? What if…?

Seri lost control of her own body. She collapsed into her mother's arms, sobbing. They both sank to the ground, still holding each other, both of them crying, both of them trying desperately to hold on to someone they loved beyond all.

A few minutes later, their sobs subsiding, Seri pulled back. She wiped her face with her sleeve. "I guess I really need to wash now."

Ninsha laughed through her tears. "I'll have Dina draw you a bath. And wash your robe. It's the least we can do."

Seri lowered her head, hands in her lap. "I can't do it, mother. I can't do everything they expect of me. I'm not strong enough."

"You are… you are the strongest young woman I know. I believe you can do anything you set your mind to."

"I'm… I'm all alone. I can't do it alone."

Ninsha put a hand on her knee. "You've mentioned Dravid in your letters. How did you lose him? And the other names you mentioned?"

In halting words, Seri told her mother much more than she had intended. To her credit, Ninsha did not express shock or horror at what her daughter had been through. Instead, she sympathized with her, cried with her some more, and offered comfort when Seri needed it most. In the end, she told almost everything.

Ninsha sat back. "Well, it seems you are in very dire straits, young lady. You cannot trust Lord Volraag, you know."

"I know. But we need him. To heal Antises. I'm the only one who can get through to him. Everything is on me."

"Not everything, surely. The fate of all six lands? That's too much for one young woman, mage though she may be."

"I'm all alone."

Ninsha squeezed her hand again. "No, you most certainly are not.

We will figure something out. More than that, you have Lady Lilitu on your side."

Seri looked up. "How can I trust her? She… she… I don't even know where she found me." To think, the Lady really had known her for her entire life, not just recently. Everything in her life seemed completely mixed up.

"Then you must ask her. She wanted you to talk to us, and you have. Now you must talk with her again." She got to her feet. "But not until tomorrow morning. For now, let's see about that bath. And then supper. Your father will be back by then."

Seri almost said, "He's not my father." But that would be cruel. Ekur had been her father in every way that mattered, just as Ninsha had been her mother. But how could she ever think of them the same? They had kept a secret from her for her entire life—a secret *about* her life.

Ninsha said she was not alone, but she had never felt more alone than that very moment.

•••••

Seri had to admit the bath was luxurious. When had she last even been able to bathe? It had to be all the way back at Forerunner's enclave. Since then, Ixchel had helped her find times to wash without prying eyes, but never a full bath, where she could relax and let the warm water soothe her tired body.

She looked up at the stone ceiling. "Who am I?" she wondered, not even sure who she was asking. "Where did I come from?"

Her mother's story had shaken her to the core. She wanted to be furious, to scream at both parents, demand to know how they could do this to her. But a lifetime of experience told her they were not at fault, that they did love her as their own, regardless of where she came from.

"It's still not right," she muttered. To keep such a secret. And the Lady! She knew, and told them to keep the secret. Why? What did she know? Seri's anger at Lady Lilitu felt much more appropriate. Despite her apparent care and aid in their brief meetings, what did she really know of the Lady? Seri imagined a multitude of scenarios involving the Lady, Curasir, night spirits, the mysterious Otherworldly man she had mentioned, and… Seri's eyes widened. The Otherworld man. Could he be the one who brought her to the Lady? Could he be… her true father?

"Get hold of yourself," she whispered. "You're imagining things.

You have no evidence." Still, the idea would not leave her head.

Talking with her mother about her losses had been comforting. Mourning them with someone else made a difference, even if Ninsha had never met Dravid or Ixchel.

If Ixchel were here, what would she think of all this? Seri had looked forward to introducing her bodyguard to her parents... but they weren't even her parents now. Sort of. She sighed. This wasn't the sort of situation Ixchel could save her from. No one was trying to stab her or drown her.

She chuckled. The first time Ixchel had saved her life, it had been from drowning. And that night, they had truly gotten to know each other for the first time, when they had first been joined by...

Seri sat up straight in the tub, sending water sloshing over the edge. The Bond. She was Bonded to Ixchel. Why hadn't she thought of that before? Everything had been messing with her senses so much lately. But why hadn't the Bond tried to destroy her when Ixchel died? Unless... it couldn't be. Seri closed her eyes and focused. She pushed aside all of her own magic inclinations. For her, the Bond had always been hard to feel, both because Ixchel was rarely in danger herself, and because everything else in Seri's life, all of the other magic stuff, tended to overwhelm it.

Was it there? She held her breath.

Yes! She could feel the Bond! Ixchel lived! And she wasn't very far, either, or so it seemed.

Seri jumped to her feet, slipped, and fell back into the tub, water closing over her head. She came back up, sputtering and gasping, but it didn't matter.

Ixchel lived.

• • • • •

Seri followed the functionary—why hadn't she caught his name?—past the palace murals again. Her anxiety level this time might be considerably higher. Concerns about Volraag and lying paled in comparison to the revelations about her own origin. Ninsha had offered to come with her, but Seri needed to do this alone. Part of her seethed inside, furious toward the Lady and even her own parents. If those she had known her entire life had kept this secret from her, how could she ever trust them again? How could she ever trust anyone?

But she also felt a little thrill: Ixchel was alive and near. That made everything better. Somewhat.

Just before they entered the receiving hall, another servant ran up behind them and whispered something to the functionary. While she waited, Seri studied another mural, this one showing the first Lord of Arazu planting the first crops after the settlement in Antises. The functionary and the servant seemed quite agitated. She heard the words "arrogance" and "unprecedented." She suddenly had a good idea what they were discussing. She gritted her teeth at the timing. She should have come sooner. But her mother had persuaded her to stay for breakfast.

The other servant scurried away, and the functionary led Seri into the receiving hall as before. After announcing her, he informed the Lord and Lady, "Another... significant guest has just arrived. I will escort him here directly."

"Is there a problem?" Lord Enuru asked.

"I will leave that for your Lordship to decide." He exited the room.

"Seri, my dear," Lady Lilitu spoke. "Did you enjoy your evening with your parents?" Did she imagine it or had the Lady placed extra emphasis on that last word?

"It was... enlightening, my Lady. I think it raised more questions than it answered."

"How so?" Lord Enuru wondered. Lady Lilitu did not look pleased. Could it be the Lord was ignorant of all of this?

Seri was saved from answering by the knock announcing the functionary's return.

He stepped inside, bowed and announced, "Lord Volraag of Varioch."

Lord Enuru leaped to his feet and took two steps forward. Even without her star-sight activated, Seri could see the magic radiating out from the man. Lady Lilitu stood more slowly, but she put her hands together, perhaps preparing some magic of her own.

Seri spun to see Volraag saunter into the receiving hall. Somewhere, he had found a tailor to adjust his clothing for his new musculature. It fit perfectly now, though he still looked odd. "I claim the right of hospitality," he called. Even in the one day since she last heard him, his voice had improved. It still sounded painful, but he had volume now.

"What is the meaning of this?" Lord Enuru demanded. "How dare you show yourself here!"

Volraag gave a mock bow. "Come, your Lordship. Do I have your hospitality or not?"

Enuru raised his hands, his fingers splayed out and rigid. For a moment, both hands shook. Then he lowered them to his sides. "You know I cannot deny you. You have three days. And once the demands of hospitality are met, you will face the demands of wrath."

"Why are you here?" Lady Lilitu demanded.

Volraag touched his chin. "As you can see, I have been injured, while pursuing Varioch's interests. I seek only a place to rest and recover."

"Outrageous," Lord Enuru grumbled. The Lady eyed Volraag with a critical glare. "You have… changed since we last met, young Lord. It is most curious."

Volraag spread his arms. "I am as you see me."

Enuru settled back in his chair. "You have taken more power not your own, I presume."

"I possess great power, all of which shall be used for the advancement of Varioch and ultimately, all Antises."

"You have murdered and stolen power, and you expect us to believe it is altruistic?" Lady Lilitu laughed as she took her own seat.

Seri wondered at the wisdom of Volraag's plan. What did he hope to accomplish here that he could not have done by remaining hidden on shipboard? She frowned. Something was missing.

"Whether you believe me or not, everything I have done and everything I will do, is for the good of all." Volraag glanced at Seri and gave a small nod. "We meet again, young mage."

"You have met?" Lord Enuru asked.

"On Zes Sivas," Seri said.

"I rescued this young woman from my despicable father's advances," Volraag added. "You may have heard of it."

No one spoke. They all knew he spoke the truth.

"You have our hospitality," Enuru said at last. "You will be taken to quarters of your own and left to yourself." He lifted a finger. "But should you leave the palace grounds, you lose the protection of hospitality. And you also lose it in three days, regardless."

"I would also be interested in discussing trade with your Lordship," Volraag said. "Our two lands have benefited greatly from each other in the past, and—"

"Your arrogance is unbelievable. There will be no trade." Lord Enuru clapped and another servant appeared. "Escort Lord Volraag to guest quarters. See to his needs, within reason."

Volraag bowed and followed the servant out. Lord Enuru grumbled, asked for Seri's pardon, and departed as well. As the door closed behind him, Lady Lilitu rose and approached Seri.

"Now. We can finally talk."

<h1 style="text-align:center">(((22)))</h1>

The Lady led Seri down another hallway to a walled garden on the west side of the palace. "We are far from prying ears here," she observed. "When I am in this garden, the servants know to stay far away."

Seri's curiosity overcame her. "Why is that?"

Lilitu smiled. "I have requested it. A lady needs some privacy from time to time." She paused. "And since I come at night on occasion, it helps promote the 'night spirits' rumor."

"You want people to believe the rumor?"

The Lady laughed. She sat on a stone bench and patted the seat beside her for Seri. "It is amusing to have people believe I am in league with something supernatural. Besides, should anyone catch me using my actual magic, they will attribute it to that."

Seri furrowed her brow. "And that is better, somehow?"

Lilitu raised one shoulder in a light shrug. "As I said, it amuses me."

Seri did not know where to begin. The incident with Volraag had thrown all of her thoughts off.

"I cannot imagine what that upstart young Lord thinks he is doing in coming here," Lady Lilitu murmured, looking back into the palace. "I do not trust him." She looked back at Seri. "Did you notice the change in him, though?"

"He looked… larger," Seri said. "And I think he held more power than before."

"Precisely. But what kind of power? It is not the magic of Antises. He has taken power from the Otherworld."

"Are the two compatible in one person?" Seri had been wondering that for some time.

"His presence would seem to confirm it. But we do not know what effect it is having on him. I suspect his body may not be able to hold all of that for long."

"What do you mean? The magic will leave him?"

"I do not know. We are in uncharted waters here, my dear. Anything could happen."

"Where did I come from?" Seri burst out, asking the one question she needed to know.

The Lady pulled a hanging vine near and fingered one of the leaves. "What did your parents tell you?"

"That you gave me to them as an infant." Seri struggled to keep her voice from rising.

Lilitu nodded. "I did. And that is all they know, and all they needed to know. They took you and they raised you, and, by all I can tell, they loved you dearly."

"They did." Seri almost choked on the words. She knew them to be true, but almost didn't believe them at the same time. Her thoughts, emotions, and beliefs all collided and twisted up within her.

"Isn't that what matters?"

"No. I mean yes. I mean, I need to know. Why do I have this… star in my eye? Forerunner called it my 'heritage.' Who are my parents? My real parents?"

The Lady pulled one of the leaves from the vine and tore a small strip loose from the stem. She did not say anything.

"Please…" Seri needed to know.

Lady Lilitu turned her face to Seri's. Once again, she saw the star, so much like her own, in the Lady's eye.

"Seri, I am your mother."

Seri's world froze. She blinked instinctively, and her star-sight activated. She saw the strange power within the Lady and a few scattered beams of colored light warping from the ground around both the Lady and herself. But all of it, all of the magic stood still, frozen in place. Part of her mind pondered that: was the magic reflecting her own feelings?

But the rest of her mind screamed in mixed protest and delight. Could it be true? Of course it could. Even Dravid had pointed out the similarity between the two of them; the Lady looked like Seri's older sister. But her mother? Was it… could it…?

Lady Lilitu's smile was smaller than usual, a sad, uncertain smile. "Nothing to say?"

"I… I…"

"It's all right, my dear. I'm sure it must be quite a shock."

"But… but how?"

"Surely, I do not have to explain childbirth to you at your age."

"No, no, that's… not what I…"

"I'm sorry. A little humor. A very little." The Lady tore the other side of the leaf from its stem and let it fall.

Seri did not know what to say. The childlessness of the Lord and Lady was a subject of much concern throughout Arazu. Many people wanted the Lord to take on a second wife, for the purpose of siring an heir. Could Seri actually be that heir? But… the Lord's power always passed to the male heir. How…? So many thoughts ran through her head.

The magic moved again. Seri reached out and grasped a dark maroon beam of light and drew its magic into her. She wasn't sure why.

"Is… Is Lord Enuru…?"

"He is not your father." Lilitu sighed. "My Lord Enuru cannot have children. This is a secret that no one outside of the high priest knows… and you now. This is why he has never taken another wife."

If. But. Then. Another cascade of thoughts paraded through Seri's mind.

"Who?" she asked at last.

The Lady tore another leaf from the vine. She held it up and looked at it. A tiny flame erupted from her finger and consumed the leaf. She let its ashes fall.

"The man from the Otherworld!" Seri exclaimed. "The one you talked about yesterday. Is it him?"

Lady Lilitu nodded. "But he was not just a 'man' from the Otherworld." She leaned in closer. "Seri, he was a god. One of our ancient gods, walking this land among us."

"Which one?"

"He never gave me his name, not his true name, at any rate."

"How… how are you not cursed?"

"Because I committed adultery?"

Seri nodded.

The Lady sighed again, and placed both hands in her lap. "I do not know. I deserve it, certainly. I betrayed my Lord and conceived a child with someone who was not my husband. By the Laws of Cursings and Bindings, I should be cursed. But I am not. Perhaps because he was a god, it did not apply? I do not know."

"That doesn't make it right!"

"I'm not saying it does, dear. I have regretted that one night for twenty years. And yet… because of that night, you are here. And you are amazing."

Seri could not sit still. She jumped to her feet and walked several feet away, before whirling back. "Then does Lord Enuru even know?"

Lady Lilitu shook her head. "Once I knew I was with child, I found ways to conceal it from him. I helped arrange for him to take an extended trade visit to Ch'olan. I feigned sickness for over a month. And finally, he was gone to the Passing when you were born. Only my two most trusted servants knew all."

"I was born during the Passing?"

"Possibly at the same moment that it took place," the Lady confirmed.

Seri didn't know if that meant anything, but it was a little intriguing. Some things still didn't add up, though. She frowned and pivoted, walking back and forth in front of the bench.

"Then the star, my heritage, comes from my… father, one of the so-called gods."

"Do not doubt his godhood, my child. He—"

"I've met them. They're not gods!" Seri snapped. "They're… they're powerful beings of magic. They're beautiful and strong and… they're not gods."

"You did not mention meeting them yesterday." Lady Lilitu raised an eyebrow.

"When I was visiting Forerunner, I saw them," Seri said, not wanting to discuss Calu, which would lead to Marshal and Volraag. "They met with him, and I saw their true forms with my star-sight." Remembering that moment, and how she felt on seeing the Otherworldly beings, she understood why Lady Lilitu would have been attracted to one. Even so…

"Your star!" Seri pointed at the Lady, not caring about propriety any more. "Yesterday, you claimed it happened after he trained you. Is that true?"

"Not when he… trained me, necessarily."

"Ugh. Don't say anything else!"

At the Lady's quiet smile, Seri threw up her hands and stalked across the garden. This could not be happening. To think she had any connection at all to those… those so-called gods disgusted her. They were cruel, heartless beings. And if they truly were the ancient gods, then they were even more cruel and despicable.

She paused. Did Marshal feel this way, knowing his father was Lord Varion? She never thought she'd have something like this in common with him.

Lady Lilitu stood and straightened. She caught Seri's eye and waited until she stopped pacing.

"A moment ago, I told you that I was your mother. In the purely physical sense, that is true. But you and I both know that I am not your true mother. Nor is that god your true father." She pointed off toward where Seri's home stood. "Your parents live right over there. Your true mother and father."

Seri did not respond. She did not trust herself to respond.

The Lady took a step closer. "I have watched you all of your life. I have delighted in every advancement you have made. I—"

Seri gasped. "That was why you arranged for my mage training! It wasn't anything I did at all! It was because I was your daughter!"

"No, no, no." She shook her head violently. "That is not true. Yes, I would have tried to help and support you in any path you chose. But you earned that on your own. You studied. You achieved. You, Seri." She gestured to her. "And look at you now! You've already advanced faster than anyone could have expected."

Seri pointed to her eye. "Because of this! And I only have that because you slept with some golden, magic… Agh! I can't even think of what to call him! None of my achievements, none of what makes me special, were because of me, or anything I did!"

"That is not true! You were the most promising student at the university in years! You may have been given an advantage when it comes to magic, but you were the one who learned how to use it. And it is how you used it that matters!" She shook her head. "I know you have not told me everything. But I also know that all of Antises owes you much already. At the very least, it was your intervention that prevented Volraag from killing more of the Lords and stealing their power."

"And now it's all on me again!" Seri ranted. "I've got the star. I've got the power. So everyone is counting on me to save them all. Maybe I'll just quit. Maybe I'll run away."

"I don't believe you would do that." The Lady smiled again. "I do not understand all that you're saying, but if the fate of Antises truly is in your hands, then… it is in good hands."

"I don't even know whose hands these are!" Seri shook her hands in front of her. Without thinking, she let magic radiate out from both of them. The plants on either side of her shook, buffeted by her power. She sank to her knees. "I don't even know who I am…"

The Lady stepped closer and placed her hand on Seri's bowed head. "You are Seri-Belit, mage of Arazu, daughter of Ekur and Ninsha. Is that not enough?"

"I don't know."

Seri sank inside herself. Everything she thought she knew, everything she thought she believed: all of it was in doubt. She could count on nothing and no one.

"Seri…"

At that moment, the nearest tower of the palace exploded.

•••••

Volraag emerged from his assigned quarters and saw Lord Enuru storming down the corridor toward him. A pair of oil lanterns on the wall exploded as he passed, his anger creating an aura of vibratory magic.

"What is going on?" Volraag called. "I heard something crash."

"Do you think me a fool?" Lord Enuru demanded. He threw a wave of magic at Volraag, who released a burst of his own power to counter it.

"The thought had not crossed my mind," Volraag answered. He spread his arms out, palms up. "I have been relaxing in the quarters you provided me. I am not responsible for whatever is happening."

"You are the only other one here with power!" Enuru stopped a few feet away, his power rolling off him in waves.

Volraag got down on one knee. "I swear to you that I have not left this room until just now."

At that moment, another explosion echoed through the palace. Both Lords jerked their heads in the direction of the blast, which sounded like it came from the opposite side of the structure. Enuru spun back to Volraag, who lifted his hands further. "I'm right here."

Enuru lowered his hands. "So it would appear."

Volraag got to his feet. "May I join you in investigating this attack? You may need help."

Enuru considered him for a moment. "Better to keep you in sight, I suppose." He gestured down the hall. Volraag turned and hurried that way, glancing back to make sure he was heading in the right direction and Enuru was following.

He smiled, despite the pain it still caused. All was going according to plan. Rathri's devices succeeded in sowing chaos and confusion. Now only one crucial step remained.

(((23)))

Lady Lilitu threw up a shield of golden fire, deflecting the bricks raining down toward them. Seri joined in, using a bit of magic to disintegrate a large chunk of debris that came too near. When the dust cleared, they looked at the shattered tower, then at each other.

"That was magic," Seri said. The Lady nodded. They both must have felt it. But who? Lord Enuru or…

"Volraag!" Lady Lilitu exclaimed. She rushed back into the palace, Seri on her heels.

They climbed two sets of stairs before reaching the destruction. Seri stared out through an open space where the tower had been. She saw no sign of Volraag or anyone else, nor had they passed anyone on the way up. She activated her star-sight and began grasping for any beams of magic she saw along the way.

At that moment, a second tower exploded.

"He must be moving fast!" Seri couldn't tell how far away the other tower was, but it didn't sound too far.

"No." The Lady frowned. "That doesn't make sense. He must be somewhere else, where he could see both of those towers and launch attacks at them."

"But why?" Seri wondered. This didn't make sense. Volraag had the sanctuary he wanted for three days. Why ruin it with an attack that… accomplished nothing more than irritating the Lord and Lady? The towers were nice, but they looked mostly decorative.

She followed Lady Lilitu down the stairs and along another hallway. "I don't think this is Volraag," she said. "What good would it do him?"

"Madmen need no reason for their madness," the Lady responded. "And I fear what he has absorbed is driving him mad." She came to a stop. "Still… you may be right. The only thing this seems to be accomplishing is to distract us."

"Distract us from what?"

A dark figure fell from the ceiling, landing directly behind Lady Lilitu. She gasped and crumpled to the floor. The figure turned toward Seri, a bloody dagger in his left hand and a sword in the other. A horrible grin split his ravaged face.

Rathri.

"What are you doing?" Seri demanded, gathering what little magic she could.

"It's called revenge, girl. Something I've been quite accomplished at for longer than you've been alive." With a flick of his wrist, Rathri launched the dagger at Seri's chest. Somehow, she managed to throw up a burst of magic to deflect it. But by then, Rathri had already charged toward her.

Seri backpedaled, tripped over her own robe and sprawled onto the floor. Rathri's sword passed just over her head as she fell.

Another person leaped over Seri's fallen body and stood between her and the assassin. "I knew it!" Seri cried. Rathri's sword bounced off Ixchel's shield.

"So. Not dead after all," Rathri observed.

"My apologies, my Lady," Ixchel said. "I was delayed trying to determine what he had done to the towers."

Seri clambered to her feet. "You're back! I don't care about anything else."

Ixchel dodged another strike from Rathri.

"All right. I do care about the assassin trying to kill us all." Seri moved to the side of the wide hallway and waited for her opportunity.

Understanding her movements, Ixchel kept the combat closer to the opposite wall. She engaged Rathri up close, then dodged backward. Seri unleashed a wave of magic. It slammed Rathri up against the wall. Ixchel lunged in and stabbed. Rathri deflected it just enough to keep it away from his chest. Ixchel's short sword plunged into his thigh. Rathri backhanded her and stumbled back.

The assassin fell into his stance in the middle of the hall. He faced both of them, leg bleeding. "Is that the best you can do?"

Unfortunately, it was the best Seri could do. She had not been able to absorb much magic in the last few minutes. She looked desperately around for more. Instead, she saw a sudden fiery build-up right behind the assassin.

Flames engulfed him. He staggered back. Lady Lilitu, still on the floor, held one hand up, wielding her mysterious power.

Rathri spun and raced down the hall. He dropped to the floor and rolled. With most of the flames quenched, he leaped back up and kept running.

Ixchel looked about to chase him, but Seri barreled into her with a desperate hug. Ixchel stiffened by instinct, but quickly responded, dropping her sword and returning the hug.

"Oh!" Seri broke loose and stumbled to the fallen Lilitu. "My Lady! Are you all right?"

The Lady lifted herself up on one elbow and put her hand on the bleeding wound in her stomach. "I will be," she gasped. "Give my magic time, and it will heal me." She looked up. "Holcan. I am glad to see that Seri's report of your death was also an exaggeration."

"I did think she was dead!"

"A necessary deception," Ixchel said. "And one that allowed me to watch out for this assassin."

"Pursue him. Both of you. I fear for my Lord's safety," Lady Lilitu ordered.

Ixchel picked up her sword and she and Seri hurried down the hall.

"How will we find the Lord?" Ixchel asked.

"When we're closer, I should be able to sense him," Seri said. "In fact, I think I sense him just ahead right now."

A strong source of magic did call to her from around the next corner. But it felt too weak to be one of the Lords. Rathri did not manifest as any form of magic she could feel. What could it be?

When she rounded the corner, Seri caught only a glimpse of something round on the floor a few feet away, glowing and trembling with power. Ixchel grabbed her. "It's one of them!" She yanked Seri back around the corner. They both tumbled to the floor.

A massive explosion of power erupted behind them, shredding the walls, roof and floor. Ixchel screamed and they both fell through the debris that flew in every direction around them.

• • • • •

Volraag paused at an intersection. "To the right," Lord Enuru growled behind him. He nodded and continued. What was taking Rathri so long? He should have been here by now!

They reached the outer hallway that wrapped around the palace, lined with the murals. "Shouldn't we find a stairway or something?" Volraag asked, stopping again.

Enuru moved up beside him. "No. Something is wrong here. Why target the towers?" He glared at Volraag. "Your presence during this attack cannot be a coincidence."

Volraag spread his hands again. "I am here with you. I'm not the one damaging your palace. Where are your guards?"

Enuru looked both ways. "They will be rushing to the destruction, hoping to help anyone that might be hurt."

"And not rushing to protect you?"

Enuru rolled his eyes. "I am a Lord of Antises. What protection do I need? My guards know better."

Another explosion shook the palace. This one came from somewhere inside the structure.

"This is outrageous!" Lord Enuru turned and ran back the way they had come. Volraag followed after him.

Enuru took another turn and started up a wide staircase. Then he came to a stop. Volraag joined him and they both stared.

A spherical object sat on a landing just ahead, shaking. It looked like it might be made of glass, but it glowed with undeniable power.

Volraag took a step back. Rathri had explained the devices, and his own power had filled them. He had no desire to be this close to one when it erupted. The fact that it shook meant Rathri had been here seconds before and activated it with a touch. It might go off at any moment now.

Lord Enuru took a step closer. "What is this sorcery?"

Volraag caught him by the shoulder. "My Lord! This is dangerous. We should fall back."

"Nonsense." Lord Enuru swept his hands in a circle, surrounding himself with an aura of magic once more. Volraag wished he had time to learn how to do that particular trick.

The device exploded. Volraag and Enuru both fell backwards down the stairs, crashing to the first floor. The blast tore the stairway apart, wood and stone. A cloud of dust settled around them.

Enuru coughed and rose to his hands and knees. "Devilry," he murmured.

Rathri appeared beside him in the dust. The assassin's already devastated skin hung in tatters from his body, along with what little remained of his clothing. Something had burned his entire body.

"Look out!" Volraag called in a weak voice.

Too late. Rathri's sword cut deep through Lord Enuru's chest.

Volraag lifted a hand and blasted the assassin with his own power. Rathri tumbled down the hall, scrambled up and dashed out of sight.

Volraag crawled to Enuru's side and struggled to help the Lord sit up. They both coughed, but Enuru spit blood. "Shall I go for your guards now?" Volraag gasped.

Lord Enuru shook his head. "It is… too late for me." He looked off into the distance. "Thank you. I was wrong to… accuse you."

Volraag looked around. "It may not be too late. Perhaps the Lady can help you…"

"No. I am in Theon's hands now."

Volraag leaned in closer. "But your power, Lord. You have no heir."

"Perhaps… it will go to my wife."

"I have sought this knowledge for years," Volraag said, his voice urgent. "You can choose, Lord. Right now. You can pass your power on before you die."

"To you?" Enuru laughed, choked and started to slump over. Volraag held him up.

"Yes, to me. Let me tell you why."

• • • • •

Jamana kept his arms wrapped tightly around Victor. The young warrior struggled against his embrace, growling and cursing. He kicked out at the ship's railing, trying to push Jamana back, but without success.

Adhi approached the two of them, eyes wide. "What is wrong with him?"

"It's the Bond," Jamana said. "Seri must be in terrible danger." The truth of it hurt Jamana much more than Victor's struggling.

"Let me go!" Victor screamed. "I have to go!"

"And do what? Swim to the mainland? You would never make it."

"I have to!"

"Is this normal for Bonds?" Adhi asked.

"Completely normal!" Victor said. "Which is why you have to let me go!"

"Do not be a fool. We care about Seri too, but you cannot charge across the lake!"

"I can try!"

Jamana groaned and held on. For the next ten minutes at least,

Victor ranted and strained against him. Finally, he sagged back, slumping against Jamana's chest.

"It's over. You can let go now."

Jamana released Victor, but stood ready to grab him again if the situation changed. But Victor collapsed to the deck, exhausted.

"Is she… dead?" Adhi whispered.

Victor shook his head. "No. The danger is passed. At least the life-threatening danger, anyway. She must be all right."

Jamana knelt beside him. "It is good. I do not want to try to hold you any longer. You are very strong."

Victor laughed. "And yet you held me back. Not bad for a mage."

"What does that mean?"

"No one thinks of mages as strong. They think of…" Victor gestured at Adhi. "That."

Adhi rolled his eyes. "There are other kinds of strength."

"You don't have to tell me that. I've seen plenty."

Jamana frowned. "Do we need to change course so that you may pursue Seri?"

"No." Victor shook his head. "We need to stay the course to Kuktarma. It's too important."

"Important enough to lose Seri?"

"I don't… I don't think that will happen. She has Ixchel with her. In fact…" Victor looked up and stared off to the east. "I think, now that the horrible danger has passed… she's safer than ever."

"Maybe Volraag is dead."

"Maybe. But I wouldn't count on it." Victor got back to his feet. "And don't forget Rathri."

Jamana glanced toward the forward cabin. "We should send an assassin to fight the assassin. Do you think he would, if we paid him?"

"He doesn't do that any more. I don't know if he's ever going to do anything at all."

"But he lets us use his boat."

Victor nodded. "At least we have that much. How long will it take us to get to Kuktarma, anyway?"

Adhi looked up at the sail. "We still have very little wind. Our progress is slow. And once there, Simbala, the capital city, is far from the coast."

Victor took a deep breath. "Not much we can do about it now." He looked toward the mainland again. "I just hope we're not too late."

<h1 style="text-align:center">(((24)))</h1>

Seri woke in her bed, but did not get up. Everything hurt. She remembered Ixchel yanking her back away from the strange device. She remembered the explosion and falling, being struck by heavy objects, hitting the ground, more objects striking her. Ixchel dug her out of the debris, using only one arm.

The Lady's servants found them there, helped them, carried Seri to her parents' home. She remembered little of what happened after that, except for hearing the report of Lord Enuru's death.

Her body's aches and pains echoed the pain she felt within. So many revelations, and none of them good.

"You are awake, my Lady? Would you like something to drink?" Ixchel's voice penetrated her reverie. She turned her head and saw her bodyguard seated in a chair, right arm held in a cloth sling.

"No," Seri started to say, then coughed. Perhaps a little water would be beneficial. Ixchel helped her rise up on one elbow and drink from a tall glass. Seri almost laughed. She always drank from that glass in this house. Her mother must have placed it there on purpose.

Seri fell back on the bed and stared at the ceiling. Ixchel set the glass down and watched her.

"Your parents have been very concerned," she said after a few moments.

"They're not my parents," Seri answered. "I mean, they are. But they aren't."

"I don't understand."

"Of course you don't. I don't either."

Ixchel fell silent.

Seri didn't want to talk. She didn't want to do anything, really.

Nothing mattered.

"Shall I tell them that you're awake?"

"No. I don't want to see anyone."

"Shall I leave?"

"I don't care."

Silence again.

Seri sighed. "Is Lady Lilitu all right?"

"She is recovering. Work proceeds on repairing the palace already, though some of the artwork is lost."

Seri wondered which murals might have been destroyed. Not that it mattered.

"The physician says you have no broken bones," Ixchel continued. "You should be able to get up whenever you want."

"I don't want."

After another awkward silence, Ixchel leaned closer. "You will have to assist me, then. Clearly something is troubling you greatly, and I do not know what it is."

"Maybe because you haven't been around."

"When you handled Rathri on the ship, I decided to remain hidden. It gave me an advantage. If he tried to sneak up on you, he wouldn't be prepared for me. I am sorry that this caused you pain. I assumed the Bond would inform you that I was near."

Seri grunted. Ixchel's hiding might make sense, but right now she didn't care.

"Volraag is gone. It appears that he—"

"Volraag used me, Ixchel." It was just the latest in a string of horrible events. "He acted like he was going to give up this portal thing, and then he used me to help him kill Lord Enuru."

"I do not see any way in which you helped him with this task."

Seri rolled her head to the side and looked at Ixchel. "I didn't tell them the truth about him, about what he did, or how we traveled with him."

"And this made them allow him in the palace?"

"No! That's our stupid Arazu hospitality. He took advantage of them."

"Then it appears he took advantage of everyone."

Seri looked back at the ceiling. "I can't believe I was so stupid. But apparently, I've been stupid about a lot of things. Maybe I get that from my father. Maybe he was the god of idiots."

"You are accusing your father of... stupidity?"

"Ekur is not my father. He and Ninsha raised me, but my birth parents are Lady Lilitu and one of those 'gods' from the Otherworld."

Ixchel did not respond.

"Nothing to say to that, huh? I can't figure out what to say, either."

"When my father abandoned me," Ixchel said in a slow monotone, "my grandparents took me in. They raised me as their own until I was old enough to enter the Holcan training. Even then, they continued to be my true parents." She gestured at the room around them. "Haven't Ekur and Ninsha done the same for you?"

Seri started to put her hands to her head, but lifting her arms hurt. "Yes, they have. But that doesn't help right now."

"How could it not?"

"You had your whole life to adjust to that. You knew all along! I only found out all of this yesterday!" Seri knew her tone was harsh, but she didn't care.

"And what of Marshal, and his father?"

"What about them?"

"Do you think it bothers him, being the son of Lord Varion? And the half-brother of Volraag?"

"Of course it does. What does that have to do with me?"

"We cannot choose our parents. But sometimes... they choose us."

"Well... I guess we all have horrible fathers, then."

Ixchel stood. "I think there is one waiting outside this room that would argue that point." She opened the door and stood aside as Ekur entered. He nodded to Ixchel and hurried to Seri's side, where he knelt and took her hand.

"My daughter, how do you feel?"

"I'll be all right." Seri felt tears welling up in her eyes, and wanted to stop them. She shouldn't cry now, not for this man, who wasn't her real father. He wasn't. He...

She began to sob. Ekur looked perplexed for only a moment. Then he wrapped her in his arms, strong and gentle, and held her while she cried.

•••••

At lunchtime, Seri found her appetite returned. She ate and enjoyed the presence of her mother and Ixchel. Watching them get to know each other was a scene she had longed for. Though she remained conflicted about her parentage, she knew that before they left, Ninsha would be calling Ixchel her second daughter.

"You have been training to fight since you were a child?" Ninsha asked.

Ixchel nodded. "I was taken from my grandparents' home into the life of a Holcan very young, as all of us were."

"A Holcan?"

"We are elite warriors in service to the Lady of Ch'olan." She glanced at Seri. "Except when we are assigned to serve another Lady."

"So you trained every day with these other girls, then?"

"Yes, there were six of us. We grew up together, studying every day, beating our bodies into submission and our minds into careful thought."

Seri kept herself from shaking her head. Ixchel had told her much of this in confidence, but she never shared much with anyone else. Ninsha had a way of pulling stories out of people.

"So you had no time to play? Your childhood was all fighting?"

Ixchel hesitated. "We... had time to ourselves on rare occasions, on holy days or when our instructors were needed elsewhere."

Ninsha smiled. "And what did you do to amuse yourselves, then?"

"Usually, we practiced against each other."

Seri snorted. "Nothing else?"

"We sought out other challenges."

"Like what?" Ninsha pressed.

"We went to the Tsonot." Before they could ask, Ixchel explained: "Deep in the jungle, far from the city, there is a deep pit full of cold, clear water. One of our instructors said it used to be hidden underground, but the water dissolved the rock over many years and exposed it to the air."

"You went swimming there?" Ninsha asked.

Seri straightened. "You told Rathri you couldn't swim!"

Ixchel ducked her head. "My Lady lied to Rathri to conceal her intent. I did the same. If he knew I could swim, he would have stabbed me. By telling him I could not, he only shoved me into the water."

"I never meant to teach you how to lie," Seri said. "I just..."

"Let her tell the story," Ninsha said. She looked back at Ixchel. "Both stories."

Ixchel nodded. "A dive into the Tsonot was a challenge, even for us."

"How far was it?"

"Perhaps... seventy feet," Ixchel admitted, shrugging. "Anyone who hesitated would be mocked and pressured. We all did it."

Seri shook her head that time. Growing up in Arazu's schools, she well knew the power of peer pressure, but none of her friends had ever pressured her to risk her life.

"The dive was only the beginning," Ixchel went on. "If you could swim deep enough, you could pass under an overhang of rock near the very floor of the pit, and then swim back up into a cavern. It was a place of great beauty, but you can only reach it through the water."

"That must have been quite a swim," Ninsha observed.

"It was very long. Most cannot make it. Some make the dive and reach the cavern only once in their lives. Two of my class never did it. Two others made it, but one injured her leg and could not complete the Holcan training. Another girl made it three times."

Seri narrowed her eyes. "How many times did you do it?"

Ixchel's eyes darted around. She did not boasting. "Five," she whispered.

Seri laughed. "No wonder you could survive falling off the ship!"

"It was not easy, even so," Ixchel said. She pointed to the scar on her side. "Falling into water with an open wound is not the same. And I had to remain under the surface while Rathri watched."

"But no one saw you at all!"

"Once the ship moved past me, I swam from starboard to port, into the ship's shadow. Only then could I rise up and breathe. Everyone was running to the aftcastle, so I dove and swam to the prow. I climbed a rope I noticed previously and arrived where the main deck joined with the forecastle.

"With everyone focused on the aftcastle, I ran across the deck and down into the cargo hatch." She looked up at Seri. "I listened to your confrontation with Rathri, ready to intervene, but you handled it well."

"I didn't think so."

"Nevertheless, your courage in facing him convinced me that I could gain an advantage by pretending to be dead. As long as Rathri did not know I still protected you, I could be in a position to surprise him."

"It worked," Seri said. "We all believed you were dead."

"Again, I am sorry. I thought the Bond would alert you."

"All of my magical senses have been mixed up since we left Ch'olan," Seri said. "I didn't realize you were alive until the night before I saw you again."

"I have caused you pain, then." Ixchel dropped down on to her knees. "I have failed you, my Lady. I should have fought Rathri to the death."

"Don't be ridiculous," Ninsha clucked. "Get up, Ixchel. Seri doesn't think you're a failure, do you?"

Seri looked into Ixchel's eyes. "You could never fail me. I know that in my deepest heart."

Ixchel got up. "You do not wish to dismiss me, then?"

"Of course not!" Seri jumped up and embraced her. Ixchel hesitated, then returned the hug.

"There, see?" Ninsha beamed. "Nothing touches a mother's heart like seeing her daughters love each other so."

"I knew it," Seri whispered.

•••••

Another day went by before Ixchel pressed Seri on their plans. "We must move on," she suggested.

"And do what? So far we've only made things worse." Seri lounged on one of the benches in her parents' courtyard. She felt better than the day before, but not by much.

"Volraag is undoubtedly on his way to the third portal. Marshal and Victor will be on their way as well. They may need our help."

Seri lifted her hand and looked at it. "Why do you suppose my skin isn't lighter? Or even golden like Calu?"

"I do not see how that makes any difference to our quest."

Seri put her hand down. "How can I go on a quest when I don't even know who I am anymore?"

"We have discussed this. You are still Seri—"

"I know, I know. I'm Seri, mage of Arazu." Seri pointed at her chest. "But who am I inside? Whose blood runs through my veins? What other hidden powers or inclinations might I have, besides the star in my eye?" She waved her hands. "Am I going to start spouting flame like Lady Lilitu? I wouldn't know how to control it! And what if I'm more like my father? Will I start trying to rule over people and demand their worship? What if worship is what fuels a god? What if I start feeling a need for it?"

"I do not think this speculation is beneficial." Ixchel looked genuinely perplexed. "Whatever physical effects you may have inherited, it does not change who you are."

"She's right, my love." Ninsha's voice carried across the courtyard.

She and Ekur approached the two girls. Ninsha sat next to Ixchel on the bench, while Ekur stood with arms folded across his chest.

"Nothing has changed about who you are, Seri," Ninsha said. "You are the girl we raised, the girl we loved. And whatever happens next, whatever you choose to do, you will have our support."

"More than that," Ekur said. "When you leave here, I'm coming with you."

"What? No, you can't." Seri looked at him in alarm. "That's… it's…"

Her father chuckled. "Are you going to say it's too dangerous? The daughter says that to her father?"

"Yes, but… I have magic, and you don't."

"I have other things." Ekur continued to smile. "Such as horses, a carriage, and contacts across all of southern Kuktarma to help us along the way." He crackled his knuckles. "I'm also still pretty good with a bow."

"That would be advantageous," Ixchel observed. "I have little experience in ranged weapons."

"Yeah, but he can't… but, but…"

"You will not leave without me, Seri-Belit."

She sighed. "I don't want you in danger, but I can't deny you."

"No, you can't. I'm your father. It doesn't work that way."

Seri smiled. "You are. You really are."

(((25)))

Marshal reached the top of the ridge and looked down. Devouring fire. If anything, the Durunim army had grown larger than before. He knelt down to keep his profile smaller, but he doubted they could see him through all the dust they were kicking up. Talinir, with his extra height, stood several feet below, and could still see over the top of the ridge. Tich scrambled up next to him.

"All right. Now I see why you were worried." She paused. "You say this army is going to invade Kuktarma?"

"If Volraag opens the portal, yes."

"Hmm. Kuktarma has some decent fighters. Not as good as Ch'olan, of course. But even so, this… this is not good."

Marshal considered. "My grandfather was able to call down enough power to destroy half of the army before," he said to Talinir. "I wonder if I can do the same."

Talinir shook his head. "I would strongly advise against it. Your grandfather had many years of experience with the power and knew what he was doing. Even so, it killed him."

"But he was… old. I'm not."

"Any time you use your magic, it tires you, does it not?"

"Yes."

"Then using that much power would, at the very least, exhaust you. Then what would you do about the other half of the army that came after us?"

Marshal nodded, conceding the point. "Then I guess, for now, we focus on rescuing Dravid."

"So," Tich said. "We sneak in, find your friend, grab him, and head back to our world."

"Well… some of us can go back," Talinir said.

"What do you mean, some of us? You can't go back?" Tich rolled over to look at him.

"No, I can go back. You're the problem here. Any human that comes to the Otherworld without their own magic is… trapped. The stars lay claim to them."

"What? You mean I can't go home?"

"It is the fate of those who dare enter without the protection of their own magic."

Tich stared. Talinir looked back with his usual grave expression.

Marshal couldn't hold it in. He burst out laughing and rolled away from his view of the army.

"I knew it!" Tich cried. "I knew that couldn't be true!"

"Talinir! You told a joke!" Marshal couldn't stop laughing.

The Eldani smiled. He patted Tich on the shoulder. "You've told me so many stories of dubious truth, I had to try my own."

"I'm glad I could educate you." Tich rolled back to look at the army again. Marshal could see the offense in her stiff shoulders. She didn't like being on the receiving end.

Marshal turned his thoughts back to the current situation. How to find Dravid? The Bond told in what direction he lay, but it could not guide them to him with that much precision. He could be anywhere among this vast army.

"Talinir, old friend. You really aren't very good at warding." At the voice, all three of them spun around. Another Eldani stood just below, smiling at them. His white hair hung long, pulled back to show off his angular face.

"Curasir."

"You remember my name. How delightful."

Marshal narrowed his eyes and braced himself. He had far more power now than during his last battle with Curasir. But at the time, the renegade Eldani had been siphoning power from Zes Sivas after murdering the Masters. He called himself a mage of sorts. Who knew what power he had now?

Curasir raised a finger. "Careful now. If you use your power against me, you'll draw the attention of… well, all of them." He pointed at the army.

"Swords it is, then," Talinir said, drawing his warpsteel sword.

Curasir drew his own, but did not advance. "If I wanted to fight, would I come alone? I could also signal everyone else with but a thought."

"What do you want?" Marshal asked through gritted teeth. He got to his feet, hand on his own sword hilt.

"Who is this guy?" Tich wondered.

Curasir spared her a glance. "Another addition to your harem? I prefer the mage girl myself, though she did seem quite passionate with the one-legged slave."

"Harem! Why you—"

"Tich, please." Marshal took a step down toward Curasir. "Again: what do you want?"

"Marshal, Marshal. It was always about you. I told you that from the beginning. We wanted you, your power, your potential. And here you are, traipsing across our world, doing nothing to hide that power. Your presence here is like a beacon of flame for those of us who know where to look. But of course, you rejected our offer." Curasir shrugged. "So we turned to your brother. And now he's opening the portals for us."

"He's opened one. He will not open another."

Curasir raised his eyebrows, always an odd look for the Eldanim. "You must know something I don't. I think he's heading that way right now, and has a very good chance of success."

"We will stop him."

"Then what are you doing here?" Curasir cocked his head.

"We've come for our friend. The one Calu took as a slave."

"Even after what I told you about the mage girl? I guess you do like this one better." He looked at Tich. "I don't see the appeal myself."

Tich started forward, but Marshal put out a hand to stop her. "We want to get him back. Then we'll leave. That's all."

"Are you sure? Because we both want the same things, Marshal."

"That's not true."

"But it is! Don't you want to end the Laws of Cursings and Bindings?"

Marshal stood still. How did Curasir know that?

"We want that as well. It's how Theon keeps you people in line. Get rid of the Laws, get rid of Theon. And let my friends, the old gods, return." Curasir gestured toward the army again.

Marshal knew there was a distinction here, but he struggled to remember it. "I want the Laws gone. But I don't necessarily want to get rid of Theon."

"Why not? They're his laws, aren't they?"

Dimly, Marshal recalled the words of Nian, his priest-friend. "The

Lords and mages created the Laws. Not Theon. He gave people a choice."

"A choice? He stripped away all the beliefs men held before him! We want to restore the choice."

"And that takes an army?"

Talinir snorted.

"Of course not. The army is to discourage any of Theon's followers from interfering, like the Lords and mages you also despise."

"Take your arguments elsewhere. You're never going to convert me."

Curasir studied him, then sighed. "No, I suppose not. I think I liked you better when you couldn't talk so much." He drew a line in the dirt with his sword, then added a few more lines across it. "No one wants a big fight right now," he said, looking up.

Marshal didn't respond.

Curasir waved his free hand. "You could fight us. We could fight you. You could reduce our army by dozens, maybe even hundreds. But in the end you would fall. It would not benefit either of us. So… what shall we do?"

"I am here for my friend."

"Of course." Curasir nodded. "I believe I can arrange something then."

"Like what?" Talinir asked.

"I will set up a meeting between you and this slave's owner."

"Calu?"

"Oh no. Calu grew tired of a one-legged slave and traded him to someone else."

"All right. What do you propose?"

"The army will not stop for another two or three hours." Curasir pointed his sword toward the southeast. "Follow along with us, as you are doing now. I will speak to the one you seek. When he agrees to a meeting, I'll come find you."

"Agreed," Marshal said. Talinir shot him a look.

"Very well." Curasir gave a mock bow, then blasted up into the air with an explosion of magic. Marshal turned and watched him descend near the army.

"We cannot trust him," Talinir said.

"We can't trust any of them. I know. But what he says is true. Neither of us wants a battle."

"So they'll try to kill you in your sleep," Tich chimed in. Marshal and Talinir looked at her. She shrugged. "It's what I'd do against someone that powerful." She looked Marshal over again. "Could you really destroy hundreds of them?"

"It's possible." Marshal turned back to Talinir. "She's right, of course."

"Which is why I'm here," Talinir reminded him.

"And why we'll take precautions going into this meeting."

"Because it's a trap," Tich said.

"Of course it is."

• • • • •

Marshal watched Curasir descend and land in a burst of dust and rock. Tich coughed. "He couldn't just walk to us like a normal person?"

"I have arranged a meeting with Vayan," Curasir announced, stepping out of the small crater he had created.

"Vayan is Dravid's current master?"

"Master would be an appropriate title. Also Owner. Lord. God."

"What does he want?" Every interaction with Curasir grated on Marshal's nerves.

Curasir gave a short wave with spread fingers. "You'll have to ask him. I'm just the messenger."

"Fine. Where do we meet?"

Curasir pointed to the southwest. "There is a small valley about half a mile in that direction. By the time you get there, Vayan should be waiting for you."

"Good. You can leave us now."

Curasir laughed. "So eager to get rid of me! Very well. I'll inform Vayan that you're coming." He launched himself into the air again, spiraling off in the direction he had indicated.

Marshal started walking, and gestured to Talinir. "Do you know anything about this Vayan?"

"Until recently, I didn't even know these so-called gods existed." Talinir shook his head.

"Vayan is one of the ancient gods of Kuktarma. He's associated with wind and pain," Tich answered.

Marshal stopped and looked at her. She held out her palms. "What? I told you I spent a lot of time in the Lord's Library in Raeton. I read everything."

"And you remember it all?" Talinir asked.

She shrugged. "Most of it."

"Huh." Marshal shook his head. He had relegated Tich to just an annoyance. Maybe he should actually listen to her stories from time to time.

"There was something about him riding an antelope or something," Tich added. "I'm not sure what that meant."

"'God of wind and pain' sounds ominous enough." Marshal started walking again. "I wonder what he'll demand in exchange for Dravid."

"Pain," Tich guessed.

After a short walk, Marshal spotted the valley Curasir had mentioned. He sent Talinir ahead to scout around it. He returned to them before they reached the valley. "There are a number of people within the valley, but no one else around," he reported.

"Not much of a trap," Tich said, "unless, of course, they have a way to hide from you."

"Is that possible?" Marshal wondered.

Talinir hesitated. "I would like to say it is not, but… their powers are still mostly unknown to me."

"All right." Marshal started down into the valley. "Watch my back."

They made their way over the uneven terrain until they reached the bottom. It really wasn't much more than a large crevasse or gorge, rather than a true valley. Curasir couldn't even get that right.

At the opposite end of the gorge, a large wooden throne had been erected. Slumped across it sat one of the golden-skinned gods, wearing multiple layers of red and yellow clothing hanging loosely over his muscular body. Marshal almost laughed at the gaudy crown and earrings.

Curasir stood beside the throne. In the shadows behind them, Marshal thought he could make out three other figures, but couldn't tell if Dravid was among them.

The god tapped a long scepter against the arm of the throne. "This is the King of Antises, Curasir? I must say I'm disappointed. I expected better clothing, at the least." He sprang to his feet and gazed down at Marshal. "The scars are tantalizing, though."

"Are you Vayan?" Marshal asked.

The god swept his scepter in a wide arc. "I am," he declared. "And who is your lovely companion?"

Marshal blinked and looked at Tich. She stared at Vayan with a look he had never seen on her face before. She dropped her coiled rope and ran one hand along the skin of her other arm, eyes never leaving

Vayan. What?

"He called her a tick, I think," Curasir offered. "Which I believe is also the name of a blood-sucking insect in their world."

"Tich," she said, her voice surprisingly husky. "It's Tich."

Vayan bowed to her. "Perhaps when I have completed whatever business your King here desires, we can explore your desires, beauteous Tich."

"I... I..."

"Stop it!" Marshal snapped. Vayan's physical appeal affected him as well. Who could deny the absolute perfection of that majestic body? But Tich's reaction was over the top. And he hated to admit it, but for some reason, it made him jealous.

Vayan gave a short nod, then reclaimed his seat on the throne. "Curasir says you wish to negotiate something with me."

"I'm looking for a friend, who may be one of your slaves. His name is Dravid."

"Dravid?" Vayan looked at Curasir, then back at the others in the shadows. "Dravid?"

With slow movements, one of them came out of the shadows, leaning on a staff. Marshal sucked in a gasp. Dravid looked... drained. Tired, but more than that. His eyes stared at Marshal without recognition.

"Oh, the cripple! Of course." Vayan looked back at Marshal. "I tend to forget their names, you know."

"What have you done to him?" Marshal cried.

"Done? Done?" Vayan looked at Dravid, then Curasir, then back to Marshal. "What do you mean? He serves me well and is well rewarded. I have no complaints."

"Dravid!" Marshal called. "Are you all right?"

Dravid lifted his head ever so slightly, his face a mask of melancholy. "I am... well."

Marshal growled. He didn't know what was going on, but Dravid's condition infuriated him. "They say you're the god of pain," he snarled at Vayan. He pointed at Dravid. "Is this how you show your godhood? Inflicting pain on those who have already suffered?"

Vayan straightened and leveled his gaze at Marshal. "I do not cause pain, little King. I take pain."

Take pain? What did that mean?

Vayan waved at Dravid. "If I have 'done' anything to this slave, it is to his benefit. I have taken his pain."

"He takes the memories of pain too!" shouted a female voice from behind the throne. "He takes all of it!"

Vayan's eyes rolled upward and the smile disappeared from his face. He tapped the scepter against the throne's arm again. A golden cone, sharpened to a point, grew from the end of the scepter. Magic of the Otherworld.

Vayan spun and leveled the scepter at the remaining figures in the shadows. "Your time in my service is at an end, girl." The cone shot from his scepter at the cowering figures. One of them gave a cry and fell. Vayan returned to his slouching position, his face a mask of indifference.

Tich gasped. The callous act had broken Vayan's spell on her, at least.

Marshal stood in shock for a moment. To kill so casually... "Monster," he whispered.

Vayan straightened his crown with his scepter. "You know, he called me that too." He pointed at Dravid. "At some point. Or was that someone else? It doesn't matter, I suppose."

"Humans are quick to throw around epithets like that," Curasir said. "One of their most annoying traits."

"Enough of this," Vayan said. "You want my slave. What do you offer in exchange?"

Marshal trembled, his anger stealing his voice. Perhaps recognizing his mood, Talinir bent and placed a hand on his shoulder. It did nothing to calm him.

"Dravid does not belong to you," Marshal said, every word a struggle. "He is coming with me."

Vayan's eyebrows went up.

"Careful, Marshal," Talinir whispered.

"And you will restore his memories!"

Vayan looked at Curasir as if seeking confirmation for the audacity. "He makes demands of me! The King of Antises demands!"

Pebbles around Marshal's feet vibrated. A few rolled away from him.

Vayan set his scepter down and folded his hands together. "I will not give you something for nothing, little King. That is not how negotiations work. You have already cost me one slave, and now you wish to take another. You must offer something of equal value in return. Perhaps the girl..."

Tich offered a very colorful suggestion that could not be physically possible, even for a god. Her language did what Talinir's whispers could not: dissipated some of Marshal's anger.

"You will not leave here with anyone else," Marshal said in a more even tone, "except your lackey Curasir there."

"Lackey?" Curasir exclaimed. "Why, I—"

A burst of laughter from Vayan interrupted him. The god convulsed in chuckles before regaining control of himself and standing.

"I like you, little King. So let us make a deal. You may have the cripple, and…" He held up a finger. "I will restore his pain to him, but I want something specific in return, something you obviously possess in great quantities."

"What is that?"

Vayan spread his hands apart, golden magic sparking between his fingers. "Your pain."

Marshal swallowed. "What do you mean?"

Vayan took a few steps nearer. "Tell me of your pain. Perhaps the day you got those scars… or, no, that's too simple." He paused, his head tilted forward, casting more of a shadow across his face as he grinned. "Tell me of your curse, and how you escaped it."

Marshal took a step back. His curse? He could not forget that. It was the reason for everything he did now. And if he told of escaping it, would he lose memories of Aelia? Even losing the memory of her death would be too much. He looked at Dravid. He had promised Seri he would rescue him. But the cost…

With a jingle, a coin purse landed on the ground in front of Vayan. He turned to look at Tich, who stood with hands on her hips. "You want pain? Take mine."

<h1 style="text-align:center">(((26)))</h1>

"Tich! No!" Marshal stepped up, intending to move between her and Vayan. But Tich pushed at him and stepped around, facing the god once more.

"I have pain like you wouldn't believe," she declared. She pointed at the coin purse. "That's part of it."

Vayan bent and picked up the coin purse. He gasped as he touched it. "Oh, yes…" He emptied the coins into his hand. "Eight gold coins, I see. Oh, I must have this story."

"You know the deal."

"Tich, you don't need to do this," Marshal said. "We'll find another way."

She looked up at him, and for the first time, he saw softness in her expression. She always held herself so rigid, so emotionless. But now he saw vulnerability, and… pain. "Marshal, please. For the past year, I've only been trying to escape my pain, my guilt. It's why I do crazy things like jumping into gateways to other worlds." She glanced at Vayan. "If he can take it away, and we free your friend at the same time, then it's something I've got to do." Her eyes glistened. "Please."

Marshal put his sword in its sheath and took her hand in his. Though rough from her sailing work, it was small and surprisingly graceful. "Then I'll stay right by your side," he promised. He turned to Vayan. "Restore Dravid first."

"And then I take her pain, and then you take him away, I suppose." Vayan sighed. "Very well. The promise of these coins is worth the exchange, I think."

Vayan walked to Dravid, who cowered at his approach. The god formed a lattice of gold magic with his hands and placed it over

Dravid's head. He sighed, closed his eyes and stood still for a moment. When he lifted the lattice and let it dissolve, Dravid's eyes went wide. He almost fell, but Talinir stepped in and caught him.

"Marshal? Talinir?"

"It's us," Marshal confirmed. "We've come for you."

"Where's Seri?"

"Enough of this!" Vayan interrupted. "My payment. Now."

Tich stepped forward. Marshal stayed at her side. Vayan approached and created the lattice again. He placed it over Tich's head. "Now. Tell me of your pain."

"No!" Dravid cried. "Don't do it! He'll take your memories!"

"It is the price for your freedom," Talinir said. "She has chosen this."

"I don't even know her..." Dravid's wide eyes darted from Tich to Marshal.

"Tell me the story of the coins," Vayan said.

"My parents were wild mages," Tich began, closing her eyes. "My mother could make anything grow. She had plants all over our house. She loved all of them. Sometimes it seemed like she loved them more than she loved us. My father, though, he could shape stone. He would put his fingers on a rock and vibrate them, cutting through the stone, making whatever he wanted."

"You don't have to tell him all these details," Marshal said.

"Yes, I do! Or the pain isn't real!" Tich's eyes flew open.

"Continue," Vayan said.

"I, I should have been happy. We weren't rich, but we had everything we needed." Tich trembled a little. "But I always wanted more. I read about all the other lands, and wanted to see them. My parents were worried, though. They warned me constantly that wild magic had to be kept secret, and since both of them had it, I might have it too.

"I never did."

Tich squeezed Marshal's hand. He looked from her face to Vayan's. The god seemed delighted with her story thus far.

"I left home at seventeen and wandered. Took up sailing. Saw all those places I wanted to see." She paused. "Except this one spot in northern Ch'olan I keep hearing about. I still need to go there someday."

"The coins," Vayan reminded her.

"Yeah." She paused. "A little over a year ago, I ended up back in Rasna. I don't even remember what port it was. We were celebrating the end of a long voyage. I spent all my earnings in two days. It wasn't much. Cheap captain didn't pay us what we were worth. The first mate, who I thought really liked me, abandoned me for another woman. I needed money and I needed a new job."

None of this had been included in any of the stories Tich had told about her life before. How much did she hide behind those stories? Marshal wondered if she was even telling the truth now. But Vayan, if he truly had the power he claimed, could probably tell the difference.

"That's when I saw the poster. Lord Tyrr was looking for wild mages." Tich stumbled over the next few words. "And... he was offering to pay."

Marshal's blood ran cold. He knew where this story went now. He almost released Tich's hand, but she squeezed his again.

"I hadn't seen my parents in years. I went to visit them. Naturally, they acted thrilled to see me, but it was obvious they weren't happy with my appearance or my life choices. And just being around them made me... resent them even more. They wanted to control me.

"So I did it. I told Lord Tyrr's men where to find them. They paid me ten gold coins, more money than I had earned in all my time sailing. I spent two of them over the next several weeks. And then I found out what Lord Tyrr had done."

Tich faltered. Vayan, though, was captivated. "Go on, go on," he urged.

"They were dead. All the wild mages he took. Someone killed every last one of them."

That someone was Volraag.

Vayan's sharp intake of breath broke the silence that followed. "Exquisite," he whispered. He pulled the lattice web away and it dissolved. He leaned back, eyes closed, mouth gaping.

"Tich?" Marshal pulled her around to face him. "Tich, are you all right?"

She pulled her hand away from him. "Of course I'm all right." The rigidity returned to her face. "Why wouldn't I be?"

"He just... he..." Marshal looked at Vayan. The god took several steps, almost on his tiptoes, then fell into his throne. He laughed and leaned back.

"I'm fine. I knew what I was doing." Tich looked at Vayan too. "So, the deal is done, right?"

Vayan waved a limp hand. "You may go, all of you."

Curasir did not look happy. "My lord, are you sure?"

"Such delicious pain, Curasir. You have no idea."

Another man emerged from the shadows, carrying a woman's body. Marshal felt his hands tremble again. The woman Vayan had killed so casually.

"Lasa!" Dravid cried. He hurried to her side, followed by the others. The large man set her gently on the ground.

Dravid wept over the dead woman. Marshal, Talinir, and Tich stood by, waiting. Even the other slave did not display emotion. He only looked tired.

Dravid pulled himself back up on his staff and took a step toward the throne. "You call yourself a god, but you're nothing!" he shouted at Vayan. "A god should care about people! You killed her because she spoke the truth about you!"

"Curasir, there is a gnat buzzing about," Vayan said, his voice thick. "If it persists, please swat it."

Marshal stepped next to Dravid and put a hand on his shoulder. "Let it go, Dravid. We can't fight him now. It—"

At that moment, Marshal felt his sword slide out from his sheath. He whirled, a second too late, to stop the other slave from taking it and charging toward Vayan with a guttural snarl.

"Tiur!" Dravid exclaimed.

The slave swung Marshal's warpsteel sword down toward the seated god. But Curasir blocked it with his own, a casual maneuver that seemed to barely occupy his attention.

"Fool," Vayan said. A lance of golden light shot out from his hand, straight through the slave's chest.

"Noooo!" Dravid screamed.

Tiur stood impaled for a moment. Then the lance dissipated and he collapsed in a heap. The sword clanged on the rock, and Marshal dove for it.

Vayan stood and clapped his hands. His laconic expression had vanished. He looked fierce and sinister once again. "You have violated the terms of our agreement by attacking me."

"We didn't attack you!" Marshal yelled. "That was your slave!"

Vayan raised a finger. "You said that I would not leave here with anyone else, besides Curasir. Therefore, this slave was part of the deal. Since you paid the price, he became a member of your party. And now he has attacked me. The deal is off."

Marshal dropped into his defensive stance, sword at ready. "Then we fight."

"Oh, no. Not me." Vayan's grin chilled him. "I'm not the arbiter of disputes here."

He paused for effect.

"I appeal to Murdak."

•••••

Dravid's mind struggled to keep up with all that had happened in the last few minutes. For the past two weeks, he had been living in a haze, the repeated sessions with Vayan draining him of so very much of himself. At least, he thought it had been two weeks. Even that seemed fuzzy. But now all of it came rushing back, restoring him, reminding him of so many things. It made focusing on the present difficult.

He watched Curasir launch himself into the air and out of the gorge. Marshal adjusted his grip on his sword, glancing around at the others. "What does that mean?" he asked. "Who's Murdak?"

"He's their leader," Dravid said. "The most powerful one."

"King of kings and god of gods," Vayan declared. "And the sole arbiter when it comes to matters of justice."

"There is no justice needed here!" Talinir said. "You killed the slave. What else do you want?"

Vayan pointed at Dravid. "The agreement has been violated. Therefore, that one still belongs to me. All that he is..." He narrowed his eyes. "And all of his pain... are mine." A chill ran down Dravid's spine. He would not submit to that again, no matter what happened.

"Right. We're not staying." Marshal waved at the others. "Talinir, help Dravid. Tich, follow him. I'll bring up the rear."

"I do not think that will be possible," Talinir said.

Dravid looked up. Dozens of heads appeared over one side of the gorge, followed by the full forms of the Durunim warriors. The only way out now would be through the entire army. Could Marshal do that? His grandfather had destroyed a large chunk of the army, but not all of it.

He looked down at the two bodies. Lasa and Tiur, dead because they resisted Vayan's evil. He had barely gotten to know them, and both of them had little to know because of Vayan's memory theft. Yet they had somewhat bonded together in their shared misery. He would miss them.

At the top ridge, the Durunim parted and several of the gods stepped up to the edge. Even from this distance, Dravid felt a surge of attraction at the sight of one of the goddesses. Then the gods parted to make room for one final figure. He stepped to the edge, then stepped off. He plummeted to the base of the gorge and landed with an explosion of dust tinged with golden light.

As the dust cleared, the god stepped into view. Taller than even the other gods, he might be pushing eight feet. His dark skin glowed with the golden power of his people. What little clothing he wore reminded Dravid of Lord Meluhha's ceremonial costume: a wide strip of maroon cloth that wrapped around his waist and thighs in multiple layers, then looped up over his left shoulder. An open white shirt of gauzy material hung over that, leaving the rest of his chest bare, except for a necklace of multi-colored gemstones. His face was clean-shaven, topped with the blackest hair Dravid had ever seen.

"What is the dispute here?" he demanded, his voice rumbling with magic.

Vayan bowed to the newcomer, presumably Murdak. He gestured to Marshal. "The scarred youth there is the King of Antises. We made an agreement over some slaves, and then one of his party attacked me. The agreement is voided, but he will not return my property."

Murdak leveled his gaze on Marshal. "What do you have to say for yourself?"

"The, uh, attacker was not a member of my party," Marshal said, his voice sounding weak and fragile in the face of such power.

"The attacker was one of the slaves that passed into his possession," Vayan countered.

"You must return Vayan's property to him," Murdak declared.

In the silence that followed, Dravid felt certain Marshal would abandon him, and he would be right to do so. The god's voice inspired obedience. To defy it would be insane.

"I do not wish to fight all of you," Marshal said at last, glancing up at the Durunim. "But I will not surrender my friend back into your hands."

Murdak studied him for a long moment. "You will not have to fight all of us," he announced. "Only me. Should you defeat me, you will all go free. Should I defeat you, all of you will be Vayan's slaves to do with as he wishes. Save one. I will choose one of you to be my slave, as compensation for my work in this matter."

"This is ridiculous," Marshal's female companion complained. Dravid still didn't know her name, even though she had given up her memories to save him. "You call this justice?"

"The justice of Murdak cannot be questioned." At the god's response, the girl quailed. Dravid didn't blame her.

Talinir bent down to Marshal. Dravid moved closer to hear them.

"I do not see an easy way out of this," the Eldani said.

"Nor I," Marshal admitted. "I may have to fight him."

"Can you beat him?" the girl asked. "I mean, I know you have Kingly powers or whatever, but he's… um…"

"I don't know. I have to try." Marshal glanced back at the waiting gods. "But I don't trust them, either. Talinir, as soon as the fight starts, I want the three of you moving as far from it as possible. Don't fight, if you're threatened, but don't just wait around either. Tich and Dravid are your responsibility now."

"I promised to protect you, not them."

"There's nothing you can do to protect me right now. But you can help them. I'm asking you, Talinir."

The warden nodded.

Marshal turned back to the gods. "I accept the challenge," he announced.

"Your acceptance was not required, but is helpful to avoid more unpleasantness," Murdak said. "Meet me up top." He turned, bent down and leaped up to the top of the gorge again. Dravid swallowed as he realized no magic had been involved in that leap; Murdak's physical prowess was that impressive.

"All right, let's go. And watch for an opening, Talinir." Marshal turned away.

Dravid tapped him on the shoulder with his staff. "Wait."

Marshal looked back expectantly.

"You need every advantage you can get in this fight. I can help you."

"How?"

"How do you feel about armor?"

(((27)))

Marshal tried to look tall and strong as he walked out to meet Murdak. He felt surprisingly comfortable in the golden breastplate and helmet Dravid fashioned for him. The magical armor would only last as long as Dravid could manage, but every advantage he could find might help.

Murdak watched him come. They stood alone in the middle of a vast open space beneath the stars. Talinir, Dravid and Tich waited behind Marshal, while most of the Durunim army surrounded the rest of the makeshift arena. Murdak held up his right hand and a flaming sword appeared in it.

Marshal glanced at his warpsteel sword. It looked like a dagger compared to his opponent's.

"I call on the stars to witness!" Murdak cried. "Let justice be done!"

"Let's get this over with," Marshal grumbled. He used a burst of power to launch himself into the air, angling toward the god. The faster he could do this, the better. Dravid couldn't keep this armor in existence for long.

Murdak watched his approach and did not move. Marshal held his sword at his side, disguising his blow for as long as possible. At the last moment, he swept a slash up from below, hoping it would be the last thing his enemy expected. But Murdak's sword parried his without effort. The impact of their blades knocked Marshal back. He used another burst of power to cushion his fall, somehow landing on his feet.

Then Murdak attacked, bringing his flaming sword down in a massive overhead strike. Marshal dodged to the left, heat rushing down his right side as the sword passed him. He threw a blast of magic at Murdak's head. The god flinched, but showed no other reaction.

"I fought one of your ancestors, you know," Murdak said, keeping up the offensive. He swung blow after blow in rapid succession. Marshal dodged as best as he could, but one of them caught him on the side. The impact knocked him off his feet and sent him rolling across the dirt. Dravid's armor held.

"When you first came to Antises, the portals were open. I challenged Akhenadom, for the privilege of keeping them open."

Marshal had never heard that story. Seri hadn't even mentioned it in all her raving about the founding. "I notice the portals are closed," he said, scrambling back to his feet.

"Yes, but I defeated him in single combat. He was the first and greatest of your Kings. So how can you hope to defeat me?" Murdak advanced toward him without any hurry.

"Maybe you haven't heard." Marshal aimed his sword at his foe and unleashed his power. "I have a Lord's magic in addition to a King's!"

The first blow knocked Murdak back several feet, but he recovered and took a step forward. Marshal focused, gritted his teeth and poured on the power. It rushed out of him in a massive wave, tearing apart the ground between the combatants and throwing up a cloud of dust that obscured them from the crowd. It felt good to unleash everything. Since the battle at the portal, every time he had used his power, he had been forced to hold back, only use a little bit at a time. Not now.

But as his power struck Murdak and pushed him back, something changed. Golden armor of light appeared all over the god, mimicking what Dravid had done, but more extensive. With this shield in place, he took another step forward.

Marshal redoubled his efforts, pushing himself as far as he could. Focusing the power through the warpsteel sword meant he wouldn't damage his own body, as he had done in times past.

But it wasn't working. The god of justice took another step forward, inexorable. Marshal couldn't even fathom the amount of strength it took to move against the power he unleashed.

Well, if he couldn't harm him directly, then he needed to do it indirectly. Marshal shifted his sword's angle. His power exploded into the ground beneath Murdak, carving out an enormous crater and throwing the god into the air.

Marshal launched himself into the air again, trying to see through the debris and dust. The flaming sword gave Murdak away. Marshal blasted the ground near him again, tossing him to the side. He adjusted his own vector and came down, sword in position.

He should have taken Murdak's head off. Instead, golden light appeared right as his sword struck, deflecting him. Undaunted, Marshal landed and whipped around, swinging at the back of the god's leg. Another segment of golden armor appeared the instant he struck. His sword ricocheted off it, throwing him off-balance.

Murdak backhanded him. Once again, Dravid's armor held, so a blow that would have snapped him in half instead only threw him a dozen or so yards away. He hit the ground uncontrolled this time and rolled.

That hurt. And so far, nothing he had done harmed his opponent.

The golden light in front of his face wavered, then vanished. The rest of his armor faded away. Dravid had done what he could. The rest was up to Marshal.

He climbed to his feet. Murdak waited, not pressing his advantage. Marshal wondered about that. Was he so confident in his power he believed the outcome of this fight to be inevitable?

Regardless, he needed to do his best. He resisted the urge to glance at Talinir. He needed to keep everyone's attention on the battle, to give them time to escape.

Both Talinir and Aelia had taught him well in swordplay. Perhaps he needed to shift the battle more in that direction, look for any openings in Murdak's defenses.

He approached the god of justice cautiously, sword ready in a defensive posture. Murdak waited. His height would be an issue, but Marshal felt confident it wouldn't create too much of a difficulty.

Without warning, Murdak attacked. His flaming sword came at Marshal from multiple directions in a succession of blows that happened so fast, he could barely keep up. He dodged and parried over and over, stepping back and back. Still Murdak advanced. Marshal let his power flow out of him in all directions, creating a barrier of sorts that helped protect him when he couldn't avoid the blows.

Even with the barrier of magic, the force of Murdak's sword striking at him still threw him off balance. Another blow upended him, tossing him on his back. Marshal lifted his sword in time for Murdak to strike it, knocking it out of his grasp. Murdak reached down and grabbed Marshal by the front of his shirt.

Marshal struggled, unleashing wave after wave of his own power, but Murdak lifted him up into the air. "Were we in your world, you would be able to harm me, though the end result would be the same." He leaned in closer. "But here in my realm? You had no chance."

He slammed his own head against Marshal's. For a moment, all Marshal could see were the stars. His vision blurred. Murdak slammed him down on the ground. Something cracked inside his chest. Then Murdak kicked him and sent him rolling across the rough ground again.

This felt all too much like his first battle in the Otherworld, against Curasir. Then he had been inexperienced with his power, but still it had saved him in the end. He still had a chance. He could still—

Murdak picked him up off the ground and punched him. He collapsed onto the ground again. By now, every part of his body screamed in agony from all of the impacts. His limbs didn't want to respond to his thoughts, what few he could muster. His mind reeled. Power. He had to use his power.

Marshal let it go. He closed his eyes and let his power erupt from his body, consuming Murdak in a whirlwind of vibratory magic. The earth exploded for hundreds of feet in every direction around them. Marshal sagged back. That was all he could do.

Dirt and debris rained down around him. As it cleared, he saw Murdak still standing above him. "Pathetic."

Marshal's consciousness fled from his body. The last thing he heard was Murdak ordering the Durunim to seize the others and deliver them to Vayan. His vision cleared for one final moment, giving him a last look at the stars above. Was it his imagination, or did one of them... fall?

It didn't matter. He had lost. Everything went black.

•••••

Dravid strained himself to the breaking point keeping Marshal's armor intact as long as he could. When the fire inside built to an unbearable agony, he had to let it go. He collapsed back into Talinir's arms.

"It's time to go," Talinir said.

"We can't leave Marshal!" Tich. Marshal called her Tich. Her real name?

"It was his request," Talinir reminded her. "He will catch up to us if he can."

Dravid's vocal cords felt blasted and dry, but he managed to croak,

"How do we escape them?" He gestured toward a large contingent of Durunim only a couple dozen yards away. Their eyes were on the duel, but they would surely notice an escape attempt.

"Carefully." Talinir lifted Dravid up. Normally, he would object to being carried, but his entire body felt like it might melt at any moment.

Talinir and Tich each took several steps backward, keeping a watch on the enemy soldiers. They made it about ten yards back without being noticed. Talinir let Dravid back down. "This is as far as we need go," he whispered.

"This is escape?" Tich pointed. "All one of them has to do is turn around and he'll see us."

"We cannot run. They will immediately pursue." Talinir bent his incredibly tall frame down and grasped two handfuls of dirt. "There is no hiding place that will conceal us well enough."

"Then what are we doing?" Tich demanded.

Talinir's eyes narrowed. "You stand within the protection of a warden of the Eldanim in the Otherworld. In a moment, you will be safer than you have ever been in your life."

Talinir turned in a circle, sprinkling the dirt from his hands as he murmured something in his own language. He looked up at the stars and lifted his hands. "I appeal to the Maker of the Stars!" he cried in a loud voice. Dravid's eyes snapped to the Durunim, but they seemed not to have heard somehow.

Talinir bowed his head and closed his eyes. As Dravid watched, the air around the three of them shimmered. A beam of pure white light erupted from the ground near his foot. It wrapped around them in multiple loops before turning back on itself. He wondered if Seri saw magic like this all the time.

"Great," Tich said. "Let's give them a bright light to help them see us."

"They cannot see us at all." Talinir opened his eyes and smiled.

"How?"

"Your people are fond of calling my people 'beings of magic,'" Talinir said. "Why should it surprise you to see one of us wield it?"

Dravid did not argue. He had seen so many forms of magic in the last few months. Who was he to say what was possible or not?

"Then why haven't you used this before?" Tich wanted to know. "Like when those monsters were trying to eat us?"

"When this is done, I will be completely exhausted and defenseless. It is not something I do lightly. By then, the enemy will be gone. I trust the two of you can avoid getting into trouble while I rest."

Dravid marveled at the light that swirled around them. He reached out with the staff and touched it. He felt a vibrating warmth flow down the staff into his hands. It was not the strong vibrations of Antises magic, nor the heat of the gods' Otherworldly magic, but something in between. A combination, a blending of both. Fitting for the race that lived in both worlds.

"Don't do that," Talinir warned. "You have a bad habit of absorbing things that you shouldn't." Dravid smiled and pulled the staff back.

"Marshal!" Tich gasped. Dravid looked up in time to see Murdak punch the young King into the dirt. Then Marshal unleashed his power in a display that matched the one his grandfather had used against the Durunim army. Power swirled around the combatants, destroying everything around them, throwing debris hundreds of feet into the air. Nothing could survive that.

But when the dust finally cleared, Murdak stood alone. Marshal lay unmoving on the ground.

"No..." Tich started forward.

Talinir caught her by the shoulder. "We can aid him best by remaining hidden."

She glared at him. "We don't look hidden to me!"

Dravid heard Murdak ordering something. The Durunim nearby turned toward them. As one, they stepped forward, then hesitated. They looked in every direction. Some wandered within a few feet of where Talinir crouched, but they looked right through him and the others.

"Do we look hidden now?" Talinir asked.

"They can't hear us either?" Dravid whispered.

Talinir shook his head. "The Durunim are blinded to us. As long as..." He hesitated. "As long as Curasir or one like him doesn't come near, we will be fine."

Dravid turned back to watch. The Durunim searched all around them, moving further and further out. In the distance, he watched Murdak pick up Marshal and toss him over his shoulder. Two other figures approached him. They might be Vayan and Curasir, but the distance made it hard to be sure. They seemed to argue for a moment or two, then fell into step behind Murdak as he strode back to the rest of the army.

"We're not just going to let them take him, are we?" Tich asked.

"No." Talinir's voice sounded grim. "We are not."

(((28)))

Talinir held the magical concealment in place for three hours. The Durunim and some of their masters searched the entire area thoroughly, but none of them saw or heard the three hidden figures. In the end, they abandoned the search and rejoined the army. After a great deal of what seemed useless re-organizing, the huge column resumed its movement. When they were out of sight, Talinir gave a great sigh of relief.

The light dissolved into a rain of tiny sparks that vanished as they struck the ground. Talinir sank to the ground as well. "Keep an eye out," he whispered. His eyes closed.

"Is he asleep?" Tich asked.

"I think so." Dravid pulled himself up with his staff. He stared after the army. He could see the dust cloud moving. It would not be hard to keep up with them.

"What do we do now?"

"As Talinir said, we wait and watch." Out of habit, he reached for his power and drew a circle of golden light in the air. He relaxed and let it dissolve. Every time he strained himself, he worried it might leave him. Forerunner had not been sure how long it would last, and Dravid had not met anyone else that could tell him.

"So… you're some kind of mage too, I take it?"

Dravid turned to find Tich seated on a large rock, leaning back against her arms. "Something like that," he said. "And you're… Tich?"

She nodded. "That's my name."

"Why did you… do what you did back there?" Dravid gestured toward the gorge.

"What do you mean?"

"When you sacrificed your memory for me."

"What memory?"

Dravid groaned. He awkwardly sank down and sat in the dirt himself. "To secure my release, Vayan asked for Marshal's pain. You offered yours instead. A story about"—He watched her reactions—"your parents?"

Tich cocked her head. "I'm not sure what you mean. My parents are wild mages back in Rasna."

Was it his place to remind her of what she had lost? Dravid didn't even know her. Better to wait for Talinir. Or Marshal. "I'm Dravid, by the way."

"I know. They've been using your name a lot. It's why we came here." She gestured expansively. "Not much of a place to visit, if you ask me. Though the view upstairs is nice." She looked up at the stars.

"It is," Dravid agreed.

"Ever been to sea?"

"Uh… no, not really. I mean, I've sailed to and from Zes Sivas, but that's it."

An awkward silence followed. "So, um, I've been here for a few weeks now," Dravid said. "What's been happening on the other side?"

"That I can help you with. I'm a sailor. I know all the news." Tich shifted onto one arm to face him. "Mandiata declared war on Ch'olan."

"What?"

"Oh, yes. I think they really want to go to war with Varioch, because of the whole killing the Lord thing, but Ch'olan is in their way. So I guess they're going to just go through them."

"That can't be right."

"Well, you know the Otherworld has invaded Rasna and Varioch, right? Everyone's just going crazy now. Won't be long until all of Antises is at war."

Dravid didn't know what to say.

Tich sighed. "That's why I came with Marshal, you know. Ch'olan was demanding to use my ship in their battles. I didn't want any part of it."

Dravid waited, but she didn't elaborate any more. After another few minutes, he asked, "What about my other friends? Do you know them? Seri, Ixchel, Victor?"

"Don't know the first two, but I know Victor. Blonde guy. Likes to use a flail."

"Seri wasn't with them?"

"You know, I think I heard that name, but I never met her. Just Victor. And then that Jamoona guy."

"Jamana?" Dravid sat up.

"That's the one. Big guy. Mandiatan. Ugly robe."

Dravid laughed. He couldn't imagine how Jamana had ended up with Marshal and company, but it was great to hear about his friend again. "And they're all right?"

"Sure. As far as I know. Of course, Victor got married."

"Really? To who?"

"Me." Tich leveled her gaze at him. "Do you have a problem with that?"

Dravid stared. Tich stared back. After a long moment, he shook his head. "You are seeing how much I'll believe, aren't you?"

Tich shrugged and rolled onto her back. "You're right. I'm not really married. I have no plans to ever get married. Though if I did…" She paused. "We came to rescue you because Marshal was Bonded to you. I guess you rescued him at some point?"

"Yes, I saved his life. I guess he saved mine now, so the Bond should be gone."

"So if I rescue Marshal… the King of Antises will be Bonded to me." She chuckled. "I could do worse."

"You… are a very strange woman."

"I am who I am."

•••••

Jamana listened to the sailors grumble on the aftcastle. Once again, their small ship stood still. The wind had come in fits and starts and gotten them within sight of the shores of Kuktarma, but now it died again. From the sailors' talk, this was practically impossible. None of them recalled anything like it ever happening.

Victor walked up beside him. "It's so hot down below," he complained. "I don't know how Adhi can sleep in this."

"That boy never ceases to surprise me," Jamana said. "Every time I think I understand him, he does something new."

Victor leaned on the railing. In the distance, they could see a pair of lights on the shore. "What do you suppose those are?"

"Farmers burning scrub brush, perhaps? I have never been to Kuktarma, but I know there are many farms near the coast."

"Ugh. Looks like we could almost swim there."

"I could not swim that far."

"Yeah, I probably couldn't, either." Victor turned around and leaned back, facing the deck. "Oh, there's Kishin."

"Who?" Jamana turned and saw a dark figure emerge on deck from the front cabin. "The owner?"

"He comes out at night to practice."

"Practice what?"

Victor only nodded, so Jamana turned to watch. Kishin drew two swords, struck some kind of pose, then began moving around the deck. He swung both swords in every direction, shifting into various stances, occasionally jumping... it took Jamana a minute or two to realize the whole thing had a pattern to it. The movements followed some sort of regimen. The longer it went, the faster Kishin moved: stabbing, slashing, kicking, dodging, leaping, rolling.

At last, he came to a stop, and sheathed both swords at once. He stood not far from them, his chest rising and falling in deep breaths.

Victor pushed off from the railing. "Come on." He walked to Kishin with his hand raised. Jamana followed.

"Interested in sparring?" Victor asked.

"No, thank you," Kishin responded. "I told your friend I wish to be left alone."

"I know, but he's gone. I'm not. Just thought I'd ask. This is Jamana, by the way. He's another mage."

Jamana lowered his head. "Thank you for letting us use your ship," he said.

When he lifted his head, he looked into Kishin's face for the first time. His eyes widened and his next words stuck in his throat. The pale, decaying skin gleamed in the low light from a nearby lantern. The man was a leper!

"I owe Marshal a great debt. This is the least I can do," Kishin answered.

"When you see the leper face-to-face..." The old man's words echoed in his mind.

"I... I have a message for you, sir." Jamana swallowed and dug around in his pockets.

Kishin frowned. "For me? From who?"

"That's... hard to explain. It was an old man I met in Mandiata." Jamana found the scroll and offered it to the assassin.

Kishin's eyes narrowed. "An old man." He took the scroll but did not open it. "What did he look like, this old man?"

"Um, very old. He had a long beard. Skin not as dark as mine, nor as light as Victor's. But I could not figure him out. I thought him a priest. Or a mage. Or both."

"He didn't have a staff, did he?"

"No, sir."

"Of course he didn't," Kishin said, more to himself. "He couldn't have gotten it back. Or could he?" He opened the scroll and read it. He stood silent. Jamana couldn't tell if he were reading the note again, or merely pondering its meaning.

"This can't—" Kishin broke off. "Huh."

He left them on the deck, strode to his cabin door beneath the forecastle, and disappeared inside. Along the way, he balled up the message and dropped it.

Jamana retrieved the paper and rolled it back open.

"What does it say?" Victor asked.

"Redemption is not offered only once in a man's life," Jamana read. "Choices remain until you die."

"Huh. So he still has a chance."

"A chance for what?"

"I'm not sure." Victor looked toward the closed cabin door. "I guess that's up to him."

• • • • •

The wind returned the next day, long enough to get the ship moving again and make it into port. Jamana looked out at a bustling city sitting beside a wide river mouth. In a few minutes, they would finally be done with ships.

"From here, we will take a barge up the river to Simbala," Adhi said, stepping up behind him. He had a contented smile on his face, and had changed from his acolyte robes into more practical and colorful clothes. "In another two or three days, I will be home."

"Do you have much family?" Jamana asked, realizing he had never spoken with the young acolyte about that topic before.

"Oh, yes. I come from a very large family." Adhi noticed the gangplank being set into position. "Excuse me, Jamana. I must arrange our transport."

Jamana watched him go and shook his head. Even though he knew this was Adhi's homeland, imagining him "arranging transport" felt wrong somehow. He had never seen the acolyte arrange anything greater than simple chores at Zes Sivas. He wondered if Adhi's magical senses had even awakened yet. Another topic they had not discussed since reuniting. What kind of friend was he?

Within a couple of hours, Jamana found himself boarding a large flat-bottom barge along with Victor. Adhi stood talking to the barge's pilot.

"Did you speak with Kishin again?" Jamana asked Victor.

"No, he didn't come out."

"Does he know we're leaving?"

Victor glanced back in the direction of the ship. "He knows. I'm not sure how, but I am sure he knows everything that's going on."

Adhi approached them. "I'm afraid there weren't any barges available with cabins today. But the weather is nice. We can enjoy the open air for a while longer."

"Makes no difference to me," Victor said. "I can sleep anywhere."

The barge did have a canvas cover mounted on poles over half of the flat surface. Four large men stood on either side of the barge, each holding an extremely long paddle.

"They will row us up the river?" Jamana wondered.

"Only until we're outside the city," Adhi explained. "Then a team of buffalo will take over."

"A team of buffalo?" Victor scrunched up his forehead. "How does that work?"

Adhi pointed to the front of the barge. "We have ropes that will be thrown to the drivers on the shore. They will hook us up to the buffalo team, which will pull the barge the rest of the way to Simbala."

At that moment, an impressive warhorse with an equally impressive soldier atop it pushed through the crowd on the dock. To Jamana's surprise, the soldier spotted their barge and came right beside it. He looked over the three of them with a dismissive glance, then turned to the pilot.

"I am Captain Parpola of the Kuktarma Defense Force," he announced. "I was told that my presence was required here. Who summoned me?"

Adhi stepped forward. "That would be me, Captain."

The Captain looked at Adhi and blinked. "You?"

"Yes, I have a special task that requires someone I can trust. I need you to ride ahead of us to Simbala. There, you will need to assemble Kuktarma's military leaders for an immediate conference with the Lord. You will have until our barge arrives to accomplish this. It should not be difficult."

Adhi glanced at Jamana and winked. Winked. Who was this young man?

The Captain stared, mouth ajar in astonishment. He barked a quick laugh. "Who are you to command one of the Lord's Captains? By what right do you make these demands?"

Adhi gave a short bow. "My name is Adhi. I am a scion of Simbala, regional overseer of the Kuktarma Defense Force, acolyte mage in training, and the seventh son of Lord Meluhha. It is by those rights that I make these demands."

<h1 style="text-align:center">(((29)))</h1>

Marshal woke in pain. How many times in his life had that been true? He was so tired of mornings like this. So tired of everything. His head throbbed in agony, muscles ached in both arms and legs, and his chest drove a stab of pain deeper inside with every intake of breath. The floor beneath him jolted, adding more discomfort to his pains.

He opened his eyes and saw a roof of dark wood planks only a foot or so above his face. Turning his head to the side, he saw iron bars surrounding him. Beyond that, he caught glimpses of Durunim warriors marching. A prison wagon of some kind, then. He pulled himself to the edge, next to the bars, his body protesting with burst of pain that almost knocked him out again. He tried to look up at the stars, but the roof of the wagon had been built with overhangs, specifically to prevent his view. Or so it appeared.

He let himself go limp again. How cruel to deny him the one thing he wanted to see. The stars might be able to help him heal faster as well. Perhaps that was why they cut off his view.

Did he at least have his power? Yes, he could feel it within him. They couldn't block that, not like that strange cave in Ch'olan. Once he was rested, he would be able to blast himself free of this cart, fight his way through the army, and meet up with the others. He just needed to regain his strength.

"Ah, you're awake. I wondered how long it would take."

Marshal opened his eyes. He knew that voice far too well. Curasir. He groaned.

"By now, you've evaluated your injuries and started making plans to escape, I'm sure. I would advise against that."

Marshal didn't bother answering him.

"Here's the thing," Curasir went on. "Your three friends are being held in a separate location on the other side of the army. Should you cause any trouble, they will be killed."

"You're lying," Marshal said. The two words caused him much more pain than he expected. He struggled for another breath.

"Why would I do that? We know your power. We know that you require… motivation to keep you in line."

Marshal didn't answer. He had told Talinir to get the other two out, but he couldn't be sure they had escaped. Curasir had him, and he knew it.

"We should thank you, actually," Curasir said. "You placed yourself into our hands. It saves us a lot of trouble finding you later."

"Why?"

"Why keep you alive? Murdak has plans for you, once we arrive in your world." Curasir chuckled. "I am not privy to them, but I'm sure it will be something impressive. Perhaps he will use you to prove a point. The King of Antises! In a cage! Behold the power of your gods!"

"I'm not… King," Marshal pointed out. If Murdak hauled him out in front of a bunch of people, they would wonder who this scar-faced stranger was.

"As I said, I don't know all his plans. But I know he has been thinking about them for hundreds of years. Whereas you?" Curasir laughed again. "If you even have plans, you make them up five minutes before you execute them!"

"It works." Sometimes.

"Is that why you're in a cage?"

Marshal groaned again—not intentionally. It just slipped out. He tried to ignore Curasir's rambling voice. The renegade Eldani babbled on for a while, apparently not caring whether Marshal responded or not. Maybe he enjoyed the sound of his own voice that much.

After a while, he finally left Marshal alone again. The cart continued to shift and shake, jerking here and there as it rolled over the uneven ground.

Curasir's mocking of his planning hit close to home. Once again, he had set out with good intentions, and look where he ended up! Why didn't he learn? His previous big plan, traveling to the Ch'olan portal, had ended with Rufus betraying him, Topleb murdered, Dravid enslaved, and Seri leaving him for Volraag.

What could Murdak want with him? According to Curasir, the gods wanted to end the Laws of Cursings and Bindings and re-establish themselves in place of Theon. Marshal's power might be needed for the first goal. After that, he would be superfluous. The six lands of Antises were held together by their joint worship of Theon, and the Laws. With the Laws gone, and each land reverting to its own pantheon of gods, there would be no need of a King. The Lords themselves might be eliminated as well. Why would the gods allow any other power other than their own?

Why couldn't Volraag see that? What did he hope to gain by opening the portal?

The cart struck a rock and bounced Marshal across the floor into the bars on one side. He moaned. The questions made his head hurt even more. He wanted to sleep, but the uneven motion would keep him awake as long as the army kept moving. He had never been more miserable.

•••••

Jamana watched the Captain ride away into the crowd, then turned to Adhi in open-mouthed astonishment.

"You can't be serious!" Victor said it first.

"We're ready to cast off!" Adhi called to the pilot. He nodded and gestured to one of the rowers.

Jamana caught Adhi by the arm. "You? You are the seventh son?"

Adhi nodded, smiling.

"The one in all of the stories that Dravid tells?" Victor demanded.

"Well, you see—"

"How could you keep this a secret?" Jamana cried. "You are little Adhi, mage acolyte, not a prince!"

"Still not a prince," Adhi said. "I'm not in line to be King. I'm not even in line to be Lord. I have six older brothers, you know."

"You know what I mean! Why did you not tell me?"

With a jolt, the barge moved away from the dock. The rowers inserted their oars into the water in unison, pushing the barge out into the river.

Adhi gestured to a lower part of the deck beneath the canvas overhang. He led the way and sat down on the only bench. Victor sat down cross-legged on the deck. Jamana remained standing, still unable to believe his ears.

"When you are raised as the son of a Lord, with many older brothers, you reach a point where you want to accomplish something for yourself," Adhi explained. "I decided to become a mage. No one else in my family took that path, so I could be sure that any success I found was my own."

"But... but you've done so many things!" Victor argued. "We've heard the stories!"

Jamana nodded. Dravid had told him many stories of the sons of Lord Meluhha. The seventh son showed up in many of them, and often did some amazing things.

Adhi rolled his eyes. "I hate some of those stories," he admitted. "You have to understand: many of them are not actually about my family, but about earlier Lords and their sons. The stories are adapted with each generation to match the current Lord's family. Even those that actually happened are often exaggerated and expanded from the true events."

"What about the one with the, uh, fourth son and the chief of the guard?" Victor asked. "Did that one happen?"

"Oh. That one." Adhi cleared his throat and pulled at his collar. "I guess that one is mostly true."

Victor hooted in laughter and fell back.

Jamana couldn't help chuckling as well. "I do not think Dravid knows this, does he?"

Adhi shook his head.

"You must let me tell him when we meet again." Jamana roared with laughter and finally sat down. "I cannot wait to see his face!"

After the laughter died down, Victor sat up. "But this is actually very good news! I was worried that we couldn't get the Master Mage on our side, but the son of the Lord! That's even better!"

Adhi agreed. "As I told the Captain, I am also the regional overseer of the Kuktarman Defense Force."

"And that means?"

"It means I'm in charge of the army... or at least one quarter of the army. The part that is stationed in and around Simbala."

"That's fantastic! Then you can call them up and march to the portal!"

Adhi raised his hand. "It is not quite that simple, I'm afraid. I must convince my father that the threat is real. Your presence will help, but it will still be a challenge. The army is mostly for show, after all. Kuktarma has not fought a real battle in generations."

Victor nodded. "Aside from Ixchel's bunch, who in Antises has? We fought with Varioch's army against Rasna, but that was the first time in… who knows how long?"

"The Mandiatan Sentinels are well armed and skillful," Jamana said.

"Who are they?"

"Guardians of the Sands. They learn their trade deep within the Djatan Desert."

"In the desert? I'm impressed."

Jamana watched the rowers for a few minutes. What a back-breaking job. At least they would not have to do it for long, according to Adhi.

"So… two or three days?" Victor asked.

"Yes, depending on the strength of the river's flow," Adhi said.

Victor reached into a pouch and pulled out his cards. "Tell me, seventh son of Lord Meluhha: have you ever played Mages & Lords?"

(((30)))

Seri took a deep breath, then pushed open the massive door into the receiving hall. Lady Lilitu sat alone in her chair, leaving the Lord's chair empty, but in its traditional place. The Lady sat with eyes downcast, her head leaning on one elbow. The room felt different without Lord Enuru in it: stark, quiet... empty. All of the palace remained in mourning. Seri had to find her way to the receiving hall on her own.

"You are leaving, then." The Lady's voice broke the silence, sounding broken herself.

"Yes, my Lady." Seri came closer. "I need to get to the high place. The portal. And do what I can to stop Volraag."

"If anyone can stop him, you can, my dear."

Seri waited. The stillness of the room disturbed her. She could feel the pulse of the Lady's power, though it felt wrong somehow. Her senses had not been working well for her since leaving Ch'olan. Volraag or Rathri, or just everything that happened at the high place, had left her confused.

"Is there something else?" Lady Lilitu asked, looking up at last.

"You have nothing else to say to me?"

The Lady sighed. "I am sorry, my child. The loss of my Lord has... disrupted me. I find it difficult to think of other things."

"And... you do not have his power?" Seri had been wondering about that.

She shook her head. "We are searching for any relatives of my Lord. So far, there is no sign of his power. Perhaps it has abandoned Arazu. We will be the first land without a Lord."

Seri wondered. Volraag could not have stolen the power, could he?

Tezan, the thief of power, was dead. Without him... But where else could it have gone? Back to the land? To Zes Sivas? It was a mystery. A mystery that would have to wait, for now. Seri needed to set out after Volraag, but not until she asked—

"I said I wasn't cursed," the Lady said, her gaze looking off in another direction. "But perhaps I was wrong. Perhaps my Lord's death, and his childlessness, is my fault. My curse. Who can say how Theon works these things?"

"But you have a child," Seri said. "I'm... I'm standing right here."

The Lady smiled, but it was a weak thing, as if her facial muscles found it exhausting to move in that direction. "Yes, my dear. And as I told you, I'm so very proud of what you've become. Even if I've given you cause to question that."

"I have a mother and father. But that doesn't mean that you and I can't... that we can't be... something to each other."

"That would make me very happy." This time, the smile looked stronger.

Seri stepped closer. "I'm sorry, my Lady. But I need to know more. Your powers, then. The star in your eye. They all came from your... lover?"

"He awakened them in me. But..." She hesitated. "He told me once that the powers were mine all along. That I must have some of the god's blood in me already."

"Then I have more than half," Seri concluded. "What does that mean? Will I be able to unlock the same powers as you?"

"I do not know, my dear." The Lady stretched out a trembling hand and a tiny flicker of flame appeared on her palm. "He taught me, instructed me. Given time, I might be able to do the same with you." She closed her fist and the flame vanished. "But we never seem to have much time together, do we?"

"I wish we did," Seri said, and meant it. But how would the Lady react if she knew...

"Perhaps when this is all over. After you've saved Antises. Even with my Lord dead, I..." She broke off. "My dear, you look very troubled. What is it now?"

"I... I must tell you the whole truth," Seri said. "It... it's my fault that he's dead."

"What do you mean?"

"I came here with Volraag. I knew he was here." The words came out in a rush. "I was trying to persuade him not to open the portal. But he wanted… I thought he was listening to me. I thought I could change his mind. But then he claimed your hospitality, and, and… I didn't know."

The Lady said nothing. She studied Seri with a severe look, so much that Seri began to feel genuine fear. If the Lady used her power against her, could she withstand it? Would she go that far, in her grief?

"I do not blame you," she said at last. "You were deceived. We all were deceived. I do wonder about how Lord Volraag did some of what he did here, but the blame lies solely with him. Not you." She sighed. "I have confessed my greatest sin to you. How can I condemn you for unintentional blunders?"

"There's more," Seri said quickly. "I need to tell you everything. You deserve to know."

Lady Lilitu raised her eyebrows. "Then by all means, tell me."

Starting from the day she left Zes Sivas with Ixchel and Dravid, Seri described the events of the past few months. She told the Lady all about Forerunner, and more importantly: all about Marshal.

Lady Lilitu stood and walked a few steps from her throne. "A King. After all this time."

"Yes, my Lady. And once we stop Volraag and the gods, he will come with us to Zes Sivas, and the land will be healed."

The Lady's eyes dropped. "I hope you are right, my dear, but I fear it is too late."

"Too late?" Seri's heart skipped a beat.

"You have experienced the shaking earth."

"Yes, but there hasn't been one in weeks now."

"But there are other signs, for those who know where to watch." The Lady gestured toward the outside. "Surely you've noticed the lack of wind lately."

"It caused much difficulty in getting here on the ship," Seri acknowledged.

"It is a calm. A calm before a storm." The Lady bent and placed her palm on the floor. "The earth does not shake. But neither does it breathe. Antises holds its breath. It is waiting."

Seri didn't understand all of what the Lady said, but it disturbed her. "Waiting for what?"

Lady Lilitu shook her head and stood up. "I do not know. For the gods to return? For the portal to be opened? Or perhaps it merely holds itself together, waiting for the King to heal it, if he can. If not… I fear for all our lands." She stood. "If the ground begins to shake again, it may very well be the last time."

Seri swallowed. After all they had done, all they had suffered, it might be too late? Antises might tear itself apart? No. She could not believe that. She would not believe it.

"I will do everything I can to prevent that," she said aloud.

The Lady nodded. "As I said to you in the garden: if the fate of Antises is in your hands..." She stepped forward and grasped Seri's hands in her own. "Then it is in good hands."

Seri felt the same argument rise up inside: that she wasn't even sure whose hands these were, that she didn't know who she was. But she pushed it back down. It could wait. For now, as Ixchel said, she had a job to do. Once it was done, she could explore these other problems.

"I think, however, that I must go with you."

"My Lady?" Seri blinked.

"Not physically." Lady Lilitu placed something in Seri's hand. She looked down. A stone. Smooth, ovoid, and altogether unremarkable.

"What is this?"

"The Eldanim have special stones they use to communicate," the Lady explained. "This is similar to theirs, but it is linked only to me. With it, I will be able to follow your progress, and you can report to me from time to time."

Seri turned the stone over in her hands. "How does it work?"

"Fire, like my power, activates the stone. When that happens, we can speak to each other."

Seri nodded, and tried to hide her excitement. Another magical device for her to examine. What could she learn from it?

"You will keep her safe, won't you?" the Lady called to someone behind her.

Seri turned and saw Ekur, her father, standing at the doors. He held a smooth, composite bow in one hand, wore a quiver on his back, and a narrow-bladed axe hung from his belt. His appearance was such a contrast to her understanding of him as a successful merchant.

"I will do all I can, my Lady," he said. He smiled. "And have you seen her bodyguard? I am certain she will be well protected."

"Go with my blessing," the Lady said. She released Seri's hands and sat on her throne again. "Return when the job is done. We have much to... explore."

Seri bowed and followed Ekur out. At the door, she looked back once more. The Lady looked so small in her throne, gazing up at the larger, empty throne beside her. It occurred to Seri that even as she wondered who she was with all of these revelations, the Lady must be wondering who she was… without her Lord.

It was the saddest thing Seri had ever seen.

•••••

Jamana missed the Conclave's audience chamber. At least there, he could sit and listen while the Masters debated. Here in Kuktarma's council room, there were no chairs. Everyone stood around a large table made of some exotic wood Jamana didn't recognize. The air felt thick and stuffy. The windows stood open, but Jamana had not felt a single gust of wind since their ship managed to make it to the docks.

Adhi seemed to be holding his own in debate with his father, brothers, and Kuktarma military leaders. Such a contrast to the quiet, thoughtful little acolyte on Zes Sivas!

Victor shifted his weight from one foot to the other and muttered something under his breath. Jamana couldn't blame him. Victor was a warrior and wanted to get to the action. All of this talking would be driving him crazy.

In other circumstances, Jamana would have been delighted to see the ones he had heard so many stories about (primarily from Dravid). Lord Meluhha he knew from the Passing. He wasn't wearing his enormous crown like then, but his very presence commanded the room with ease. He stood at one end of the table, flanked by his first, second, fourth, and fifth sons. Together with Adhi, that made five out of the seven. Were the other two busy elsewhere in the land?

"The army has not been called forth in our lifetimes," the second son argued.

"Or in my father's lifetime," Lord Meluhha added calmly.

"Yet is it not for this exact situation that we even have an army?" Adhi asked.

"I have read of the founding of Kuktarma," the first son said. "And of the institution of our defense force. Nowhere did I read of an invasion from another world, led by ancient gods."

"The nature of the threat is unique, to be sure, but it is still a genuine threat to Kuktarma."

Jamana glanced at the four military leaders at the other end of the table. They had not said much of anything so far. The discussion centered on Adhi and his father and brothers.

"Be reasonable, little brother," the fifth son said. "Even you must admit this story is not very credible."

"The warning came from the King of Antises," Adhi countered.

"I have heard nothing from Zes Sivas about a new King," Lord Meluhha said. "While I do not doubt your intentions, my son, that particular claim does not stand up without confirmation from the Conclave."

"The Conclave is down to three Masters, because Antises is under attack! They are hesitant to move, afraid to confirm the new King because of what happened with the false one."

"Exactly. We must be careful not to embrace another imposter."

"Whether Marshal is really the King or not is beside the point!" Victor burst in. "We have seen what is coming, and are here to warn you!"

"You raise a very good point," the fifth son said. "What proof do we have of this? Only your word."

"I will vouch for their honesty," Adhi said. "And I heard the words and saw the signs of the King who accompanied them."

The first son raised his hands until all eyes turned to him. "Let me be clear," he said. "We have Adhi's testimony, which is but what he heard from others. And we have these two witnesses." He held a palm out toward Jamana and Victor. "One comes from the army of Varioch, and the other is an acolyte mage, friend to my little brother. You are not the most reliable of sources."

"What cause would we have to lie?" Jamana asked. "We come from two different lands, with no animus toward your own."

"Exactly," Adhi said. "What harm would befall us if we called forth the army, and this turned out to be nothing at all?"

"It is a great deal of trouble and work," Lord Meluhha said. "Not to mention the lost labor from those who are called away from their normal employment to march to the east for this possible incursion. Harvest is only a few weeks away. We cannot afford to have those who would be working it lay down their implements and take up their spears."

Adhi spread his arms. "I thought you would be reasonable, Father, after what you saw at the Passing. You know Volraag is a madman. You know what he did there. He seeks more and more power. We must stop him."

"My son, I do not believe you have fabricated this story. But the decision is not merely mine. You have command of a quarter of our forces, but to gain the rest, you must convince your brothers."

"What would it take?" Adhi demanded, looking across the table at the first son.

His oldest brother scratched his head. "Under Kuktarma law, cases that do not fall under the Laws of Cursings and Bindings require three witnesses for confirmation. You have but two."

"I do not count?"

"Your witness is only what you have heard," the fourth son reminded him.

"Then I will be the third witness." Everyone turned at the sound of the voice. A cloaked figure stood among the four military commanders, who stepped back. Jamana had not noticed him there. No one else seemed to have noticed him either.

"Who are you, sir?" the first son asked. "By what right do you speak here?"

"I am a witness to what these have said." The cloaked figure moved around the table and approached the Lord and his sons. "I am from Ch'olan, and fought there against Volraag and his minions at the high place there. You have three witnesses. Will you aid your brother now?"

"Again, who are you? What do you have to gain from this?"

"I have nothing to gain and everything to lose." The cloaked figure stood before Lord Meluhha and his second son. He reached up and pushed back his hood.

"Kishin!" Victor gasped.

Jamana stared. The assassin stood with hands by his side, palms open. The other brothers backed away from his diseased appearance.

"Do you know me, Lord Meluhha?"

"I… do not know any lepers. Why do you come before me like this?"

"Because, while I fully support these others in their quest and beg you to listen to them, I have my own desires."

"What are they?"

"Redemption. Justice. Forgiveness."

"Who are you to want such things from me?"

Kishin knelt. "I kneel before you, Lord Meluhha, as the man who"— He choked, swallowed hard, then continued—"as the man who murdered your third son."

(((31)))

Jamana tried to calm Victor down. "He is seeking, he—"

"What did he think was going to happen?" Victor ranted, stalking in a circle while they waited in the hallway outside the council room.

After Kishin's revelation, it was all Adhi and his brothers could do to keep Lord Meluhha from killing him then and there. "If you kill him, one of us will be cursed!" Adhi screamed when the Lord put his hands around Kishin's neck. The Laws of Cursings and Bindings had no exceptions for avenging.

In the end, Lord Meluhha ordered Kishin locked away until he could decide what to do with him. The discussion about the army was over, at least for now.

"I don't know," Jamana admitted. "But he wants to atone for his past sins. The note talked about redemption."

"I know he does. It's why he helped us in Ch'olan and let us use his ship. That doesn't mean he needs to go around confessing to family members of those he's killed!" Victor slapped his hand against the wall. "Especially when we're in the middle of trying to save the world!"

Adhi emerged from the council room. He wiped sweat from his forehead as he approached. "Well, we didn't see that coming. At least my father is not tearing the room apart any more."

"Do you think we still have a chance?" Victor asked.

"I don't know. I'm not going to bring it up with him again today. Maybe not even tomorrow. We'll need to give him time to calm down."

"I need to speak to him," Jamana said abruptly.

"I don't think that's a good idea," Adhi said. "As I said, he's—"

"Not your father. The assassin. Kishin. I need to speak to him."

Adhi frowned. "Do you think that wise?"

"We'll be leaving soon. I need to talk with him about the old man. The one who sent him the note."

Victor stared at him. "What are you talking about?"

"I met this old man in Mandiata. He helped me escape before I met you. And he... he was a mage of some kind. And a prophet I think." Jamana paused. "He told me I would meet a leper and to give him that note. Kishin seemed to know who he was."

Adhi tilted his head. "All right. I'll see if it's possible. This way." He led them through a series of hallways and down a few stairs to storage rooms below the palace. They passed four guards in the hall, then approached a door where two more guards stood ready.

Adhi spoke with the guards, then turned to Jamana. "They will let you in, alone."

One of the guards checked Jamana's robe for weapons, then opened the door. "Knock when you want out."

Jamana stepped through the door into a small storage room with no other exit. Kishin sat against the far wall. A single candle sitting on the floor provided meager light to the otherwise empty room.

"What do you want, acolyte?"

Jamana stepped closer as the door shut behind him. "I want to know why you did this. And what you know about the old man."

Kishin eyed him for a moment, then shrugged. "Very well... I have spent my life in pursuit of my own desires, doing whatever I wanted. I even called myself a god at one point." Kishin snorted. "I thought I was free. But that was a lie. Then..."

"Your curse was lifted." Jamana squatted down to face the assassin.

Kishin nodded. "I had to choose, then. Choose not to kill. It was so hard. And in the end, I fell again."

Jamana didn't understand all of it, since Victor's explanation of Kishin's story had been a little vague. But he grasped enough to get the basics of what Kishin meant. "You were cursed, then free, then cursed again."

"And the old man warned me. I met him, after my curse was lifted. He frightened me. He knew all about me. Spoke about grace and choices. I thought if I helped Marshal, I could make up for my past sins. But I failed even at that."

Jamana wanted to ask more about the old man, but Kishin kept talking. Better to let him unburden himself.

"Then you gave me that note. I still have choices. So I made one."

"Why? Why confess to the Lord? What good does that do?"

Kishin shook his head. "I don't know. I cannot atone for all the deaths I have caused. But this one... it was so wrong. A killing for someone's jealousy, nothing more. And since we were here, and you needed another witness... it felt like the right thing to do."

"They don't know what to do with you," Jamana said.

"Of course they don't." Kishin snorted. "I've killed someone. I should have suffered with a curse from Theon as punishment. But I didn't. So now the Lord wants to punish me, but he can't. Magic causes all kinds of trouble, doesn't it?"

Jamana waited a moment before broaching the subject again: "The old man. Did he... do any magic when you met him?"

Kishin looked up. "He did not use magic like you mages do, but... he knew my name. He knew all about me. If that is not magic, I do not know what it is."

"He knew me too," Jamana said. "And I could tell: he was full of magic."

Kishin's gaze grew more intense. "Did he tell you his name?"

"No, he would not. But he acted like I should know him."

"He did the same to me. Do you suppose... do you think he might be Akhenadom?"

Jamana almost lost his balance. He stabilized himself with one hand on the cold stone floor. "Akhenadom? No, no. Why would you think that?"

Kishin shrugged. "Incredible power. Been around a long time. Implies we should know him. Just thinking."

"He would have to be over a thousand years old!"

"Is that impossible? Considering how much we've learned about the gods and magic and such?"

"I suppose not..." Jamana shook his head. "No, no, it can't be him. We have record of Akhenadom's death, and his final words. His grave is on Zes Sivas."

"Then I have no idea who he is, or what he's up to."

"He called himself a servant of Theon, and spoke of defeating the false gods."

Kishin shook his head and looked at the floor again. "Then I don't know why he has bothered with me."

"He said a lot of people need to do a lot of different things. I guess you're just one of them."

Kishin gestured at the room. "It doesn't look like I'll be doing much of anything."

"I'm sorry."

Jamana didn't know what else to say. After a few moments of silence, he got to his feet and moved back to the door.

"Acolyte."

Jamana turned back. "Yes?"

"If you see Marshal again..." Kishin looked up at him. "Tell him about all this. Tell him about the old man. I have a feeling it might be important."

"I'll do that."

Jamana knocked on the door. As the guard opened it, he cast one last look at the leper assassin. At this point, he certainly did not look like the efficient terror he had once been.

●●●●●

Dravid looked up as Talinir approached. At least in this world, the Eldani didn't give him that weird sensation of being taller than his visible height. Of course, here he actually *was* taller. Much taller.

"Did you learn anything?" Dravid asked.

Talinir squatted to be closer to his eye level. "The army has been moving, and we'll have to hurry to catch up," he reported. "And Marshal is being held in a cage on a wagon. Barbaric."

Dravid frowned. "How are they keeping him from using his powers to escape? That doesn't seem like it would hold him."

"Who knows? Some other form of magic we don't know about? Threats? Promises? We don't have enough information."

"So what are we going to do?" Tich asked, sliding off her stone seat.

"I don't know yet, but we need to get moving." Talinir picked up his gear that he had left behind while scouting the army.

Dravid and Tich followed suit, but neither had much to carry. A few moments later, they started walking, led by the tall warden. Tich sped up to walk next to him.

"So, Tallman. How are we going to rescue Marshal?"

"Talinir," he corrected.

"I like Tallman better."

Dravid tried not to smile.

"It will not be easy to get to him," Talinir said. "He's near the middle of the column, with many Durunim warriors on either side of the wagon. And, of course, there are the wagon drivers. I don't doubt that the gods or Curasir check in on him from time to time as well."

"The wagon drivers might be slaves," Dravid pointed out. Already, Talinir and Tich were three or four strides ahead of him. Keeping up with the warden would not be easy.

"Yes, I had considered that. But I don't see how it helps us."

"What about when they stop for the night? Or whatever it's called here?" Tich asked.

"You would think that would be our best chance," Talinir agreed. "We'll have to wait and see how well he's guarded. Even so, I am unsure how to proceed. If they've done something to his powers, that could be a significant problem in escaping the army, once we free him from the cage. There are so many unknowns here."

"Sounds like we need more information."

"That's what I said at the beginning."

Dravid stopped. He could not keep up. The others were fifteen or twenty yards ahead of him and gaining. "Talinir?"

The warden glanced back, then stopped. "Dravid! I am so sorry." He came several steps back. "I did not make allowances for your... unique condition."

"For my one leg. It's all right. You can say it."

Talinir looked about, then shook his head. He came back to Dravid, turned around, and crouched. "You will have to ride my back."

"I'm not a child."

"If we are to have any hope of rescuing Marshal, we must keep up with the army. This is the most efficient method I can think of to keep us moving at their pace. Please, Dravid."

Dravid knew he was right, but that didn't change how it made him feel. He handed Talinir the staff and clambered onto his back. The Eldani rose up into the air. Dravid's vision blurred for a moment at the sudden rush of height, perhaps a remnant of his head injury.

Talinir set out again. He handed the staff to Tich, who put it to good use in keeping up with the warden's long strides. To keep himself from getting dizzy, he looked up. The view was much better, anyway.

As he often had in the weeks since coming here, Dravid wondered about the stars. Marshal and Talinir almost worshipped them. In fact, that had become a wedge between Marshal and Seri, who, like Dravid, admired their beauty, but nothing more.

"Talinir, who is the Maker of the Stars?" he asked, remembering the warden's appeal during their hiding.

"He is the One Beyond, the One Over All," Talinir answered.

"Is he Theon?"

"I… hesitate to say that for sure. I have limited knowledge of your people's theology. From what I do know, they appear similar, at least."

"Then perhaps we worship the same god."

"Perhaps." Talinir seemed reluctant to discuss the topic, as he did anything connected with the stars. How could someone be so infatuated with something and yet not want to talk about it?

"Hey, backpack boy," Tich called. "Since you're just relaxing up there… The others said you told good stories. How about sharing one with us to pass the time?"

"My stories may not interest you as much…"

"Come on. Got anything with something scandalous?"

"As a matter of fact…" Dravid took a deep breath. He didn't much like this story, but he had heard it many times. "One day, the third son of Lord Meluhha noticed a woman of Arazu visiting the great city of Simbala…"

• • • • •

"My brother was not a wise man," Adhi said in response to a question from Victor.

"What actually happened to him?" Jamana asked. The three of them sat together in Adhi's spacious quarters, waiting for Lord Meluhha's pleasure.

"It was a woman of Arazu," Adhi said, looking off in the distance. "Arun saw her in the marketplace. He fell in love, or whatever you wish to call it, in that moment. She was young and beautiful, full of life, and delighted at everything she saw. But she was being escorted by an older man who was clearly her father."

"Uh-oh." Victor rolled his eyes.

Adhi nodded. "So though my brother approached her in his usual winning way, the father rebuffed him and forbade him from speaking with his daughter. Said she was promised to a wealthy merchant in Arazu.

"My brother, though, could not take no for an answer, and so enlisted the aid of my fifth brother. He managed to distract the father long enough for Arun to persuade the girl to come with him into the palace. There, he overwhelmed her with our wealth and status."

"Where do you come into this story?" Victor asked.

"I was two years old at the time."

Jamana chuckled. "If Dravid were telling it, the 'seventh son' would show up and warn the older brother about his actions."

"No doubt that is the way the story goes with other tellers, but I'm simply telling the truth," Adhi said.

"So the father found out, and hired Kishin?" Victor asked. "That seems… excessive."

"It was more than a simple fling," Adhi explained. "The girl became pregnant. Her father was furious. He even persuaded Lord Enuru to send a letter of condemnation to my father. It threatened to undermine our two land's relationship. Apparently, the merchant to whom the girl was promised was one of Lord Enuru's closest associates.

"And then the girl died in childbirth."

"Oh." Victor looked out the window. "Yeah, I guess I might want to kill someone too, if that happened to someone I cared about."

Adhi nodded. "And so he did. The leper assassin's fame was enough that the father found a way to contact him and offer payment." He hesitated. "I do not think the storytellers know about the assassin's identity, or even the leprosy part of it. The concept of an assassin who operates outside the Laws of Cursings and Bindings is sensational enough."

"And so he killed your brother."

"He did. My father was filled with grief. He spent two years seeking for the assassin. He sought out everyone he could find with a curse, because of course he must have been cursed. But he never found the true killer."

"And now he has," Jamana said. "But what can he do about it?"

"I don't know. I am terrified he will either kill him or do something that brings about his death. Either way, the curse will fall on one of us. I am hoping his love for those of us who still live outweighs his need for revenge."

"I suppose he could just keep him locked up forever," Victor said.

"He might. I do not think that would cause a curse. But to have him here, always… it would eat at my father every day. And probably some of my brothers as well. I do not know how long they could endure it."

"I guess the only way to truly get rid of an assassin is to hire another assassin to do it," Jamana observed.

Adhi gave him a horrified look. "Don't say that to my father! It's bad enough as it is!"

(((32)))

Seri had not expected traveling with her father to be so pleasant. In fact, it was easily the most pleasant time traveling she had experienced since leaving Zes Sivas. It made her feel somewhat guilty to be enjoying travel without Dravid.

First, and most obvious, she got to ride in a carriage most of the time. Ekur always traveled in style, and saw no reason to skimp this time. Ixchel found this a little uncomfortable. She kept climbing back out of the carriage and walking alongside it. Seri, for her part, enjoyed the ride. Arazu's roads were smooth and well kept for the most part, so she did not experience much jostling. Considering how sore she still felt from the disaster at the palace, it was a blessing. She and Ixchel, who would never admit it, both needed time to heal.

Second, Ekur knew the best places to stop. For the first few nights of their travel, Seri slept in a bed each evening. Twice they stayed at inns in small towns, and twice at the homes of Ekur's business partners. In each place, they ate well and slept better.

At the second of these homes, they first heard about the caravan.

"A great multitude, out of Mandiata," Ekur's friend told them at the supper table. "They've crossed the Nadu river and are turning east. You should overtake them before long."

"Whatever are they doing?" Ekur wondered.

"From what I've heard, they're on some kind of pilgrimage. Their new Lord, the one without powers, is leading them." Ekur's friend shrugged. "Maybe they think he'll regain his power this way."

"A pilgrimage… to the high place?" Seri asked.

"No doubt. Can't think of anywhere else they'd be headed to."

Seri and Ixchel exchanged looks. A crowd of Mandiatans on their way to the high place? With an army of Durunim set to emerge? That could not end well.

That night, Seri placed Lady Lilitu's stone on the edge of her room's fireplace. After a few moments, it glowed a dull red, and the Lady's voice spoke from it: "What is it, my child?"

Seri told her about the caravan. The Lady seemed interested, but they had little to discuss. When they finished, Seri discovered she could pick up the stone, without feeling any heat. Curious. She activated her star-sight and studied the stone. She could see red and purple lines of magic woven throughout the stone's surface, but could find no sense of how it worked. Just another example of how much Seri still did not know. In some ways, that excited her, because she could continue to grow and learn. The depths of magical studies available to her continued to increase.

The third reason Seri found traveling to be more pleasant was harder to admit. Ekur would never be mistaken for a warrior. Compared to others she knew, such as Ixchel and Victor, he wasn't very impressive when it came to stature and intimidation. And yet with him around, Seri felt... safe. She knew it did not make logical sense, but there was a comfort while this man was near: this man who had kept her safe for all of her life, whose love had been proven through little things day by day for so many years. The longer they traveled together, the more ashamed Seri felt for ever doubting him. Regardless of who had impregnated Lady Lilitu, this man, Ekur, was her father. And he would take care of her.

Every morning, Seri placed her hand to the ground and concentrated. Back in the city, she hadn't been able to trust anything from her magical senses. With enough focus now, she could locate Volraag, but he seemed further away than he should have been. Every morning, his trail grew fainter, though not from distance. Something else, some other magic users perhaps, were interfering with her senses.

Ixchel chafed at Ekur's long visits along the way. "We stop before night falls," she complained. "We should be pressing on. Isn't time of the essence?"

"Even with the stops, we're moving much faster than we would on foot," Seri pointed out.

"But Volraag and Rathri will not be stopping at all."

Seri didn't know how to answer that. Ixchel made sense, but she was loathe to tell Ekur to speed things up. It felt like complaining about a precious gift.

As it was, things changed again a couple of days later, when they met the caravan.

•••••

Night among the Durunim army wasn't much better than day. Of course, "night" and "day" were arbitrary terms in the Otherworld. Marshal wasn't even sure how his captors measured the passage of time.

Without the jolting of the wagon's movement, he hoped to sleep. But the agony in his head and chest prevented him. The chest pain especially concerned him. He felt sharp pain with each deep breath, but short breaths didn't provide enough air. He felt along his chest area and found a large section tender to his touch, though all of it felt tighter than usual. Cool air whispered through the cage, but he couldn't stop sweating.

Something had broken inside: one of his ribs, he assumed. And the broken edges had caused more damage, affecting his breathing. Every time he managed to doze off, he woke up soon after with a sharp cough, or a deep gasp for air, either of which caused another sharp pain in his chest. At times, his heart accelerated, making relaxation almost impossible.

Starved of rest, his mind wandered in strange places. Friends and foes together looked at him in pity or berated him for his failures. Aelia and Murdak, Topleb and Tich, Seri and Volraag: he saw them all in combinations that made no sense. Some of them were dead. Weren't they?

At one point, he rolled to the side, feeling a little more lucid, but being on his side only made his chest hurt even more. He rolled back, but not before noticing someone watching him. Vayan.

"You don't look very well, King of Scars," the god observed.

Marshal wanted to respond with something snarky, but couldn't muster the strength.

"After the beating you took from Murdak, what pain you must be experiencing." Marshal couldn't see his face, but he imagined Vayan licking his lips.

"My pain," he whispered.

"Yes, it is. But you don't have to endure it, you know. Any one of us can heal you."

Marshal didn't see anyone lining up to help him.

"I could do it."

Marshal rolled his head to look at Vayan.

"I could heal you… if you let me have your pain."

"How… much?"

Vayan reached out and moved his hand slowly in front of Marshal. "Your chest wound is the most serious. But I will heal it, if you let me take the pain of your defeat at Murdak's hands."

Marshal tried to consider what that would mean. He would not remember losing the fight. He would not even know why he was in this cage. But he had no real reason to hold on to that memory, did he? In the greater scheme of things, how important was it?

Still, he rebelled at the thought of letting Vayan take anything from him. The man disgusted him. And who knew if he would keep his word? He might pull other memories away, memories that Marshal did not want to lose. In his weakened state, he would not be able to stop Vayan once he began.

"No."

"Be reasonable," Vayan argued. "You're only going to get worse without help. Your lips are turning blue, by the way."

"No."

Vayan took hold of the bars of the cage and leaned in. "You cost me, King of Scars. I will require payment in full eventually. Maybe another day or two of this pain will change your mind." He released the cage and stalked away.

Part of Marshal's brain told him something about those last sentences must be very important, but he couldn't grasp it. He shifted again, trying to get his head and chest to the highest point in the cage, nearest the front of the wagon. Maybe the angle would help him breathe.

Breathing was important. He needed to keep doing that. Even though it hurt.

Everything hurt.

• • • • •

Jamana looked out over the city of Simbala. He could see many similarities between it and his home city of Tenjkidi. The Kuktarmans held to similar architectural ideals: mostly flat roofs, brick construction, large clusters of similar buildings. The more he studied it, the more organization he could see. The city had been laid out in a very specific grid formation. But the biggest difference confused him a little: an enormous wall circled Simbala. He had noticed a wall around parts of the coastal city as well.

"Is the wall common to all cities in Kuktarma?" he asked aloud.

Adhi glanced up from the papers he had scattered across a wide table. "It is," he confirmed.

"Were the builders worried about attacks from outside Antises?" Victor asked, "Or were relations with Arazu that problematic?"

"Neither." Adhi found the paper he sought and picked it up. "The walls are to prevent flooding. Every Spring, the rivers of Kuktarma run wide and deep with new life. Some years, it is enough to spread across miles of land. The cities are walled to keep it out."

"Huh." Victor scratched at his beard. "I wouldn't have thought of that."

"You are a soldier, my friend. Your instinct is to think of enemies." Adhi sighed and set the paper down again. "But my brothers are right. Kuktarma has not fought against real enemies in our lifetimes. Even if we take an army to the portal, I don't know that it would be enough to make a difference."

"Every bit will make a difference," Victor insisted. "Look, I saw the fighting between Varioch and Rasna. Many of those soldiers had never fought before, but when it came down to it... they did. Your people will do the same."

"But is it worth it?" Adhi gestured to the papers in front of him. "As much as I believe in this cause, I must count the cost."

"I think every bit will help," Victor said. "And we'll have Marshal. His power alone may be able to turn the tide. If your father came..."

"I do not believe that will happen."

"It is more than military numbers," Jamana said. The others turned to look at him. "What we are facing is not just an invading army. It is an invading belief system. The leaders of this army want to be our gods. They want our worship."

"How do you fight a belief?" Victor asked.

"That is why we should be there. The more of us that show that we do not want them here, the better. We will show them that they will not just walk in and demand our allegiance." Jamana clenched his fist. "We will show them that we stand for our lands as they are, for Antises as it stands, for Theon, for our way of life."

Adhi studied him for a moment. "That is well said. Perhaps that is the argument we need to make to my brothers: not that we must fight, but that we must take a stand."

"Yes!" Victor seized on it. "And we may not have to fight at all! If Seri stops Volraag, the portal won't even be opened!"

"But we must prepare for every eventuality." Adhi gathered the papers into one stack and picked them up. "My father is not listening to anyone right now. Let us visit my brothers, one at a time, and make our case. We may not be able to bring our entire army, but as you said: every bit will help."

He started toward the door, then paused. "We have delayed long enough. Regardless of the outcomes of these visits, I will give the word. We march out with whatever we have in two days."

(((33)))

"Do you see him yet?" Dravid asked.

"No. I said I'd tell you when I do," Tich answered irritably. She sat on top of a tall outcropping, watching in the direction of the Durunim army.

"Sorry, I'm just worried." Dravid looked around at the barren landscape. "If Talinir gets caught, it's just the two of us out here, with no way to protect ourselves, no way to get back to our world..."

"We'll build a house out of rocks," Tich said. "That'll keep the monsters out. And now we can find water. We passed a stream yesterday. Food will be a little more difficult, but I think we can survive." She looked back at Dravid with a raised eyebrow. "Of course, since it will be just the two of us, and you've got your... problem, we'll need more help eventually. We'll have to have some kids."

"What?"

"You, uh, are just missing the leg, right? Nothing else?"

"No!" Dravid wanted to yell something else, but he bit his lip. Infuriating woman.

"Just teasing, Dravy." Tich slid down from the outcropping. "Talinir's here, by the way."

The tall figure of the Eldani warden appeared a few seconds later. He looked around, then settled in beside them in the alcove they had chosen for this night.

"How does it look?" Dravid asked.

Talinir shook his head. "It's not much better. There are many Durunim camped around his cage. It might be possible to get to him, but releasing him and getting him out without detection... I just don't know."

202

Dravid created a small dagger out of golden magic. "I can get the cage open quietly."

"Yes, but getting you into the camp would create its own set of problems." Talinir sighed. "We need to find out more: more about Marshal's current condition, how they're keeping him from using his powers, how often they check on him."

"So we need a spy," Tich said.

"Yes. Perhaps someone among the slaves. Dravid, did you meet any others? Any that might help us?"

"The only two I knew much at all were Tiur and Lasa. If only they hadn't both died..." Dravid let the dagger dissipate and looked down. "The only other slaves I met, while still under Calu's control, were cowardly and angry. I do not know if we can find help there."

"Then I'll have to do it," Tich said. She stood up and brushed dust from her hands. "When should I start?"

"What do you mean?" Dravid asked.

"I'll be the spy. I'll go in, hang out with the slaves, act like I'm one of them, and find out what I can. They do have new slaves show up sometimes, right?"

"Well... yes," Dravid admitted. "Every so often, they raid a village on the other side and steal new slaves, but..."

"But what?"

"Can you act like a slave?"

Tich snorted. "Act like a slave? How hard can it be?"

"Your appearance, for one thing," Talinir said.

"Your attitude," Dravid said. "It's about the attitude."

"What do you mean?" Tich looked back and forth between them. "Both of you."

"You're too... self-assured, confident," Dravid said. "These slaves are beaten down, tired, hopeless. You can't walk in among them with your swagger and snark."

"So who's got snark?"

"And your appearance goes with that," Talinir added. "You would need to keep your head down, slump your shoulders. You have to look like a slave, like someone who has no hope in this world. Or any other."

"This is depressing."

"There's nothing pleasant about slavery." Dravid scratched lines in the dirt with his staff, trying not to think too hard about his time as Vayan's slave.

"I can do this," Tich declared. She got to her feet, then underwent a transformation. As Talinir suggested, her head went down, her shoulders slumped, and she shuffled away from the other two. When she looked back at them over her shoulder, her eyes were haunted. She looked for all the world like someone who had lost everything. Then she abruptly straightened up and became the old Tich again. "So what do you think?"

Talinir studied her for a moment. "Lose the rope."

• • • • •

Another day of travel with the army, and Marshal felt only worse. He struggled for every breath, fighting the tightness and pain in his chest. The speed of his heartbeat alarmed him even more. It couldn't keep going at this rate forever.

His only interactions today had been with the slave that brought him water every few hours. She was a quiet thing who didn't say much, which was just as well. Marshal didn't feel much like talking.

Vayan was right. Another day like this, and he'd give anything for this pain to end. Unless, of course, he took the other way out. He wasn't even sure how to stop fighting, though. He couldn't just stop breathing. Everything hurt so much, he couldn't imagine doing something to make it hurt more, even if only for a little while.

Yet what other way out did he have? The broken rib had damaged something inside him, something that affected his breathing and heart rate. It wouldn't heal on its own; it was getting worse. In time, it would likely kill him. But how long would it take? Would one of the gods decide to keep him alive for whatever purpose Murdak had in mind?

With that question, he realized his thoughts were his own again. These moments of lucidity came and went with the pain and exhaustion. Most of the time, his thoughts made no sense at all, and hallucinations marched through his psyche.

"Marshal?"

Oh, the hallucinations were back. Wonderful.

"Marshal, it's me. Tich."

That was different. They usually didn't talk much, except to berate him for his failures.

"Theon's pillars, Marshal. You look awful."

He turned his head and blinked a few times. It really did look like Tich standing outside his cage, though she looked even more disheveled than usual.

She looked around in a hurry. "I can't stay long. One of them will notice."

Notice? "Are… you… here?"

"Am I here? Of course I'm here. What do you mean?" She peered in through the bars, then winced. "I'm guessing there's more wrong with you than I can tell, what with your scars and all. Is that why you haven't busted out of here?"

"You." Something still didn't make sense here.

"Me. Yes, me. I'm here. Devouring fire. What have they done to you?"

The hallucination looked like Tich, and talked like Tich. But Tich was a prisoner, along with Dravid and Talinir, somewhere else in the column. So she couldn't be here. Therefore, not real. He closed his eyes.

"All right, try to listen to me, at least. We're following the army and keeping hidden. Talinir let me come in and pretend to be a slave so I could check on you." She looked around in a hurry again. "Once I tell him your situation, we'll work on a rescue plan."

Of course she couldn't be real. Rescue provided something to hope for, another way out beyond death or Vayan. Exactly what his brain had been thinking about. It wouldn't fool him.

"Marshal, you… I don't remember what happened with that god when we came for Dravid, but… I remember that you stood with me, helped me. No one's done that in a long time." The hallucination sounded sincere. Interesting. "So I guess what I'm saying is… no matter what it takes, I'm going to help get you out of this."

She reached through the bars and stretched until her fingers brushed against his hand. "We'll rescue you. I promise."

She pulled back and glanced around one more time. "I'd better go. If I can get back in without suspicion, I will. Until then… um… hang on."

The hallucination hurried or faded away.

That last bit was nice, but proved it had to be a hallucination. Tich would never act that way, show such concern. Would she? He had held her hand while Vayan took her memory. That had been nice. She wasn't Seri. She didn't look as nice as Seri. And certainly didn't understand him as well as Seri. But holding her hand had been nice.

If it had been real, if Tich and Talinir and Dravid really were free, then nothing was stopping him from using his powers. Except, of course, the fact that he was dying.

Maybe… maybe there was another way out.

Marshal lifted his hand until he touched the dark wood ceiling. Everything hurt so much. He tried to concentrate, but it wasn't working. He closed his eyes and took several deep breaths, nearly losing consciousness with the pain of each of them. But the pain served to clear his murky thoughts for at least a moment or two.

He focused all his concentration into his index finger and let his power flow. Splinters of wood and sawdust rained down on his face. He sputtered and coughed, and his hand fell back to his side. He blinked a few times until his eyes watered enough to clear out the dust. At last, he could see.

It worked. His focused power had drilled a small hole, about an inch in diameter, through the ceiling. Starlight shone through it. He wanted to blast it open much larger, but that would attract too much attention.

Months ago, the Eldanim had channeled that starlight to heal Marshal from the brink of death. He didn't know what they had done, but maybe, just maybe, it would help him now.

At the very least, it gave him something to focus on. He could see the light. And if he rotated his head enough, he could make out two or three different stars.

"Please," he whispered.

And with that, he drifted off into unconsciousness of some kind. It wasn't sleep, not really, but at least he couldn't feel the pain quite as much.

<h1 style="text-align:center">(((34)))</h1>

"There must be thousands of them!" Seri exclaimed.

"Two thousand, perhaps," Ixchel said. "But still an impressive number."

Their view of the Mandiatan caravan was spectacular. They came over a hill and looked down into a wide, flat plain, most of which appeared golden with late summer wheat. But a huge mass of people were making slow progress between the base of the hill and the actual crops. They came from the north and were turning east on the same road that stretched out in front of Ekur's carriage.

"We'll be losing at least one percent of that crop," Ekur murmured. "Crowd that size can't help overflowing into the fields and tramping down some good grain, not to mention those that'll just take what they want from the edges. We're losing too much as it is. No wind. No rain."

Seri couldn't help but smile at her father's practical observations. Of course that would be his first consideration. She examined the crowd's composition. For the most part, they seemed to be common people, almost all of them on foot. Here and there, she saw wagons carrying supplies (and a few people). Occasionally, a rider on horseback worked his way through the crowd until finding an open spot and galloping past. From here, she couldn't tell if the riders were part of the pilgrimage, or just trying to get past it.

Ekur turned around to look at the girls. "What should we do?"

"We can't go around them, can we?"

He shook his head. "Not without trampling some grain ourselves."

"Let's see if we can make our way through to the front," Seri suggested. "I want to understand what they think they're doing."

"All right." Ekur nodded to his driver, who flicked the reins. The two horses pulled the carriage down the hill toward the crowd. It did not take long before they were in amongst the pilgrims and had to slow to a crawl. At this point, they might be faster on foot.

Seri watched the pilgrims until she spotted a young woman who looked a little younger than herself. She beckoned to her. "Would you like a ride for a few minutes?" She kept smiling until the girl finally nodded.

The carriage moved slow enough that the girl was able to catch hold and pull herself up next to Seri. She gave a nervous smile, then noticed Ixchel with her sword and shield. Her eyes got a little wider.

"This is Ixchel," Seri said. "She protects me. I'm Seri, a mage here in Arazu. What's your name?"

"I am Itri, my lady."

"What a pretty name! So much nicer than mine. Itri, can you tell me what's going on here?" Seri gestured at the crowd.

"We are on a pilgrimage, my lady, to the high place in Kuktarma." The girl's voice was lyrical and pleasant, though Seri could tell she was still nervous.

"From Mandiata?"

"Yes, my lady."

"You don't have to call me 'my lady.' Seri is fine."

"As you wish… Seri."

"There you go!" Seri patted her on the knee, then felt stupid. That had to have appeared wildly condescending. "What is this pilgrimage about?"

The girl glanced at Ixchel again before answering. "Lord Bakari says the world is changing, that… that the old gods are returning. One of them, Nummotem, is with him now, at the head of our pilgrimage."

Seri and Ixchel exchanged looks. One of the gods was already here?

"Fascinating," Seri said, somehow keeping her pleasant demeanor. "And what do you hope to accomplish with this multitude?"

"Lord Bakari says that when the gods arrive, we who are there to meet them will be rewarded." Her words came in a sudden rush. "It has been such a hard year, my la— Seri. With the earth shaking, and the murder of Lord Sundinka, and, and…"

Seri nodded. "I know. It's been hard everywhere."

"But when the gods come, they will set everything right. Nummotem promises. And we will be rewarded."

"That's amazing." Seri considered for a moment. She wouldn't be able to turn this caravan back to Mandiata, not when their own Lord was leading the people. She might have to do something more drastic.

"The Lord travels at the head of the caravan?" she asked.

Itri nodded. "He is there with Nummotem. I only saw them from a distance."

"Who else is with them? I may know some of them."

"Oh! There are the mages. One wears robes just like yours!"

"Blue?"

"Yes, my lady. The other wears, um, purple, I think. And also Nummotem's assistant Harbinger." She wrinkled her forehead. "He may be a god also. I'm not sure."

"Thank you, Itri. You've been very helpful."

A few minutes later, the carriage was forced to stop for a while because the crowd grew too dense. Itri thanked them for the ride and hopped off. Seri turned to her companions.

"We have to do something about this."

"What do you propose, my Lady?" It always sounded different when Ixchel called her that.

"I don't know. The key is Lord Bakari. He's been swayed by this god. How can I change his mind?"

Ekur climbed over into the back with the girls. "Are you seriously considering confronting this god?"

"I know what they can and can't do while here," Seri said. "Or, at least, I know some of it."

"My Lady, we could not even defeat Forerunner," Ixchel pointed out. "How can we defeat one of his masters?"

"We don't necessarily have to defeat him. Just... I don't know. Stop him from bringing all of these people along." She brightened. "All we need to do is expose his true motivations!"

"And how do we do that?" Ekur asked.

"We'll need to get close to him. Maybe pretend to be joining the pilgrimage." Seri pointed at her father. "You could say you've been sent by Lady Lilitu to investigate!"

"Perhaps, but will this god not realize who you are?"

"He won't know me."

"What about the mages?" Ixchel asked.

"The purple one must be Master Korda... or at least I hope it is. The other one.." Seri frowned. "Itri said he had blue robes, so he's a full mage. I can't know whether he was ever at Zes Sivas while I was there." She growled and stamped her foot on the carriage floor. "Why does everything have to be so complicated?"

"Master Korda is the one who sent us on this quest," Ixchel pointed out. "Would he not be an ally now?"

"I would think so, but... he's here. With that god. I don't know what that means."

"He may just be following his Lord," Ekur said.

Seri mused on that. "Could be. I just don't know how he's going to react to us showing up here and now."

"There's only one way to find out."

Seri pulled back from Ekur. "Are you serious? I would think you'd be advising me to stay away."

Ekur shrugged. "You've been among Lords and Masters since you left home. This is where you seem to shine."

Seri smiled. "I've never thought of myself as a diplomat."

"Your father is right," Ixchel said. "You have negotiated with and persuaded many important people since we met."

"All right..." Seri thought for a moment. "Let's see if we can talk to Master Korda first. Maybe he can let us speak with the Lord. The longer we go without confronting the gods the better."

"And now we have a plan." Ekur smiled. "Let's do it."

●●●●●

Seri waited, shifting her weight from one leg to the other. "He should have been back by now," she muttered.

"Give him time," Ixchel said.

"I am giving him time. He should have been back by now." Seri turned and pretended to knock her fist against the carriage. She had never been good at waiting, and now that her father might be in danger...

"It is good that you are concerned for your father. But all he is doing, as a merchant of Arazu, is seeking an audience with one of the leaders of this expedition. There is no danger inherent in this action."

"And yet we're surrounded by danger. You know it, and I know it. I just don't know if he knows it."

"Then you will be pleased to know that he's coming back."

Seri spun back around. In the dim twilight, she saw two figures approaching. The shorter one with the bow on his back was her father. And the other...

"Master Korda!"

The enormous Mandiatan mage came to a halt and his mouth dropped open. "Seri-Belit?" He looked down at Ekur. "This is your daughter? That wanted to meet a Master mage?"

Ekur inclined his head. "She is my daughter, and she did want to meet a Master: you, specifically."

Master Korda chuckled, then turned back to Seri. "You are, perhaps, the last person I expected to meet along this way. What are you doing here?" He glanced around, nodded once to Ixchel, then returned his gaze to Seri. "Have you found… the one you were sent to find?"

"It is a long story," Seri said. "My father's servant has built a fire over here." She gestured toward a glow coming from behind the carriage. "Shall we sit and exchange stories, Master?"

Master Korda regarded her for a moment, then nodded. They made their way to the fire. At their approach, the carriage driver rose, bowed, then moved several yards away to keep watch without overhearing their discussion. Ixchel also stood some distance from the fire, but close enough to listen.

Seri again wondered where to begin, and once again decided to start from the beginning. "From Zes Sivas, we traveled to Varioch," she began, and related the story of her travels. This time, she did not leave anything out, except for personal things, like her growing relationship with Dravid.

When she described Forerunner, Master Korda interrupted several times, pressing her on details about him. "There is one here with us, very similar," he observed. "Though he goes by the name of Harbinger."

"Forerunner hinted that he was not the only one sent to prepare for the gods' return," Seri said. She went on with her story, until she reached the point of meeting Marshal.

Master Korda leaned forward eagerly. "Do you believe it is he?"

"I do." Seri nodded. "He may not have had all of the King's power when we first met, but he does now. There is more to explain." With the Master's approval, she went on, telling of all that happened at the Ch'olan high place.

"And this is why the gods are leading your people to the other high place," she explained. "Because Volraag will try to open it."

Master Korda nodded. "Nummotem has said the other gods would return. I assumed the high place would serve for their arrival. But I did not know of Volraag's involvement."

"It takes a Lord's power to open the portal," Seri said. "He has that now, and more."

"But Nummotem's power equals that of a Lord, at least, though it is very different."

"I don't think his power will work. I think it has to be the magic of Antises. That's why they tried to recruit Marshal at first, then turned to Volraag. That's what Curasir was saying, anyway."

"And this Curasir is the same Eldanim that visited us on Zes Sivas? The killer of two Masters?"

Seri nodded. "He and Volraag are in league. And Volraag has his assassin with him, the one who killed Lord Sundinka, and his own father." She lowered her head. "And Lord Enuru."

"Lord Enuru has fallen as well? This is dire news. Tell me."

Seri skipped over her own travels with Volraag and told only of what had happened that fateful day in the palace.

Master Korda stood and paced in front of the fire. "Then we do not know what has become of the magic of Arazu. This is a great loss."

"If we can't find it, what of the Passing?" Seri asked. "The earth hasn't shaken in a long time, but…"

"But the land needs healing," Mater Korda finished. "If this new King comes to us, that will help, but without the magics of Mandiata and Arazu, I fear it will not be enough."

Seri looked at the fire, how it crackled, but no breeze stirred it. "Lady Lilitu said that Antises has stopped breathing. That we are in the calm before a storm."

"It is possible." Master Korda stared into the darkness. "I have felt this uneasiness lately, beyond my concern over these gods. Something is happening beyond what we can detect."

Something occurred to Seri then. What if she could detect it? Her star-sight gave her insight into many things. Maybe she could find the life of Antises and see what was transpiring.

"Volraag is on his way to the high place," Ekur broke into the silence. "Could he have hidden among this crowd?"

Seri blinked. She hadn't even thought of that.

Master Korda chuckled. "I would think his pale skin would stand out among our people."

"No, he's very good at hiding," Seri said. "And it wouldn't take much. A hooded cloak. Then he and his assassin could travel unnoticed among you all."

"What good would that do him? He can travel faster alone."

Ekur shrugged. "It was just a thought."

Seri thought it was a good one. Volraag would find perverse delight in hiding among the people whose Lord he had murdered. She had been unable to detect his presence the last few days, but these gods were no doubt confusing her senses. Volraag could be only a few feet away and she would not know it.

"We must speak with Lord Bakari," she said. "And explain the true purpose of these gods."

"I do not think that would be effective," Master Korda replied.

"Why not?"

"Lord Bakari has been deep in the counsel of Nummotem and Harbinger, even before I returned to Mandiata. That is why I sent your friend Jamana back to Zes Sivas. It has not been… safe. I have had to feign excitement about the current plan myself."

Seri took a quick intake of breath on hearing about Jamana. Well, at least he was back on Zes Sivas. Even with the earthquakes, it might be one of the safest places to be right now.

"But now you're not alone," she said. "With what I can share, surely he'll listen to reason."

Master Korda cocked his head. "Do you think he will listen to a foreign mage over one of our people's ancestral gods?"

Seri almost blurted out that she was part "god" herself, but resisted the urge. Master Korda made a good point.

"Don't we have to try?" Ekur asked.

No one answered him for a few moments. "I think we should make the attempt," Seri said at last. She looked up at Master Korda. "But if you argue on my side, it could put your position in jeopardy."

"That is true."

"Then I'll have to do it alone." Seri got to her feet. "All I will need from you is an introduction."

"It will take more than that," Korda said. "I will have to get him to meet you without the gods around."

Seri took a deep breath. "I can handle it. Send him."

●●●●●

Seri twisted her hands together, around and around. Master Korda would bring Lord Bakari to meet her at any moment. Why had she agreed to this? Agreed to it? She'd suggested it! What had she been thinking? She had already tried to change one Lord's mind—Volraag—and that had been a spectacular failure.

What could she say to Lord Bakari that could make any difference at all? And why would he listen to her at all?

A few moments earlier, she contacted Lady Lilitu with the stone and updated her on the situation. The Lady agreed with her attempt to persuade Lord Bakari, but warned that he would be difficult to persuade.

"Bakari is not like other Lords," the Lady explained. "He was raised to become a Lord, to receive his father's power when the time came. But instead, his father was murdered and the power stolen. Bakari is a Lord without power: unique in the history of Antises. He is desperate to hold on to what standing he does possess. If he sees anything you say as a threat to his grasp on the Lordship, he may react in a very negative manner."

"But wouldn't he want revenge on Volraag, the man who killed his father?" Seri asked.

"That is likely. But not if it comes at the expense of his current status."

Every time Seri talked with the Lady, she struggled again with her own identity. While traveling with Ekur, she knew him as her real father. Nothing else mattered. But talking with Lady Lilitu, who understood her magic as well as the intrigue of the six lands… it made her feel like she belonged there, in the palace, with someone who understood her. Her real mother.

"They come," Ixchel said. Her voice startled Seri out of her worry. As before, Ixchel waited just outside the circle of firelight. Ekur decided his presence could not help, so he waited by the carriage.

Master Korda entered the firelight, followed closely by Lord Bakari. The young Lord looked barely older than Seri herself. She had only seen Lord Sundinka for a few days during the Passing months ago, but she could see the family resemblance immediately.

Lord Bakari glanced over her, then turned to Master Korda. "Why have you brought me here to talk to another mage?" he demanded. "And a girl, at that! Do we not have enough mages?"

"Your Lordship!" Seri said, a little too loud. "I asked Master Korda for an audience with you. I have news of your enemy Volraag!"

Lord Bakari gave her a longer look. "You are not one of my subjects, nor are you one of his, unless I miss my guess. What can you tell me?"

"I know where he is, what he is doing, and where he is going."

"Explain."

Seri bristled a little. This was hardly the proper protocol of an interview with a Lord. She didn't consider herself on Bakari's level socially, but he should still show her more respect than this. She took a deep breath and calmed herself.

"I have confronted Volraag in Ch'olan and followed him here to Arazu."

"And why would you do this?" Lord Bakari folded his arms over his chest.

"Master Korda tasked me with searching for the lost King of Antises. In my search, I ran into Volraag and discovered his plans."

Lord Bakari tapped his foot. Impatient fool! Seri gritted her teeth and went on.

"As you may know, Volraag started a war with Rasna. This war was over the high place between their lands."

At the words "high place," Bakari's face shifted ever-so-slightly from impatience to interest.

"Volraag opened the portal to the Otherworld there, and then traveled to the high place in Ch'olan, where I met him. He attempted to open that portal as well, but we stopped him."

"I see where this is going," Lord Bakari interrupted. "So he is traveling to the third high place now? Good. We will find him there and capture him ourselves."

"But don't you see?" Seri asked. "He's trying to open the portals!"

"What of it?"

"Aren't you leading these people to the high place because the gods want the portal to open?"

Bakari scowled. "What are you trying to say, girl?"

"These… gods you're following are allied with Volraag!"

"The gods are here to deliver us!"

"This is why Volraag killed your father and stole his power. He needed a Lord's power to open the portals!"

"This is a serious charge," Master Korda broke in. "Perhaps we should consider this, Lord."

Bakari unfolded his arms and paced to his right. "It seems very convenient to me. No, no. We travel all this way and then this girl shows up and tries to tell us we're on the same side as our greatest enemy?"

That was it. Seri unleashed a burst of magic into the fire, scattering sparks and ashes. "I am not just some girl! I am Seri-Belit, mage of Arazu, and you will listen to me!"

"You think the title of mage will convince me? The mages let

Volraag kill my father!"

"Lord, surely—" Master Korda began.

"That is enough from you, Korda!" Bakari pointed without looking at him. "You have been reluctant to embrace the gods all along! As for you, mage of Arazu…" His voice dripped with contempt.

Ixchel stepped into the firelight, hand on her hilt, eyes fixed on Bakari.

"You have not given me one good reason to believe anything you say!" Lord Bakari pointed at Seri. "You may call yourself what you wish, but I have no cause to trust you."

"I am more than just a mage!" Seri pulled in a little more magic, probably all she could find on short notice, and let it flow through her voice. It worked for Forerunner. So why not? "I am the daughter of Lady Lilitu, ruler of the land in which you now stand! I am her mage, and you will listen to me. I have found the lost King of Antises!"

"Oh, really?" A tall figure approached the firelight. Ixchel whirled, starting to pull her sword free. He stepped into view, taller and more strongly-built than Master Korda or any other man Seri had seen outside of Calu. His bright clothes were topped with a strange animal pelt hanging from his shoulders.

Seri swallowed, trying to keep herself from trembling. The power radiating from the newcomer was familiar… and overwhelming.

"Tell me of this King," said Nummotem.

(((35)))

The god loomed enormous in the firelight. Seri looked to Ixchel and shook her head. Swords would be of no use here.

Nummotem got down on one knee, and still could look Seri in the face. "Interesting," he observed, his voice rumbling with power. "You have a star in your eye."

"As do you," Seri said, seeing the glimmer.

"Ha. I do not know you, little mage. I am the inimitable Nummotem. Who do you claim to be, and"—he held up a finger—"what is your bloodline?"

Ekur stepped in behind Seri, bow and arrow at the ready. Again, she gestured for him to back off. Starting a battle of any kind at this point would not end well.

"As I said," Seri began, trying to keep her own voice under control again, "I am Seri, mage of Arazu. I was birthed by the Lady Lilitu. My… father was from your world."

"Indeed. You are not one of mine, obviously." Nummotem ran his fingers over his bearded chin. "Nayana and Ishker have enjoyed dalliances with mortal women in the past. Perhaps you are one of theirs."

Part of Seri wanted to ask for more details. The chance to discover her real father's identity might not come again any time soon. But even as she thought it, she felt Ekur stir behind her. He was her real father. That was all that mattered. Wasn't it?

"So. Tell me of this King."

"What do you want to know?" Seri asked. She needed more time. Time to think. Time to come up with a way out of this situation. Convincing Lord Bakari was a lost cause. Now her only goal had to be

217

getting out of this alive.

"Everything. Who is he? Where is he now?"

"I do not know you." Seri folded her own arms across her chest. "Why should I tell you anything?"

"Are you mad, girl?" Lord Bakari exclaimed.

Nummotem held out a hand to calm him. "It is a fair question. She is not of Mandiata and would not know me." He glanced back at Bakari. "Not that any of you remembered me well."

Bakari actually bowed. Bowed! A Lord of Antises, and he bowed. Seri wanted to smack him.

Nummotem picked up a piece of wood from their pile, waiting for the fire. He held it up before his face. "Everything has a soul, little mage," he said. "Life exists in everything around us, even our very words. And even this piece of a tree you have severed from its source."

"What—"

"Sh, sh, sh." Nummotem held out the wood across both his hands. As they all watched, it trembled. Seri activated her star-sight and looked closer. What magic was he using? She could see something flowing from his hands into the wood. It wasn't the vibratory magic of Antises, but neither was it like the golden magic which Dravid and Forerunner used. Something in between, perhaps?

So intent was she on analyzing the flow of magic, she almost missed it when the wood sprouted. Three pale roots sprang from one end and two narrow branches from the other. Nummotem turned the miniature tree upright and lowered it to the ground. The roots dug hungrily into the dirt. Nummotem released it and held out his hand as if to display his work.

"Devouring fire," Ekur whispered.

Manipulating the life within a plant? How was this done? And if he could do this, could he do it to other things? Animals? People?

"Life exists in all," he repeated. Then he snatched the tiny tree back out of the ground and threw it into the fire. Seri stifled a cry. "And it exists only at my pleasure!" He rose to his feet. "Now you know who I am. And I know who you are. Tell me what I want to know, or you will see another display of my power that you will not enjoy."

Seri glared at him. "You and your other gods will never rule Antises again! Even now, there are plans unfolding in both worlds to stop you!"

Nummotem studied her. Seri could only imagine how ridiculous she looked standing up to the massive figure. "In both worlds, you say?

Thank you. So your King is in the Otherworld. No one else would have the power to travel there."

Seri felt a chill in spite of the fire. She kept her face still, determined not to give anything else away. "I do," she said.

"You?" Nummotem laughed. "You're a child. A mage, perhaps, but the mages of this world are toddlers playing with forces they've never understood." Master Korda stirred at that. "And you are the least of those. You think your bloodline makes you special?"

"No." Seri felt the ground tremble. She wasn't sure whether she had done that or if it came from Master Korda. Lord Bakari glanced around uneasily. "I have told you who I am and what I can do. Whether you believe that or not is your decision." She turned to Bakari. "And I have told you the danger you face with this man. Again, it is your decision to believe or not."

Ixchel stepped up beside Seri, sword and shield at ready. "And my Lady does not lie."

•••••

"You are loved, Marshal. You are valuable. You have a purpose in this world." Aelia's words. Marshal mouthed them with dry lips. She often asked if he believed her when she repeated it. Most of the time, he believed the first one. Aelia always loved him. But the other two? What value and purpose did a Curse Boy have?

Now, as the wagon's jostling sent more pain surging through his body, he held on to the words. Although this time, he had more trouble with the first one. Mama was dead. Who loved him now? His friends cared about him. But could he call that love? Victor. Talinir. Seri.

The Durunim and their masters thought him valuable. Why else keep him around? Seri and her mage friends thought him valuable, because of his power. No one really valued him for himself, though.

As for purpose…

"You do not appear to be dying."

Marshal turned his head. The wagon had stopped, though he hadn't noticed. Murdak stood beside it, crouched down low to peer in at him. Another god stood beside him, an odd one: thinner and less… impressive than the others.

He did feel a little better today. The tiny bit of starlight must have helped. The hallucinations seemed to have mostly faded. And his breathing, while still excruciatingly painful, had stabilized somewhat.

"As long as you survive, that is all that matters to me." Murdak straightened as if he would leave.

"Why?" Marshal managed.

"Why what?"

"Why do you… need me?" Marshal pushed through the pain to speak. Having only recently obtained a voice, he wasn't going to give it up because it hurt.

Murdak crouched down again. "Your power could have served us. You could have been a part of all this. We helped lift your curse for that very purpose. Since you chose to oppose us, I must make an example of you."

Marshal puzzled over that for a moment. How had they helped lift his curse? Oh. The eidolon that had killed Aelia. He assumed it had been Curasir, but it could have been any of these denizens of the Otherworld.

"My curse?" He still wasn't sure what that had to do with anything, though.

"The Laws of Cursings and Bindings were linked to our world, keeping us trapped," Murdak said. "When your curse went away, all of that magic became weakened. Now, for the first time in a thousand years, we can return. And we owe it all to you."

"But… the Laws… aren't gone."

"No, they aren't. But it's only a matter of time. Once we have established ourselves over Antises, we will find a way to remove them, or perhaps turn them to our favor. The basic concept isn't bad, after all. We have enough diverse powers to figure something out, I'm sure."

Marshal wrinkled his brow. Diverse powers? The gods all seemed the same. Or did they? Vayan had that pain thing. Maybe they each had another power, unique to them? He knew vague ideas about the ancient gods, that each one of them represented something, like the sun or harvest.

The strange god bent and reached toward Marshal, his hand crackling with black fire. Murdak grabbed his arm and pulled him back. "No, Ne'gal. I don't know what that would do to him, but it's not time to experiment."

What kind of power did this strange god have? As Marshal looked into his face, he felt a sudden chill. The god's eyes held no warmth, no brightness whatsoever. Despite his golden skin, he seemed as dark and disconnected as the Durunim.

"What's… your power?"

Murdak chuckled. "You've experienced it already." He reached under the wagon and lifted it with one hand. "My power is nothing less than... power itself. I am the strongest of us all. Accepting a challenge against me was perhaps the most foolish thing you could have done."

He let the wagon drop. The impact jarred everything within Marshal. He choked and struggled for breath. He had meant to ask the other god, not Murdak, but the answer was... interesting.

"You will still serve us, though in a different way. Your failures will show all the futility of resisting us. It is the only reason I need you. No other purpose matters, regardless of what Vayan or Curasir may tell you." He laughed and strode away.

Purpose. Yes, Marshal had a purpose. Or rather, other people had purposes for him. Slave? King? Savior? Failure? Would the decision be made for him? Or could he decide his own purpose for himself? He managed to suck in another breath of air. For now, his purpose was to stay alive, even if it served Murdak's plan. Alive, he could still choose.

●●●●●

"You need to get me to him!" Dravid demanded. "I can heal him!"

Talinir sat on the ground and crossed his long legs. Dravid thought he looked ridiculous. Tich picked up her rope and watched the two of them. Her report on Marshal's condition had Dravid ready to head back to the Durunim camp on his own.

"You can't go into the camp, Dravid. You'll be recognized right away."

"I know. That's why you need to hide me, like you did before."

Talinir sighed. "It doesn't work that way."

"Why not? Can we not move while you're hiding us? What?"

"That's part of it. I don't know how to explain this to you." Talinir thought for a moment. "When you want to use your magic, what do you do?"

"I summon the magic and I use it." Dravid paused. "Well, that's the way this new magic works. For the magic of Antises, I would have to find some and absorb it first."

Talinir nodded. "My magic doesn't work that way."

"Why not? Everyone always says the Eldanim are 'beings of pure magic' or something like that."

"There are many things that everyone says that aren't true." Talinir gestured at his face. "Because we are beings of two worlds, we are not understood. It is just the way we were made. We have various abilities, most of which involve shifting between the two worlds." He pointed up. "We are bound to the stars, and they heal us. And sometimes, every so often, they help us. Like when we hid after Marshal's battle."

"But you said it was the Maker of the stars, not the stars themselves," Tich broke in.

Talinir bent his head to one side, then back. "It is... a debatable dissimilarity."

"So your magic is inconsistent and can't be depended on," Dravid said. "That's what you're saying."

"If that is how it appears to you, then that is as good an explanation as any."

Dravid threw up his hands. "But we need to help Marshal!"

"I agree. I just don't know how yet. I need to think." The Eldani warden unfolded himself and stood. He moved about a dozen yards away to look toward the army.

Dravid leaned back against the rock. He noticed Tich watching him. "What?"

"Can you really heal him?"

"I think so. I've used this power to heal before. In fact, it was him." Dravid chuckled without meaning to. Healing Marshal had created the Bond, which is why Marshal had come to rescue him now. But here they were, back in the same situation.

"Your power is kind of like those god people, right?"

"I absorbed it from one of them, yes."

"So one of them could heal him if they wanted to. And they're not." She scowled. "Hailstones of fire. None of them deserve to be called a god."

Dravid couldn't argue with that. He scratched at the back of his hand. He had a scar there. Looked like a burn, but he couldn't remember where it came from. A chill swept over him. If he couldn't remember... Vayan had probably taken that memory. And hadn't restored it when he gave back the others. How many other memories was he missing?

"What else can you do?"

"Excuse me?"

Tich waved a circle in the air. "You can make that gold kind-of-see-through stuff, and you can heal people. Anything else?"

Dravid frowned. "That isn't enough?"

"I dunno." Tich shrugged. "Just wondering."

Dravid thought for a moment. "I wonder." He concentrated and summoned the magic. As always, heat rose up inside, but he was getting more used to that now. He tried focusing the power through all of his fingers, drawing threads of gold in the air. He crossed one hand over the other, attempting to weave the threads together. He succeeded in making a big mess.

He dismissed the power, then summoned it again. He tried again, attempting a weave. This kind of detailed work was much harder than it appeared, very different from the simple shapes he had created so far. Once again, the result was a chaotic tangle.

Every time he dismissed the power, it took a few moments for the construct to fade, and then summoning it again took a little longer. He forced himself to remain calm. Taking his time was the only way this might work.

"What are you doing?" Tich asked.

"I'm trying something." Dravid's fingers got tangled and he grunted. And tried again.

"I can see that. But what is it?"

"I'll tell you if I make it work."

"You could just tell me now, so I'll stop bothering you."

"Ugh. I'm trying to do what Vayan did." Dravid shook his hands. Why was this so hard?

"Why would you want to do that? Didn't he absorb pain or something?"

"And take memories too."

"And you want to do that?"

Dravid's tore apart his latest attempt and let it dissipate. "It's not... I just want to test my limits."

"Test away."

"I'm trying!" Dravid pushed away his irritation and kept working on his idea. After another dozen or more tries, he managed to make a lattice, but it was too stiff to fit over someone's head. He groaned and started over, trying to regulate the rigidity of his constructs, something he had never attempted before.

After another half hour of experimenting, he managed to make strands that could bend. Then he had to start all over on making the lattice. Talinir returned and watched him for a while, then left to go find more water.

Eventually, he created a flexible lattice he thought looked similar enough to what Vayan had made. He looked it over one more time, then turned to Tich. "Come help me test this."

"What?"

"Let me test this on you."

"You want me to let you try to mess with my head?"

Dravid rolled his eyes. "I can't do it to myself, and Talinir is… well, he's not human."

Tich approached and examined his work. She shrugged. "Well, it can't make me any crazier than I already am. Go for it."

Dravid placed the lattice over her head, then hesitated. What had Vayan done next? He kept his fingers contacting the magic. "Tell me a story. Something painful, but not much."

"And if I tell you, you steal my memory of it?"

"If it actually works, then I can give it back, like Vayan gave mine back."

"Right."

Dravid waited a moment. "Come on. Just a small story."

"I stubbed my toe on that rock over there."

Dravid rolled his eyes. He was already having difficulty holding on to the construct, since it had taken so long to make it. "A little longer than that, please."

"Did I ever mention how my mother died when I was four years old? She caught the plague from a book in the library. That's when my father told me never to go there again. I didn't listen, of course."

"You said your parents were… wild mages." Dravid wrinkled his brow. He couldn't feel anything happening through the magic.

"I did? Oh, I suppose that's true. Obviously, they weren't healers, or she wouldn't have died."

The heat and pressure build-up grew too much. Dravid sighed and let the lattice dissipate. He sat back down. "Was any of that actually true?"

"No, not really. But I'm not giving you a true story. Those are rare."

"Not for a normal person, they're not!"

"I never claimed to be normal."

Dravid rubbed his face with his hands. Either the magic knew she was lying, or he had done something wrong, or… he didn't have that kind of power.

"What good would it have done if you could do that?" Tich asked. "You never explained that."

"I don't know. I just… I need to do something to help Marshal. My powers aren't doing what I need them to do."

Tich cocked her head. "You can make just about any shape you want with that stuff, huh?"

"If I work at it." Dravid let his head fall back against a rock. All the frustration had worn him out.

"Why not make yourself a new leg?"

(((36)))

"Now." Nummotem loomed over Seri. "I've been patient long enough. You—"

An arrow slammed into Nummotem's left shoulder. He jerked, but did not fall. Seri whirled to see her father fitting another arrow to his string. "Seri. Run."

"I agree," Ixchel said, backing up.

Nummotem slammed his foot against the ground. Roots exploded from the earth around it and began writhing toward all three of them, twisting and squirming like a bundle of serpents. Ixchel slashed through one of them, but they kept coming.

"Mortals. You always think you can stand against the power of a god. So foolish." Nummotem lifted his hand and rotated it. The writhing roots duplicated his movement and rose up into the air.

"No." Arms encircled Nummotem from behind and lifted him off the ground. "After all, we're just toddlers."

With her star-sight still on, Seri could see when Master Korda used his power. Ribbons of many colors erupted from his arms and circled back into Nummotem's chest. She heard bones shattering before the god screamed.

"Run!" Ekur shouted again. This time, she obeyed.

Seri glanced once over her shoulder, wondering about Master Korda, but she saw only a bright golden light. Whatever magic Nummotem was using overwhelmed her star-sight. She turned back, blinking. Ekur ran beside her, Ixchel behind.

A yell echoed behind them. A yell of pain or a yell of triumph? Seri couldn't even tell who was yelling. She stumbled and kept running. Voices came from every direction as people reacted to the yell. She spread her hands and absorbed every beam of magic she could find as they ran.

"Which way are we going?" Seri gasped.

"Away from him," Ekur said.

"I don't know if we—"

"Roots," Ixchel interrupted.

Roots? Seri barely had time to process the word before something grabbed her ankle. She came to an abrupt stop and fell face-first into the dirt.

"Owww." She spat dirt and tried to get up. Whatever grabbed her ankle wouldn't let go.

Ekur spun back to her side and whipped out his narrow-bladed axe. He hacked down by her foot. Seri managed to roll over and see the tree roots wrapped around her ankle. Nummotem was many yards behind them, and could still control plant life. How far did his power extend?

Ixchel grabbed her arm and yanked her to her feet as the clutching root came free. Ekur slashed down at another one that kept moving toward them. Seri snatched the purple beam of light that erupted from the ground near it.

"This is disturbing," Ixchel muttered. Seri knew what she meant. Fighting enemy warriors was one thing. Fighting tree roots, though? At least they weren't deep in a forest. They could get away from the trees here... but that meant running into the open where they would be seen...

"Keep moving!" Ekur urged. They scrambled away from the nearest trees.

"Look up!" Ixchel's yell jerked Seri's head up. A golden glow arced into the air from behind them and came down in their direction. Nummotem? Leaping or flying? Seri tried to run faster, but her robes had not been designed for this.

Nummotem landed only a few feet behind them. The impact rattled the ground at their feet and Seri nearly lost her footing again.

"We cannot flee," Ixchel said. She faced Nummotem, sword and shield at the ready. Ekur stepped up beside her, pulling an arrow back.

"But we can't beat him," Seri whispered. In that moment, she knew what she had to do.

Nummotem spread his arms. His shoulder showed no sign of the arrow injury. "What is this? You cannot run from a god."

Seri stepped in between her protectors, gently pushing them to the sides. Had she absorbed enough magic? It would have to be enough.

She had bragged she could do this, after all. Behind Nummotem, a crowd of curious onlookers gathered. Murmurs filled the air.

"You laughed at my claim a moment ago," she said. "Do you wish proof now?"

Nummotem eyed her. A golden glow radiated from his body, providing illumination all around them. "This should be amusing. What did you have in mind, little mage?"

Seri took a deep breath and lowered her head. She had done this on her own only once, in a moment of desperation on Zes Sivas. "Life is everywhere, you say?" She closed her eyes and concentrated, reaching out with her magical senses. Yes. Yes, it was true. Thanks to Nummotem, life was everywhere, awakening, listening to his commands. She felt the life of the grass, the trees, the nearby wheat field.

But she reached beyond it, knowing she could find what she looked for. And then she did. The life of Antises itself. It felt much… smaller than it did on Zes Sivas, but she found it. Without Nummotem's life-enhancing power, she probably wouldn't have reached it. She smiled.

"I'm waiting," Nummotem said. "Where is this proof?"

Seri's eyes snapped open. She gathered up all the magic she had absorbed and forced it between the life of Antises. As before, a scream struck her ears, though she couldn't be sure of its source. She pulled the magic apart. "Stand closer!" she cried, hoping Ixchel and Ekur understood. She wrapped the magic around all three of them.

"What's happening?" Ekur shouted.

Purple fire and darkness enveloped them. Seri yanked it the rest of the way and released the magic.

She blinked and looked up into a sky filled with enormous, beautiful stars.

"Where are we?" Ekur gasped.

"Father, Ixchel… welcome to the Otherworld," Seri answered. She looked around and breathed a sigh of relief. No sign of Nummotem. She didn't think he could make that trip on his own. Otherwise, why wouldn't the gods have always been going back and forth with their world?

She stumbled as a wave of fatigue swept over her. Ixchel caught her arm, but she waved and pulled loose. She found a fallen tree trunk and sat down. "Sorry. That took a lot out of me."

"What did? What have you done?" Ekur stared first at the incredible sky, then at the battered and broken landscape around them.

"Seri has transported us to the Otherworld," Ixchel said. "It is a place of magic, inhabited by the Eldanim, and also the so-called gods."

"They're from here? Why would we run here?"

"Nummotem and the others can't travel freely from world to world," Seri said in a faint voice. "That's why they need Volraag to open the portal."

Ekur continued to stare, turning slowly in all directions. "I didn't think... I never knew..."

Ixchel scampered on top of a rock outcropping for a better view. She kept her sword and shield at ready.

"We can't stay here very long." Seri lifted her head enough to get another look at the stars. "If we use too much magic, it will attract monsters."

She said this more to remind herself. The temptation to stay and look for Dravid was so compelling. But of course, she had no way to find him, and the Otherworld was... well, it was an entire world.

"How do we... can you get us back?" Ekur asked.

"Yes," Seri said with more confidence than she felt. "But I need some time to recover. And we'll need to move away from here so we don't go back to the same place."

Ixchel looked down. "So our location here corresponds to the locations in our world?"

Seri nodded.

Ixchel returned to looking around. "Being able to come and go from here would provide immense tactical advantages."

Seri couldn't help but chuckle. Of course Ixchel would think that way. She looked up at Ekur. "Father, you may as well find a place to sit down. There's not much to do for now."

Ekur tore his eyes away from the stars and looked at Seri. "Are you all right, my child? You said this took a lot out of you..."

Seri smiled. "I'll be fine. I just need to rest." She patted the trunk beside her. "Sit down. Let's watch the stars."

Ekur set his bow aside and joined her.

"I see no signs of any threats at present," Ixchel announced.

"The stars are... amazing," Ekur said. "I wish your mother were here to see them."

"So do I," Seri admitted. "So do I."

●●●●●

"What did you say?" Dravid took his hands away from his face.

"I knew a sailor in Rasna whose leg got bit off by a shark," Tich answered. "The ship's carpenter made him a wooden leg. Kind of a peg-thing. He stomps around just fine. So why not use your magic to make yourself one of those?"

"I don't... I..." Dravid considered, then shook his head. "No, it wouldn't work. I can't maintain a construct for more than a few minutes."

"How long?"

"It depends."

"On what?"

Dravid glared at Tich. Except she was right. He sighed and looked down. She was asking questions about his powers that he should have been asking all along.

"I thought it was based on the size of the construct, but the armor I made for Marshal was probably the largest I've made. And I kept it solid for around fifteen or twenty minutes. That might be the longest I've done it."

"So." Tich took a step back and glanced toward the army. "We get you near the army, you make yourself a leg, we walk to Marshal's cage, you let the leg thing go, heal Marshal, then make yourself another leg, and we walk out."

Dravid rubbed his face again. He still felt dry and parched from all his experimenting. "That... might work. But I'll need at least a day to practice."

Tich shrugged. "It's only Marshal. King of all Antises. He can wait another day."

Dravid scowled. "It was my idea to heal him!"

"And it's a good idea."

"Then why are you trying to make me feel guilty?"

"It's one of the only things I'm good at." Tich toyed with the end of her rope. "I just... I want to be useful here. You know?"

Dravid knew. For months, he had felt useless following Seri around. He became a slave to save her life, so it hadn't been useless. But now... he was back to being the cripple someone had to help get around. Tich's suggestion made sense. And it might help him not feel so useless any more. Of course, that depended on if he could actually do it. And if Talinir would let them.

Once Talinir returned, Dravid took a long drink of the water he brought back, then explained the concept to the warden. He did not appear impressed.

"You'll have to prove you can even make the leg before we can consider this."

"I know," Dravid said. "I'll work on it during our next stop."

Talinir glanced away. "The army is moving. We should get going as well."

Dravid reluctantly climbed on to Talinir's back again and the three of them set off. While he rode, Dravid considered the ideas. A strong part of him urged caution, not to get his hopes up. But another part couldn't help explore the possibilities. If he could fashion a new leg, and it worked... then maybe, just maybe he could learn how to maintain it for longer. An entire day? Someday?

Talinir shifted beneath him. He looked toward the army, its dust cloud just visible in the strange starlight.

"We're coming, Marshal. I'm coming."

(((37)))

Seri ran her fingers through the dirt. The brief trip to the Otherworld and back had exhausted her, but she felt unsettled. Something was wrong. Something important felt just out of reach. Like she had almost discovered… something important.

Ixchel's shadow fell across her, lengthened by the early morning sun. "The caravan has moved on," she said. "We should be safe from the ones leading it, at least for now."

Ekur got up and stretched. Seri watched her two companions, feeling disconnected, like she didn't even belong here. Surreal.

"What will we do now?" Ekur wondered. "Do we follow the caravan? Or… what?"

"We should be able to move faster than them," Ixchel said. "We can go around and still reach the portal before they do. They are traveling quite slow."

"As long as it's a wide circuit around them. I don't want to get anywhere close to that… god. Or whatever he was."

"Agreed." Ixchel set her shield down and knelt next to it. "Do you agree, my Lady?"

Seri fingered the dirt of Antises. When she traveled, what did she actually do?

"My Lady?"

Master Hain taught her in using magic with living things. He told her to find the gaps between the life and force the magic between it. In her first visit to the Otherworld, she had done something similar by desperate instinct. And now she had repeated it.

"Seri?" Ekur also leaned in to look at her.

"It shouldn't work," she said aloud.

"But it should," Ixchel countered. "We are but three, on foot and not slowed by small children and—"

"Not that."

The other two waited, watching her. Seri barely recognized that she had confused them. Something was more important. She needed to articulate it.

"I took us to the Otherworld and back."

"Yes," Ekur agreed. "It was quite the experience, though I can't say I'd like to repeat it."

"I shouldn't be able to do that. It doesn't make sense."

"Yet you have done it. More than once." Ixchel's matter-of-fact response annoyed her for some reason. She pushed the feeling aside and kept trying to track down the elusive mystery.

"I used magic. I forced magic in between…" In between what? "The life of Antises."

"Antises is alive?"

"Yes. No." Seri frowned. Surely the land had life. But not of itself. The life of Antises was its people, its animals, its plants. Wasn't it?

"If you are opening a path from one world to another," Ixchel said, "and you are using magic in between them, then is it not simply between the two worlds?"

"But there's nothing between the worlds." Even as she said it, Seri felt it couldn't quite be true.

Ekur looked at Ixchel. "When we went through, both times, I saw this world and then that one, with all the stars."

"But…"

He hesitated. "But there was a moment, less than a second maybe, when we weren't in either world. Or so it seemed to me."

"Purple," Ixchel said. "I saw purple. My Lady, you've spoken often about the importance of colors in your magic. Is the purple what you are referring to?"

"Purple. Yes." The Masters wore purple robes. And that color range —magenta and the various shades of purple—represented the most powerful magic. And the weakest. It still confused her, especially since her instructor in that arena had been Curasir, not someone she could trust. How much of what he had taught her had been true, and how much of it had been his way of toying with the little girl mage?

She missed Master Hain. Even Master Korda would be helpful right now. Or Jamana. Or Dravid. Where was he right now? Still enslaved in the Otherworld? Maybe she should have stayed there and searched for him.

She shook her head. Not the point, Seri! Focus! Between the worlds. Why did two worlds even exist? Maybe there were more than two. But not like these two. After all, the Eldanim belonged to both worlds. They could see in both at the same time.

"The worlds are bound together," she said aloud. Yes. Connected in some way that made them essential to each other. Curasir told Marshal the binding of magic to Antises had stripped it from the Otherworld. "That can't be right."

"They're not bound?" Ekur asked.

"No, I found magic in the Otherworld. That's how we came back here." Or had she? Now that she thought about it, she couldn't remember finding any magic there. But she had enough to get back home. How? She didn't have that much stored up. Yet even as she thought it, she realized she felt full of magic even now.

"I absorbed magic when we crossed over," she said. She lifted her head and looked at the other two. "There's magic between the worlds. That's what binds them together."

"Like our Bindings?" Ixchel asked.

Seri gasped. She scrambled to her feet. "Of course. Where else did the original Masters and Lords get the inspiration for the Laws of Bindings? They were learning from the Binding between the worlds! And they... they..." She wrinkled her brow. Something still didn't add up. Curasir said the Otherworld was the source of Antises' magic. And while she didn't trust him, she couldn't deny what she had seen there at Zes Sivas. The maelstrom of power. What did it all mean?

"I need to try something." She closed her eyes and reached out for the magic.

"What should we do, my Lady?"

Ugh. Interruptions. "Just... just wait here, both of you. I'll be back soon."

"Back? Where are you going?" Ekur's voice rose.

"Close. Very close. If I'm right."

Seri embraced the magic, pulling everything within herself upward. She reached out and began to push, but this time she limited the force of her probing. Nothing happened. Scowling, she pushed harder. In her mind, she saw an opening appearing, a portal back to the Otherworld. No. Too much. She released the power and the opening closed. She pushed again, trying to find the balance between too little and too much.

Purple. The magic needed to be purple. Her hands shook. Yes. They needed to. More. Her arms shook too.

"My Lady?"

Seri crossed her arms, then pushed out to either side, palms outward. She opened her eyes and saw purple. Flames of purple. She stepped into them.

Pain enveloped her body and she screamed. Flames encompassed every inch of her body, flames that did not consume her, but burned all the same. It had been her screams, every time! Yet she never experienced pain, not like this! In that instant, her mind disconnected from her body; it was the only way to survive the unbearable pain. Maybe that had saved her in the previous trips. She just didn't remember the pain.

"I need to remember," she told herself. "I need to know what's going on here."

In that moment, she felt Antises. All of Antises. She floated within the magic that bound it together, that bound it to the Otherworld and maybe more. And something was terribly wrong. Antises was in pain. The magic, the power that held it together was unraveling, just as she had seen at Zes Sivas. Unraveling. Coming apart.

And yet... She could see that it could be fixed. Something was missing here. Her vision seemed to extend for immense distances, though she couldn't see any way to measure anything here. And there... something was missing. A gap within the purple flames. A place where something else belonged. And that gap was the source of the problem. The source of all the problems.

"Oh, this is interesting."

"Lady Lilitu?" How? She hadn't activated the stone.

"You're floating in fire, daughter. The stone activated on its own."

"Can you... see what I see too?"

"No, my dear. But I can sense what you're experiencing. I told you Antises was on the verge of coming apart. Doesn't it look that way here?"

The purple flames frayed at the edges. The magic could not hold long. Soon, very soon, it would fail. What did that mean for Antises? Or the Otherworld? Would they be torn apart? Could one exist without the other? What would happen to the Eldanim?

"Fools," Lady Lilitu murmured. "Always blind to the side effects of their meddling."

Seri's mind could not maintain the disconnect any longer. She felt her body again, and felt the burning, the pain, the devastating, all-encompassing pain.

"Seri? What is happening? Seri!"

She screamed, her vocal cords igniting as the flames spread within her, burning her from the inside as well as the outside. Agony unimaginable.

She fell to the ground. Purple swallowed up by blackness. Then nothing.

•••••

Dravid focused the magic into the shape he wanted, trying to match his good leg. He had considered making it just a peg, like the sailor Tich mentioned, but since he had the ability, why not an entire foot? He couldn't make an ankle joint, of course, but a foot-sized base would still provide better balance.

He shaped three legs before he satisfied himself with the work. He held up the finished result.

"How will you attach it?" Tich asked.

Dravid blinked. He hadn't thought about that. He placed the magic construct next to his stump. "How did the sailor attach his peg leg?"

Tich shrugged. "Straps of some kind, I think."

Dravid considered. He could make straps, sort of. He had done it with Marshal's breastplate, but that had wrapped around his back. Easy. How could he do it with his leg? He placed the construct into position, then began shaping the golden magic upward, wrapping it around his stump. Would it be enough? He continued all the way up to mid-thigh to be sure. He squeezed it together against his skin right up to the point of being painful.

He held a hand out to Tich. "Help me up?"

She grabbed his hand and pulled. Dravid rose up... on two feet. For the first time in months. Tich released his hand and he stood. Alone. Unaided. The emotion of the moment flowed over him. He could stand. He swallowed hard against the lump in his throat, complicated by the already-rising heat within from maintaining the magic.

"Are you going to walk or just stand there?"

Dravid snorted, then hesitated. Should he step forward with his good leg or the construct one? Putting all his weight on the construct right away would be a good test, but... Argh. Make a decision! He lifted the construct leg and moved it forward a few inches. He shifted his weight and took a quick step with his good leg.

The pressure against his stump felt beyond strange. But the construct held. He took another pair of halting steps.

"There you go!" Tich exclaimed. Talinir nodded his approval.

He moved the construct leg forward again. It struck against a rock and promptly threw him off balance. He wavered, threw his arms out for stability, but lost it. He toppled forward. He would have landed face-first in the dirt if Talinir had not caught him.

He released the magic and the construct leg evaporated. Dravid watched it go and sighed.

"That was a good start," Talinir told him, helping him get seated again.

Dravid nodded. "It worked. But only on a perfectly flat surface. I don't know how I'll be able to walk across this." He spread his hand to indicate the rocky surface of the Otherworld.

"It's a start," Talinir repeated. "When you first learned to walk as a child, did you run across uneven surfaces without trouble?"

"Did you walk just fine your first time at sea?" Tich added.

"I suppose not." Dravid's real concern was maintaining the construct. It had taken him a good ten minutes to create the leg, leaving only a few short moments to try it out. He could get faster in making it, as he had with Marshal's armor, but the short time frame in which to use the leg might make the whole rescue mission implausible.

"Let's get some sleep," Talinir said. "The army will move out early again tomorrow, and we'll need to be ready."

Dravid and Tich agreed and found appropriate sleeping places.

"What's going on in our world, Tallman?" Tich asked with a yawn.

Talinir stood watching for a moment. "We're in Arazu now," he said. "Beyond that, I can't tell much. Farms. Crops. I can't tell how close we are to the portal, but it can't be too much further."

"Just wanted to make sure it was still there." Tich rolled over and faced the other direction.

Dravid waited until Talinir had settled in. Then he reached out in front of his face and concentrated. He formed a ball of magic the size of his fist and set it on the ground. He watched it, feeling the usual heat and dryness build up inside. How long could he keep it? He resolved to practice until he could not stay awake. He had to get better.

•••••

Even though he rode on Talinir's back for most of the day, Dravid felt exhausted the next evening. He spent much of the ride the same way he had spent the previous evening: creating small constructs and seeing how long he could maintain them. Each time, he tried to push it further. Yet he never got much longer than fifteen minutes.

"If we don't rescue Marshal, can we even get back to our world?" Tich asked.

Dravid looked up. He had dozed off. "Where's Talinir?"

"He went to scout the army again. So can we?"

"Can we what?"

"Get back to our world without Marshal."

"I don't know. If the portal is opened, we could go through it, but this whole army might be in our way." Dravid scratched the scar on the back of his hand. "I think Talinir can travel between the worlds, but I don't know if he can take anyone with him."

Tich nodded. "Makes rescuing Marshal kind of important, doesn't it?"

"Yeah." Dravid looked away. He hadn't even thought of that aspect, but he couldn't deny it. They had to rescue Marshal. His abilities might be the only thing that could help, but he couldn't make them work the way he needed.

With a whisper of sound, Talinir appeared beside them. "Things are changing," he announced.

"What do you mean?" Tich asked.

"When the army stopped for the night, the gods held a meeting." Talinir bent and sketched a rough outline of the Durunim camp layout in the dirt. "They all gathered here, toward the front of the camp, along with most of the army itself."

"What about Marshal?"

Talinir stabbed his finger down in the middle of the camp. "He's here. While the gods and their followers are meeting, the slaves are left to set up all of their tents and such. Only a handful of Durunim wander the rest of the camp to keep an eye on things." He glanced over his shoulder. "I was able to get within a dozen yards of Marshal. There are two Durunim stationed beside his cage."

"We can take them," Tich said with confidence.

"Perhaps. But then we'd need to carry Marshal out." Talinir looked to Dravid. "I think your healing power will still be needed here."

Dravid looked at the dirt sketch. "You think they'll have another one of these meetings?"

Talinir nodded. "We are getting very close to the portal. I think they're making their final plans. We'll stay closer tomorrow evening and watch. If they do meet again, then it's our chance. We need to take this opportunity while it's available."

"I'll be ready," Dravid said, though he didn't believe it.

"With this change, you won't need to walk in," Talinir pointed out. "I'll get you most of the way. Then while I handle the guards, with Tich's help, you get to Marshal and heal him enough to free himself."

Dravid considered. He would still have to move fast when the others went after the guards. And the construct leg took a lot out of him when he might need it for healing. He grasped his staff. "I'll do what needs to be done."

Talinir gave a short nod. "Good man. Let's get some rest. One day from now, we're getting Marshal out of there."

(((38)))

Three days with the trickle of starlight made Marshal feel significantly better. He still ached everywhere, and that broken rib threatened more damage with every movement. But at least the shortness of breath and tightness in his chest had faded. It still hurt to breathe, but he could bear it. Somewhere during his times of incoherence, he had urinated on himself. Multiple times, maybe. The smell added to the general discomfort.

He pushed himself over to his side again, something he had only been able to accomplish during the past day. A Durunim guard stood not far away. Another waited on the other side of his cage. Just like the previous evening. Something was happening, but they weren't leaving him alone.

Marshal let himself lay back and reached up to the dark wood ceiling of his cage. He thought he knew now. And maybe it would work.

In their time together, Seri had tried to teach him about his magic. He knew, of course, that vibration was the foundation. But Seri's Master told her everything vibrates in its own way, at its own speed. The mages of the past studied the vibrations of different things, and that led them to more control.

For three days, while his body slowly healed, Marshal had studied the ceiling. He put his hands on it and felt its roughness, its imperfections, its... life. Seri told him wooden objects, though no longer part of a tree, still held some life within them. The ceiling held a tiny spark, though it couldn't be much, probably because of its age. Yet he felt it. And the more he studied it, the more he understood it. He even began to sense its own vibration.

So caught up was he in the study, he almost didn't hear the footsteps approaching. He looked to the side and froze.

That strange god, Ne'gal, stood beside the cage, alone.

"What do you want?" Marshal asked. Murdak had stopped this one from touching him before. Yet now he stood here without Murdak. This could not be good.

Ne'gal did not answer. His lifeless eyes focused on Marshal's scarred face. He looked morose, his mouth downturned in a perpetual frown. Such a bizarre expression for one of the gods. His pale hair was long, tied back at his neck. He wore dull robes, also different from any of the other gods. In his left hand, he held a mace topped with the head of some kind of feline predator. His right hand... his right hand crackled with black fire, as it had before.

Without a word, he lifted the hand and reached toward Marshal.

"I don't think so." Marshal shoved toward the god, unleashing his power. Ne'gal somersaulted backward, thrown back several dozen yards. The Durunim guard stepped toward Marshal.

He placed both hands on the ceiling. Blasting Ne'gal had wracked his broken body with pain, nearly knocking him unconscious. If he used his power that way again, he would be out and unable to defend himself. He needed a less violent way to escape.

Where was that vibration? There. He coaxed the wood's vibration toward him, then focused on it. If he could... only... He closed his eyes just in time. The wood ceiling fell apart, collapsing into dust.

Marshal coughed. Despite the danger and his pain, he felt elation. He had done it! He found the vibrational frequency of an object and controlled it!

Pushing against the agony, he sat up for the first time in over a week. His body screamed in protest, and some of it may have escaped his lips.

One of the Durunim guards stepped up, looking down at him, sword at ready. Marshal hesitated. He might be able to stay conscious with one more blast, but he had at least three opponents here.

Talinir appeared out of nowhere, right behind the guard. His warpsteel blade stabbed up through the guard's chest. He fell without a sound.

Ne'gal stood up and walked without hurry toward Talinir. The Eldani warden dropped into a defensive stance, waiting for him.

The second guard rushed around the cage, only to trip and sprawl into the dirt. Tich stepped into Marshal's vision, holding the other end of the rope wrapped around the guard's ankle. She waved at him, then grabbed the rope before it was yanked out of her hands. The guard jumped back to his feet, dragging her forward, still off-balance.

Ne'gal stretched his hand out toward Talinir, who swung his sword from the god toward the Durunim, seeing the armed guard as the greater threat. He was wrong.

Marshal reached out and blasted the stumbling guard just enough to throw him into Ne'gal. The strange god caught the Durunim and immediately dropped him.

But the Durunim guard twitched and lay still. His sword rolled out of his hand. His eyes stared upward at the stars. Dead? At a single touch from Ne'gal?

Marshal wavered and almost passed out. A hand reached through the side bars and steadied him. "Let me heal you," Dravid said. "Where should I focus?"

Marshal sighed in relief. He relaxed and gestured. "Chest. Ribs."

Dravid's brow wrinkled. "All right. I'm not entirely sure how this will work, but…" He placed his hand in the middle of Marshal's chest.

Marshal tried to keep an eye on what was happening with the others. "Don't let him touch you!" he called in a weak voice.

As before, a glow spread from Dravid's hand, enveloping his chest. Warmth spread throughout his body. The glow increased, brighter and brighter. "This'll attract too much attention," Dravid muttered, but kept pouring the golden magic into Marshal's chest. He felt a snap inside, but no pain. He gasped and took in a deep breath, both without difficulty. Dravid pulled his hand away as the light faded. He slumped back against his staff.

Marshal climbed to his feet. When Dravid had healed him the last time, he had been near death, yet sprang up full of energy and life. This time, he felt rejuvenated, but some aches and pains lingered in other parts of his body.

Tich had retrieved her rope and stood beside Talinir, facing off with Ne'gal. The death god, or whatever he was, had not made a sound through the entire encounter. He stood before them, hand rippling with that black fire, dead eyes watching them without emotion.

"Cut his hand off," Tich suggested.

"This has been a bigger disruption than we intended," Talinir said. "We need to get out of here, quickly."

"Fine by me," Marshal said. He jumped out of the remains of the cage, landing next to Tich. He waved at Ne'gal and blasted him back again. This time, his power use caused no pain. He smiled.

"Come on!" Talinir took two steps, bent over and lifted Dravid, then led the way out of the camp. Marshal and Tich ran after him as fast as they could.

"Are you all right with this?" Tich asked, glancing at him.

"I feel great!" Marshal answered. And he did. Though pains lingered, Dravid had healed what incapacitated him. Running, though he hadn't done it in a week or more, felt fantastic.

Behind them, a clamor arose. Pursuit would be swift. They would not escape the enemy that easily.

•••••

The dry, uneven surface of the Otherworld erupted in tiny dust clouds with every step they took. Dravid, from his position on Talinir's back, watched behind them.

A small band of Durunim warriors had gathered at the ruined cage, then set out in pursuit. Their long legs were the equal of Talinir, and faster than Marshal and Tich. They would catch up in a short time. He pointed this out to Talinir.

"Let me know when they're almost here," Talinir said. "We turn and fight then. But for now, we put distance between us and the camp."

Dravid watched the enemy warriors draw nearer and nearer. He counted five of them in this grouping. During his time as a slave, he tried to avoid the Durunim as much as possible. Their light-absorbing skin was only the beginning of their strangeness. To his knowledge, he had never heard one of them speak. He saw them forcing slaves to work, slapping them around sometimes, but never yelling or giving orders. Only the gods did that.

When the Durunim were close enough, he alerted Talinir. In one smooth motion, the warden lowered him to the ground, drew his warpsteel sword, and pivoted to face the pursuers.

Marshal turned to help also, but even before he could lift his hands, Talinir struck. The warden spun under the first Durunim's clumsy attack, deflected its sword arm upward, and stabbed it through the chest. Keeping the body between him and the other four, he yanked his sword free, then darted back a few steps.

With Talinir clear, Marshal unleashed his power, blasting the remaining Durunim off their feet. Dravid winced at what sounded like bones breaking. With pursuit already underway, Marshal apparently saw no reason to hold back on his power.

"Keep moving!" Talinir ordered. When he swung back around to run, Dravid could watch their pursuit again. Another small group of Durunim raced after them, but it would take them much longer to overtake the escapees.

Then he spotted another dust cloud leaving the army and coming in their direction. It was moving very fast and somewhat erratic. Only one chariot driver he knew drove like that.

"We're about to have a lot more trouble, Talinir."

"What is it?"

"Vayan."

"Do we turn and fight?" Marshal asked.

"Keep running! We'll fight when they get here, but we must get as far from the camp as possible!"

A few moments passed as they all tried to keep their balance on the uneven terrain, moving as fast as their legs would carry them.

"Wait! Stop!" Marshal stopped running. Tich, who was trailing him, stopped as well. Talinir had to turn around and come back.

"I can get us home right now." Marshal held out his hand. "Give me your sword, Talinir."

"Too late!" Dravid cried.

Vayan's chariot, carrying two people, rushed toward them. Marshal turned and unleashed a blast of power, but the chariot swerved out of the way. The next instant, Vayan released the creature that pulled his chariot. The chariot itself rolled on for a few seconds. The wheels dissolved and it became a platform shooting across the ground. The platform dissolved also, leaving Vayan and Dursa, the goddess who often visited his tent, standing alone.

"Eldani!" Vayan shouted. The horse-like creature lunged forward at Talinir. He dropped Dravid, but couldn't get to his sword in time. The creature slammed into him, throwing him back.

"This is madness!" Marshal stepped toward them. "You're not Murdak. You can't defeat me."

"I never planned to, your majesty," Vayan responded with a short bow. "My companion, on the other hand…"

The goddess, wearing perhaps even less clothing than the last time Dravid had seen her, stepped forward. He averted his eyes. "Marshal, don't look at her!"

"Why shouldn't he?" Dursa asked. "Doesn't a king know his own mind?"

"I… I'm not afraid of you," Marshal said.

"You shouldn't be, King of Scars." Dursa moved toward him. Without even looking at her, Dravid could imagine her suggestive movements. He swallowed hard. How to free Marshal from this?

"Come, Dravid," Vayan said. "Return to my service. We have so much to discuss together." His former master walked toward him, looking as unconcerned and flamboyant as ever.

Dursa reached out and touched Marshal's scarred face. "And you can come with me, your majesty. Murdak need not take you now. You can stay in my tent, where we can work to unite our peoples."

Dravid summoned his magic and formed a shield. He spared a glance for Talinir. The warden seized the creature by its horns and tried to hold it back.

Vayan laughed. "What is this? You think to use our own power against me? I'm not here to attack you." He spread his arms wide. "I'm here to recover my lost servant, my friend. We're only a day away from crossing into your world. We should do it together."

"We are not friends," Dravid hissed, still trying to keep his eyes away from Dursa, though it became more difficult by the second.

"You men are pathetic!" Tich announced. She threw her rope around Dursa and yanked her back.

"Marshal, save me!" Dursa pleaded.

"Release her, Tich! Now!" Marshal's hands balled into fists and the ground began to shake.

"What is wrong with you? She's the enemy!" Tich yanked again and Dursa stumbled. She fell to her knees. Marshal blasted the ground on either side of the two women with a howl of rage.

Dravid held the shield up before him as Vayan approached. He could think of only one thing to do, and he wasn't entirely sure it would work.

"Come, Dravid." Vayan reached out and took hold of the top of the shield. It began to dissolve. "Tell me of your pain again."

Dravid let the shield dissolve to reveal the golden dagger he had formed behind it. Vayan's eyes widened. Dravid stabbed forward into the god's chest. "Try this pain!"

"Vayan!" Dursa cried, turning toward him. Tich kicked her from behind, and she sprawled into the dirt.

Releasing the rope, Tich stomped on the goddess' back and leaped forward in front of Marshal. "Got to break her spell on you somehow," she muttered. She grabbed Marshal's head and kissed him.

Dravid caught only a glimpse of it before Vayan shoved him away. He lost his balance and tumbled down, rolling in the dirt. The god grasped the magical dagger and dissolved it with his touch. Blood poured from his chest and he stumbled to his knees.

Dravid rolled onto his elbow and looked around. Talinir ran toward them, blood dripping from his sword. Vayan knelt bleeding. Dursa pulled the rope loose and climbed to her feet. She stood tall and proud, casting her eyes first on Dravid and then on Marshal, who shoved Tich aside. Dravid couldn't help it. Her beauty captivated him. Shouldn't they go back now? If he could just be near her…

Talinir leaped past them all and placed his sword against Dursa's neck. "Your charms do not work on me. Release the others. If you say a single word otherwise, I will cut your throat." He leaned in. "And my blade moves faster than anything else here."

The goddess glared at him, then waved her arm. Dravid blinked. What had he been thinking? He looked at Vayan, barely breathing on the ground now. For a moment, the thought crossed his mind that he could do something, save the god's life. But even as he thought it, a last breath left Vayan's body and he fell still.

"Tich! I am so sorry!" Marshal ran to her and helped her back to her feet.

"I should hope so." Tich glared at him, then at the goddess. "Crazy." Then she looked toward Dravid. "'Try this pain'? That's the best you could come up with?"

Dravid snorted. He found his staff and pulled himself to his feet.

"What do we do with her?" Talinir asked, looking at Marshal.

"I have some ideas," Tich offered.

Marshal rolled his eyes and released Tich's hands. "Send her back. On foot. Dravid and I will face the other direction until she's gone."

Dravid nodded his agreement. Marshal and Tich joined him to wait while Talinir sent Dursa on her way.

"She wasn't all that beautiful," Tich complained.

"It's her power," Dravid said. "She manipulates the minds of men."

Tich looked over her shoulder and folded her arms across her chest. "I wonder if there's a male god who does the same to women."

"If they had sent him after us, we'd all be dead," Marshal observed.

Dravid chuckled. Tich narrowed her eyes, trying to determine whether she'd been insulted or complimented.

Marshal staggered. He waved away Tich's offer of help and found a seat on the ground.

"Sorry. Still very tired and sore. Only my magic got me through all that."

"Should I try to heal you some more?" Dravid asked.

"Not right now. It's hard to pinpoint where I'm hurt."

Talinir stepped up. "She's gone. What now?"

Marshal let out a deep breath. "Let me rest a moment, then loan me your warpsteel sword." He looked up at the stars and sighed. "And then I think it's time we left the Starlit Realm. Maybe for the last time."

(((39)))

Volraag stood before the final high place. "I've come all this way, Rathri," he announced, "and I'm still not sure what I'm going to do."

The third high place differed again from the previous two. A wide stone stairway led straight up a tall hill. At the base, the stairs were at least thirty or forty feet wide. Though made of granite rather than the crumbling limestone of the northern high place, the stairs still contained many broken and shattered portions. The ascent narrowed as it went up, pausing at a platform after several hundred steps. By then, it was only around twenty feet wide. At the top, where Volraag stood, it narrowed to ten feet wide.

Jutting out in the center of the stairs stood a tall dais, topped by a narrow pillar. To reach it, Volraag had to reach the top of the main stairway, then turn and ascend another narrow set of stairs ten more steps. From here, he could see for miles in every direction. Most of the countryside here was flat, though a few short hills could be seen in the distance. Kuktarma owned most of what could be seen, though a good portion of the northernmost view probably belonged to Arazu.

At the very top of the stairs stood the portal, or at least what Volraag assumed to be the portal. A half circle of stone rose from the left side of the hill, towering at least twenty feet high from the hill's peak. Volraag guessed it had once been a complete circle, though he couldn't tell for certain. He hoped the missing half wouldn't cause problems if the portal were opened. From his position on the dais, he faced what would be the exact center of the portal if it were open.

The pillar contained the familiar stone recesses where he could insert his hands and use his power. He placed his hands in position, then removed them.

Rathri, who stood at the base of the dais steps, tapped his sheathed blade against the rock. "Isn't this why you came?"

"It is." And yet… He looked down at his palms. The power he now held frightened him sometimes. He could almost feel it bursting out of his body, so much did it contain. Did he truly need more?

Rathri sat down on one of the steps facing the stone half-circle. "You wanted to destroy the system. Take down the Lords, who use their powers only for themselves. You swore to be different." He almost sounded bored. Not for the first time, Volraag wondered what Rathri wanted out of all of this.

"A Lord should serve his people, not prey on them." Volraag repeated the line from his speech at his father's funeral.

"So this is the final step. Open the portal. Allow the old gods to return. Theon and his Laws will be swept away. The entire system of rule in Antises will be upended. Just like you wanted." Rathri paused. "And you gain even more power for yourself."

The assassin was not wrong. Yet Seri's words from the ship still troubled him. "How do I know the gods will allow me to continue to rule Varioch?"

Rathri shrugged. "We've had this same discussion multiple times. You don't know. You can't know. But they're gods. They want worship, not rule. And besides…" He picked up a piece of broken rock from the steps and tossed it at the stone half-circle. "With all the power you're gathering, you should have little to fear from them."

Volraag let an aura of vibration radiate out from him, rattling pieces of broken rock. "Do I have enough?" He knew he did not equal his half-brother yet. And Marshal had done things he couldn't… or at least hadn't tried yet. Then there was Curasir, the mysterious Eldani who had first given him this idea. He seemed able to travel between the worlds at will, without one of these portals: another power that Volraag did not possess. If Curasir served the gods, they would obviously be more powerful than him. That did not fill him with confidence.

If he did not open the portal, he had traveled all this way for no reason. Well, that was not entirely true. His visit to Arazu had been somewhat productive at least. Perhaps he should continue into Kuktarma, find Lord Meluhha, and add to his power in that way. It made more sense, after all. Then he could return home and finish off Lord Tyrr. Lord Rajwir would be his only competition then, and he could be made to see reason.

On the other hand, the power he had absorbed from the god Calu intrigued and thrilled him. More than his Lord's magic, it gave him a sense of… immortality. Invulnerability. Or at least it had, until Victor hit him with that flail. He rubbed his chin with the memory of the injury. What had gone wrong there? Why had that particular weapon hurt him so much?

He needed more power. The power to be invincible. The power to be a god himself.

Yet still he wavered. "I need more time to think," he said aloud.

"Then perhaps that will settle your mind." Rathri pointed.

Volraag turned to look. What direction was that? South… west? From Kuktarma. A large group of people moved into sight. As he watched, the crowd grew larger and larger. Birds moved in lazy circles over the organized marching. "What is that?"

"I could be wrong, of course." Rathri stood and stretched. "But that has all the appearances of… an army."

•••••

Jamana stared. "Is that it?" He turned in the chariot to look at Adhi standing beside him. "Is that the high place?"

Adhi nodded. "This is the first time I have seen it, but it can be nothing else." He waved to the next chariot, which bore Victor and Nijamu, Adhi's second-oldest brother.

At his command, the two chariots moved alongside one another and came to a stop. Around them, Kuktarma's army, or at least the half Adhi and his brother commanded, came to a slow halt as well.

"I see no enemy, little brother," Nijamu noted.

"Of course you wouldn't," Victor said. "We got here in time. Volraag hasn't opened the portal yet. And Seri may have stopped him altogether!" He frowned, then turned toward the north. "But… she's not here. Not yet." Jamana puzzled over that for a moment before remembering Victor's Bond to Seri.

"What shall we do then?" Adhi asked.

Nijamu gazed up at the high place. "Let's move in closer, and set up in a defensive position while we wait to hear from our scouts—ah, here comes one now."

A young man rode up toward them from the direction of the high place. "Your lordships!" he called. "Two men have climbed the stairs to the high place. I have seen no one else in the area."

"Volraag and Rathri," Victor growled. "What happened to Seri? Why don't I feel anything toward her right now?"

"What do you mean?" Jamana asked.

Victor leaned toward him. "Normally, with this Bond, I get a sense of her direction, and also a sense of whether she's in any kind of danger. It yanks at me if she is, but if she's all right, then, I have this…" He gestured at his own chest. "…kind of, I don't know, a feeling of peace in my gut. But right now…" He looked toward the north again. "I don't feel anything. And that worries me even more."

Adhi and his brother gave orders and the army began moving again. As the chariot rolled on, Jamana watched the high place draw nearer.

"Do people often come to this site?" he asked.

"Not often. It is a place of antiquity. Scholars come here to study it from time to time, but there is nothing of value here." Adhi gestured around. "The ground is rocky and dry here. It's not useful for any crops, when better lands are reasonably near."

Jamana continued to watch the hilltop. If he squinted against the late afternoon sun, he thought he could see some kind of shape at the top. And then it grew brighter. At first, he believed it to be some effect of the sun, but as the brightness increased, it became evident that something else was taking place.

"Do you see that?"

Adhi nodded. The brightness faded, but a light of some kind remained at the top of the hill.

"The portal is open," Adhi said. "We must prepare to fight."

<h1 style="text-align:center">(((40)))</h1>

Volraag took his hands from the pillar and watched. As anticipated, the portal filled the stone half-circle and continued as if the stone did also in a complete arc. The stone did not seem to make any difference.

Rathri got to his feet and stood watching also. Minutes ticked by.

"Where are they?" Volraag growled. He looked back at the Kuktarman army taking its position in the plain below, then back toward the portal. "What's taking so long?"

"Perhaps... we arrived before they were prepared?" Rathri suggested.

"With all our delays on the ship, and then in Sandu-Emuq? I thought we would be too late as it is."

Rathri gestured toward the army. "We still arrived before anyone else on this side."

Volraag looked back at them and put his hands on his hips. "And who is that, anyway? Not my bastard brother. I would sense his presence." He paused. "In fact, I sense no one of power anywhere near us. No mages, no Lords. Lord Meluhha is not with that army. So why are they here?"

Rathri drew one of his swords and extended the blade into the portal, then drew it back. Volraag watched him, frowning.

"When I opened the first portal, you wanted to go through it," he recalled. "But you didn't try at the second portal, and don't seem interested now. What changed?"

Rathri shrugged. "At first, it was a mystery, but now we know what lies beyond. I am content to wait."

Volraag wondered. Rathri's motivations had been a mystery to him throughout their acquaintanceship. Back in Varioch, he professed his desire to stay close to Volraag so that he would absorb some of his magic, as often happened to those close to a Lord. He promised it would make him a more effective assassin. But now that he thought of it, Volraag had seen no evidence that such a thing had happened.

At the second portal, Rathri had fought against all their enemies, but it had not escaped Volraag's attention that he seemed especially interested in killing Seri. And when Seri joined them in their travels, Rathri had worked against her at every step, threatening her and keeping her from Volraag.

Not that he minded, most of the time. Rathri was a very effective servant, irreplaceable in his job, especially with the loss of Kishin. For years, Volraag had hired both assassins, amused that neither knew of the existence of the other, at least until recently.

"It might be worth one of us going through, to find out what's happening on the other side," he suggested.

Rathri cocked his head. "I can go, if you want me to." He pointed back toward the army again. "But should I leave you up here alone with all of them out there."

Volraag smiled. "With all the power I contain, I could destroy all of them."

"Yet you have not declared war against Kuktarma. Would that not result in many curses unleashed?"

Volraag ground his teeth. Always the curses. His enormous power and the desire to use it made him forget sometimes: using the power still had consequences. "Stay then," he growled.

Rathri nodded and took a seat on the steps again, watching the Kuktarman army. Volraag sighed and sat next to the pillar. Sunset drew near. Would that make a difference to the denizens of the Otherworld? He honestly didn't know. He only hoped he wouldn't have to stay awake all night, waiting to find out.

● ● ● ● ●

Jamana wandered about the Kuktarma military encampment, feeling completely out of place. Victor fit right in with all of these soldiers, even though he came from another land. Adhi—little Adhi!—was busy giving commands to soldiers. He still couldn't get over that. Seventh son indeed.

"So why am I here?" he muttered. He had traveled to Zes Sivas to deliver the book. He came with Adhi and Victor thinking Master

Korda would want him to continue in opposing the gods. But what had he done to oppose them? It had been a fine journey, but he could think of nothing he had contributed to the effort.

Even his appearance marked him as a complete outsider. These ridiculous robes. He had been so proud of them on his first day at Zes Sivas. Now they looked absurd. And they made him sweat. Late summer heat would be bad enough, but the continued lack of wind made it even worse. The air never moved. At least the approaching evening promised to bring a break from the heat, if not the stillness.

He wanted to see this out. He wanted to see Volraag and the gods defeated. But more and more, he found himself without a role to play in this story.

A hand touched his shoulder. "Ah, mage? Sir?"

He turned to face a young soldier he didn't recognize. "Can I help you?"

"Someone wants to speak to you." The soldier pointed to a nearby tent where a cloaked figure sat before a low fire, holding a staff across his knees.

Jamana wrinkled his brow and approached. He did not know anyone else in this army. Why would they want to speak to him? And why would anyone build a fire in this weather?

"Come, young acolyte. Keep an old man company in this lonely place." The figure by the fire looked up and his cloak fell away.

"You!" Jamana stared at the old man who had traveled with him back in Mandiata.

"Oh, good. One always appreciates being remembered."

Jamana hurriedly sat down by the fire, ignoring the extra bit of heat. "How did you get here? Why are you here? How did you know about the leper?"

"Ah, delivered my message, did you? Well, that's one thing that's gone right. Not much else has thus far." He paused and looked up toward the high place. "But unless I miss my guess, everyone who needs to be here will be here soon."

"Does that include Seri?" Jamana had no idea if the old man knew Seri, but Victor's words about her still troubled him.

"Now, now, I don't know everything. That would make me Theon. And I assure you I am not he." He stirred the ashes of the fire with the end of his staff. "Oh, I found a new staff. It'll do until I get my old one back. Like it?"

Jamana spared the staff only a brief glance. He scooted a couple of inches closer. "Who *are* you?"

The old man eyed him with those ancient eyes. "I told you that I am a servant of Theon. What more do you need?"

"A name."

"Why? I don't expect you'll be calling for me any time soon."

"But—"

The old man leaned forward on his staff. "I'll tell you what. After this current situation is over, and you've discovered why you're here, I'll tell you my name."

Jamana caught his breath. It was as if the old man knew what he had been thinking. As before, his knowledge seemed supernatural. A servant of Theon he might be; in fact, Theon might be speaking to him directly. How else could he know the things he knew?

"Now." The old man tapped the ground with his staff. "Since I do not know everything, perhaps you can help me out. Regale me with your exploits since last we met."

"What?"

"Tell me what you've been up to." The old man's eyebrows narrowed. "I know you're smarter than that."

In spite of his bafflement, Jamana obliged. He told the old man everything he could think of, from the moment they went their separate ways in Mandiata until now.

He groaned on hearing about Kishin's actions. "That idiot," he muttered. "That wasn't what I meant at all. Still, there's time, I suppose."

"Time for what?"

"Time for him to find his purpose in all this mess."

Jamana hesitated. The old man smiled at him, as if knowing his indecision. "Why is Theon letting all this happen?" he burst out. "You say you're his servant. Do you know?"

"Why is he letting this happen? Why did he allow the mages and Lords to create the Laws of Cursings and Bindings? Why does he not strike down these so-called gods and forbid their return?"

Jamana nodded. He wondered all of these things.

"I am his servant, young acolyte Jamana." He tapped the ground with the staff again. "I am not his plaything. Theon does not control my actions. Nor yours. Nor Lord Volraag's over there. He gives us the choice." He paused and rubbed his scraggly beard. "You believe Theon created mankind, do you not?"

Jamana nodded.

"Did he create them as his puppets? For him to delight in how men and women moved about while he pulled the strings?"

Jamana frowned and shook his head.

"He will not force anyone to do anything. That goes against his very character."

"But are we not forced by the Laws?"

"The laws of Theon? No. The Laws of Cursings and Bindings? Yes."

"But they are merely a reflection of his laws," Jamana argued. "The mages and Lords implemented his wishes."

"Did they? Then why did they take away man's choice? Are you free to worship Theon?"

"Yes, of course."

"Are you free not to worship him?"

"I… I'm not sure." Jamana thought of Kumadi and Lord Bakari. "There are those who do not worship him."

"But are they free to break his laws?"

"I guess not."

"The choice is what matters, Jamana. If we have no choice, we are puppets. And that is not a god worth worshipping."

A young boy approached them. "Um, mage Jamana? Commander Adhi has been looking for you."

"Go with him." The old man gestured. "We will speak again, acolyte. The end draws near."

As Jamana got to his feet and followed the boy, he thought he heard the old man whisper, "And then I can finally rest."

(((41)))

Jamana found Victor, Adhi, and his brother talking together outside the command tent, still being erected. Victor waved as he approached. "Got some news here," he called.

"Seri?"

"Uh, no. Still nothing there." Victor glanced toward the north. "I know she's near, but... nothing else."

Jamana nodded. Seri's fate concerned him, but there seemed nothing they could do about it.

"Many of our scouts have returned," Adhi said. "The news is... unusual."

Nijamu folded his arms and stared at Jamana with narrowed eyes. "And I can't help but wonder how much this one knew about it already."

"He did tell me about it back on Zes Sivas," Adhi intervened. "He wasn't keeping it a secret."

"Keeping what a secret?" Jamana had no idea what they were talking about.

"The caravan from Mandiata. They're not far."

Oh. That. Jamana hadn't given it much thought in quite a while.

"What are they doing here?" Nijamu demanded.

"They are led by Lord Bakari and the god Nummotem," Jamana said. "They consider it a... pilgrimage."

"To what end? Our scouts said it did not appear to be an army. Just ordinary people."

"To welcome the gods as they return, I assume."

Adhi pinched his fingers across his eyes. "If an army emerges from that portal, and we're here to fight them, a huge number of ordinary people in the way could lead to a lot of…"

"Dead ordinary people," Victor finished.

"You should have told me about this," Nijamu said. "We should have taken this into account with our plans."

"How soon will they get here?" Jamana asked.

"They're moving slow," Adhi said. "Not for another day at least."

"Then we have time." Victor pointed out over the plain. "We can shift our army so that we're between them and the high place."

Nijamu pointed back at the high place, now barely visible in the twilight. "If enemies are going to emerge from that, we need to be in the best position to fight them when they reach the bottom of the hill."

"Can't we do both?"

"It's possible," Adhi said. "We will need to consider it thoroughly. At first light, I want us ready to shift our position. By then, we should know where we need to be."

"I'll inform the officers." Nijamu strode away.

Jamana sighed, still feeling a little out of place. "The people following Lord Bakari are desperate and hopeful fools," he said. "Volraag's murder of our Lord and theft of his power unnerved everyone. And when this god showed up, he played into those fears." He looked from Adhi to Victor. "They are innocent people."

"We'll do everything we can to protect them." Adhi nodded and looked away. "I sincerely wish my father had listened to us."

"Maybe the bad guys won't show up at all," Victor suggested. "I mean, we don't even know who's up on top of that hill, do we?"

"I sent two scouts to climb the stairs as far as they could go," Adhi said. A young soldier erected a camp chair and he sank into it.

"And?"

"One did not return at all. The other came back with a stab wound and died soon after we found him. He never saw his attacker."

"Sounds like Rathri." Victor toyed with the handle of his flail. "I don't know how we're going to deal with him. For that matter, how do we deal with all of these magic people? Volraag, or these gods? I had hoped Marshal and Seri both would be here before we were. Without them, we're in serious trouble."

"We have no defense against the power of a Lord." Adhi looked far older sitting in that chair in the gloom. "And we don't know anything about the power of the gods."

Jamana glanced back into the camp, thinking about the old man. "Maybe we have more on our side than we know."

Adhi looked up. "How can you think that?"

"I have to have faith." Jamana spread his hands. "It's all I have left."

•••••

Volraag peered down the side of the hill. Though the open portal provided a constant glow, he could not make out much of anything. Aside from the stairway on the western side, the entire hill seemed devoid of any remarkable features or even much in the way of plant life. Curious. The Ch'olan portal had been surrounded by jungle.

He strode back in front of the portal, rubbing his bare arms. At this height, even in summer, the air became cool at night. It would not grow cold enough to bring true discomfort, but he found it annoying. At least the lack of wind worked in their favor for once. "Nothing with which to build a fire," he grumbled.

"No need," Rathri said, stretching. "Perhaps you should get some rest, Lord Volraag. I'll keep a watch on the portal."

"Madness. All madness." Volraag looked up at the pillar. "I should shut it down. What good is it doing?"

The portal shimmered. A tall figure emerged, the gleam reflecting from his long white hair. Curasir.

"It is about time!" Volraag took the first step up toward the pillar, so he could be on the same level as the Eldani. "Where are your masters? Where is the power I was promised?"

Curasir regarded him, a smile without pleasure on his lips. "Greetings, son of Varion. I am delighted you have accomplished the task you were given."

"I have." Hearing his father's name in this place irritated Volraag more than he cared to admit. Varion had nothing to do with any of this.

Curasir stepped to the edge of the stairway and looked down. His eyes swept over the plain. "I see that others have come as well, though not the ones I'd expected. At least not yet."

"They are nothing."

"No, they're not." Curasir glanced back at him. "But your brother is. He's near. And he'll do everything he can to stop us."

"Why? What does he gain from it?" Volraag shook his head and looked down the stairs, half expecting to see Marshal striding up toward him. "I do not understand him."

"It is often difficult for those who have created their own form of morality to then understand those who embrace a different form. Marshal thinks he fights some great evil, perhaps imagining himself a mighty hero of some kind."

"There are no heroes. We do what we must, to change what we must." Volraag looked back at Curasir. "What now?"

"Now? The gods return, son of Varion. The gods return."

"And what does that mean to me?"

Curasir ran a finger along his eyebrow. "You have pleased them well in opening the portals. They were disappointed in your failure at the northern one, of course, but they are willing to overlook that."

"If Marshal shows up, we might have a repeat of that," Rathri pointed out.

"I think he'll be too late," Curasir said. "They arrive tomorrow."

"And the power I was promised?"

Curasir took a step closer and leaned in as if sharing a confidence. "Until you've met Murdak, you haven't seen power, let me tell you."

"Murdak?"

"One of my masters." Curasir stepped back. "You'll meet him tomorrow. And his friends." Curasir laughed and stepped back again. "So many friends." He stepped back into the portal. "Tomorrow." He vanished into the glowing swirl.

•••••

Marshal stumbled. Despite his words to Dravid and his earlier euphoria, he did still suffer from numerous aches and pains, some of them quite deep. After all the trauma his body had endured over the past year, he wondered if he would ever be free from pain again. A brief burning sensation across his face seemed to answer him.

Tich turned to him with a look of concern. Before she could say anything, he shook his head. "I'll be all right. Let's just keep moving."

"I was just going to say that since Talinir can see both worlds, you'd think he could have told us that we were going to land in the middle of a stream," she responded.

The Eldani warden, leading the way, glanced over his shoulder. "I didn't realize that getting your feet wet was such a concern for a sailor."

Marshal chuckled. Although he already felt the pull to go back and look at the Otherworld's stars again, he felt a huge sense of relief being back in his own world. The transition between the two now happened so easy. Except, of course, that he had to borrow Talinir's sword to do it. The gods had taken his warpsteel sword.

In fact, the more he thought about it, the more he missed the sword. He missed the comforting weight of it on his side. He knew he would miss the ability to channel his power through it. How could he get another one of those? The Eldanim seemed very protective of them. In all his time around them, even at their city, he had only ever seen three of the blades: Talinir's original, which had ended up with Kishin, the one Talinir carried now, and the one Marshal had taken from Hanirel.

"At least you got to clean up in the stream," Tich said. "Improved your smell a bit."

Marshal couldn't argue with that. Cleaning his body and his clothes made him feel at least human again.

"How far is the high place?" Dravid asked.

"It can't be far," Marshal said. "The gods were making their final plans, as if they expected to cross over any time now."

After crossing over into this world, the party had slept well for the first time in what felt like weeks. With the morning's light, they set out toward the portal.

Talinir bounded up a short hill and stopped. "Very, very close," he called back. It was actually a relief to see Talinir in this world again, not having to crane their necks to look up at him. Some things about the Eldanim just didn't make sense in Marshal's head. How could he be two different heights, yet still see in both worlds?

Marshal and Tich joined Talinir, followed by Dravid. They looked down into a wide plain, barren of growth save for patches of a sparse grass with thin sharp points. In the center of the plain, perhaps a mile away, towered a narrow hill. And at its top, they could all see the open portal.

"Seri didn't stop him," Dravid said.

Talinir pointed toward the southwest side of the plain. "But it looks like Victor and Jamana were successful in rallying Kuktarma." He frowned. "Though it's a much smaller army than I would have expected."

"They won't stand a chance against the one that's coming," Tich said.

"I'm here now," Marshal said. "And I'm shutting that portal down." Nothing else mattered. He would protect Antises from those gods. At the thought, he chuckled to himself. Maybe he was acting like a King, like Talinir described, after all. Or maybe he just had the power to help, so he should.

"Should we meet up with the others first?" Dravid asked.

"We'll head in that general direction. They should come out to meet us and then we can approach the high place together."

The small band moved down the hill and into the plain. As they walked, Marshal contemplated the high place. Its location on top of the hill made it more difficult, but he felt confident he could bury it as he had the one in Ch'olan. But Seri's failure troubled him. Where was she in all of this?

A familiar vibration tickled his feet. Marshal stopped and looked around. The others kept walking for a few feet, until they noticed he had stopped.

"Marshal?" Tich cocked her head to look up at him. "What is it?"

The ground trembled. This time, everyone felt it.

(((42)))

"Did you feel that?" Volraag looked down at the granite steps, sure he had felt them tremble. He lifted his head and glanced around. Rathri was nowhere in sight. Idiot assassin. The sun was rising, the gods were coming, and Rathri had disappeared.

At the same moment, he sensed something else. A tremor, not from the ground, but within. An indication of someone approaching... "Marshal."

Volraag scrambled to the top of the stairs next to the pillar and looked out over the plain. There. Emerging into view toward the northwest, he saw a small group of people. Marshal was among them. He knew it beyond certainty.

His hands shook as he released a short burst of power. This time would be different. Marshal would not thwart him here. Things had changed. His power had grown. And soon, he would have powerful allies to fight with him. Let Marshal connect with the Kuktarmans. It would not change anything.

The stairs beneath his feet shook. Volraag stumbled and fell to one knee. No question now. Everything was shaking. It didn't feel as bad as the earthquake back home in Varioch, but he hadn't been on top of a narrow hill at the time, either.

He glanced back at the portal. Chunks of rock tumbled off the half-circle that formed one border, but the portal itself didn't move. If everything else fell away, would it remain suspended in air?

The narrow stairs and pillar worried him more. He slid down the stairs, trying to maintain some sense of dignity, though he felt sure no one could see him. If the pillar fell over, he would lose the chance to close the portal. Or open it again. In fact, it might seal this portal forever… or leave it open forever.

•••••

Jamana listened to the grumbling from soldiers as he walked through the camp again. He couldn't blame them for being annoyed. After working hard yesterday to set up this camp, they now had to shift the entire thing further north, because of the approaching Mandiatan caravan.

He stopped before a row of tents. The old man had been here last night; he knew it. But there was no sign of him anywhere. He stopped a few soldiers, but none of them knew anyone like he described. Most were baffled that he would be asking after an old man in the middle of an army of young warriors.

What now? Jamana walked to the edge of the camp and looked toward the high place. The portal still gleamed in the early morning sunlight. At least nothing had emerged yet.

His legs wobbled as the ground shook. Was it Volraag? Marshal? As the shaking intensified, he knew. Earthquake. He got down on his hands and knees and waited. At least out here, nothing could fall on anyone. All around, the panicked voices of the soldiers filled his ears. Jamana guessed the earlier quakes at Zes Sivas had not been this strong in Kuktarma. Strange that he was experienced with this situation.

The shaking's intensity decreased bit by bit and came to a stop. All told, the quake had lasted no more than a minute. Yet Jamana knew from experience it had felt much longer to everyone else.

He got to his feet and looked around. No one seemed hurt. A quick glance toward the portal didn't show any change. He looked out over the plain. A handful of people were getting to their feet several hundred yards away. The earliest parts of the Mandiatan caravan?

No. One of them was tall… Eldani.

A grin split his face and he broke into a run.

•••••

Marshal let a flow of power radiate from his palms down into the ground. Maybe he could counter the trembling of the earthquake with a different vibration. Whether it worked or not, the shaking subsided and stopped.

"Hailstones. That was… different," Tich said.

"Too familiar for me," Dravid said as Talinir helped him get up.

"First one in a very long time," Marshal murmured. He looked at the ground for a few moments more, then got to his feet.

"The ground is supposed to be solid, not move like the deck of a ship." Tich's face looked much paler than usual.

Marshal dusted off his hands. "This is part of the big problem," he explained. "Antises is coming apart because the magic has been… misused. Well, that's Seri's theory anyway."

"You have another one?" Dravid asked.

"No." Marshal shook his head. "I don't know what it all means. I'm just trying to get things done. And right now, the priority is Volraag." He pointed toward the high place again.

"Then let's not waste any more time," Talinir said. They had only walked a few more yards when the Eldani warden cocked his head and noted, "Someone is coming this way."

Marshal looked and chuckled. It would be hard not to notice the large figure in orange robes rushing across the plain toward them. "Jamana."

"What?" Dravid looked up. His mouth dropped open. "How…"

A few moments later, Jamana pushed past Marshal and seized Dravid in an enormous bear hug, lifting him off the ground.

"Huh," Tich said. "I guess they know each other."

"Very good friends." Marshal looked at the other faces coming toward them at a more leisurely pace. It was easy to spot Victor, pale-faced and yellow-haired, among the darker Kuktarmans. He waved.

The two groups met, and Marshal embraced his friend. "I was worried you might not make it," Victor said. He glanced at the others. "I see you found him. And survived a trip with Tich along. Well done."

"Thanks, Vic. I like you too." Tich shifted the rope on her shoulder.

"Seri?" Marshal asked.

Victor shook his head. "No sign of her. And the Bond is… acting strange."

"Who is this Seri person, anyway?" Tich wondered. "Seems like all of you are mooning over her."

Behind him, Marshal heard Jamana babbling away to Dravid, telling him of his journeys. "…And from Zes Sivas, we set out for Kuktarma."

"Adhi!" Dravid exclaimed. "No robes for you?"

Jamana laughed. "I have been waiting for this moment! Everyone listen!"

Marshal and the others turned to face him.

"It would not be appropriate to wear my mage robes now—" Adhi began.

"No! Be quiet! You will not deny me this!"

Adhi lifted his hands in surrender, a smile growing on his face as well.

Jamana gestured. "Dravid, Marshal, Talinir, Tich... may I present to you the regional overseer of the Kuktarma Defense Force..."

"This is ludicrous," growled Nijamu.

"AND..." Jamana raised his voice. "The seventh son of Lord Meluhha... your friend and mine... Adhi."

Marshal raised his eyebrows and looked at Dravid. The look on his face could not be described. He didn't move, didn't speak.

"Oh, great," Tich observed. "We went to all that trouble to rescue him, and now you broke him." She waved her hand in front of Dravid's face.

"You... you can't..." Dravid stammered.

Adhi made a short bow. "And this is Nijamu, second son of my father Lord Meluhha, also a regional overseer. We have brought our two regions of the defense force." He turned to Marshal. "But I'm afraid it will not be enough. I hope your presence will make the difference."

Nijamu eyed him. "They're telling me you're actually the King of Antises. Is that true?"

Marshal winced. "I do not claim to be King. But I am descended from the Kings and possess their power."

"Good enough." Nijamu nodded. "Power is what we're lacking here."

Marshal looked toward the hill. "Volraag?"

"He's there," Victor confirmed. "Along with Rathri."

"Let's pay them a visit."

• • • • •

Volraag got to his feet and looked over the stairs and platforms. The earthquake did not seem to have caused much more damage than already existed. But Marshal was out there. He could see the Kuktarman army shifting to meet him, changing their position for some reason.

He heard the ripple in the portal before turning to see it. Curasir stepped out again.

"Why the delays?" Volraag complained before he could speak. "Marshal is here. We must move quickly!"

"That is precisely the reason for the delay." Curasir stepped to the edge of the platform and looked down at those below. "An opportunity presented itself."

"An opportunity?"

Curasir looked back at him. "A way to deal with Marshal. And his other friends, if I am right." He walked back to the portal's edge. "But first, there is someone who wishes to meet you."

The portal shimmered again. A tall, dark gold skinned man stepped through, wearing a maroon cloth wrapped around his waist and thighs in multiple layers and looped over his left shoulder. He adjusted his open white shirt of gauzy material and straightened a necklace of multi-colored gemstones.

"May I present the king of all kings and god of all gods, Murdak." Curasir bowed low before the newcomer.

Unsure, Volraag also bowed. He looked up at Murdak, easily the tallest man he had ever met. The god glanced down at him with indifference. "This is the one?" he asked Curasir.

"Yes, your majesty. This is Lord Volraag of Varioch, the one who opened the portals for us."

"Hmm." Murdak looked out over the plain and took a step onto the platform. "He doesn't seem cut from the same cloth as his brother."

Volraag felt a surge of anger. "What's that supposed to mean?"

"It means," Murdak said, turning his head but not really looking over his shoulder, "that in the grand scheme, you are... insignificant."

Volraag looked at Curasir, then back at Murdak. He clenched his fist. "Insignificant? I opened the portals! I possess more power than any man alive!"

Murdak finally looked at him. "Except your brother, of course. And you have failed to stop him at every turn. He's here even now, I believe."

"Yes." Volraag shook his head and tried to relax. "Yes, he is. But I will deal with him. He will not—"

He broke off as two more of the gold-skinned gods emerged from the portal, both male. Volraag would have thought them the perfect embodiment of masculinity had he not already seen Murdak. One of them walked to the edge of the platform and watched the people below. The other, who wore clothing that reminded Volraag of Lord

Enuru, stepped beside Murdak and turned to face him.

"We have a plan to deal with the scarred King," Murdak said. He nodded to Curasir, who slipped back through the portal. Murdak turned his attention back to Volraag. "You, however, have now served your purpose."

"I opened the portals!" Volraag repeated. "I was promised power. You cannot dismiss me like a servant!"

"Yes… power." Murdak lifted a hand, then let it fall back to his side. "I believe you have power that does not belong to you."

Volraag clenched his fists again. The rocks around him began to vibrate. "This power is mine. It's been in the hands of the wrong people for too long!"

"You misunderstand me. I care not how much of… that kind of power you take for yourself." Murdak pointed at him. "But you took power from one of my people. Calu, I believe? That was a step too far." He cocked his head. "And unforgivable. Devir, take it back. Now."

The other god, Devir, stretched out his hand. Volraag gasped as a tightness congealed within his chest. "What…" Before he could finish his question, the tightness erupted out of him, rushing away. Power drained from him, the power he had taken weeks ago in Ch'olan. His physical body shrank back to his normal proportions, his clothes growing loose. And just like that… the power was gone. All of his Lord powers remained, but nothing more. He gasped again and collapsed to his knees.

Murdak nodded. "That will do. Now let's deal with the King." He turned away.

"No!" Volraag leaped back to his feet, his power surging. "You will not treat me this way! I opened the portal, and I can close it again! You need—"

Murdak spun around with surprising speed and seized Volraag by the neck. "I need what? You? Your ego is pathetic." He glanced at the pillar. "The portal is open, and it will stay that way. Your service, your usefulness to me… is at an end."

Murdak took two steps to the edge of the platform, carrying Volraag with him. "Farewell." With a flick of his wrist, he tossed Volraag over the side of the hill.

(((43)))

Marshal strode toward the hill, flanked by Victor, Dravid, Jamana, Adhi, Talinir, and Tich. Nijamu remained behind, ready to give orders to his army if needed.

"Where is Seri?" he muttered to himself.

Victor heard. "She's somewhere close, I think. It's so weird, Mars. My Bond with you never behaved this way." He shook his head. "I know she's near, but I can't tell anything else."

"Volraag is not alone any more," Talinir noted.

Marshal looked up the stone stairs. Several tall figures moved about at the top of the hill, silhouetted against the glowing portal. One of them stepped to the front and put his hands on his hips. Marshal came to a stop.

"Hail, scarred King!"

Murdak.

"Is that one of… the gods?" Adhi asked.

"That's what they call themselves," Dravid said. "All I know is that they're powerful. And cruel."

"Only one god is true," Jamana murmured.

"Murdak!" Marshal called. "You are not welcome here. Return to your world and do not trouble ours."

Murdak spread his arms wide. "But this is also our world. Your people worshiped us in times past. They will again."

"We do not want you here. Go back." Marshal released a burst of power that shook the hill. "I buried the Ch'olan portal. I'll do the same to this one."

"No." Murdak shook his head. "You will not."

"You doubt my power?"

"I doubt your will." Murdak glanced over his shoulder and beckoned. A squad of Durunim emerged from the portal and spread out around him.

"Do it now!" Victor urged. "Don't let him bring any more through!"

Marshal gathered his power, preparing to unleash it. He took a deep breath, feeling it course through his entire body. He relished the thought of releasing it, ripping this hill apart, tearing it down to nothing.

"Will you kill us all, scarred King?"

In answer, Marshal released a short burst of power. Several of the granite steps halfway up the hill exploded, raining shards of stone.

"What about now?" Murdak called.

Marshal raised his hands to unleash it all, then stopped. Curasir stepped up beside Murdak. In his arms, he held a body.

Dravid knew first. "Seri!"

Marshal refocused, then bent his knees in a crouch. Victor put a hand on his shoulder. "What are you thinking?"

"I'm going up there. One wide blast will knock them all down and I'll grab her and be back."

"No. Look!" Dravid cried.

Another god stood beside Curasir, with his hand outstretched inches from Seri's face. Ne'gal.

"I assume you know what my friend here is capable of." Murdak's voice carried out over the plain. "Stand aside as my army descends, or she dies."

"What is wrong with her?" Dravid murmured. "Where's Ixchel?"

"What do we do?" Jamana asked.

"There's nothing we can do," Marshal answered. He let his power die down.

"Are we sure about this?" Adhi asked. The others turned toward him. "I don't wish anything to happen to Seri, either, but... do we sacrifice all of Antises for her?"

"I do," Dravid said.

Adhi gestured back toward his army. "As my father's son, I have a responsibility to defend our land, as does my brother. Do we allow an army to invade it to save our friend? I don't know if I can make that decision."

"You can't be serious!" Victor bounced on one foot and clenched his fist.

"Talinir... any ideas?" Marshal asked.

The Eldani warden shook his head. "You know as well as I do what is at stake here. The decision must be made by whoever has the highest authority." He looked from Marshal to Adhi and back.

"I'm waiting!" Murdak called.

"Theon's pillars! I never wanted this!" Marshal took a deep breath. There would be no going back from this. "Adhi."

"Yes?"

"Do you—" Marshal stopped, then tried again. "I am the King of Antises. Do you accept this?"

"I accept it, if you are making that claim here and now."

Marshal grimaced. "I am."

Adhi gave a short bow. "Then the decision is yours. My troops are at your command, King Marshal."

Marshal ran a hand through his hair. No turning back now. Responsibility. Selfless. He stepped away from the others and looked up. "Murdak! What will it take to release my friend there?"

"I didn't say anything about releasing her. The only negotiation right now is whether she dies here and now."

"Then she lives."

"As you say." Murdak waved. Ne'gal took a step back from Seri, but stayed close. Around them, Durunim warriors streamed down the stairs, coming toward Marshal and his friends.

"I think we just lost," Victor said. Marshal couldn't argue. His first act as King, and he handed over the kingdom to the enemy.

●●●●●

Volraag groaned and shifted his weight. The act made him slide several more feet down the side of the hill.

Everything hurt. The impact from his fall hadn't been that severe, but the stripping of his power had torn and bruised muscles throughout his body. His left arm hung useless by his side, and his other limbs weren't much better.

Above, he heard Murdak's voice challenging Marshal, and what came of it. Though he couldn't see, he understood what took place. His idiot half-brother gave up the world for the sake of a girl. Volraag would have laughed if he weren't in such pain.

He lost consciousness for a moment or two. Then another voice came from above, a rasping, hated sound he would recognize anywhere.

"I pledge fealty to the great god Murdak," Rathri declared.

"And what good is that, twisted one?" Murdak asked.

"My sole purpose in life is to kill and destroy as many humans as possible. You seem more… efficient at it than those I have served before."

Volraag suppressed another groan. He had known Rathri's predilections, used them for his own purposes for many years, but to hear him state it outright… it chilled him.

After a moment of silence, Murdak spoke again. "You are able to pass among them as a spy more effectively than my soldiers ever could. Perhaps I can use you."

"Whatever you wish."

"Make a good start of it. The scarred King down there. He has a number of… friends, I suppose. Bring me their heads. I want him to suffer before I end him."

Murdak's voice grew fainter with the last few words. Volraag reached up with his right hand, trying to pull himself up a little higher. Instead, his movement sparked a miniature landslide. The dirt and rocks beneath him slid away, taking him with them. He scrabbled for any kind of handhold, a foothold even, but found nothing.

Volraag slid, overbalanced, and flipped over a few times, before coming to a grinding halt somewhere much further down the hillside. His pain overwhelmed him this time, and his consciousness drifted away.

●●●●●

Marshal and the others watched the Durunim descend the stairs. When they reached the base of the hill, they turned to the right and marched toward the north side of the plain.

Nijamu raced up on his chariot and came to a sudden stop, throwing dust over the watchers. "What are we doing?" he demanded.

Adhi walked toward him. "Marshal has decided to claim his position as King of all Antises," he explained, pointing. "He has given us the order to stand down and wait."

"What? Isn't this why we came? Whose side is he on?"

Adhi stepped up next to the chariot and explained in a low voice. Nijamu looked up at Marshal. "I thought my next oldest brother a fool when he risked everything for a girl. He died for it." He shook his head. "But you… risking all of us? All of Antises?"

Marshal didn't answer. He couldn't.

"Listen." Victor stepped to his side. "There has to be a way to stop this. Still want to blast your way up?"

"Of course I do. But I can't. I can't let her die."

Victor looked up at the hilltop. "What's the deal with this god that made you stop, anyway?"

"His very touch is death."

Victor nodded. "That could be a problem."

"Don't forget Murdak beat you to a pulp," Dravid added. "We are far outmatched here."

"That true?" Victor asked. Marshal nodded.

"How did she even end up there?" Jamana wanted to know. "And what is wrong with her?"

"She was with Volraag," Marshal said. "I never should have let them leave together. If I see him again…"

"The death god has moved away," Victor noted. "Maybe we could get up there fast enough."

"Now you'd be in the middle of the entire army, not to mention the gods," Talinir said. "Think carefully before taking any reckless action." He glanced up. "And don't forget Curasir. He's not without power himself."

"Anyone else have any ideas?" Marshal asked. He took a step back as a pair of tunaldi bounded down the stairs with Durunim riders. One left the stairs at the middle platform, leaping and sliding down the steep side of the hill.

"I dunno. I'm kind of with the soldiers here," Tich admitted. "I know you're all friends with this girl, but…"

Marshal frowned at her. She raised her hands in surrender. "She's your old girlfriend or whatever. I get it. No one wants her dead. But you just claimed the kingship of all Antises. Doesn't that mean you now have a responsibility for all of us? Not just her?"

"She's not wrong," Adhi said quietly.

"I'd also like to point out that you're thinking too direct," Tich said. "The hill has more than one side, you know."

"You're suggesting coming up behind them?" Dravid asked. Tich shrugged.

"The hillside is steep, but not insurmountable," Talinir said. "It might work."

"They'd see us, though," Victor argued.

"Not if we came up directly behind the portal. They can't see through it."

"But how do we get around back without them noticing?" Victor bounced on one foot again. "Don't get me wrong. I want it to work, but I don't see how."

"We are out in the open here, and they can see all around," Jamana said.

Marshal put his hand on his face and found himself tracing his scars. Had he really come so far, all for nothing? The scars. Losing his mother. Fighting Curasir. The army. Losing his soldiers. Fighting Volraag. Losing his grandfather. The beating he took from Murdak. Finally claiming the kingship... only to lose it all. Because of a girl. Because of... Seri.

No. He had lost too many people already. He could not lose her too. If he had a responsibility to Antises, he had a responsibility to its people even more, and that included Seri.

"Talinir."

"Yes, Marshal."

"You can do it, can't you?"

"Do what?"

"Get behind the hill without being seen."

Talinir hesitated. "I can. But alone."

Marshal looked back at the Durunim army coming down into his world. Many of them carried large bundles. They would have had to leave their supply wagons behind in the Otherworld; they'd never make the trip down those stairs. Would they rebuild new wagons here or just carry all they needed? And where would they go from here? How many would die now?

"Do it. Wait until you hear me, then move up. I'll attack them at the top, try to save Seri—"

"No." Victor shook his head. "We've already established your power isn't enough."

"I have to try!"

Victor snapped the chain of his flail. "We have one weapon here that we know can harm a god." He smiled. "Launch me up there. I'll take them down."

"Regardless," Talinir said. "I'll be waiting." He slipped away. Marshal lost sight of him before he took a dozen steps.

"How does he do that?" Jamana asked.

"Do you have a plan now?" Dravid wanted to know. "What are we doing?"

"We're going to try to rescue her," Marshal answered. "As soon as Murdak descends. I'll save my rematch with him for later."

"What do you want us to do?" Adhi asked.

"And me!" Dravid insisted. "I need to help!"

"Have the army stand ready," Marshal said to Adhi. "I don't know if an attack will be wise just yet, but... be ready." He turned to Dravid. "I... don't know what you can do to help. I'm sorry."

Jamana put his hand on Dravid's shoulder. "Let the warriors fight. We will support them in other ways."

Dravid shoved his hand away. He stretched his hands apart and formed a rough golden blade. "I can fight! You know I can!"

Jamana's mouth hung open. He hadn't been aware of Dravid's abilities, apparently.

"I can't..." Marshal looked around at all of them. "I don't doubt you, Dravid. Or any of you. Tich. Jamana. I just don't know how to use all of you in this situation."

"Then maybe we'll make our own way!" Dravid turned and moved away as quickly as he could with his staff. Jamana followed him.

Tich looked at Marshal and shook her head. "Your first few decisions as King aren't going so well, you know. Hope that's not an omen or anything."

"I'm doing the best I can."

She nodded. "I'm sure you believe that. And that's why you need your friends." She turned and called to the other two. "Hey! Mage boys! Wait for me!"

"It... I..." Marshal didn't know what to say.

He looked at Victor, who shrugged. "You're trying something. That's all I asked for."

"Hail, King of Scars!" Marshal turned back to see Murdak descending the stairs with the latest squad of Durunim. "Thank you for your cooperation. Ne'gal remains above to ensure it stays that way." He stopped and looked about him. "It is good to be back. Thank you. For giving us this world again."

As the god continued on his way, Marshal turned back to Victor. "This is it."

• • • • •

"But what can we do?" Jamana repeated.

"Talinir went around the back," Dravid said. "We should do the same."

"Uh, I hate to point out the obvious," Tich replied, "but Talinir is sneaky weird magic guy. We're not."

Dravid kept moving. "We'll just have to circle around further, to keep from being obvious."

"Won't that take a long time?"

"Yes. So keep moving."

Tich looked at Jamana and shrugged. The two of them followed Dravid.

(((44)))

Marshal allowed his power to build up once again. "It will probably work best if you hang on to my back," he told Victor.

"Are you sure?" Victor scrunched his forehead. "I'm bigger than you."

"That's the reason. If I hold on to you and blast off, I'll just lose my hold. You have to hold on to me."

"I'm having second thoughts about this…"

"Come on. The longer we wait, the bigger the army."

Victor rolled his eyes and stepped behind Marshal. He wrapped the chain of his flail across Marshal's chest and held on to both ends. It wasn't exactly comfortable, but it wouldn't be for long.

At that moment, the roar of a crowd erupted behind them. Both of them turned. The noise did not seem to be coming from the Kuktarman army, but from beyond it. Marshal couldn't make out anything.

"The caravan from Mandiata?" Victor suggested.

"Must be. Adhi will have to deal with it. Come on."

Once again, they braced themselves. Marshal took a deep breath, then forced the power to erupt below his feet. He had done this numerous times, especially in the Otherworld while fighting Curasir. But he had never done it with another person clinging to his back. Victor's weight threw off everything he thought he knew. He made sure to use more power than needed to launch. The force of it threw them into the air, but also flipped them, almost sending Victor tumbling head-first back toward the ground. Marshal threw out more power and managed to stabilize their flight, but sent them far higher than he meant to.

277

The chain bit into his chest, still sore from his previous injuries. He put a hand on it, but instead touched the ball on the end of the chain: the Ranir stone that Calu had fused into it. It felt warm to his touch, and a curious sensation ran through his his whole body, not unlike when Dravid healed him. The stone held some form of magic within, something of the Eldanim.

From this height, he could see everything. Mandiata's caravan had indeed arrived from the northwest. Kuktarma's army stood between them and the high place. The Durunim army continued to assemble directly north of the hill. Marshal winced when he saw the size of the army already, and more continued to pour down the stairs. Adhi's forces were easily outnumbered five or six to one, and they had an equal number of ordinary people in the caravan that would need protection.

As they hit the apex of their flight, Marshal focused on the high place, trying to discern what awaited them. Durunim kept emerging through the portal. He couldn't make out Curasir, but knew he had to be there. Seri lay unmoving to the left side of the portal. Ne'gal stood a few feet from her, watching their approach.

"We're going to land hard!" Marshal yelled over his shoulder. "Hit the ground and I'll throw a burst of magic in all directions!"

"Got it!" Victor shouted in his ear.

The top of the hill rose to meet them.

• • • • •

Volraag regained consciousness, though he had no idea how much time had passed. It felt like only seconds. The pain probably woke him again. Everything hurt.

"What have we here?"

His heart skipped a beat. Rathri. Afraid to move and cause another avalanche, Volraag turned his head just enough to look toward the voice.

The assassin stood poised only a few feet away, seeming to have no trouble maintaining his balance on the scree and loose dirt. He took a step closer and drew his sword.

"Rathri," Volraag managed to croak, his mouth dry from inhaling too much dust. "Help... me."

"Help you? I'm beyond you now, little Lord." Rathri took another easy step and lifted his blade. "You were a means only to an end, and that end is here."

Volraag tried to summon his own magic, hoping to throw out enough to stop the blade that descended towards his head. But nothing happened.

At the last moment, another sword inserted itself, deflecting Rathri's blade away and into the dirt. The assassin stepped back. Volraag twisted his head to see… Talinir. Marshal's Eldani friend.

"You again?" Rathri snarled.

"Again. We have unfinished business."

Rathri ran up the side of the hill, his footsteps barely moving any of the scree. He circled around to be above Talinir, drawing his second sword as he did.

Talinir, unimpressed, shifted across the steep side of the hill just as effortlessly. He dodged Rathri's first stroke, then feinted once. Rathri stepped back, giving Talinir the opportunity to move level with him.

The two warriors faced each other, staring with an intensity that felt almost palpable.

An impact resounded from the top of the hill, shaking everything.

• • • • •

Dravid considered stopping and shaping himself a temporary leg again. He might be able to move faster. Seri was in danger. Seri needed help. And he couldn't do anything, because of his stupid limitations. A tremble ran through the ground beneath him.

"Whoa." Tich's exclamation made him glance back. Marshal and Victor were in the air, shooting skyward. What must that be like? If he could do that, he wouldn't need to walk.

"Someday we will learn this trick," Jamana said.

"How?" Dravid snapped. He kept moving.

"The Masters can do it at Zes Sivas," Jamana replied. "You've seen it. One day, we will be Masters too."

Dravid shook his head. "You might, but not me. I gave that up, Jamana. And no one will train me, anyway."

"You have a… different magic now, though."

"A lot of good it's doing me here." Dravid looked up, watching Marshal and Victor descend toward the peak. "Come on! We need to help!"

• • • • •

Marshal gasped as he struck the granite platform. It was always a struggle to determine how much power he should use to slow his fall, and carrying Victor made it much harder. As the rock shattered all around them, something twisted in his right knee. He barely maintained his stance.

Victor dropped to the ground as instructed. Marshal swept both arms out, releasing power in all directions at chest level. The stairs leading to the activation pillar erupted. Durunim flew in every direction. Some fell back into the portal, some tumbled down the stairs, and a few disappeared over either side of the hill.

Marshal pulled himself back up, though his knee protested. Ne'gal stood unfazed.

"Victor!" Marshal aimed a concentrated burst of power at the strange god. It didn't push him away, but kept him from advancing toward Seri's prone form.

Victor scrambled to his feet. He charged toward Ne'gal, flail spinning.

Marshal took a limping step toward Seri. Fiery pain erupted across his back and he stumbled, almost plummeting headlong down the stairs. His knee gave out and he fell, but caught himself with both hands. He turned to look behind him.

Curasir wiped blood from his sword. "I should have just stabbed, I know. Murdak will be disappointed in me." He sighed. "But I still think there's hope for you, Marshal. We can still work together."

Four more Durunim soldiers emerged through the portal.

●●●●●

Rathri and Talinir dueled across the side of the hill. Volraag watched in awe as the two fleet-footed combatants exchanged blows, leaped, dodged, and scurried. They somehow maintained their balance on an angled surface threatening to slide out from under Volraag's prone body at any moment.

A rumble sounded from above again. This time, a pair of Durunim soldiers appeared, tossed like rag dolls from the summit. Yet even in their descent, they managed to twist around and land on their feet, sliding for a bit before coming to a stop. They stood on either side of the existing duel. Both spotted Talinir at the same time and drew their swords.

•••••

"Look!"

At Tich's cry, Dravid craned his head. He spotted the four tall figures fighting on the side of the hill, less than halfway up its slope.

"Talinir is outnumbered!"

Jamana stopped. "We can't climb this. And what will we do when we get there?"

"We have to try!" Dravid jammed his staff into the side of the hill and pulled himself up. His foot slipped right away, almost sending him down again.

"We don't even have any weapons!" Jamana argued.

"Speak for yourself!" Tich sprang past both of them, swinging her rope above her head. She had fastened a weight of some kind on the very end and launched it upward.

The rope wrapped around the only gnarled leafless bush protruding from the hill's slope about ten yards up. Tich yanked it tight, then pulled herself up, foot by foot.

"There has to be another way!" Dravid summoned his own power, but stopped short of forming anything. What could he possibly make to help them ascend?

•••••

Marshal pushed himself up, trying to get to his feet. His knee wouldn't hold his weight without excruciating pain. His back burned with agony. The torn fragments of his shirt grew wet with his blood.

"Oh, look at that," Curasir observed, looking out past him. "Plants, of all things, pushing a way through your pitiful army. That will be Nummotem. He always did love to show off his power."

Marshal spared a glance at Victor. His rotating flail kept Ne'gal and the Durunim at bay, but he had yet to strike the death god. Seri remained unmoving. No sign of Talinir.

"At the rate you're going, the rest of your body will end up matching your face." Curasir took a step back and allowed two of the Durunim to move in towards Marshal. "You really are the King of Scars, aren't you?"

Marshal gritted his teeth, lifted a hand and blasted one of the Durunim off the hilltop. He turned the blast on Curasir. The strange

Eldani held up his sword and absorbed the blast. Marshal had forgotten he could do that. Something about that sword. It wasn't a warpsteel blade, was it? It didn't look like Talinir's., but Curasir used it for all kinds of things.

"That's the problem with the gods and their healing power. Well, except Ne'gal over there. He doesn't exactly do any healing. But the rest of them… it doesn't completely heal, does it? After what you did to me in our battle a few months ago, it took a lot of healing to get me back on my feet. And still"—Curasir gestured toward himself—"I have aches and pains inside. I assume it's the same with you."

The second Durunim hacked down at him. Marshal blasted him into the air, then poured on the power as he struck the activation pillar. It exploded into a million shards of rock. The portal flickered, but did not vanish.

"Creative," Curasir noted. "That's one of the things I like about you. So unlike your brother. He was so… simple in his thinking."

"Was?" Where was Volraag, anyway? And Rathri? Marshal shot a quick look over his back.

Curasir gestured. "Oh, Murdak tossed him over the side, after taking back the power he stole. I don't think we'll be seeing him again."

Marshal leaned on his hands again. He let the power flow out into the granite platform. Everything shook. The remaining stairs to the missing activation pillar collapsed.

"Again, creative. But what are you going to do? Bring down the entire hilltop with all of us on it?" Curasir slammed his sword down into a crack between the stones. At once, the platform stopped shaking as the sword absorbed the power again.

"This is pointless," Curasir went on. "I told you that before too. We can fight." He gestured toward Victor and the other enemies. "They can fight. One of us will lose. So what? What does that accomplish?"

Marshal stayed on his one knee. As long as he didn't put all his weight on the other one, he would be all right. "If it gets you to shut up, it's worth it."

Curasir threw back his head and laughed. "Oh, this is delightful. You are so much more entertaining than my usual company." He thumbed at one of the silent Durunim with a grin. "I'm so glad you escaped from that cage." Then the grin faded. "But you killed Vayan. That was a mistake. I don't think Murdak will forgive that."

"I'm not asking him to."

"No, I suppose not." Curasir sighed. "Which means it's better if I kill you." He saluted Marshal with the sword. "I won't make you suffer."

<h1 style="text-align:center">(((45)))</h1>

Volraag lifted his right hand and concentrated. He released a short burst of power, taking the legs out from under one of the Durunim. His delight in accomplishing that much disappeared as he slid further down the hill. The warrior he struck slammed face-first into the scree and tumbled down the hill. Volraag himself came to a stop, now sideways, looking up.

At least he wasn't completely useless. Rathri and Talinir continued their dance across the hillside. Neither seemed able to gain advantage over the other. But Rathri's movements had purpose. He kept maneuvering Talinir closer to the remaining Durunim warrior, who waited with sword drawn.

Volraag considered trying to blast that one too, but his last effort had cost him. He wasn't sure he could summon enough of a blast to reach that far now.

"You said humans did this to you!" Talinir shouted at Rathri. "How? What happened?"

"It is not your business!" Rathri growled. "Only that they must suffer."

Volraag had no idea what they were talking about.

One more feint made Talinir step back, almost within range of the other opponent. The Durunim lifted his sword.

A golden spear slammed into the side of the hill inches from the Durunim's foot. Talinir glanced back, realized his danger, and let himself slide down a few feet. He dashed to his left, circling around Rathri.

"Yeah!" Volraag turned his head to look down. Only a few feet away, a woman he did not recognize stood on the scree, holding on to a rope with one hand, the other lifted in the air. Had she thrown the spear? At the base of the hill, he spotted two other figures: a mage, and… was that Marshal's one-legged friend?

Rathri saw them as well. Volraag turned back in time to see him gesture at the Durunim warrior. "Bring me their heads." The Durunim leaped into the air and launched himself toward the two at the bottom.

•••••

Dravid's eyes widened. Forming the spear and tossing it to Tich had seemed like a good idea at the time.

"Run!" Jamana cried, starting to move. Then he came to an abrupt halt, remembering Dravid couldn't.

Dravid released the magic of the spear, letting it dissolve. But it was taking too long! He'd never be able to regain his power and form anything new before the Durunim reached them.

"Forgive me, my friend!" Jamana grabbed Dravid's staff and yanked it away. Dravid wavered, threw out his arms for balance, and fell backward. Jamana stepped between him and the charging warrior.

The Durunim sword came down. Jamana smashed it out of the way with the staff. The dark warrior paused, as if surprised that this human would dare try to stop him. Then he swung again and again, shifting each time. Jamana wielded the staff with surprising effectiveness, but he couldn't keep it up for long. The Durunim was too fast.

Dravid felt his power return. He called to it, trying to form something—anything—to help his friend.

•••••

Still on one knee, Marshal watched Curasir advance toward him. If only he had a sword! He should have borrowed Victor's. But a quick glance in that direction showed Victor had enough trouble of his own. Several more Durunim emerged from the portal and encircled him. Ne'gal stood still just outside the circle, watching as Victor spun, trying to keep up with all of these opponents.

With no other options, Marshal focused his power at Curasir directly. Again, Curasir absorbed the power with his sword. But at least it gave him pause. Marshal growled. His back still burned. His knee throbbed in agony. And so many other aches and pains throughout his body continued to protest.

How much power could that sword absorb? Did it have a limit? Regular swords could only absorb so much before they exploded. Maybe even a warpsteel sword. Curasir's sword was something different. Still, what else could he do? Marshal poured it on.

Curasir took a step closer. And another. He lowered his sword until the point aimed at Marshal's face.

Marshal reached out and clapped both palms against the flat sides of the blade. He let power flow into it, as much as he could.

"It's a shame, such a shame," Curasir said. "You could have been a part of all this. You could have been… so much more than you are. A true King among the gods." He shook his head. "Instead, you'll die as King of nothing more than scars."

He thrust the blade forward.

Something slammed into the side of Curasir's head and he stumbled back a step. He wiped a trickle of blood from his cheek and looked past Marshal. "What is this?"

Marshal took a quick look, then stared. A glow of pure white light floated a few feet away. Shards of rock whirled about it, forming multiple rings of debris. Another piece came loose and shot at Curasir, who managed to duck this time.

In the center of the light floated… Seri.

• • • • •

Seri had no idea what was happening. Her last conscious thoughts had been of unimaginable, unbearable pain. Then blackness, only blackness for a long time. When she finally woke up, everything had changed.

She heard yells, rumbles, the clang of weapons. Her eyes fluttered open. A clear blue sky stretched above. It would be peaceful if not for the sounds. And the hard rock surface beneath her. What did it mean? Where were Ixchel and her father?

She sat up. But even as she did, new sensations overwhelmed her. Magic. Magic filled her entire body, infusing every single iota of her being. Her skin glowed. Her hair rose from her scalp without a breeze to move it. She turned her hands slowly to look at them, and found herself lifting up into the air.

How could she have absorbed this much power? From the stuff between the worlds? More importantly, how could her body contain this much? It was far more than she had ever taken in before, even while siphoning from Marshal. Master Hain warned her against this.

Yet she felt... whole. Healthy. Rejuvenated. Not a hint of the pain remained.

She spun in a circle as she rose. In response, loose shards of rock and dust rose up to join her, spinning around her, forming loops of debris. She laughed in delight. The sensation reminded her of when she and Marshal had joined hands and power. Except this time, she was doing it alone.

Only then did she think to look at her surroundings. A hilltop. The portal! Victor. Durunim. Marshal... in danger! With the slightest of thoughts, she sent a chunk of rock flying at Curasir.

"Seri?" Marshal stared at her, kneeling at the edge of the granite platform.

"I don't know what's happening!" She blinked and activated her star-sight. Marshal glowed with his enormous power, so much he still couldn't possibly comprehend it. The portal's appearance altered as well, its edges looking like a ring of fire that threatened to erupt outward. Curasir possessed some power of his own, though it was difficult to make out behind the sword. An aura of multicolored light moved with the sword.

She looked down at herself. Light shot from her body in every direction. She had absorbed so much power, it was leaking out, erupting from her all over the place.

Marshal took advantage of everyone's amazement, launching a burst of power at the Durunim around Victor. Two fell back through the portal and four others tumbled off the side of the hill. A strange figure, one of the gods, remained standing.

Seri's body shook. This was too much. Everything inside of her vibrated, as if it all might fly apart at any moment.

"Marshal! I can't hold it in!"

•••••

Dravid pulled the magic into a long shape, another spear. The quickest weapon he could imagine. But it came apart in his hands, dissolving even as he tried to shape it. "No!"

The Durunim's sword lodged into the staff just enough to yank it out of Jamana's hands.

Dravid could see Tich almost at the base of the hill, descending faster than she had gone up. But she wouldn't be in time.

An arrow slammed into the Durunim's shoulder, staggering him.

A familiar, colorful figure dashed past Dravid and Jamana, blocked the Durunim's next stroke with her round shield, and stabbed him straight through the chest.

"Ixchel!" Dravid screamed in excitement.

Ixchel yanked her sword from the Durunim as he fell. An unfamiliar Arazu man approached them, another arrow at his bowstring.

"Where is Seri?" Ixchel demanded.

Dravid pointed to the hilltop, then pulled his hand back to shield his eyes. A bright light radiated from the high place, hiding the portal and everything else.

"What do they have up there?" Jamana wondered. "A star?"

•••••

Marshal kept an eye on Curasir, but glanced at Seri again. What was happening to her? Can't hold what in? The brightness expanding from her kept growing in intensity.

Seri did not possess her own magic inside, he reminded himself. As a mage, she drew magic from Antises itself, wherever she could find it. But this…

"Fascinating," Curasir murmured.

"Let it out!" Marshal yelled. "Release it!"

Seri threw her arms wide. Marshal couldn't "see" magic the way she could, but the air warped around her. The spinning debris erupted outward, but then returned right back to where it had been. Seri looked at her hands, her face a mask of desperation. "It's not working! I absorb it right back!"

The magic needed to go somewhere else. Through the portal, maybe? Or, he could let her blast at him. Could he absorb it from her? He had never done anything like that before. He shielded his eyes from the bright light. Power didn't flow into him; it flowed out.

But it flowed into Curasir's sword.

"The sword!" He pointed at Curasir. "Aim everything at the sword!"

Without hesitation, Seri brought her hands together and aimed at the sword. Marshal dove out of the way as the power erupted from her. The air sizzled around him.

Curasir's sword became like a living thing in his hand, shaking with the power that flowed into it. He stared at it for several moments, open-mouthed. The sword grew brighter as Seri's brightness decreased. It was working.

Curasir released the sword and scrambled back into the portal. Marshal aimed a quick burst of power at him, but it struck the stone where his feet had been.

The sword's brightness increased exponentially. As Seri settled back down onto her feet, the sword rose into the air. Bits of dust and pebbles began to revolve around it now.

At last Seri stopped, letting her arms fall to her sides. She sagged, but stayed on her feet. The sword radiated light almost too bright to look at, but Marshal couldn't help it. He felt drawn to this blade. Something about it called to him. If he listened, he almost felt sure he would hear words…

"Uh… a little help?" Victor called. "Death god still standing here!"

Marshal reached into the light and grasped the sword's hilt. Whatever else it might be, the sword was a tool, and he needed it right now. He concentrated on his power, aiming the sword at Ne'gal. Pure magic burst from the blade, a beam of Antises magic, far more focused than what Marshal could create on his own. The beam struck Ne'gal in the chest and pushed him back.

The god reached forward, trying to push back against the magic. Marshal inched toward him and kept concentrating. At last, Ne'gal couldn't resist. He dropped his arms. The magic threw him off the hill and across the plain for hundreds of yards before he arced down toward the ground.

Marshal let the sword drop down and leaned on it, still unable to put weight on his knee. He chuckled and looked up at Victor. "I thought your flail would take care of him?"

"I never got a hit on him!" Victor complained. "He wasn't moving that fast, but I couldn't get him!"

Seri stumbled toward them. "I have no idea what's going on," she said, "but it is so good to see the two of you."

Victor grinned. "Same to you." He shielded his eyes from the bright light still radiating from the sword. "What do we do with that?"

"We destroy this portal once and for all," Marshal answered. He plunged the sword down into the granite platform.

(((46)))

Jamana watched the light at the hilltop become almost too much, then fade. What was going on up there?

Tich approached the group, rolling up her rope. "What's happening? Are we not climbing the hill now?"

"Who are you?" Ixchel demanded.

"This is Tich," Jamana intervened. "She's a friend."

"There are stairs around the west side of the hill," said the archer. "It will be much faster." He started in that direction without waiting for a reply. Ixchel went with him.

"There's an army over there," Dravid said.

"If I have to fight through an army to reach my Lady, I will do so," Ixchel answered. She quickened her pace.

"Who are they?" Tich asked.

"Ixchel is a friend," Jamana explained. "I don't know the other one."

"I'm going with them," Dravid said.

"What about Talinir?" Tich wanted to know.

Jamana looked up. The Eldani warden continued to duel Rathri back and forth across the side of the hill. How they kept from sliding down, he couldn't imagine. Then something else caught his eye.

"There's someone else up there, not far," he said.

"One of the weird dark ones?" Tich asked. She glanced at Dravid, who hastened away after the other two.

"No," Jamana said. "It's a human." He ran toward the hill.

Tich threw up her hands. "Will someone make up their mind around here? Are we all going in different directions?"

● ● ● ● ●

Marshal wanted to study the sword, learn everything he could about it, practice with it. But the portal remained open. An army of Durunim and their god-masters already assembled below. Thousands of people were in danger. His people. His land.

"Get down the stairs!" he snapped at Victor and Seri. "This is going to be messy."

Seri looked ready to argue, but Victor pulled at her robe's sleeve. "Come on. Remember the last one!" The two of them hastened off the platform. Marshal hoped they could get out of range in time.

Everything still hurt. His knee throbbed. He still couldn't stand on it. The cut on his back might be the worst. He couldn't tell how deep it was, but the pain from it threatened to overwhelm him. His blood soaked what was left of his shirt and down into his trousers.

No more time to think. He allowed his own power to radiate out from his whole body, hoping to protect himself from what happened next. Then he focused on the sword, willing it to release its power again.

The granite exploded outward in every direction. Marshal's power protected him from the worst of it, but a few smaller shards penetrated his makeshift shield, adding some minor cuts to his injuries. He kept his focus. The entire upper platform of the high place disintegrated, blown apart and out. Debris rained down in every direction.

The glowing portal itself remained intact and upright. It settled down onto the new top of the hill. Marshal frowned. He kept up his focus through the sword. More dirt and rock erupted. He would tear down this high place if he had to destroy the hill one piece at a time.

•••••

Volraag screamed as an avalanche of rocks and dirt roared toward him. The scream helped him push past the mental barriers preventing him from using what power he had left. It erupted out of him in all direction, pulverizing rock and shoving dirt aside. The effort knocked him loose from his precarious position and sent him sliding further down, almost to the base of the hill.

Even in the chaos, he couldn't stop marveling over the two masters of combat dueling above him. The avalanche did nothing to stop Talinir and Rathri. Both of them leaped into the air, launched themselves from chunks of stone falling from the hilltop, dashed through clouds of dust, and kept up constant attacks and defenses against each other. Both were bleeding from a number of small cuts, but neither had suffered serious injury yet. Volraag had never seen anything like it.

After their first short arguments, the combatants had fallen silent. No shouts. No taunts. No sneers. No grunts of pain or effort. Back and forth, they executed a mute but deadly dance, defying that force which pulls everyone toward the ground.

Beyond the duel, Volraag saw more eruptions occurring at the top of the hill. More rock and dirt rained down. One enormous slab of granite broke loose and skidded down the side of the hill. Pushing an ever-growing cascade of scree ahead of it, the slab accelerated in its descent. It must have been at least a dozen feet wide and maybe half as long.

A split-second before it arrived, both Rathri and Talinir vaulted into the air and landed on the slab itself. As it continued its headlong rush, tilting wildly back and forth, the two combatants leaped at each other. Both seized the wrist of the other's sword hand and fought for control. They swayed left and then right, yet maintaining their balance somehow on the plummeting slab.

Only then did Volraag realize his danger. Using his right arm, he managed to sit up, but it wasn't enough. The slab would crush him in moments. He fought to regain concentration, to summon his power once more, to save his life.

"I've got you." Two strong arms encircled Volraag's chest and pulled.

Together, Volraag and his would-be rescuer tried to move out of the slab's path. He strove to help, but his limbs still wouldn't obey his thoughts. Chunks of rock were already striking both of them. The torrent of loose dirt threatened to bury his legs. The slab drew ever closer at a fantastic rate, carrying its two adversaries in their unending struggle.

They were almost there, but it wouldn't be enough. The edge of the slab was going to hit them.

Volraag screamed again, unleashing one short surge of power at the granite only inches from crushing him. The stone flipped into the air, missing him and his savior by inches.

Talinir and Rathri flew into the air, separating from each other. Both lashed out with their blades as they tumbled through the clouds of debris, but neither sword struck anything more than rock.

The last thing Volraag saw was the assassin and Eldani warden tumbling in different directions away from the slab, which flipped entirely and smashed into the open ground of the plain. Then another chunk of rock struck his head and all went dark.

•••••

Seri hastened down the stairs after Victor, as fast as her feet would take her without tripping over her robe. As she did, she tried to understand. This was obviously the high place. Volraag must have opened it. Marshal and Victor had arrived too late, but were trying to stop it.

Below her, on the plain, she saw the Durunim army toward the north. Straight ahead, toward the west, she saw crowds and crowds of people, though she couldn't quite understand who they were or what they were doing. Many looked like soldiers, but more didn't.

"Victor! How did I get here?" she gasped, pausing to catch her breath on one of the steps.

Above them, an eruption occurred, launching rock and dust in every direction. Some of it tumbled down the stairs toward them.

"Look out!" Victor grabbed her hand and pulled her to the side to dodge a large chunk of rock. They couldn't dodge everything, though. Without Victor's help, Seri would have lost her balance and followed the rock down the stairs at a much faster rate than she'd like.

When the short avalanche dissipated, they resumed their rapid descent, though now they had to watch their steps even more. "I don't know how you got here," Victor said a few moments later. "Just that the bad guys had you."

How was that possible? When she lost consciousness, maybe she fell into the Otherworld again. Had the gods found her there and brought her back? And what about Ixchel and Ekur?

They reached the halfway platform and paused to catch their breath. Much of the debris had stopped here, requiring them to climb over some loose granite to resume their descent.

The hilltop erupted again. "He just couldn't wait until we got down, could he?" Victor grumbled.

They both kept moving. When the next wave of debris caught up to them, Seri used some of her remaining magic to push aside any large chunks of rock. Even so, they both had to stop and kneel to keep from losing their balance. As soon as it subsided, they rushed down the final stairs toward the base of the hill.

Victor stopped on the final step, putting his hands on his knees. Seri stepped out onto the rough grass and breathed a sigh of relief. Above, she heard Marshal blast away another piece of the hill. They wouldn't be out of danger until they moved further out. She turned to tell Victor, and saw two figures running around the side of the hill toward them.

"Ixchel! Father!"

Before Seri could take another three steps, Ixchel caught her and whipped her into a spinning hug. Ekur followed, a relieved smile on his face.

"Oh good," Victor said. He stretched and looked up at the hill again. "I was wondering where she was."

Seri laughed. She still wasn't entirely sure how all this had come about, but at least they were together again. Everyone was here: Ixchel, Ekur, Marshal, Victor…

And then she saw him. Stumbling along, far behind Ixchel but hurrying as fast as he could. "Dravid."

Ixchel and Ekur released her and stepped back. Seri took a step toward Dravid. Ixchel turned toward Victor. And that's when everything went horribly wrong.

"Seri! Look out!" Victor's yell made her turn. Debris cascaded off the steps again, but not enough to cause concern.

Then she saw him. The strange-looking god Victor had been fighting at the top of the hill. How had he gotten here so fast after being blasted off by Marshal? He stood only steps away, rushing toward Seri, arm outstretched, black fire crackling on his fingers.

She took a step backward and tripped over a chunk of granite. Dravid yelled something. Ekur tried to pull out his axe. Ixchel leaped between Seri and her attacker. Victor raced toward them, pulling his flail out.

"Ixchel! Don't!" he yelled.

But Ixchel had no knowledge of this god's power. She battered away his outstretched arm with her shield and stabbed beneath his armpit. Ordinarily, a killing blow. As the strange god slid off her blade, he reached past it. One finger brushed the top of Ixchel's sword hand.

She collapsed in an unmoving heap next to Seri.

(((47)))

Marshal took a break to let the dust settle. He gave it an extra push with his power, trying to get some clean air to breathe.

Every time he unleashed his power through the sword, he destroyed a layer of the hill, making it two or three feet shorter. So far, the sword had not depleted its store of magic; Marshal only used his own power to protect himself from the chaos. But it was taking too long. The portal still stood. It moved down with him each time he destroyed part of the hill, but otherwise, it didn't change at all.

The portal in Ch'olan had been flat, allowing him to bury it without much difficulty. This one's vertical alignment might prove more difficult.

At every pause, one or more Durunim appeared through the portal. Some tried to attack him, while others ran to the side of the hill and tried to escape. The attackers he blasted back into the portal. He didn't concern himself with the escapers. Curasir had not re-appeared.

He glanced down the stairs. Seri and Victor had reached the bottom and others came to meet them. The dust and debris clouded his vision, preventing him from seeing anything more.

Enough. He took one last deep breath of clean air and then focused again, this time including more of his own power through the sword. Wave after wave of power erupted around him. His descent, along with the sword and the portal, accelerated. The hill shrank, sending its pieces flying in all directions.

• • • • •

Seri screamed and released more of her magic at the bleeding god. He staggered back, leaving him wide open for Victor. The flail, expertly swung, smashed into the god's chest and took him off his feet. He flew several feet, rolled across the ground, and lay still.

Seri scrambled to Ixchel and grabbed her arm. The shield fell away. "What did he do to her?"

Victor staggered to them and dropped to his knees. "Marshal called him the death god. Said his very touch could kill."

"No, no, no, no." Seri pulled Ixchel's head into her lap. Was she breathing? She couldn't tell.

Loud explosions came from the hill. Victor looked up. "Marshal's really going at it now. We need to get further away."

Seri ignored him. She patted Ixchel's face, trying to wake her. Ekur approached, but stood silent behind her.

Dravid arrived at last and let himself collapse next to them. He reached out, his hand glowing. "Let me try to help her."

Seri nodded. Out of the corner of her eye, she saw a chariot break free from the Kuktarman army and come toward them.

Dravid placed his hand on Ixchel's head and closed his eyes. The glow spread across her face and hair. Dravid's face scrunched up. Nothing happened.

"I don't— I think… it's not working." He opened his eyes.

"You will not give up!" Seri stared into his eyes, those eyes she had longed to see for so long. "Keep trying, Dravid."

"I've only been able to heal when I knew the injury, or at least where it was." He coughed from the dust that swirled around them. "I don't know what's wrong with her. I… don't think she's breathing."

"No, I can't accept that!" Seri grabbed Dravid's hand. Any other time, she would have found that highly distracting. But only Ixchel mattered right now. She placed her other hand on Ixchel's forehead and focused.

Master Hain taught her to sense the life within something. She needed to find the life within Ixchel. Maybe she could hold on to it or bring it back or something.

"What are you doing? You can't just sit here!" The voice sounded familiar, but not the authority of it. Seri opened her eyes and looked up.

"Adhi?" Seeing her young acolyte friend from Zes Sivas on a military chariot had to be the strangest thing that had happened yet.

"Seri. Good to see you," he answered in a rush. "But you may have noticed Marshal tearing apart the hill behind you. This is not a safe place."

"Ixchel is hurt, maybe even dead," Dravid told him. "We can't move her."

Seri went back to focusing on Ixchel. Where was the life? It had to be here. It had to. Adhi argued with Dravid and Victor, but she ignored the conversation. "Ixchel. Where are you?" she whispered.

A glimmer of life caught her attention. There. Maybe. But so small. And getting smaller.

•••••

Volraag's eyes came open, then shut again, clouded with dust. He coughed hard before realizing someone still had arms wrapped around his chest, pulling him backwards.

"If you're awake, you could help by moving your feet," an unfamiliar voice said behind him.

His heels were dragging on the ground as his rescuer tried to pull him along. He tried working his legs, taking steps of some kind. But his muscles remained weak, and he hindered their progress more than helped. A blast of power would launch them further away, but when he tried to access it, he found nothing. The power still vibrated within him, but he couldn't seem to use it.

"Just keep still then," the voice said.

Volraag couldn't see much of anything through the dust. All around, debris rained from above. A few rocks struck both him and his rescuer. Most were tiny, but at least one impact would leave a bruise on his leg. Behind him, he heard a pained grunt as one of the larger rocks hit his new friend.

"Marshal's speeding up his destruction. I'm not sure we're going to get far enough away in time. Theon help us."

Volraag echoed the sentiments.

•••••

Seri pulled at the tiny spark of life she found within Ixchel. But it continued to drift away from her. In moments, it would be gone beyond her reach.

The explosions and avalanche of destruction continued, but she ignored it all. The others would deal with it. She had to do something here. Her Bond to Ixchel demanded it. But more than that, Ixchel was counting on her. They were friends. Sisters.

The ebbing life continued to slip away. She needed something else. Something...

Dravid. His power could heal.

"Dravid, let your power flow!"

"I don't know where—"

"Into me! I'll guide it!"

Without another question, Dravid obeyed. Seri gasped as his golden magic flowed from his hand into hers. It felt so different! Warm almost to the point of discomfort. Her throat, already parched from the dusty air, grew drier still.

She shook aside her analysis of the effects and focused on Ixchel again. Where was it? Where was it? The life. Was she too late already? No. There. Almost gone completely. Seri forced Dravid's power toward that spark of life, encircling it in her mind: a golden sphere surrounding a glowing spark. She pulled on the power, drawing it back toward herself. That was the advantage to Dravid's power. Once the magic of Antises left her, it could not be pulled back in any way.

"Is it... is it working?" Dravid asked.

"Yes. Quiet, please." Ouch. The dust and the magic side-effects tore at her throat.

Ixchel's life spark resisted her, starting to pull back against Dravid's power. Seri concentrated even harder, braced herself mentally, and yanked it as hard as she could.

Ixchel lurched into a sitting position with an enormous gasp. She blinked against the dust and coughed over and over. Seri seized her and wrapped her arms around her. Tears streamed out of her eyes, forming dark rivulets down her dust-covered cheeks.

It worked. It worked. Ixchel lived.

●●●●●

Marshal couldn't see much through the clouds of dust and debris. But he knew the hill had been greatly reduced, at least. Time to deal with the portal itself.

The sword focused his power in a more direct flow. But now he wanted to unleash it in a much broader swath.

He inhaled deeply through his nose to avoid the dust, though it didn't help much. No matter. He could breathe when he finished the job.

The power flowed out of him in an enormous surge. If he hadn't been hurting so much from his injuries, he would have marveled at how easy this had become. Months ago, he would have to concentrate to throw out one burst of magic. Now, it came out with barely a thought.

Holding his own position, he blasted away at the ground beneath the portal. Using his power this way, it did not take long to excavate an enormous area. As he deepened and widened the hole, the portal fell, bit by bit.

This process actually made no sense to him. Logically, no matter how deep he buried the portal, if it remained open, wouldn't the dirt and rock just pour through it into the Otherworld? But somehow, it had worked with the portal in Ch'olan. Maybe the portal's magic required open air to work? Or sunlight? Regardless, this was the only method he knew.

Once the portal, still upright, fell below ground level, he switched tactics. Now he had to bury it. He used his power to push dirt and rubble into the hole. He dumped an enormous amount down around it before he realized he couldn't do all of this from one position. He would have to get up and move around the hole to push material in from all sides.

Except his knee wouldn't allow him to walk right now. Frustrated, Marshal knew he needed help.

With the clouds of dust and debris still settling, he had to wait. He had no way of telling how far the others had retreated while he worked. For that matter, he didn't know where the enemy might be, either.

Just as the thought came to him, four Durunim emerged from the dust, charging him from all directions. One of them slashed his sword right away, catching Marshal's left arm with a short gash. He threw his arms outward, unleashing power in all directions. Unfortunately, the act pulled apart the wound on his back again.

Marshal yelled in pain. He clapped his right hand over the cut on his left arm to slow the bleeding. Not much he could do about his back. He coughed again. All this dirt would be getting in his wounds too. That couldn't help.

He turned his head left and right, eyes darting around. He was vulnerable here. He couldn't work on burying the portal while trying to guard himself from attacks. Another reason he needed help. But no one could even see him in all this dust.

A thought occurred to him. He held his palms out near the ground and rotated his torso left and right. As he did, he allowed the barest whisper of power to radiate out from his upper body. It took more concentration to keep the power level so low than it did to increase it. To his delight, the dust clouds blew away from his vibratory wind, clearing the air in the immediate area.

The dust clouds swept back, revealing a wall of Durunim warriors only a few yards away. They had advanced through his destruction using shields to protect themselves. Now they stood ready with spears poised. As the dust swept further, more and more of them appeared.

Marshal's heart sank. He could blast them all away, and might even succeed. But if any of the gods approached, it would take all of his power to hold them off. And the portal remained open. He heard movement down in the pit. More enemies might still be coming through it.

A hand rested on his shoulder. He almost blasted it away before he realized Talinir stood beside him. He took another quick look. Talinir had never appeared more bedraggled than now, bleeding from multiple cuts across his entire body.

"I told you, Marshal. I promised to protect you." The warden stepped between Marshal and the Durunim, raising his warpsteel sword in challenge.

At that moment, the earth shook. Marshal almost fell. The shaking did not come from him.

The ground shook again. And then erupted.

(((48)))

Jamana lost his footing. What was happening? Marshal finished destroying the high place. Didn't he? Why was everything shaking again?

When he first pulled the injured man from the side of the hill, Jamana hadn't recognized him. Then he had used magic to save them. In the chaos, Jamana hadn't even noticed his own magic senses reacting. It was Volraag.

It would be easy just to let him go. To run away and save himself. No one would even see. Dravid took off after Ixchel. And Tich… where had she gone? Regardless, Jamana stood alone, pulling their hated enemy to safety. His mind screamed at him, reminding him this man killed his homeland's Lord. This man started a war. This man endangered all of Antises with his actions over and over. This man must have done something to Seri, even.

But it didn't matter what his mind screamed. His conscience, his heart, would not allow him to leave Volraag behind. "That's the difference," he told himself. "Mercy. These gods kill without mercy. I will not be like them."

He stumbled and released Volraag. They both fell prone as the ground shook. "What is he doing now?" Volraag cried.

Jamana pulled himself up on his hands and knees, wincing. He tried to ignore all the bruises he suffered from falling debris while dragging Volraag. He looked around. Cracks appeared in the earth.

"I don't think Marshal is doing this."

•••••

Seri released Ixchel and wiped her face with the back of her hand. Together again. She laughed. Then her gaze settled on Dravid.

He was here, really here. Marshal rescued him, like he promised. He looked the same as ever, except that now his beautiful smile was surrounded by weeks of facial hair growth. She reached out and Dravid took her hand in his again. But this time, the warmth in their touch had nothing to do with magic. She opened her mouth to say something.

And the earth shook.

"What now?" Victor exclaimed.

All around her, the others fell to their knees. Only then did Seri notice someone had flipped Adhi's chariot onto its side to shield her and Ixchel from the avalanche. Debris piled up against the chariot and spilled around its sides. That could have been disastrous. She needed to thank Adhi for that. And why was he in a chariot, anyway?

All of these thoughts rushed through her mind in the brief moment between the first tremble and the second, which came far stronger. In that moment, she knew. Marshal wasn't causing this.

"Antises holds its breath. It is waiting," Lady Lilitu said. The calm before the storm.

The storm had arrived.

● ● ● ● ●

Marshal scrambled on his hands and knees. An enormous crack opened right beside him, dirt and rock collapsing into it. Talinir sidestepped away from it. Two of the Durunim were not so lucky and plunged in as the crack spread toward the north. The earth shook, its intensity growing by the second.

Three of the Durunim chose that moment to make their attack anyway. They lurched across the uneven, shaking ground and threw their spears. Marshal lifted his hand to blast them out of the air, but Talinir intervened. He whipped into the spears' flight path with unbelievable speed. He deflected two of them with a sweep of his sword and seized the third one in mid-air. He spun and launched it back at its thrower.

Marshal didn't see what happened next as another shock sent him face-first into the dirt. He pushed up, spitting, but even that much took effort. The ground shook even more, tearing itself apart everywhere he looked.

"Tell me you're not doing this!" He looked up, surprised to see someone standing even as the earth tilted under her feet. Tich.

"It's not me!"

She knelt beside him and put an arm around his shoulders. He winced as it came in contact with the gash on his back. "So this is Antises tearing itself apart, like you said." She pulled him up to his knees. "Come on. Let's try to find some solid ground."

Inch by inch, Tich helped Marshal move away from the portal. After only a couple of steps, the shifting earth knocked him down again. Somehow, Tich stayed on her feet and helped him back up. Three more steps and they both fell. This time, as she helped him up again, Marshal took a quick look around.

Talinir followed not far behind them, keeping his sword at ready and watching the Durunim. For their part, the enemy army had its own problems... as did everyone else. No matter where he looked, Marshal saw no one staying on their feet. Durunim, Kuktarman, Mandiatan. They all fell to the shaking ground. Worse, more cracks were opening, some of them several feet wide. Screams filled the air as people struggled to escape.

"We gotta keep moving," Tich urged, taking another step.

"Why? Where can we go that's safe?"

Tich looked around as well, her balance shifting with each tremble of the earth. "I... I don't know."

Marshal shook his head and let himself slide back down. "Nowhere. Nowhere is safe any more."

•••••

Seri clung to Dravid as the earth convulsed about them. Even during the most violent quake on Zes Sivas, it had never been this horrible, this violent.

Beneath Adhi's overturned chariot, a crack opened. The chariot shifted, then tumbled down. Victor scrambled back from the edge. Ixchel and Ekur helped pull Dravid and Seri away. Together, they crawled toward the Kuktarman army. But even there, she saw no hope. No one could stay on their feet. Devastation. Screams. Cries of anguish. Shouts. Death. She closed her eyes against it all.

Lady Lilitu had been right. Antises had held itself together for as long as it could. Now it was tearing itself apart, and nothing could stop it.

Or could it? It could all be fixed. She knew it. Hadn't she seen that, in the space between? Something. Something missing. Something that could pull everything back together.

On the first day she arrived at Zes Sivas, so long ago, she saw the first of these quakes. It seemed so tiny now. The Masters had been so concerned, yet so analytical about it all. Ridiculous theories spouted forth, even blaming the Eldanim. But they knew. She knew. It was the missing King and his power. Without it, the Passing never achieved what it was meant to do. And now they were paying for it.

But they found the King. Her eyes flew open and she grabbed Dravid with her other hand.

"Marshal!"

"What about him?"

"We have to get to him. He's the only one who can stop this!"

• • • • •

"Can't you do anything?" Tich lost her balance again and caught herself with her palms next to Marshal.

He shook his head. "I don't... I don't think I can."

But he could try, couldn't he? During the short tremor earlier, he thought he could try using a different vibration against the vibration of the quake. But that was a small tremble. This...

Tich reached for him, to pull him back up, but he pushed her hand away. "No, I'll try." She gave him a searching look, then nodded.

Marshal took a deep breath. Everything still hurt, perhaps more than ever. After all the shaking and flying debris, bruises ached all over the place. The gash across his back and the cut on his arm burned. His knee throbbed. A quick glance showed it to be swollen much larger than normal. Even his facial scars burned.

He spread his palms across the earth, though it wouldn't stay still even now. Closing his eyes, he concentrated, trying to understand the vibration of the quake. At first, it felt chaotic, shifting without rhyme or reason.

"Are you doing anything?" Tich asked.

"Not yet. Give me a minute."

It wasn't all chaotic. There. A rhythm. A very strange one, but he could feel it. Then he lost it. "Hailstones!" His eyes flew open in time to see a wave of dirt and debris washing toward them. He let a brief burst of power flow out, tearing the wave apart.

"Let me know if something like that comes toward us again," he said. He couldn't spend time watching.

"Yeah. You got it." Tich sounded almost as unsettled and vulnerable as she had when facing Vayan. Even as he recalled that moment, she reached out and placed her hand on top of his. He looked into her face for a moment. What an unusual woman. Dealing with her pain had altered her, taking away some of the sarcastic and defensive edge. Except she hadn't really dealt with it; she had forgotten it. What would happen when she learned the truth?

He shook his head. Why were these thoughts in his way now? He closed his eyes and focused again.

The rhythm. Find it. He could do it. There. Definitely a pattern. A rough, uneven syncopation, but repeating itself every few moments. That had to be it.

Now. He needed to release his power in a rhythm to counter that one. And it had to be precise. If he messed up, he might throw it off and lose the rhythm entirely. Or he might alter it.

He waited until what he considered the point of ending or repetition for the rhythm. He let loose a short burst, countering the first few vibrations of the rhythm. He waited until it repeated again, then did the same thing, this time adding another pair of vibrations, again countering the quake's rhythm.

"I felt that," Tich said. "I think it stabilized us for a second or two." She squeezed the back of his hand.

Marshal took another deep breath and tried again. And again. Each time the rhythm repeated, he added more to his own pattern, his own rhythm of vibrating magic, radiating down from his palms. After a dozen or so repetitions, he had it. He kept it going, letting his power flow in the pattern, countering the earth's vibrations.

"It's working!" Tich released his hand and stood up.

Marshal opened his eyes and looked around, but kept the flow going. He and Tich crouched and stood on an island of solidity in a sea of shaking earth. He was making a difference, but only in a small circle of ground around the two of them. Good for them, but worthless to everyone else who remained in danger.

He gritted his teeth and tried to increase his power output, pushing out the boundaries of the stable ground. He had no idea what he was doing. Countering the pattern required constant concentration. How to expand it? More power was the only answer he could conceive.

His power flowed into the ground, more and more of it. Yet the stable earth increased by only a few inches. All right. He had more power. He increased it again. And again. And again. But no matter how much power he unleashed, their safe zone barely increased.

"You're doing it, Marshal." Talinir's voice this time. He must have joined them. Marshal kept his eyes closed and kept pushing himself.

"It's not enough," he whispered. "I don't have enough power."

Then he missed one beat in the rhythm. The ground heaved up beneath his legs, tossing him forward toward an open crack.

(((49)))

"How can we possibly get to Marshal? I can't even move!"

Seri ignored Dravid's words and stared across the plain. Marshal's power called to her from that direction. She couldn't see him right now, but his power was unmistakable. "We have to try!" she repeated.

"You will not go anywhere without me," Ixchel said from the other side. She crawled beside Seri and took hold of her arm. "We'll go together."

"Wait." Seri turned her head to see her father watching them, next to Victor. "Go," he said. "You can do this." She nodded, locked eyes with Victor for a moment, then turned back.

Ixchel crawled, pulling Seri as she did. Dravid came along, doing his best. He dropped the staff to have a free hand. Together, the three of them inched along the trembling earth. Seri guided them, sensing Marshal's presence ahead. Lying on the ground with the constantly shifting terrain, no one could see more than a few feet away.

Consequently, Ixchel almost fell into an enormous crack before she saw it. She stopped and scrambled back, Seri helping to pull her.

"Can we get around it?" Seri asked.

Ixchel craned her neck to look. "It seems to extend a long way in both directions." She pushed back another few inches. "And it's growing."

Seri thought for a moment. There had to be a way across. If only…

"Dravid. Build us a bridge."

• • • • •

Jamana slipped. His left leg went over the edge of a foot-wide crack in the earth. He grabbed hold of Volraag and used the Lord's weight to pull himself back. Volraag grunted, but said nothing.

Neither of them knew what to do. The earth convulsed around them in every direction. Jamana couldn't see anyone on their feet, not even the sure-footed Talinir. In fact, he couldn't see anyone at all.

He looked south, toward the closest edge of the plain surrounding the former high place. Should he try to go that way? Trees swayed as if buffeted by strong winds. One fell, ripping an enormous chunk of earth out with its roots. They would find no safety there.

"Nowhere safe," he muttered. "Nowhere at all."

Volraag rolled to look at him. "An acolyte mage? Do I know you?"

"No." Jamana didn't feel like trying to explain his relationships with those who did know the young Lord.

"You saved me." Volraag struggled to speak while everything shook around him. "If we survive this, you will be well rewarded."

"Keep it." Jamana kept trying to watch for others. "We may not survive, anyway. I am thinking no one will survive."

"This will pass," Volraag insisted. "It always does."

Jamana watched the nearest crack expand another few inches, dirt tumbling down into it. "I'm not so sure it will."

"You'll see. We'll be all right. I can—oh."

Jamana turned to see why Volraag had broken off. At last, he saw someone on his feet, only a couple dozen yards away. He lifted a hand to wave, then realized who stood there.

The leper assassin.

•••••

"A bridge?" Dravid stared at Seri. "I can't make a bridge."

"It doesn't have to be elaborate," Seri said. "Just… you know, like a plank we can crawl over." She gestured at the crack.

Dravid eyed it dubiously. This crack had to be three feet wide now. Plus, the edges couldn't be stable, so a bridge would have to be more like six feet long. At least. He had never made anything that big. And it would have to be stable enough for all three of them to cross it.

"I don't… I can't…"

Seri squeezed his hand. For a moment, he forgot everything else. The world itself might be tearing apart. Ancient gods with sinister designs might be a short distance away, together with an army of magical warriors. But he was here, with Seri, holding her hand. Let the world end. At least they were together.

"You can do it," Seri urged. "I believe in you."

How could he argue with that?

She caught his gaze and looked directly into his eyes. Well, as much as she could with everything shaking. "I love you."

Dravid swallowed. Now he had no choice. Make the bridge or fail Seri. Do something improbable, or do something unthinkable. He released Seri's hand and flipped himself onto his back, his head resting not far from the crack's edge.

He closed his eyes and reached inside himself. The power waited for him. Still there. Because of its strange nature, he always worried it would run out, or fade away. But that didn't matter right now. He focused and lifted his hand into the air. A tingle of warmth rushed up his chest and throat. Golden magic began to form.

Dravid considered how wide to shape his bridge. A foot would be too narrow, but if he made it too wide, he didn't think he could maintain the entire thing. He settled on his own width, somewhere around a foot and a half. He could crawl on something like that. Seri probably could too. And he had no worries about Ixchel.

Dravid bent the end of his bridge down, to plant it into the earth on the other side of the crack. Then bit by bit, he added to it, making it longer and longer. After a minute or so, it extended out over his face. He tried to ignore the undulating surface beneath his back.

"It's getting worse," Ixchel observed.

"Shhh," Seri said. "Give him time."

Inch by inch, Dravid forged his bridge. By the time it reached three feet long, he could already feel the negative effects of using this power. The warmth in his chest and throat grew to an uncomfortable heat. He pulled and pulled on the magic, drawing out the width and length he needed. Was he making it too thick? Could he cut back on that? Or could he get it too thin? Everything he formed seemed practically indestructible. He had held someone aloft with a small circle of it one time. That girl back at Forerunner's home. What was her name again?

Agh. He didn't need to remember that. Focus!

"You're doing it," Seri whispered. "Keep going."

Dravid glanced over his shoulder at the crack. Had it grown wider? He breathed in through gritted teeth and kept going. The bridge grew unwieldy, and he flipped it down over his leg. He pulled more and more of the golden power into being.

"Almost there..." Seri's words barely penetrated his consciousness, so intent was he on his work. The heat grew. His chest tightened. He closed his eyes against the warmth behind them.

"That should do it," Ixchel said.

Dravid opened his eyes and looked down. The bridge stretched longer than his height. It had to be enough. Before he could move, Ixchel seized the bridge and thrust it out over the crack. It reached the other side with room to spare. She pressed down on it; it did not give.

"Go," Dravid told Seri. "I'll be last."

"I knew you could do it," she said before crawling forward.

The earth continued to shake as Seri ventured out on Dravid's bridge. Ixchel glanced at Dravid, then stayed close to Seri, ready to leap forward if the bridge failed. Dravid almost laughed. What could she do if that happened? He had to keep it intact, or they would all die.

"It's very strong," Seri called back. In a brief lull in the tremors, she hurried the rest of the way and reached the other side. Dravid would have breathed a sigh of relief, but he couldn't breathe at all. The tightness in his chest cut off his air.

He waved at Ixchel to go on. She nodded and hurried across.

Dravid tried to suck in air, but couldn't. He had to let the magic go. But Seri might need him! He crawled onto the bridge. At least he could still crawl. In fact, the last time he had crawled like this might have been soon after he lost his leg, back on Zes Sivas, in the tunnel where he and Seri watched the Passing.

Spots danced before his eyes. He couldn't breathe. The heat reached unbearable levels, as if fire might explode from his chest or spew out of his mouth.

He couldn't do it. With his last shred of willpower, he released the magic. The bridge dissolved beneath him as he gasped a mouthful of cool, sweet air. And he fell.

Something grabbed the back of his shirt. Another hand seized his arm. He flailed forward and found dirt. The edge! Ixchel! With her help, he scrambled up and over, rolling onto unstable but flat ground at last. He sucked in huge droughts of air over and over.

Seri crawled beside him. "See? You can always do more than you think you can."

"When..." he gasped, "when did you get so wise?"

"I've always been wise. You just never noticed."

"Right." Dravid chuckled. "I just need to rest a moment."

Seri looked away. "We may not have time. I think Marshal's in trouble."

•••••

Marshal stared down into the abyss as it rushed up to claim him. At the last moment, he jerked back. Talinir, of course, caught him. Together with Tich's help, he climbed backward and they moved away from the crack.

"Try it again," Tich suggested.

Marshal groaned. Finding the rhythm and countering it had taxed him mentally and physically. He didn't relish starting the process over.

"I don't think I can do much," he answered, but he placed his palms down and felt for the rhythm again. There. No. Had it changed? After a few moments of concentration, he decided it hadn't. It was still the same.

He took another deep breath, then lost it when it created a brief pain in his chest. A memory of his earlier injuries? Or something still there? He pushed past it and started his counter vibrations again. After several false starts, he got it. Once again, he set up his own rhythm opposite that of the earth, stabilizing the immediate area around him.

Talinir and Tich both got to their feet. "This is good," Tich said.

"Not much," Marshal gasped.

"It's a start," Talinir said. "From here, you can—"

"I can't do anything else! No matter how much power I pour into this, I can't stabilize any further. I can't stop it all!"

Talinir fell silent. Good. Marshal didn't need more useless encouragement.

"So… if you can't stop it… and it doesn't stop on its own…" Tich paused. "What's going to happen?"

"I don't know," Marshal answered. The more probable answer terrified him. Seri said Antises was coming apart, that the quakes would only get worse. Was this happening everywhere now? What about in the cities? Would all six lands be destroyed? "It's all my fault," he whispered. If he had gone to Zes Sivas with Seri right away when they met… maybe he could have prevented this. Maybe Topleb and Rufus would still be alive. Maybe…

"Someone is crawling this way," Talinir said. "Three people."

"Good or bad?" Tich asked.

"One of them is Seri. I can tell by the robe," Talinir observed.

"I repeat my question."

Marshal rolled his eyes at Tich. "Get her here, Talinir. She might be able to help."

Talinir nodded and took off across the trembling plain. Marshal maintained his counter-rhythm, but tried to watch the warden's progress. His sure-footedness seemed uncanny. He took short steps, sideways dashes, long leaps in unerring combinations to keep moving across the ground that would not stay still.

In a few moments, he returned, carrying Seri on his back. She slid off onto the stable ground, and Talinir bounded away again. "Theon's pillars," she exclaimed. "What a relief." She knelt onto the earth and took several deep breaths. Looking up, she noticed Tich. "Oh, hello. I'm Seri."

"So I've heard."

Marshal tried not to laugh. In truth, it was getting harder to maintain his rhythm with all of this happening around him. If he lost his concentration again, he might not be able to regain it.

"Your back!" Seri exclaimed. "Are you all right?"

"It's not too bad."

Talinir returned again, this time with Dravid. He also dismounted, with Seri's help and breathed a sigh of relief. A few moments later, Ixchel joined them without help.

"Dravid!" Tich laughed. "You leave me alone for five minutes and come back with the ladies. Are you sure you're not a sailor?"

"Who are you?" Ixchel asked.

"This is Tich, another friend," Marshal interrupted. "Can we please focus on the problem here?"

Seri stepped to his side and put her hand on his shoulder. "What are you doing right now?"

"I'm trying to counter the… shaking. Using an opposite vibration."

"But he can't get it any further," Tich added, gesturing around them.

"That was good thinking," Seri said. "But it's going to take more than that."

"What will it take?" Marshal's vision blurred for a moment.

"The Heart of Fire."

(((50)))

"Maybe he didn't see us," Jamana said, trying not to draw attention to himself.

"Too late. Rathri has excellent vision," Volraag said quietly.

The assassin leaped over an upward fold of earth, drawing nearer to them.

"We are both dead, unless you can stop him," Volraag observed.

"Me? You're the Lord!"

"I am… but I can't use my power."

Rathri stepped calmly over a narrow crevasse and drew his sword.

Jamana looked around in desperation. No one else came into view. "You blasted that rock up there, just a few minutes ago!"

"I know. Believe me." Volraag coughed. "I'm trying. But I can't do it. You're a mage, aren't you?"

"I'm an acolyte mage!' Jamana's voice rose. "And we don't have power like you do! We have to draw it in from somewhere! I'm too far from Zes Sivas. I need another source! I need—"

He broke off as Rathri picked up his pace. He would be on them in seconds. A source of power. He needed… a source of power.

Jamana clamped his hand onto Volraag's shoulder. "This better work." He could feel the power roiling about inside the young Lord. So much power. Keeping his eyes on the advancing assassin, Jamana concentrated as Master Korda had taught him. He reached for the power, pulling it toward him.

At first, it resisted his pull. Rathri bounded toward him now, raising his sword.

The power flowed into Jamana, almost wrenching his own shoulder as it shot up his arm.

Rathri leaped, sweeping his sword in a wide arc over his head and coming down at the crouching duo.

Jamana held his other hand up and Volraag's power exploded out of it. It caught Rathri directly in the chest, stopping him in mid-air. Jamana pumped his arm. The power doubled itself. Rathri flew back through the air, losing his sword. He hit the pulsating ground, rolled three times, and plunged into a huge opening.

•••••

Despite his reassurance, Seri worried about Marshal's back. The gash looked horrible. What remained of his shirt hung from his body, completely drenched in blood. That couldn't be good for him.

She wanted to tell him everything, to explain all she had learned over the past year or so, starting with her training on Zes Sivas and leading up to her experience from a few days ago. Every detail seemed vitally important. But there was no time.

"Listen, I saw it all: the magic that holds Antises together and binds it to the Otherworld," she said in a rush. "There's a hole in it. I think the Heart of Fire belongs in that hole."

Marshal shot her a look, but kept his hands to the ground. She could feel the power pulsing out from him into the ground, holding off the destruction that surrounded them.

"I don't know what you mean," he said.

"The Heart of Fire. It's the King's power. When he releases it at the Passing, it forms this… this glowing ball of fire or something, surrounded by all of the Lords' powers."

"How does this help us now?" Talinir asked.

"You can patch the hole!" Seri insisted. She knelt beside Marshal. "At least temporarily. I'm sure that will stop the shaking. For a while, anyway. Until we can get everyone back to Zes Sivas and do it properly."

Marshal grunted. Sweat beaded along his forehead. Maintaining a specific rhythm of power couldn't be easy. "I don't even know how to form this Heart thing, let alone know how to use it here."

"I can help you. Remember? When we join our powers together, we can do more. And I can open the way to where your power needs to be."

"No," Ixchel said.

"What?"

"The last time you did that, we lost you. I will not let it happen again."

Seri looked up at her. "Ixchel, we're talking about saving the world here."

Ixchel stood rigid. "It is not my job to save the world. My job is to protect you."

"What exactly happened the last time?" Dravid asked.

"I guess I fell through or something," Seri said.

"She was concentrating, fell to the ground, and vanished," Ixchel answered. "We did not see her again until she appeared here as a prisoner of the gods."

"So she fell into the Otherworld," Dravid concluded. "But this time, she would have Marshal with her."

"I would advise against it," Talinir spoke up. "There is still a very large contingent of the Durunim in the Starlit Realm, hoping to still enter here. If you fell through, exhausted from whatever you're trying to do, you might not survive."

"Then I'll be their anchor." Dravid crawled next to Seri. "If the two of you can do so much, let's see what happens when you combine my power too."

Seri nodded. Marshal's grandfather had told her Dravid was a key to all of this. It made sense.

"When this starts, whether it works or not, Marshal will not be able to keep up his current action," Talinir pointed out. "We should be prepared for that." He looked to Tich and Ixchel. "The three of us must guard the three of them."

The two women exchanged glances and nodded.

Seri shifted and allowed Dravid to move between her and Marshal. He placed his hand over their clasped hands and closed his eyes. A golden glow radiated out and wrapped around all three of their hands.

"Now?" Marshal asked.

"Yes." Seri took a deep breath. Just before Marshal let his power erupt, she remembered. "Oh, I should also mention that this might be painful."

•••••

Marshal let his rhythm go and focused on Seri instead. As before when their powers merged, he began to see things the way Seri saw them. Dravid was there too, but Marshal could barely perceive him. Instead, he stared in awe at the power that swirled around them. A chaotic rainbow of colored beams circled Seri and Marshal, sweeping about at tremendous speeds. A rushing roar filled his ears.

Then Seri did something he had never seen before. She reached forward with her left hand, grasping. Purple beams of light surrounded her hand. "Imitate me!" she yelled. Marshal reached out with his right hand. He wasn't certain about how to do the same thing, but Seri must have been working through him somehow. His hand also became surrounded by purple.

"Now! Pull it open!" Seri wrenched to the left as Marshal did the same on the right, pulling and pushing. Instead of an opening into the Otherworld, he saw more purple. But this purple danced about like flames. "This is the painful part!" Seri warned. She leaned into the flames and pulled all of it back around the two of them.

Marshal braced himself. Seri screamed beside him, so loud and shocking he almost released her hand. Yet he felt no pain himself as the purple flames enveloped him. Seri appeared to be in absolute agony, but Marshal felt only a tingling sensation across his skin. Why did it hurt her and not him?

And then he knew. He experienced no pain because he belonged here. This place... it wasn't even really a place, was it? They were between. They existed within the magic, the binding force of Antises itself. He belonged because his magic, the magic that permeated his body, belonged. His power, his very nature as King, yes, King of Antises, made him a part of all of this. Part of the purple flames. Marshal almost laughed at that. He wondered what it would look like if he weren't seeing it as Seri did.

One moment later, he perceived the chaos. Antises unraveled here just as it shook apart in the primary world. Everything was disintegrating. The flames waved in bizarre combinations, fraying on all the edges. He felt no pain himself, but Antises did. If something did not change, it would all come apart, and soon.

Seri pulled on his hand. He turned to see her pointing, pointing at something in this... not a place. He saw a gap. A hole. Something belonged there.

He belonged there.

•••••

Dravid held on with everything he had within. His vision blurred, then re-focused, then blurred again. With each transition, he saw things different. He saw Seri and Marshal kneeling here on the broken plain, trembling along with him. Then he saw the other two floating in what looked like purple flames. Then he saw both scenes at the same time. He closed his eyes to avoid the confusing sights.

"What's happening?" Tich asked.

"I don't know," Dravid said. He could feel Marshal's power cascading through his body and back out again, looping through that one hand. At the same time, he pushed his own power out, not so much to create a physical object, but to bind their three hands together. He concentrated, extending that binding down into the earth, hoping it would keep them here, no matter what else happened.

A strong tremor shook them all. Ixchel grunted behind him, no doubt annoyed she couldn't maintain her footing any longer.

Heat and tightness formed within his chest. Not again. He had hoped the magic's side-effects wouldn't be as severe without forming something physical. No such luck. If anything, the effects were more severe.

How long would Marshal and Seri take? Could he hang on that long?

• • • • •

"He is untrained. Unprepared for this."

Seri flinched at the voice of Lady Lilitu. The flames had activated the stone again.

"Rest easy, child. Since your last visit to this place, I have learned more. I am helping you, blocking most of the pain."

"Thank you." Seri had been willing to endure the pain again, if that's what it took, but after a first wave of agony, it faded. Now she knew why.

"This boy cannot be our King," the Lady observed.

"Quiet. He'll hear you." Seri shot a look at Marshal. He appeared focused on the gap in the flames.

"He cannot hear me in this place, nor you. Words cannot travel here."

"Then how can I hear you?"

"The stone links our minds, Seri. We are communicating in a whole new way."

"Oh."

"You must understand that this boy will fail."

"What? No, he's our only hope. He's the King."

"He doesn't know what he's doing. He is damaged." The Lady paused. "No, Seri. You are our only hope."

"Me? I got him here. The rest is up to him."

"While you are touching, you can absorb his power, can't you?"

"I... yes, but what difference does that make?" Seri watched Marshal reach out toward the gap. She closed her eyes to focus on the conversation.

"You can take his power. All of it. You have the training. You know how to wield it. You can save Antises."

"What? No, I can't."

"You can. You must. Everything is falling apart, Seri. Sandu-Emuq is being torn apart as we speak."

Seri gasped. "My mother!"

"I have dispatched a servant to check on her. Thus far, the palace and the sturdier buildings around it seem to be all right, but many of the poorer areas of town have collapsed altogether. People are dying. You must take control!"

"No... I can't..."

"All of Antises depends on your actions here, daughter. I pray you make the right decision."

Seri did not respond. She opened her eyes and looked at Marshal. His scars. His current injuries. His inexperience and stubbornness. Maybe the Lady was right.

(((51)))

In his mind, Marshal approached the gap in the magic. He had no sense of actual movement, but with his thoughts, he now found himself right before it. The wrongness of the gap offended his senses. His physical body felt only the continuing tremors in the primary world. But his magic senses, those innate abilities to feel other sources of power and their strength, screamed at him.

Two years ago, Marshal had been walking through the woods around his home town of Drusa's Crossing. He spied one enormous oak that drew him toward it. Beautiful, towering, yet something felt off about it. Only when he walked around to the other side of the tree did he see: lightning had struck here, splitting off almost half of the entire tree. From one side, it looked fine. But from any other angle, it looked glaringly wrong.

This was the same. If he didn't focus on the gap, everything looked chaotic, but that could be the way things always were here. But when he looked at it, he knew. He sensed it. Wrong.

He looked to Seri for help, but she had her eyes closed. He squeezed her hand, but received no response. She didn't seem unconscious, but neither did she seem aware of her surroundings. Marshal wasn't sure what that meant, but his focus turned back to the gap.

He had to do something about this. Seri said the Heart of Fire belonged here. But he didn't even know what that meant. He lifted his right hand and released a burst of power.

As always, vibrations ran through his arm, hand, and fingers before the power left him. To his surprise, as it left him, the magic appeared like bright fire—not white necessarily, but pure and powerful. It flowed into the gap, then tore apart in every direction, dissipating until no sign of it remained.

Marshal frowned and forced a stronger burst of power through his hand. Again, the pure fire exploded out from him. Again, it ripped itself apart in the void that swallowed it.

For a moment, he considered pulling his other hand away from Seri to help focus his power. But he didn't really need to use his hands, did he? It was so easy and natural to point at things, he often forgot his power could flow out from any part of him.

He took a couple of deep breaths. With each one, minor aches inside his chest combined with the burning on his back. Everything hurt lately.

Marshal opened himself. Bright fire erupted from his chest and flowed into the hole. More and more poured out of him. The vibrations in his body enhanced all of the pains he already experienced. A fresh flow of blood warmed his back. His senses told him to stop the flow, but he kept it going. This would take everything he could give.

The pure fire flowing out of him congealed together in the gap. It formed a rough ball of fire in the middle, growing and growing as his deluge of power continued. It pulsed like a living thing, an extension of his body, of himself.

The Heart of Fire.

Exhaustion washed over him. How long had this day been already? Only yesterday he had been rescued from the gods and healed. Today, they traveled to the high place. He fought Curasir and then tore it all down. Expending that much power, even with the sword, took a lot out of him. And now he focused on doing even more, throwing out more power than he had ever done at once. He didn't know how much more his physical body could handle.

•••••

Dravid shook with Marshal, his body vibrating with the enormous power that flowed from the King. Combined with his own power's side effects, he struggled to keep the other two anchored. He kept his eyes closed, hearing the others discussing the situation, but unable to take part.

"The ground is not shaking quite as much," Ixchel said.

"Marshal's back is bleeding again." That was Tich. A moment later, he heard tearing of cloth. Maybe she was trying to make a bandage. He felt movement next to him.

"Careful," Talinir warned. "Do not disrupt them."

"Someone's got to do something about this," Tich argued.

A pause followed, then Talinir said, "Here. I will do it."

Their voices faded. Tich said something else, but Dravid couldn't make it out. Why couldn't he hear?

The tightness in his chest grew until he almost couldn't feel the heat any more.

• • • • •

"He's doing it!" Seri exclaimed. "The Heart of Fire! He's doing it!"

"Let us hope it is enough." Lady Lilitu's voice sounded resigned.

"It has to be."

"If he falters, you must be ready to take over."

"He will not falter."

"Your faith in him is commendable. I hope it is well placed."

Seri watched the Heart grow. Despite her arguments to the Lady, she couldn't deny the temptation to take at least some of Marshal's power for herself. If he did struggle, wouldn't it be her responsibility to take over? A trickle of his power already flowed through their clasped hands. It would be so easy to increase that trickle…

No! She already knew the consequences of absorbing too much power. Just being here again was dangerous, let alone being connected to Marshal's magic.

"Seri… some of the homes around the palace are starting to collapse."

Mother!

• • • • •

The Heart grew. Marshal stared, his mouth open. He wanted to get closer, to merge himself into it. Yet as long as he continued to pour his power into it, he couldn't move. Never in his life had he seen anything so awe-inspiring.

All of his aches, pains, blood loss, and exhaustion were taking their toll on him. His whole body shook with the power as it flowed out of him. As beautiful as it appeared, as much as he wanted to continue, he knew he couldn't do it for much longer. He wasn't sure how much power even remained within him.

The Heart nearly filled the hole. The bright, pure fire flickered out and around it, joining with the purple flames in every direction. As it did, the chaos began to stabilize. The pure flames weaved their way in and out of the purple, creating an intricate pattern everywhere Marshal looked.

He couldn't tell whether anything changed in the primary world. He had no idea whether he had done what needed to be done or not. With one final effort and burst, he stopped the flow of power.

The Heart of Fire pulsed within, binding Antises together. But it wasn't enough. Marshal could still see unraveling taking place, though nowhere near as widespread as before. Seri was right. To fully heal Antises, it would require his power and that of all the Lords. Together, they could do it.

But he wanted more than that. The Passing was a temporary solution. The power always returned to the Lords. What he had done here would probably be temporary, as well.

The flames built all around him and Seri, both purple and pure, dark and bright. The sight continued to transfix him.

"How do we get back?" he asked. No answer. "Seri? Seri?"

At that moment, a burst of fire from the Heart itself shot out toward him. His eyes went wide. The fire struck him in the chest.

Everything went white.

(((52)))

Seri gasped. A blackness flooded over her consciousness, but she pushed it aside somehow. She opened her eyes to the primary world, the real world. One final tremor ran through the ground beneath her and then faded. The earth grew still.

"My Lady? Are you still there?" She released Marshal's hand and fumbled for the stone in its pouch at her belt.

Ixchel's strong hands grasped her shoulders. "You are the only Lady here, my—Seri. Are you all right?"

"Yes, but I was talking with Lady Lilitu and—" Seri broke off. Both Dravid and Marshal lay face down on the unmoving ground. "Oh, no."

Tich rolled Marshal over, letting his head fall into her lap. Talinir bent down and examined him. "He still breathes," he announced. "Beyond that, I cannot tell much."

Seri reached for Dravid, her hand trembling. Ixchel helped her roll him over as well. She patted his cheek, but he did not react. Like Marshal, he continued to breathe, but gave no indication of what might be wrong with him.

"Maybe they're both exhausted," Seri suggested. "They've... been through a lot."

"What happened to you three?" Tich asked.

Seri did her best to explain about Marshal and the Heart of Fire. She didn't elaborate on her conversation with the Lady.

"What about Dravid?" Tich gestured toward him. "You didn't mention him. Was he there?"

"No, he... he was our anchor here. Without him, I'm not sure if we would have made it back."

"*You* made it back, anyway," Tich muttered, looking back at Marshal's unconscious face.

"We must give them time," Talinir said. "Time and rest." He stood up and looked around. "This world has been shaken. We must see what remains."

"What about in the Otherworld?" Tich asked.

Talinir frowned. "It… nothing much has changed there. Many of the enemy remain on that side, now unable to come through." He turned to look northward. Seri thought she heard him say "Him?" But he didn't go on. Perhaps she misheard.

She rubbed the stone with one hand and ran her hand through Dravid's short hair with the other. Her anxiety for her friend and her mother competed within her. But Dravid was here. He had to take priority for now. She put the stone away.

"Ixchel, find our other friends. Let's get these two somewhere more comfortable."

●●●●●

Jamana wiggled his fingers, staring at his hand. All of that power had come through him. What a sensation. All of his finger joints ached, but otherwise, he felt fantastic. Marshal and the Lords did this kind of thing all the time. Maybe it had grown routine to them. Jamana found it exhilarating.

"Quite the rush, isn't it?"

Jamana blinked. He had almost forgotten Volraag. And then he realized something else: the ground wasn't shaking.

He got to his feet and looked around. Devastation met his eyes in every direction. The earth lay torn and shredded. Cracks and crevasses of every size criss-crossed the plain. In some places where earth had been shoved together, it formed jagged peaks and outcroppings.

Closest to him, he spotted a small huddle of people. Talinir towered over them. He would probably find Marshal and the others there. Much further away, he saw many people from Kuktarma and Mandiata moving about. They did not appear to be fighting, but he couldn't tell much from this distance. What about the enemy? He turned anxiously to the north.

To his surprise, the Durunim and their masters appeared to have pulled back during the chaos. He could barely make them out. Perhaps they had decided against confrontation for now.

Volraag coughed, then pushed himself to sit up. "I am frankly amazed we survived that," he said, his voice gravelly. "What now, acolyte?"

"My name is Jamana." He paused. "And now? Now maybe you'll listen to Seri and Marshal."

Volraag snorted. "Why should I do that?"

Jamana waved. "Because they were right? Because they told you all this would happen! What could you possibly have gained from this?"

Volraag did not answer.

"You're going to have to come with me." Jamana swallowed, hoping he sounded more confident than he felt.

"Why?"

"For one thing, I saved your life. You're Bonded to me now, I am thinking." Just the thought made Jamana smile. Dravid would find that hilarious, at least.

Volraag started to reply, then paused. At last he snorted again. "If my half-brother has his way, all such things will be going away, anyway. So why should I worry about that?"

"Marshal needs your help." Jamana pointed to the devastated earth around them. "You see all this? It will happen again. And next time, it may not stop. Antises will destroy itself until a proper Passing takes place. That includes the King's power and all of the Lords' powers." He scowled. "And since you stole a Lord's power, that means you're needed."

Volraag lay still. Whatever happened to him had hurt him and worn him out, from what Jamana could tell. Even if he wanted to, he probably couldn't get far. But things would be so much simpler if Jamana could persuade him to stay of his own volition.

"From what I can tell, the gods used you to get them here, and then abandoned you. Am I right?"

No answer.

"What else are you going to do? You're all alone here." Jamana waved in both directions. "Your only ally just tried to kill us. No one else wants you."

"And you do?"

"Yes." And for the first time, Jamana knew he meant it. "I want you here. I want you to do the right thing and help save Antises."

"You're Mandiatan." Volraag coughed again. "I took your Lord's power. If I die, it will revert to his bloodline, not mine. You have every reason to want me dead."

Jamana leveled his gaze at Volraag. "Maybe I do. You deserve to die, or at least suffer some horrible curse, for what you've done. But I think Marshal is right, after all. People shouldn't always get what they deserve."

"Shouldn't they?"

"No." He shook his head. "It's called mercy. And it's something this world has been lacking for a long time."

• • • • •

Seri watched as Adhi's men lifted Dravid and Marshal into a hastily-constructed wagon. They moved with extreme care, as Adhi explained to them exactly who they were carrying. Even so, Seri couldn't help but worry at each step of the process.

"We will give them the best of care," Adhi said. "They have saved all of us." Seri glanced at him and shook her head. Even with all the unbelievable things that had happened in the past few days, seeing Adhi commanding soldiers had to be one of the craziest. How could she have misjudged him that much?

"He is not who we thought, is he?" a voice said behind her. "But this is better, I am thinking."

Seri spun around with a cry. "Jamana!" The next thing she knew, she had been lifted off her feet in an enormous embrace. When he set her back down, she didn't let go. He patted her back and chuckled.

At last, she leaned away from him and looked up at his face. "I have missed that grin," she told him. "You have no idea."

"And I have missed you, little Seri." He looked past her. "Are Dravid and Marshal...?"

"They're alive," she answered. "Other than that, we don't know much. Talinir thinks they might just be exhausted from their magic use, but I'm not that tired myself, so I'm not sure if that's it. And, and... oh, there's too much."

"I am certain. But I need to speak with you about something right away." Jamana's grin faded.

"Oh, ah, all right. But I need to speak with my father first. It's... urgent." Seri pointed toward Ekur, who came around from the other side of the wagon, along with Ixchel.

"Your father?"

Seri introduced Ekur and Jamana, then pulled her father aside. "Ixchel, find out what Jamana needs to talk about. I'll be right back."

"That—that will not—" Jamana stumbled over the words before looking at Ixchel with a much weaker grin. Seri would have laughed if her thoughts hadn't been so scattered and worried.

"Father, I, uh…"

"Yes, daughter?" Ekur looked amused.

"I don't know how to say this." Seri took out the stone and rolled it around in her hand. "I was talking with Lady Lilitu during all of… that." She waved toward the open plain. "And she told me about the quake back home."

"It spread that far?" Ekur's eyebrows went up.

Seri nodded. "This was probably felt all over Antises. It's why Marshal was the only one who could stop it… oh, I'll explain that later. I'm trying to tell you that the Lady said the homes around the palace were collapsing. And then I lost contact with her."

"You are worried about Ninsha."

"Yes! I'm worried about both of them. Aren't you?"

Ekur took her hand. "Do you remember all the letters you used to write to us?"

"Of course, but—"

"We paid attention to those, Seri. You talked about the quakes at Zes Sivas and the worry that they would spread. So I took action."

"Action?"

"I built a special room in our home with walls of the thickest granite, fastened all together with solid iron. At the first sign of the earth shaking, Ninsha would have gone to that room."

"It… you think it is that strong?"

Ekur's smile broadened. "I like to think it could stand up against the Lords' magic. I consulted with all of the most skilled builders in the six lands. I am sure she is safe."

"Oh!" Seri fell into her father's arms.

"I believe Lady Lilitu can take care of herself," Ekur added. "But you should try to contact her again to be sure."

Seri held him tight. "I will," she murmured. But for the moment, all she wanted was to hold him and be held. All of her insecurities about her identity and parentage vanished in moments like this. Her father listened to her, fought to protect her and her mother. What else did she need?

<h1 style="text-align:center">(((53)))</h1>

Jamana politely told Ixchel he would wait for Seri to return, though what he had to say did concern her as well. Ixchel didn't seem to mind.

While he waited, Jamana strolled along the fringes of the crowds, asking questions. Apparently, after the quake ended, the two groups worked together to help each other, both the Kuktarman army and the Mandiatan caravan. Nijamu and Lord Bakari seemed to be leading the efforts. Jamana wondered about Nummotem. Had he abandoned the caravan to join his fellow gods?

He considered looking for Master Korda, but the prospect of running into Komadi discouraged him. Best to wait until he could take Seri or Marshal with him.

"Well done, acolyte," a voice called out.

Jamana turned and was somehow not surprised to find the old man. He displayed a staff. "Got my staff back," he announced. "It always finds its way back to me."

"That is… good. What do you want now?"

"Merely to congratulate you."

"For…?"

The old man smiled. "For your actions with the fallen Lord. You did the right thing."

"Maybe. But now I must convince the others."

"You will succeed." The old man nodded. "Have faith."

"In Theon?"

"Yes, and in yourself. You can be persuasive when you put your mind to it."

Jamana had never considered himself persuasive. Most times, he went along with the leadership of others.

The old man grasped his upper arm. "You will do this. And soon we will all unite in fighting for Antises."

"All of us?"

"All of us. I will see you in Simbala." He released Jamana and turned away.

Jamana blinked. "Simbala? I wasn't planning to go to Simbala again."

"You will," the old man called over his shoulder.

Jamana shook his head. Every encounter. Every time. He returned to find Seri and her father speaking with the others: Talinir, Adhi, Tich, Victor and Ixchel. Adhi's presence made him hesitate. After their experiences with Kishin, Adhi might be the least amenable to dealing with Volraag. Maybe he should wait until Marshal woke up. But if he waited too long, Volraag might change his mind and run.

"Jamana! There you are!" Seri exclaimed. "What did you need to tell me?"

"It concerns all of us," Jamana answered. He looked around the circle. All of them had suffered from Volraag's actions. He would have to make the case to Seri and hope she could persuade the others. They waited for his words.

"Seri, you have said we need another Passing. Is that correct?"

"With Marshal taking part, yes. We need all of the power returned to Antises to heal it."

"Will that be enough?" Adhi wondered.

"I don't know," Seri admitted. "But it would definitely help. Marshal wants to do more, but we have to start somewhere."

"Then we will need the power of the other Lords as well," Jamana said.

"Yes, that won't be easy. That's why I tried to persuade Volraag to help us."

Jamana took a deep breath. "I believe he is now ready to do so."

"What do you mean?" Victor demanded, his eyes narrowed.

"During the shaking, I rescued Volraag. He is now Bonded to me, and is willing to do his part in returning his power to Antises."

For a moment, no one responded.

Talinir and Ixchel drew their swords almost simultaneously. "Where is he?" Ixchel asked.

Jamana held up his hand. "We have to discuss this first."

"What about Rathri?" Seri asked.

"Oh, I, uh, dealt with him," Jamana said. "Haven't seen him since."

"You did what?" Victor, his hand on his flail, looked dumbstruck.

"Ha! I knew you had it in you, Bashful!" Tich hooted.

"Bashful?" Seri looked at Jamana.

"Rathri will not bother us any longer," Talinir announced. "He is gone from here."

"What does that mean?"

Talinir only shook his head, but kept his eyes on Jamana.

"Even without his assassin, Volraag is dangerously powerful," Seri said. "You're lucky he didn't harm you, Jamana."

"And he is a liar," Ixchel added. "We cannot trust anything he says."

"Where is he?" Victor repeated.

"Things have changed. The gods took some of his power," Jamana explained. "He is injured and alone. He will not be a problem."

Ixchel shook her head. "He is a liar."

Seri brushed dust from her robe. "Jamana, I know you mean well, but… I already tried to convince him, and failed."

"It's different now." Jamana folded his arms across his chest. "You must trust me, Seri. This is what our struggle is all about."

She wrinkled her brow. "What do you mean?"

"Hasn't Marshal talked about ending the Laws of Cursings and Bindings?" Jamana looked around the circle. "Isn't this all about setting people free to make their own choices?"

"Volraag must still face the consequences of his actions," Talinir declared. "Whatever Marshal wants to do, there is still the need for justice."

"But no mercy?" Jamana asked.

"Mercy is both laudable and moral," Adhi spoke up at last. "But as a leader of my people, I am responsible for justice, as is Marshal now that he has claimed the Kingship. We cannot allow Volraag's crimes to go unanswered."

"He may still pay for his crimes one day," Jamana agreed. "But for now, we need him. And he is willing."

The others all looked from one to the other. One by one, they all turned to Seri. She blinked and stepped back. "You're asking me to make this decision?"

"Without the King available, you are the next logical choice," Adhi said.

"Why? You just said you're a leader!"

"I am a leader here in Kuktarma. But only a minor one. This situation affects us all. As the highest-ranking mage, you have the authority here."

Seri looked around, as if she expected someone else to step up and take the responsibility away from her. Finally, she sighed. "All right. I suppose… Marshal will make the final decision, of course. I'm sure we all agree on that." Nods answered her. "Then… we'll show him mercy for now. But we'll have to watch him closely—"

"I'll guard him," Victor interrupted. He patted his flail. "We already know what I can do to him."

Seri nodded. "All right. You're his guard." She glanced toward the crowds. "But we don't tell Nijamu about this. And especially not the Mandiatans. We'll have to keep him hidden."

"Agreed," Adhi said.

Jamana unfolded his arms and sighed. "I knew you would do the right thing, Seri-Belit." He grinned. "It is good to have someone you can count on."

"Um, you're welcome. I guess."

Jamana glanced in the direction he had left Volraag. "We will need a healer to look at him also. He's not in very good shape."

"Makes it easier for me," Victor noted.

•••••

Marshal did not wake for another day, and then only for a few minutes. He spoke briefly to Tich and Seri, who waited by his and Dravid's beds, then fell back asleep.

He woke again the next morning. This time, the first face he saw was Jamana's.

"Ah, good," the acolyte said. "Welcome back again."

Marshal rubbed his face and sat up with a wince. Pain combined with pulling told him someone had stitched up the gash on his back. He saw similar work on his arm. Of course the Kuktarman military would employ trained healers.

"Dravid?" he asked.

"Still unconscious," Jamana replied, his face lowering. "No one knows what is wrong with him."

Marshal started to stretch, but stopped when he felt the pulling on his back again. He would have to take things easy for a while.

Jamana got to his feet. "I'll arrange for some food. And once you are feeling all right, there are many who wish to speak with their new King."

Marshal groaned as he left. The gods had forced his hand, making him declare his Kingship to save Seri. And now he would have to deal with everything that went with it.

Glancing around, he had to admit the Kuktarmans also knew how to build a tent. With the straight walls, he almost felt like he was inside a house. The abrupt sound of raindrops striking canvas made it more obvious.

Jamana returned a few minutes later, somewhat damp, along with Victor who carried a waterskin and a tray of food. Marshal's stomach growled at the smell.

"I guess I haven't eaten in… what? Two days?"

"At least," Victor replied, handing him the tray. His searching gaze made Marshal uncomfortable.

"I'm fine, Victor. Other than the obvious wounds, I'm not hurt. Just exhausted."

Victor nodded and pulled up a camp chair. "Seri updated you yesterday, I think?"

Marshal took a large bite of bread and nodded. "A little," he said after chewing. "I doubt she told me everything." After downing some water, he kept eating. Victor told him more about the Kuktarmans and Mandiatans working together. The Durunim army had pulled several miles away and did not seem to be doing much of anything just yet.

"So who all wants to see me?" Marshal asked.

"Lord Bakari of Mandiata is most insistent on an audience," Jamana said.

"What for?"

Victor and Jamana exchanged a look.

"Clearly, there's something else I don't know about yet," Marshal observed.

"It's Volraag," Victor said. "He's here."

"What?"

Jamana stepped in and explained. "And Seri said you would make the final decision," he finished.

"In fact, it's time for me to go back to guard duty," Victor said. "I've been trading off with Talinir."

"Send him here," Marshal ordered. "I want his advice. And Seri too." He set aside his empty tray and stood up. "Once I've gotten cleaned up and talked with them, I guess I'll have to talk with this Lord Bakari."

Once the other two left, Marshal walked to the washbasin sitting on a narrow table. He splashed water on his face, found a towel, and did his best to make himself more presentable. He noted someone had already cleaned his face at least once; otherwise his scars would be caked with dirt from the destruction of the high place.

He sat back on his bed and listened to the rain fall outside. Volraag. Once again, his half-brother was at his mercy. Except this time, everyone knew about it. And everyone had an opinion about what he should do.

"I don't want to make decisions for other people," he said aloud.

"Then you should not have accepted the Kingship," Talinir said, pushing aside the tent flap as he entered.

"I had to, you know that." Marshal scowled at the warden. "It was the only way to save Seri."

"And as a consequence, you now have responsibilities you cannot ignore."

"Wonderful."

"You've missed the good results, as well."

Marshal stood up. "What do you mean?"

Talinir pointed outside. "The Mandiatans came here to welcome and worship the gods. Instead, they are gathered around here, working with the Kuktarmans. Why is that?" When Marshal didn't answer, Talinir went on: "Because of you. Because word has spread that a King is here and he saved them all. You accepted the responsibilities and the people are following you. You have given them hope."

Marshal lowered his head. Talinir meant the words to encourage him, but it seemed an even heavier weight to bear. How could he represent the hope of an entire people?

Seri entered a moment later, looking bedraggled from the rain. Marshal forced a smile for her. He understood her and Dravid's connection, but he couldn't help his admiration for her. If he did have to be King, people would be expecting him to get a queen at some point, to continue the line or whatever. Seri would make a superb queen. Then again, if he succeeded in getting rid of the power, maybe he wouldn't be King that long.

"I know what you're going to say," she said in a rush, "but everyone was looking to me. I didn't know what you would think, so I left the final decision to you. And we do need him, Marshal. For the Passing."

Marshal opened his mouth to answer, but another figure pushed his way into the tent. "If he can see all these other people, he can see me!" he snapped at someone outside, before turning to face Marshal.

"Lord Bakari, I presume?" Marshal asked.

The young Lord put his hands on his hips and scrutinized Marshal. "You are not what I was expecting," he said. "If not for the testimony of everyone else here, I would certainly not believe your claim."

Marshal sighed. "Do you require proof of my power?" He released a tiny spurt of magic into the ground, vibrating the tent.

"That will not be necessary. For now, I accept your Kingship." He paused. "So long as you turn my father's killer over to me."

Marshal opened his mouth, then shut it. How could he respond to that? Out of all of his crimes, Volraag's most egregious was the murder of Lord Sundinka and the theft of his power.

"Might I make a suggestion?" Talinir interceded

"Of course." Marshal tried not to appear too relieved.

"I recommend a hearing. Do you remember when you stood before the high council of the Eldanim?"

Marshal nodded. He suspected Talinir brought that up to impress Bakari more than to remind him.

"It would be something like that. You would preside, as King." Talinir took a step toward the center of the tent. "The prisoner would be brought out and all those with knowledge of his crimes would accuse him. He could speak in his own defense, and then the King could render judgment. This is how things are done outside of your Laws of Cursings. Since Volraag is exempt to the magic law, he must face your law."

Marshal looked to Bakari. "Would you accept this?"

The young Lord scowled, but shifted his weight from one foot to the other. "I... suppose it would be acceptable. But I would prefer you simply give him to me."

"Why?" Seri piped up. "If you kill him, you would get your power back, but you would also bring down a horrible curse on one of your children."

"I have no children."

"Yet. You will at some point. And the Laws will wait."

"She speaks the truth," Marshal said. He was living proof of it.

Bakari nodded. "Very well. This afternoon?"

Marshal looked to his two advisors. "Will that work?"

"It depends on the weather." Seri gestured to the ceiling, where they could all hear the rain increasing.

(((54)))

The hearing had to wait until the following day. The rain continued off and on throughout the entire day and into the early hours of the night.

Marshal stayed within his tent for most of it, discussing the situation with Seri, Talinir, and Jamana. Tich joined them, but said little. When he was certain he understood everything he needed to know, he went to visit Dravid.

"He continues to sleep," the healer told them. "I am doing all that I can. He will drink water when offered, but will not accept food. If he continues like this for too long, he may starve."

Marshal looked at the peaceful face of his friend. "I don't understand this," he said to Seri. "You and I channeled much more power than he did. Why are we all right?"

"His power is different. I don't know." Seri knelt beside Dravid and smoothed his hair back. "Besides, you're a Lord and I'm a..."

"A mage?"

"Yes, of course."

"Does that make a difference, though?"

"There must be a reason the Lord's powers pass on through their bloodline." Seri looked off in the distance as if thinking it through herself. "Maybe you have an affinity for the power that lets you channel it better."

That made sense. Except mages didn't pass on power through their bloodlines. He was about to bring that up when Seri stood. "Whatever it is, I'm not giving up on him."

"Of course not." Marshal touched Dravid's chest. "I can feel his magic within still."

Seri nodded. "It's there. And that must mean that he's still there too.

335

I have to believe that." She sniffed. "I have to."

"He... he'll come out of it." Marshal didn't know what else to say. Seri didn't answer, her head bowed. Was she crying? "I believe it too."

Seri sobbed. Marshal moved beside her and put his arms around her, feeling more awkward than ever. "He'll come back to us," he said as Seri continued to cry. "Dravid is strong. And... we'll find some priests and ask them to pray for him."

Seri nodded and pulled away from him. She wiped her eyes and straightened up. "I'm sure of it." She left him there and hurried away.

Marshal looked down at Dravid. "You have no idea how lucky you are. I'm the King of all Antises, and she prefers you, a one-legged mage acolyte." He laughed at himself. "You're a good man, Dravid. Come back to us."

•••••

Marshal watched the crowds gather. He shifted in the makeshift wooden chair some of Adhi's people had thrown together for him. They hadn't constructed it for comfort, especially considering the bandaged wound on his back. He hoped this wouldn't take too long. Talinir and Seri stood to either side of him. He looked for the other familiar faces: Jamana, Adhi, his brother Nijamu, Seri's father Ekur, and Tich. She winked at him. He blinked in reaction. What did that mean?

Lord Bakari stood near with another mage in purple robes. Marshal didn't recognize him. Around him gathered many of his people. Large numbers of the Kuktarman defense force also stood by, curious to see the new King and hear his judgment.

Victor approached Marshal's seat, escorting Volraag. His half-brother's appearance shocked him. He had lost all of the bulk he gained from stealing power, though he still stood taller and stronger than Marshal. His left arm rested in a sling, and bruises dotted his exposed skin. His shirt hung in tatters. Yet despite it all, he held his head aloft, a look of confidence radiating from his face. Victor and Volraag came to a stop a few yards from Marshal, standing in a circular open area before his seat.

Talinir stepped out into the circle. "We are gathered for a hearing into the crimes of this man, Lord Volraag of Varioch. High King Marshal of Antises will preside over this hearing," he announced in a loud voice. Murmurs swept through the crowd. Volraag laughed.

"Who is first to accuse this man?" Marshal asked. Another, lower murmur whispered its way around him, no doubt at the strangeness of his voice.

Lord Bakari almost leaped forward. "I accuse this man of the murder of my father, Lord Sundinka of Mandiata, and the theft of his power that rightfully belongs to me!"

"I never touched your father," Volraag answered.

Lord Bakari lunged forward, but Victor stepped in his path.

"Hiring or coercing others to do the action makes one just as guilty as doing it yourself," Marshal gave his prepared answer. Everyone knew this topic would come up. Whether Volraag did something with his own hands or Rathri's or Tezan's, it didn't matter.

As Lord Bakari backed off, Seri stepped out. "I accuse this man," she announced. "Of murdering the wild mages of Rasna."

"What?" Tich's exclamation caught Marshal's attention. She stared, open-mouthed, shock and confusion waging war on her face. Marshal clenched his fist. Why hadn't he remembered to talk to her about this? After Vayan stole her memory of it, she didn't realize her parents were dead.

"You have no proof of that," Volraag said.

"You will have your chance to speak after all the accusations have been leveled," Talinir said. "For now, keep silent." Volraag smiled and nodded.

"I accuse him of starting a war with Rasna for his own selfish ends," Victor offered. That one hadn't been on the list they'd gone over the night before, but Marshal could see the point.

Nijamu stepped forward. "I accuse him of endangering all of Antises with his actions. He opened the portal to the Otherworld and welcomed an invading army!"

Marshal nodded and waited a moment until the crowd grew quiet. "These are the accusations," he announced. "The accused—"

"Wait!" Seri interrupted him. "What about you? Don't you have accusations to add?"

Marshal lifted his hands for silence. "This man stands accused of multiple crimes. Anything he has done to me is inconsequential compared to those. I will not add to his crimes."

"How generous," Volraag sneered.

"He sent an assassin after us!" Victor shouted. "He tried to kill Marshal and his mother!"

Marshal kept his hands up. Why were they bringing this up? He didn't want it addressed right now. Volraag's crimes against Antises were all that really mattered.

Once the crowd quieted down again, Marshal lowered his hands. "I repeat: I will not add to his crimes here. The current accusations are enough."

Victor grumbled, but said nothing loud enough to be heard.

Marshal nodded to Talinir. "The accused may now speak in his own defense," Talinir declared.

Volraag stepped away from Victor and stood in the center of the circle. He turned his back to Marshal and faced the crowd. For a moment, he said nothing, turning his head back and forth, as if looking for someone.

"I am a Lord of Antises!" he cried. "As such, I can face no judgment aside from the other Lords." He pointed to Marshal without looking at him. "I do not recognize this... bastard as our King. In fact, not one Lord of Antises has recognized him. As such, he holds no authority over me!"

"I recognize him as King!" Lord Bakari shouted.

Volraag leveled his gaze at Bakari and chuckled. "If you are a Lord, show me your power."

Bakari lunged forward again. This time, his own mage joined Victor in pulling him back.

Volraag laughed and looked back over the crowd. He gestured outward, palm up, with his good hand. "Since no authority here exists, I need not answer these accusations." He paused and let the crowd grumble. "Nevertheless, my good name has been maligned, and I will speak to that."

Volraag pointed and swept his finger across the crowd. "How long have we all suffered? How long have each one of you suffered under the rule of Lords who care only for themselves? Rulers who see all of you as insignificant, barely worthy of their attention?" He rotated to face the Kuktarmans. "Your Lord seems most interested in siring as many sons as possible, and then encouraging them to produce more and more grandchildren. It has become your land's pastime to regale one another with these stories, has it not? Have you never wondered at the elite selfishness behind all of that?"

He turned to face the Mandiatans. "And your Lords! Have they not built themselves the most enormous palace in all Antises? Strictly for their own pleasure? Did your Lord Sundinka not spend his time trying to prove his manhood in ridiculous hunts for wild animals? When did he spend time on you?"

A few shouts of outrage from both sides melded into loud murmurs. Marshal couldn't help noticing that many of the murmurs seemed to be agreeing with Volraag.

"My own father, the previous Lord of Varioch, was a monster!" Volraag cried. "He used his power for his own selfish delight at every turn. And throughout the history of Antises, his behavior has been the rule, not the exception! For generations, we have been lorded over by unworthy leaders who behaved without restraint on their basest of impulses. They committed crime after crime, knowing they were free from retaliation, since the curses do not apply to them! Worse, they allowed their own children to suffer curses in their place!"

The crowd stood silent. Marshal watched their faces. Volraag was swaying many of them. He had been raised a Lord. He knew how to speak. Marshal's own voice still sounded odd to everyone, regardless of what he had to say.

Volraag's palm came up again. "All that I have done, every action I have taken, was for the good of Antises. Too long have we suffered under these unjust Lords. I set out to end their rule, and end it I shall! And"—his voice rose louder and louder to be heard over the crowd— "and I have done absolutely nothing that would bring a curse on any of my offspring! I will not do that. I will never do that!"

The crowd roared, some in agreement, some in anger. Lord Bakari looked ready to rip Volraag's head from his shoulders. Marshal released a surge of magic through his foot, sending a tremor rolling through the ground beneath the crowd. The roar faded to mumbling.

"This is your defense?" Talinir asked when it grew quiet enough. "You have not addressed any of the specific crimes."

"Why should I?" Volraag ran his hand through his hair and lifted his chin. "The people know that I am on their side and act on their behalf. And as I have said, you have no authority over me."

Marshal stood. He could not give an eloquent speech to sway the crowd his direction. He knew that. But he could address the issue of authority.

"You do not recognize me as King, then?" he asked Volraag.

Volraag snorted. "Of course I don't."

"But you did say you would recognize justice from other Lords."

"There are no other Lords here." Volraag smirked at Bakari.

Marshal took a step toward him. "Who inherited the power of Lord Varion?"

"What?"

"When Lord Varion died, who inherited his power? Did you?"

Volraag's brow grew dark. "You know the answer to that."

Marshal slammed one foot on the ground and let another tremor spread out from it. "From my mother and grandfather, I inherited the powers of the King!" he called out. He slammed his other foot down, trying to ignore the burst of pain in his knee, and produced yet another tremor. "But from my father—Lord Varion!—I inherited the powers of a Lord!"

He stared Volraag in the face. "Who then is the true Lord of Varioch? By your own definition, a Lord has the land's power. Who possesses Varioch's power?"

"You do," Volraag answered through clenched teeth.

"Then I stand able to render judgment on you, by your own words." Marshal stepped back and reclaimed his seat as a hush fell over the rest of the crowd.

"Is there anyone else who wishes to speak in defense of this man?" Talinir asked.

No one said anything.

"Then the King, also the Lord of Varioch, must now render judgment." Talinir bowed his head to Marshal and took his position beside the chair again.

Marshal hesitated. He knew what he had to say here, but after Volraag's speech, he didn't know how it would be received. Would it cause problems with the people here? For that matter, Lord Bakari would not like part of it. Why did everything have to be so complicated? Responsibility. Selfless.

"They're waiting," Seri whispered.

Marshal glanced at her, then looked at the other faces of his friends. Jamana and Victor looked encouraging, Talinir his usual impassive self, and Tich… Tich was nowhere to be seen. An urge to leave all of this and find her seized him. But he could no longer act for the benefit of only one person, could he? He had responsibilities now. He glanced back at Seri. Ironic then that he accepted those responsibilities strictly for the benefit of one person.

"You are valuable," his mother's voice echoed in his mind. And if he was valuable, then all people were. He stood up, his knee still protesting.

"Volraag, you have heard the accusations against you: murder, theft, endangering Antises itself. Yet you do not deny these accusations.

Instead, you try to justify them." Marshal hoped the message of his words would be heard, despite his odd voice. "For these actions, you deserve the harshest of judgments."

Volraag only glared back at him, daring him to execute the supposed judgment.

Marshal turned to Lord Bakari. "Lord of Mandiata, yours is the most grievous hurt. Your land's power should rightfully be returned to you. However..." He spread his hands wide. "We have no method of doing so, save for killing Volraag in the hope that the power will go back to its rightful owner."

"Then kill him!" someone in the Mandiatan crowd yelled. Several others took up the cry, but grew quiet when Marshal lifted his hands.

"Who would kill him? Who would take on a curse?"

No one answered. Marshal noticed the purple-robed mage whisper something in Bakari's ear. The Lord stepped forward. "You could do it," he said. "The King is above such things."

"I am not. I might not be cursed, but should I have children, one of them would suffer for my actions."

"That is the rule of Lords," Bakari countered. "Not the King. He is above it all. No curse will fall."

Marshal turned to Seri. "Is that true?"

"I don't know," she answered, her eyes wide. "I've never heard it before."

Jamana pushed up beside Seri. "Do not trust this!" he whispered. He pointed toward the purple-robed mage. "Bakari has appointed Komadi as his new Master Mage. He is loyal to the gods and cannot be trusted."

Marshal nodded. "I believe you, but I cannot confront him here in the middle of all this. What can I do?"

"The answer came from your own words," Talinir said. He stepped back into the circle. "As you all heard, the King is also the Lord of Varioch. Perhaps the King's child would not be cursed. But the child of the Lord of Varioch most certainly would." He looked back at Marshal. "As we well know."

"You cannot set him free!" Lord Bakari cried.

"I have no intention of setting him free," Marshal answered. Talinir stepped back and Marshal took his place. He took a deep breath. "The King has a responsibility to all of Antises. Its fate, its destiny, are in his hands. As such, I must make the decision that benefits Antises, and all its people. Here is what we will do. The mages of Zes Sivas will call for a new Passing to heal Antises. What I have done here is not enough. When Volraag releases the magic of Mandiata in this Passing, it will return to its natural place."

"As will that of Arazu," Seri added.

Volraag cocked his head. "Arazu? I do not have the power of Arazu."

"But... but Lord Enuru died while you were there..."

Volraag laughed. "You think he passed his magic to me? I wish he had, but it did not happen."

Seri's face blanched. "Then where is it?" she whispered. "Without it, we cannot save Antises."

"What about after that?" Lord Bakari wanted to know. "What will happen to him then?"

"We will hold another hearing in front of all the Lords and mages," Marshal said. "We will decide his final fate then. Is that acceptable to you?"

Bakari considered for a moment, then nodded.

Marshal repeated the question for Nijamu, Seri, and Victor. Each agreed to the plan. Then Marshal looked at Volraag. "You have heard the conclusion. You will be guarded well until you pass on your stolen power. Do you have any final words to say for yourself?"

Volraag pointed off toward the northeast. "Only that you are all fools, worrying yourself over me, when that enormous threat looms over us all. Have you forgotten the army of magical beings? Led by actual gods, each one with power to equal or exceed yours?"

"I have not forgotten at all," Marshal answered. "And that is why we must hurry to Zes Sivas and resolve the problems with Antises' instability. Only then can we stand solidly together against the invaders."

Talinir stepped up again. "The King has spoken. Let all hear his words and consider."

(((55)))

It took Marshal over an hour to escape from the crowds and go in search of Tich. He finally found her alone in the ruins of the high place. She sat on a large slab of granite, her knees drawn up to her face.

"Tich? Are you all right?"

She shifted her legs and wiped at her eyes. "Why wouldn't I be? Just didn't like the big crowd, that's all."

Marshal took a seat on the slab near her. "I understand. I couldn't stand it myself."

Tich snorted. "Better get used to it, King-man."

"Hailstones. I hope not."

They sat in silence for a while. He looked out over the devastation. He had caused a lot of this in tearing down the high place, but then the earthquake had shaken things much further. No telling how far these granite chunks from the stairs and platform were scattered.

"If I have my way," Marshal said at last, "I won't be King for very long. We'll return all of the magic to Antises itself. No more King. No more Lords. Well, maybe Lords still, but they won't have magical powers."

"Is it true?"

"It's what I want. If Seri and the others can figure it out."

"No, what was said back there. Did Volraag murder the wild mages?"

"Yes." Marshal finally looked at her face. Reddened eyes looked out past damp cheeks. He swallowed against a sudden ache in his throat.

"How? How could I not have heard of this?"

"Do you remember what happened with, with Vayan in the Otherworld?"

Tich wrinkled her brow. "I remember that Dravid killed him."

"Before that. When we first met him."

She looked away. "Something happened. You stood with me. I don't remember anything other than that."

"He stole your memory, Tich. The memory of your parents' death." Marshal didn't know any other way to explain it. "You gave it to him."

"What? Why would I do that?" She looked back at him with those red-rimmed eyes.

Marshal scooted a little closer to her. "He demanded that we give him one of our painful memories in return for setting Dravid free. He wanted the memory of my scars." He pointed to his own face. "But then you stepped in and offered him yours."

"I don't have any scars."

"Not on the outside, no." Marshal reached forward and brushed a tear from her face. "But we all have pain inside. Scars of another kind. He took your memory of what happened."

"Then they really are dead."

Marshal nodded.

Tich slammed a fist down on the rock. "My brain is still trying to tell me that it's not true. Like whatever that god did to me doesn't want me to know. And it hurts."

"My mother was killed in front of me." Marshal hadn't meant to tell her about that, but the words tumbled out anyway. "She died in my arms."

Tich looked up at his face. She lifted a hand as if to touch his scars, then stopped. "Is that when this happened?"

"No, that was earlier. Different scars."

Tich lowered her gaze and her hand. "Does it get less painful? Over time?"

"I don't know. Mine hasn't." Because of everything else that had happened that day, Marshal had not ever talked with anyone about Aelia's death. Not Seri. Not even Victor. "Every day, I remember her and what she always told me."

"What was that?"

"That I am loved. I am valuable. And I have a purpose in this world."

Tich snorted a little, but didn't say anything.

"I need to remember those things," Marshal went on. "If I don't... I may as well kill myself."

"Like you would do something like that."

"I tried once. Victor stopped me."

Tich's head slowly turned to look at him. She searched his face as if to be sure he was telling the truth. Then she nodded before looking away. A long silence followed.

"I guess," she said at last, "maybe it's good that I don't remember the details. Maybe there's something else that causes more pain."

"I could… tell you if you want me to. I heard what you told him."

"No." She shook her head. "I had a reason for getting rid of it. I don't want to know. This pain is bad enough." She paused. "It's like a curse, I guess. Living with it all."

"I lived with a curse most of my life."

She looked at him with a cocked eyebrow this time. "Now you're just making stuff up."

"No. I was cursed most of my life. My mother's death lifted it. That's how much she loved me."

Tich looked away. "It must have been nice, to be loved that much."

"It was."

Tich leaned against him. Marshal stiffened at first, then put his arm around her shoulders. After another long silence, he said, "You can live with the pain, Tich. You're one of the strongest people I've ever met."

She chuckled. "Devouring fire. Have I got you fooled."

"Maybe."

"Yeah, maybe."

The wind kicked up and blew a lost shred of clothing across the ground below their feet. Marshal watched it twist and writhe like a living thing.

"The point I'm trying to make is that you don't have to deal with it alone," he said.

"I've been alone a long time."

"Then maybe… maybe it's time to change."

"I might just do that. You gonna be here a while?"

"I'm not going anywhere."

• • • • •

"…and he claimed he does not have Lord Enuru's power. Where could it be?" Seri felt strange, as always, talking to a rock, but at least it worked.

"We have no choice but to wait for it to be revealed," Lady Lilitu's voice answered.

"I suppose." How could no one know where immense magical power had gone?

"Your mother has already begun the work of repairing your home," the Lady went on. "She has taken in three families whose homes were more damaged. They are all working together."

Seri smiled. That sounded just like Ninsha.

"I must go now, but I will undoubtedly see you at Zes Sivas.'

"Goodbye." Seri took up the stone from the edge of the fire and replaced it in its pouch. Dealing with the Lady continued to confuse her, especially after the quake. Lilitu's advice to take Marshal's power troubled her.

A gentle rain began to fall again. Ekur would be pleased. The healing Marshal accomplished brought the wind back, and with it, the rain. But did it have to rain this much?

She entered Marshal's tent, followed by Ixchel, to find a meeting already underway. She looked around at Adhi, Nijamu, Ekur, Jamana, Marshal, Tich, and Talinir. Victor remained guarding Volraag for now.

"As soon as the quake ended, we dispatched messengers to our father," Adhi explained, "informing him of the Durunim army, its composition and location. He will assemble the rest of our army."

"We have also sent messengers to Arazu explaining the situation to them," Nijamu said.

"With a personal message from me," Ekur added.

"We hope they will also send troops." Nijamu glanced at Seri.

"The Lady seemed receptive," she reported. "Once she has your more detailed information, I am sure she will help."

"What about the Mandiatans?" Marshal asked.

"They will be returning home," Jamana reported. "But Lord Bakari promises to meet us at Zes Sivas."

Marshal nodded. "And that is where we must go. But we'll travel via Simbala, to persuade Lord Meluhha to go with us."

"I believe he will listen to us," Adhi said.

"Lord Rajwir will no doubt agree also," Seri said, "once we are able to contact him. Lord Tyrr may be a problem, though."

"We'll deal with him when we have to. Is there anything else I'm missing?" Marshal looked around at all of them.

"A better sense of humor," Tich answered.

"What, specifically, do you want us to do?" Nijamu asked. "Even if the other troops arrive, I do not think we will be a match for the gods."

"No, you probably won't." Marshal glanced up as the rain's

intensity increased, pounding on the tent's roof. "At the moment, we don't know what they intend. I would go out to face them myself, but Seri believes the situation with Antises itself is more dire."

"We cannot endure another one of those quakes," Adhi agreed. "So far, we have counted fifty-seven dead among the Mandiatans, and twenty-three among our troops. Dozens more are missing in both camps. There is no telling how many lives were lost across the six lands if this quake was everywhere. You must go to Zes Sivas."

Seri put her hand to her mouth. She hadn't heard those numbers.

"For now," Marshal concluded, "keep scouts watching the enemy closely. Send messages to me when they move. I'll return as soon as I can."

"Don't forget there is likely an even larger army in Varioch or Rasna right now," Talinir said. "That portal remains open."

"I haven't forgotten," Marshal said, a little too sharp. "We have many problems. But we have to take them one at a time." He straightened, looking a little taller as he gazed from one face to the next. "Make no mistake. Though we have lost much, we have won a victory here. The portal is buried and no more enemies can come through. By our actions and… and the grace of Theon, we have done well. I'm proud to be with all of you. I could not ask for better friends and allies."

"We are with you," Adhi said.

Seri agreed. "Whatever it takes."

Epilogue

Three weeks later...

Jamana entered and looked around the room. Deep within Simbala's palace, a stone stairway led down to an even lower level, warmed by an enormous fireplace. The old man he had met so many times before waited there, leaning on his staff. As he descended the stairs, Jamana saw Seri and Ixchel waiting with him.

"You took your time," Ixchel said. "You told us to meet here at noon."

Jamana gestured toward the old man as he took the last step. "It was his idea. He asked for you all."

All three turned toward their host.

"What is all this?" Seri asked. "Who are you and why did you want us?"

"We must wait," the old man answered, raising a finger. "Two more must join us."

"Ah, yes..." Jamana glanced back up the stairs. "I am thinking that may not be as easy as you think."

"Have faith."

An awkward silence followed. The old man looked up and smiled. "Ah, here we are."

The others looked. Adhi entered the room at the top of the stairs, escorting a hooded figure, hands tied in front of him. Not until they were halfway down the stairs could Jamana be sure of his identity.

"I have done as requested," Adhi said. "But my father will be furious if he finds out."

The other man lifted his tied hands and pushed back the hood.

Bright eyes surrounded by diseased skin stared at the old man. "You again," said Kishin. "What do you want from me this time?"

"Everything and nothing." The old man tapped his staff on the stone floor. "Thank you for taking such good care of my staff, by the way."

Kishin's eyes narrowed. "I didn't—"

"Have a seat, everyone. To explain what I want from you, I must first tell you a story."

Jamana and Adhi found chairs. Kishin remained standing.

"When Akhenadom led the six tribes to this land, he did not act alone," the old man began. "He had the full support of his sister, Aharu, the first High Master Mage of Antises, along with all the other mages. Some of you know this."

Jamana had read much of her story in *A History of the Lords' Betrayal*. Where was the old man going?

"Before the six lands were established, before the Laws were enacted, Akhenadom and the mages banished the old gods to the Otherworld. They have been plotting ever since to return. We knew this would happen."

"We?" Kishin asked.

"But one of the old gods escaped the banishment. While Akhenadom and the mages were distracted, he made his way to Zes Sivas. Though the citadels had not yet been built, everyone knew it to be the heart of Antises. It held great magic, far beyond anything they had seen before. And this god, Murdak, came to claim it for himself."

"Murdak?" Seri exclaimed. "I mean, I knew they claimed to be gods, but... they're really that old?"

The storyteller nodded. "Only one man dared to stand in Murdak's way. Nehesy, son of Aharu, an acolyte mage and priest himself, no older than Jamana here."

Jamana had never heard this story. He knew the names. Nehesy succeeded his mother as High Master Mage, but history recorded very little of him beyond that.

"How?" Adhi asked. "How could an acolyte stand against a god?"

"He did not do much," the old man said. "In fact, Murdak beat him ruthlessly, breaking his arms, his legs, and other bones within his body. However... his actions delayed Murdak just enough for the mages to return and defeat him. In the end, he was banished with the rest of his kind."

"Fascinating," Kishin said. "Why do you tell us this?"

"In return, though Nehesy lay broken and bleeding, Akhenadom spoke the word of Theon over him: 'For your zeal and courage, Nehesy, I give you a covenant of a perpetual priesthood. Your power will not wane until your foe is defeated for the last time.'"

Jamana drew in a swift breath. Did that mean what he thought it meant?

"Murdak's final defeat approaches," the old man said, lifting his staff. "And though my body is aged and frail, my power has never waned. I, Nehesy, have served my god faithfully until this moment. And now I require your help."

No one spoke for several seconds.

"Incredible," Adhi said.

"That is hard to believe." Ixchel shook her head.

"Nevertheless, it is true."

"I believe him," Jamana said in a soft voice. "It explains many things."

"Seri-Belit, I asked you here so that you would understand why your acolyte friends will not be returning with you to Zes Sivas," Nehesy said.

"Oh, ah, thank you." Seri paused. "But, um, perhaps when there's more time, you could... teach me some things?"

Nehesy smiled but did not answer.

"We're not going to Zes Sivas?" Jamana asked. He exchanged looks with Adhi.

"Let's say you are who you say you are," Kishin growled. "What do you want us for?"

"Your new King and his friends will go to Zes Sivas to save Antises from itself." Nehesy looked around, locking eyes with each one of them. "The four of us... will save Antises from the gods."

For more information on Antises,
upcoming books, and more,
visit timfrankovich.com

(Sign up for the newsletter and you'll get access to free
short stories, featuring the origin of Kishin!)

If you enjoyed this book, please post a review on Amazon,
Goodreads, B&N, or wherever you find books!
There's no better way to spread the word.

Glossary

Caution: These listings may contain minor spoilers.

Aapo - Kishin's household servant

Adhi - A mage acolyte from Kuktarma, studying on Zes Sivas.

Aelia - Marshal's mother who willingly sacrificed herself to lift his curse. Daughter of Evander.

Aharu - Sibling of Akhenadom. Founder of the priesthood. First High Master Mage of Antises.

Ajaw - Lady of Ch'olan. Wife of Lord Rajwir. Commander of the Holcan.

Akhenadom - Called "the Great." At the time of the Great Cataclysm, he led six people groups from their original homes to the land of Antises. He introduced them to the worship of the one god Theon, and presented to them Theon's Book of the Law. In return, the six people groups proclaimed him the first King of all Antises.

Albus - A soldier in the army of Varioch. Cursed for murder and assigned to the curse squad. Killed in battle.

Alpin - Former Master Mage of Varioch. Murdered by Curasir.

Amnis River - A branch of the Trebia River that flows along the western side of Varioch and its southern border with Rasna.

Antises - The union of the six lands of Rasna, Varioch, Ch'olan, Mandiata, Arazu, and Kuktarma. Ruled from the island of Zes Sivas in the middle of Lake Litanu, which borders all six lands.

Arazu - One of the six lands of Antises. Arazu is located on the eastern side of Lake Litanu, between Mandiata and Kuktarma. Arazu is the smallest of the lands, but claims the oldest culture and strictest traditions.

Arun - Third son of Lord Meluhha of Kuktarma.

Atzam - Captain of Kishin's ship

Bakari - The young Lord of Mandiata. Son of Sundinka. The first Lord of a land without possessing any magic power (due to Volraag's theft).

Balaes - A blacksmith in the village of Drusa's Crossing. Father of Careen.

Book of the Law - A compilation of the moral and ceremonial laws of Theon, written by Akhenadom.

Calu - The name of an ancient god of Rasna, associated with wolves.

Callus - A conscript in the Varioch army, twin brother to Gallus. Assigned to the curse squad. Killed in battle.

Careen - A young woman of Drusa's Crossing. Daughter of Balaes. Was in a relationship with Victor prior to his departure.

Cassian - General of Varioch's army. Placed in charge of the war with Rasna by Volraag.

Cataclysm, Great - The event which motivated the six people groups to follow Akhenadom. Details about it are apocryphal at best. Descriptions range from earthquakes to volcanic eruptions to extreme weather events to floods, perhaps a combination of all of these.

Cato - A young man of Varioch who seeks out Forerunner.

Chimon - An elderly priest at the temple in Woqan.

Ch'olan - The northernmost of the six lands of Antises, bordered by Varioch and Mandiata. Ch'olan is known for its fierce warrior traditions and its stone monuments, especially pyramids.

Conclave of Mages - The organization of magic-using professionals based in the Citadel of Mages on Zes Sivas. The Conclave is led by six Master Mages - one from each land - and includes numerous lesser mages of varying degrees of proficiency.

Curasir - A scheming member of the Durunim, who can make himself appear as one of the Eldanim.

Curse-stalker - A large reptilian creature that is drawn to magic. Since the primary sources of magic encountered by most common people are those who are cursed, this gave rise to the idea that these creatures only hunted cursed individuals. Curse-stalkers possess two long tongues that excrete some form of acid while absorbing magic energy.

Cyra - Volraag's concubine.

Devir - The name of an ancient god of Arazu.

Diabol - The devil. Rarely mentioned in the religion surrounding the worship of Theon. Mostly used in epithets.

Djatan Desert - A large desert marking the eastern extent of Antises, primarily connected with Mandiata, but also bordering Arazu.

Dravid - A former mage acolyte. Lost his leg during one of the earthquakes on Zes Sivas.

Drusa's Crossing - A village in the mountains near the border between Varioch and Ch'olan.

Dursa - The name of an ancient fertility goddess of Kuktarma.

Durunim - Former members of the Eldanim whose physical form has been changed through an unknown process. They now wage war against the Eldanim on behalf of mysterious masters.

Efesun - A large town in Varioch, located on the shore of the Trebia River, near the Great Plains.

Ekur - Father of Seri. Husband of Ninsha. Merchant.

Eldanim - A magical race of non-human beings. Eldanim exist both within the primary world and the Otherworld (or Starlit Realm). This creates a strange dichotomy for human eyes, as their physical shape within each world is different. For their part, Eldanim can see both worlds at the same time. Their physical appearance within the primary world is similar to humans, though generally taller with much sharper, angular features. One eye appears all black, with tiny pinpricks of light. Their physical appearance in the Otherworld is several feet taller.

Eidolon - An apparition, often seen as a misty human-like form. In reality, the eidola are Eldanim or Durunim who have shifted their primary essence into the Otherworld. "Eidolon" is the name used by residents of Varioch and Rasna. In Arazu, they are called **Gidim**. In

Ch'olan, they are called **Tzitzimitl**.

Eniri - A young woman of the Eldanim who resides in Intal Eldanir. She works in the healing profession.

Enuru - Current Lord of Arazu, husband of Lilitu.

Edin Na Zu - A phrase of uncertain origin in Arazu. Used as an epithet. Has some connection to the Djatan Desert.

Evander - Father of Aelia, grandfather of Marshal. Died in the Starlit Realm.

Forerunner - A mysterious man who possesses a strange magic unlike the usual magic of Antises. Sent to the land of Varioch.

Gallus - A conscript in the Varioch army, twin brother to Callus. Assigned to the curse squad. Killed in battle.

Ganak - Current Master Mage of Kuktarma. Part of the Conclave of Mages on Zes Sivas.

Gidim - *see* **Eidolon**

Gnaeus - A conscript in the Varioch army, cursed with a twisted hand. Assigned to the curse squad. Remained at Forerunner's old camp.

Great Plains - A wide, open area of land on the western side of Antises, bordering Varioch. Generally considered to be the location of Intal Eldanir.

Hain - Master Mage of Arazu. Part of the Conclave of Mages on Zes Sivas. Mentor to Seri.

Hanirel - A member of the Durunim, who can make himself appear as one of the Eldanim.

Harbinger - A mysterious man who possesses a strange magic unlike the usual magic of Antises. Sent to the land of Mandiata. It is probable that others like him or Forerunner were sent to each of the six lands.

Hauk - A boatman who works for the mages on Zes Sivas.

Harunir - A member of the Eldanim, resident of Intal Eldanir. Husband of Indala, father of Eniri.

Holcan - An order of female warriors in Ch'olan, trained from an early age in multiple fighting techniques. Usually assigned to guard and escort the Lady of Ch'olan (wife of the Lord).

Indala - A member of the Eldanim, resident of Intal Eldanir. Wife of Harunir, mother of Eniri.

Inkil - A news broker in Woqan. Often employed by Kishin.

Intal Eldanir - The primary city of the Eldanim. While floating above the ground, it can be shifted from the primary world to the Otherworld (and back).

Ixchel - A young member of the Holcan. Assigned by Lady Rajwir to serve Seri.

Jamana - A mage acolyte of Mandiata. Serves on Zes Sivas under Master Korda.

Janaab - A name used by Evander during his wanderings in the Otherworld.

Junia - A young woman of Varioch who seeks out Forerunner.

Kanna - A small town in Varioch, near the border with Rasna.

Kawal - A man of Woqan. Kishin's second murder.

Korda - Current Master Mage of Mandiata. Part of the Conclave of Mages on Zes Sivas. Mentor to Jamana.

Kishin - An assassin of Ch'olan. Cursed with a form of leprosy.

Komadi - A mage assigned to the Lord's court in Tenjkidi, Mandiata.

Kombori - A port city of Mandiata, downriver from Tenjkidi.

K'uh - A word for magic in Ch'olan. An ancient belief (pre-Antises) connected magic with each individual's life force. This led to human sacrifice in some communities.

Kuch - Blademaster of Ch'olan. Responsible for training warriors, including the Holcan.

Kuktarma - One of the six lands of Antises, bordered by Arazu on the north, and the sea on the south. Known for its walled cities and the antics of the current Lord's sons.

Lasa - A human slave of Vayan.

Laws of Cursings and Bindings - A set of magical laws put in place by the first Conclave of Mages. Anyone who willingly violates one of the moral laws of Theon, as described in the Book of the Law, receives a magical curse appropriate for his action. Magical Bindings are formed between family members and other close relationships. In addition, special Bindings are created when someone rescues another person from serious danger or potential death.

Lilitu - Lady of Arazu. Wife of Lord Enuru. Sponsored Seri's membership in the Conclave of Mages.

Lake Litanu - A huge freshwater lake in the center of the six lands of Antises, bordered by all. The island of Zes Sivas is in its center.

Lords' Betrayal - An event that followed the creation of the Laws of Cursings and Bindings by the Conclave of Mages. The first six Lords of Antises twisted the Laws to attempt to exempt themselves from the curses. Instead, curses for their actions fell on their children.

Lucia - A young woman of Varioch who seeks out Forerunner.

Mages & Lords - A card game popular throughout Antises (with some variants) dating back to the Lords' Betrayal. Small deck with limited cards. On a player's turn, he flips over the top card of the deck, then decides whether to play it or put it back on the bottom of the deck. Object of the game is to collect either six Lords & King or six Mages & High Master Mage.

Makaan - Former Blademaster of Ch'olan. Mentor to Kuch and Kishin.

Malena - A woman from Rasna who serves Forerunner.

Mandiata - One of the six lands of Antises, bordered by Ch'olan and Arazu. Known for exotic wildlife, elaborate architecture, and high respect for the dead.

Marshal - Son of Aelia and Varion (rape). Grandson of Evander. Half-brother of Volraag. Inheritor of the powers of both a Lord (Varion) and King.

Meluhha - Current Lord of Kuktarma. Father of seven sons, whose escapades have been documented (and exaggerated) in dozens of stories that his people delight in repeating.

Merish - A conscript of Varioch. Stole a sword and received some form of mental damage as a curse. Rarely if ever speaks. Assigned to the curse squad. Remained at Forerunner's old camp.

Mukuy - A man of Woqan. Kishin's first murder.

Murdak - The name of an ancient leader of the gods of Kuktarma, associated with justice and strength.

Ne'gal - The name of an ancient god of Kuktarma, associated with death and decay.

Nehesy - Son of Aharu. Second High Master Mage of Antises.

Nian - A priest of Mandiata. Decided to go on pilgrimage to all six lands of Antises. Never made it to Rasna.

Nijamu - Second son of Lord Meluhha of Kuktarma.

Ninsha - Mother of Seri. Wife of Ekur.

Nummotem - The name of an ancient god of Mandiata, associated with nature.

Otioch - Leader of Varioch's Remavian Guard. Confidant of Volraag.

Otherworld - A parallel world separated from the primary world. Similar in shape/geography, but lacking most water and vegetation. No sun or moon, but lit constantly by enormous stars of varying colors, leading to its other name, the **Starlit Realm**.

Passing - An annual event on Zes Sivas, where the King and Lords of all six lands are instructed to surrender their magic power for one hour. The power returns to the land temporarily and seems to keep it from breaking apart.

Plecu - Current Master Mage of Rasna. Part of the Conclave of Mages on Zes Sivas.

Raeton - Capital city of Rasna. Known for spectacular pillars.

Rajwir - Current Lord of Ch'olan. Husband to Ajaw.

Ranir Stone - A stone given by Aelia to Victor. Aelia used it for sending a message to the Eldanim. The magic involved is unknown. Appears as an ordinary rock.

Rasna - One of the six lands of Antises, bordered by Varioch on the north, and the sea on the south. Known for the Pillars of Raeton and little else.

Rathri - An assassin employed by Volraag. Appears to possess a leprosy-style curse similar to Kishin, but claims to be one of the Eldani wardens like Talinir.

Regulus - One of the three Consuls who control the economic power of

Varioch.

Reman - Capital city of Varioch.

Remavian Guard - Elite warriors of Varioch, recognized by their red capes. In service to the Lord and his household.

Rufus - A conscript of Varioch. Once stole food from his neighbor and received the curse of a twisted foot, causing him to limp. Assigned to the curse squad. Tried to kill Marshal under threat from Rathri. Killed Topleb, was cursed again, then killed by curse-stalkers.

Sakouna - The first Lord of Mandiata, from the time of the founding of Antises. Apparently, he had a monkey.

Sandu-Emuq - Capital city of Arazu.

Sekou - A Master Mage who wrote extensively about wild magic.

Seri-Belit - Mage of Arazu. Prefers just Seri. Possesses the unusual ability to "see" magic due to a "star" in her eye.

Simbala - Capital city of Kuktarma.

Simmar - Former Master Mage of Kuktarma. Murdered by Curasir.

Sipak - A legendary beast of the sea, described in stories of Ch'olan.

Siratel - An elderly woman of the Eldanim. Appears to have the ability to foresee a person's future to some extent.

Starlit Realm - *see* **Otherworld**

Sundinka - Former Lord of Mandiata. After his power was stolen by Volraag, he was murdered by Rathri.

Talinir - A warden of the Eldanim.

Tenjkidi - Capital city of Mandiata.

Tezan - A wild mage who, under the control of Lord Tyrr, attempted to convince everyone he was the lost King of Antises. Fell under the control of Volraag, who used him to steal power from Lord Sundinka.

Theon - The god worshipped (or at least acknowledged) by the majority of Antises.

Thrummers - Insects about one centimeter in length. Bites like a mosquito, but less painful. Mostly harmless. Especially attracted to those with magic, as it absorbs tiny amounts of magic when it bites. The insect's abdomen glows in response with an intensity and color based on the magic's potency.

Tich - A young sailor on Kishin's ship. Originally from Rasna.

Titus - A young man of Drusa's Crossing.

Tiur - A human slave of Vayan.

Topleb - A conscript in the army of Varioch, originally from Ch'olan. Assigned to the curse squad. Killed by Rufus.

Trebia River - A river that flows on south along the western edge of Varioch, next to the Great Plains.

Tunaldi - A ferocious beast of the Otherworld, comparable in size from a hippopotamus to an elephant. Carnivorous. Attracted to magic.

Tungrorum - A small village near the border between Varioch and Ch'olan.

Tyrr - Current Lord of Rasna.

Tzitzimitl - *see* **Eidolon**

Tzoyet - Current Master Mage of Ch'olan. Part of the Conclave of Mages on Zes Sivas.

Varioch - One of the six lands of Antises. Bordered on the north by Ch'olan and the south by Rasna. Known for aggressive leadership.

Varion - Former Lord of Varioch. Father of Marshal (by rape) and Volraag. Murdered by Rathri.

Vayan - The name of an ancient god of Kuktarma, associated with pain and wind.

Victor - A young man from Drusa's Crossing. Best friend of Marshal.

Volraag - Current Lord of Varioch. Son of Varion. Half-brother of Marshal. Stole power from Lord Sundinka of Mandiata.

Wolf - A conscript in the Varioch army. Assigned to the curse squad. Later revealed to be **Calu**.

Woqan - Capital city of Ch'olan.

Zes Sivas - An island in the center of Lake Litanu. Center of magic and authority for Antises. Most of the island is covered by the Citadel of Kings and the Citadel of Mages, two interwoven fortresses.

Acknowledgments

While writing *Until All Curses Are Lifted*, I had a rough outline of the series that, at first, was a trilogy. Once I finished it and started outlining the second book, I realized three books wasn't enough for this story. The challenge came in writing middle books that still told a complete story without just being "a continuation." I hope I've succeeded.

Even with an outline, stories and characters often take twists that you never see coming. Some of the relationships that exist by the end of this book are an example of that. And now that I'm working hard on the final book, I realize that there has to be payoff for all of these things. It's fascinating and exciting. At the same time, I can't help but wonder if some things that aren't fully addressed might lead to another book or books set in this same universe later on...

A very special thank you to my wonderful wife, Denise, for supporting my heavy focus on writing this year. As I write this, for example, I'm working on writing the final book of this series, editing the second book in my other series, planning out the book launch with advertising and all that involves, and finishing up the details on this book, of course. Being an independent author is a lot of work!

I love my beta readers! Stephen Tallman, Allen Perkins, Jamie Woleben and Kristi Lindgren: your support and feedback is highly appreciated. Continued thanks to David Farland and the Apex Writers Group for education, enlightenment and encouragement. And for those who post reviews on Amazon and Goodreads - you're the best!

If you want to keep track of my progress, you can connect on timfrankovich.com, my Facebook author page, Twitter, etc. But the best way, which keeps you informed and gives you exclusive previews, is to sign up for my newsletter. (There's a form on the website.) You even get free short stories, which, for some reason, are harder for me to write than novels. Plus, you get to see covers and excerpts before anyone else!

About the Author

Tim Frankovich has been exploring fantastic worlds since third grade, when he cut up a grocery sack and drew a Godzilla-meets-superheroes story. Since then, he's gotten a little bit better at the writing part (not so much with the drawing).

His goal as a writer is to transport readers to another world, make them care deeply about characters in dire situations, and guide them deeply into life itself.

At the moment, he is probably suitably conscious somewhere in Texas with his beloved wife, awesome four kids, and a fool of a pup named Pippin.

www.ingramcontent.com/pod-product-compliance
Lightning Source LLC
Chambersburg PA
CBHW051601100726
47898CB00001B/188